Sunset at 20:47

PETER KINGSMILL

ISBN:172440850X
ISBN-13: 9781724408501

DEDICATION

This book would not have been written without the undying support of my spouse, dearest friend and hard-working partner Valerie May Kingsmill.

ACKNOWLEDGMENTS

Valerie Kingsmill, whose oil painting of a sunset scene makes up the background of this book's cover, joined Maureen Reed, Sarah LaFreniere and Lynda Erlandson as my "beta reader" team, and I thank each of you for the encouragement and perceptive suggestions. Special thanks are due to my cover designer, Rae Ann Bonneville, who kindly but firmly reinforced in me the importance of having a professional proofreader apply the polish to a finished work!

08:35 JULY 12

Crap.

Anderson pulled the shift into neutral and stumbled up the step onto the gunwale and across the widening gap to the wharf, grabbing the stern line from the well deck behind the wheelhouse as he went.

The small pontoon barge he had been towing had not wound up where he had wanted it to be. A gust of wind at the last moment had caught the barge and taken it away from the wharf, so instead of coasting gently around the end of the wharf where he could grab the towrope and tie it up properly, the barge was now drifting slowly away and offering to take the 37-foot launch with it.

Murphy's Law never fails, he thought, hurriedly putting a hitch on the dock post before stepping back onto the launch and retrieving the loose end of the towrope from the small afterdeck. *Every effing time ya come into dock, the effing wind blows — wrong!*

Anderson spent the next ten minutes putting all the floating things back where he wanted them, securing the launch, and pulling and shoving the barge around the end of the wharf by hand and along to the shore where he could put down the ramp and eventually unload the baby trackhoe, leftover cement sacks and miscellaneous tools.

Back onboard the launch, he checked the engine gauges and shut down the diesel before he went forward into the small cabin and poured the dregs of lukewarm coffee from his thermos into his travel mug. He wedged his six-foot frame onto the bench at the little table and filled out the bill for his services: (1) dig trench for footings for cottage porch, and (2) make forms and pour concrete for footings. He had thought the cottager would also want him to at least ferry the lumber for the new porch down the lake, but Mr. Jorgenson had decided to save a buck and take his two-by-sixes across in the little fishing boat he used to access his cottage. *Whatever.*

After slipping the bill into an envelope, grabbing his thermos and locking the launch cabin, Anderson limped down the dock to his old Ford Ranger. As he got in, he quietly cursed his left foot which was sore as hell where the trackhoe had partially run over it a couple of days ago when he was loading it onto the barge. That was on him, he realized; it's usually thought of as stupid to pull the control lever on a powered machine when you are standing beside it. Doc had said there wasn't much he could do to help the foot - he was just to stay off it for a couple of weeks.

"Stay off it. Yeah, right!" he muttered as he turned the truck's ignition key and started off up the road. His house, shop and rather untidy yard were only a couple of hundred yards up from the dock, but he had things to do in the village and didn't feel like walking the two blocks from home to Main Street. Besides, he wanted another cup of coffee and felt too lazy to make it at home.

In Spirit River, it was, in fact, morning coffee time. Typically, it was coffee time from after breakfast clear through to lunch when everyone went home until afternoon coffee, but things did speed up at the Zoo around 10:30 every morning. And this morning, it seemed even busier than normal.

There was still a place at his usual table near the back (he tried to avoid sitting by the window because the glare from the sun made it hard to see the faces of the table rats). "Hey guys. And gals," he said, in deference to Marion who had joined her husband at the table this morning. She and Arnold were always together, but usually not at the coffee shop, since they ran the gas station together and were loath to shut it down for a break on a weekday morning. Maybe that's got something to do with so many people here this morning, he wondered.

"A couple cops are hanging around this morning," said Arnold, as if in answer to Anderson's unspoken thoughts. "Anita's missing, or at least she hasn't been home for two nights."

The young guy who drives logging truck for the sawmill passed his cup to the waitress for a refill. "Well, not like it's the first time she's done that." He added, "Maple Falls is only half an hour away, and we all know she hangs out there a lot, dancing up a storm usually; maybe she found herself a temporary squeeze."

"Well, yeah, maybe," Marion commented. "But the cops say they've talked to all her friends and they say they haven't seen her. No texts, nothing; Fred and Georgina are beside themselves this time."

Fred Antoine worked at part-time and casual jobs around town. He was sought-after as a loader and forklift operator and sometimes filled in at the mill. He was also a skilled welder, but he was mostly interested in trapping and fishing. His wife Georgina worked most nights at the Spirit Inn Lounge on the shore of the lake, where the tourists and some of the young cottagers play on summer evenings. Their 23-year-old daughter Anita was pretty and well-liked by everyone in town, but she had a reputation as a party-girl.

"Can't be at all easy for Georgina." Anderson had a soft spot for Anita's mom, although he kept that a secret from her and everyone else.

Marion glanced sideways at him, before continuing the conversation: "Not sure if it's a good thing or not that Fred's home from the bush; he's not much use to Georgina when there are problems that can't be solved with whiskey. And with Anita, he's always yelling at her when he gets a skin full; makes you wonder if he's not part of Anita's problems. It's like she doesn't want to grow up."

Arnold took the last mouthful of his coffee and stood up. "Come on Mum," he said to Marion, "time to go earn a buck; I have that cottage lady's old Accord to fix and I'm pretty sure I don't have the parts." He held the door for his wife, then turned back: "Anderson – wanna drive to Maple Falls with me on a parts run?"

"Why not... I need to pick up some fuses for the trackhoe anyway. Maybe I'll get a real haircut too – haven't had a decent one since I shaved off my winter beard, and that was months ago."

"Okay. I'll go check for the parts, and if I'm going to town I'll come back here and pick you up. Shouldn't be more than ten minutes."

***

The half-hour drive to Maple Falls was uneventful. Anderson mused to himself about the Anita situation a little, but he knew enough about her to figure she was likely off on a little love adventure (or maybe the world's biggest hangover) and would eventually turn up at home.

His thoughts turned to the lake and the Protected Shorelines committee that he sat on, along with his chauffeur beside him. "Hey, Arnold," Anderson spoke up over the screech of the wind from the old crew cab's badly-sealed windows. "How did last week's meeting go? I was finishing off some concrete at the Jorgenson place and didn't get back in time."

"It was okay, I guess." Arnold shifted in his seat, got out his pack of Number Sevens and selected a cigarette. "It's nice that those university guys have offered to help, but sometimes I think they forget that we, too, actually live here along with the birds and fish. The conversation gets a little off-track, in my mind anyway."

Anderson handed him his lighter. "Yeah, they certainly mean well, and some – especially that gal from New Brunswick – know a lot of stuff. Of course, the cottagers, who don't really live here either, take in every word they say as some kind of new-found gospel and forget that people have hunted and fished Awan Lake for over a couple hundred years before they showed up. When's the next meeting?"

"Third Wednesday of next month, as usual. They want to

do a public meeting with some guest speaker from the west coast that the university folks admire, but our local gang isn't all that happy about it. Jeremy, for one, thinks we're not ready for that yet, and I agree with him. Time ain't right yet."

Anderson chuckled. "Definition of an expert is someone with an airline ticket and a briefcase in one hand and an invoice in the other." He sighed. "To keep everyone happy, we'll probably have to let that happen, though maybe we can put it off until next spring. Maybe I can get Barker to find a corporate sponsor to pay for it – he seemed happy with the job I did out at his island a couple of months ago and apparently he has lots of bigwig connections."

Arnold took a quick drag on his smoke, and broke the conversation: "Say, Frank, have you any thoughts on this Anita thing? Knowing her, it seems a little early to worry much, but I keep seeing stuff on the news that makes me realize the world isn't always a friendly place for young girls even in the bush land of little old Canada. Especially for girls with a little colour."

"Mmm. Frankly I've been sitting here pissed off about the grief and hassle that little chick causes her Mum all the time," Anderson admitted. "And it's hard to know where to start when it comes to looking for her. Have the cops talked about a search yet?"

"Not that I heard this morning. I guess she's now officially a 'missing person' but I think most of the searching has been on Facebook and texting with friends." Stubbing out his cigarette and closing the side window against the light sprinkle of rain that had just begun, Arnold continued: "Perhaps you and I should stop in at the cop shop in Maple Falls and let them know we want to help. Maybe they'll tell us something." He pulled into the Napa parking lot and shut off the engine.

"Sounds like a plan," Anderson responded. "Let's get our stuff and go do that – just before we stop for a quick beer at that pub Anita hangs out at when she leaves Spirit River and hits the big lights. Maybe we'll learn something."

5

The search for parts was more or less successful. Anderson had to buy a different fuse holder to accommodate the only fuses they had in the store. "The joys of owning old machinery," he had muttered to himself. Their visit to the police detachment was even less fruitful. The officers had no new information (that they would talk about anyway) but they did take down the two men's names and contact information in case they wanted help in the Spirit River area where Anita lived.

The visit to the pub was no more productive. Although Arnold and Anderson had been there before, it had been seldom and nobody recognized them. Even the most general question or comment was met with silent shrugs. Anderson felt acutely aware of his away-back-when Métis roots, but nobody knew – or would have cared – in that place, so he didn't play that card. "I must be getting old," he grumbled to Arnold. "Places like this were a lot more fun when I was twenty... now that I'm pushing a half-century they just make me feel tired."

The men left after one beer, stopped at Timmy's to grab a "I'm so hot you can't drink me for at least 20 minutes" coffee and a portable chicken burger and headed home. The conversation drifted to speculation on whether the Ottawa Red Blacks would be able to repeat their Grey Cup win a couple of years ago, and when the city fathers of Toronto would try – again – to destroy the Canadian Football League by replacing the Argonauts with an American team and an NFL franchise.

By the time they arrived back in Spirit River, the drizzle that had begun earlier had settled in and the surface of Awan Lake was living up to its indigenous name – foggy. Arnold dropped his passenger off by the Zoo where he had left his little truck and went down the street to rejoin Marion at the garage. Anderson dropped the invoice he had prepared earlier into the post office and drove the two blocks back to his house and workshop near the docks.

Anderson's house was more than a little strange, many folks thought. It had been built somewhat over a hundred years ago, as a small boat-builder's workshop. It was perhaps thirty feet wide and seventy feet long, with a big set of hinged doors facing the street where the old builder had brought in his lumber and rolled out his beautifully-crafted wooden boats, gleaming with varnish and brass and boasting the shiny black classic gasoline marine engines of that time. Boats from Awan Lake used to be found on the canals and lakes of cottage country all over the province. These days, there were still a very few left, lovingly restored by craftsmen with endless time and deep pockets, who showed them off at boat shows in Toronto and even down into the states.

Anderson had bought the building for a song some twenty years ago. It was perfect for him, and while he was a good hand at fixing stuff, and he deeply admired the work of the old craftsmen who had gone before, he was inclined to favour more modern materials: he liked his boats made of aluminum or fibreglass or even steel, because he was not particularly fond of endless sanding and painting and re-jointing planks and caulking seams.

He had taken over the back thirty feet of the building as his house. From the outside, the house part was only identifiable by a single door on the side and a few not-very-big windows on the sides and back. The workshop part was comfortably messy, as might be expected of a single male as its inhabitant: "I know where everything is," he would tell visitors, "but it's a good thing I work alone." Although there was room in the shop for his work launch, he had never put her in for the winter; he left her down by the dock where she was lifted out for winter, and worked on her there. His shop was always full of small boats, or machinery like the trackhoe, and perhaps the occasional engine or two. Wooden workbenches lined the walls; they were pretty much all covered with "stuff".

The house part, though, was a different story. When the door from the workshop (or the "front" door) closed behind them, visitors found themselves almost in a different world, and not one they might have expected from the big craggy-faced man who lived there. Pine walls and open-rafter ceilings, broad clear-coated hardwood plank floors, warm scatter rugs, a couple of paintings on the walls, a cozy small kitchen, and off to the side what was obviously a bedroom, except it was really just another space, not a closed room. There was a long built-in desk and bookcases along one wall, with a computer at one end. There was a substantial wood-burning space heater on the other side of the room and a couple of easy chairs; the main piece of furniture was a gigantic old plank table with a variety of twice-as-old wooden chairs. The table was full of newspapers, magazines and engine parts (except at the kitchen end where there was typically a coffee cup and the plate left over from Anderson's breakfast).

It was not a woman's house. But Anderson didn't really care, because he had everything he wanted there and a live-in woman was not one of the things he wanted.

16:30 JULY 12

When he got back from his trip to Maple Falls with Arnold, the late afternoon was too soggy, foggy and depressing to go and off-load the trackhoe from the barge, walk it back up the street to the shop, and service it, so Anderson opted to open his second beer of the day and potter around in the shop. He called it cleaning up; most would have called it re-organizing the chaos. He worked distractedly; his thoughts turned to the missing Anita, her rather useless (and maybe worse) father Fred, and of course, to the long-suffering mother, Georgina. Anderson, like everyone else, had more questions than answers.

At about 18:00, he shut off the lights in the shop and went into the house where he made a fresh pot of coffee and a couple of fried eggs on toast. He pawed through the morning's Ottawa Citizen while he ate, then took his coffee to the computer and checked emails and his Facebook account. His computer time clock said 19:10 when his doorbell rang.

Anderson went to the front door and opened it without hesitation. Even though he had email and a smartphone, most of his neighbours and clients still just came to the door if his boat was at the dock and his truck was nearby. "Hi," he said cheerfully, and "come in out of the rain, please!" as he stepped back from the door.

His visitor was forty-ish, well put-up, athletic with blond hair tucked up under a green ball cap. And she was really very pretty. But he didn't have a clue who she was. "Can I pour you a coffee?"

"Well, no thanks, not at this time of day." She seemed nervous and a bit out of breath. "But a glass of hot water would be nice... I paddled across from our island and it's a pretty cool, dank evening. I'm a bit chilly."

"I'm surprised you could even see where you were going with that fog."

"The fog sort of comes and goes," she replied. "And besides, I do have a little handheld GPS – two actually 'cause there's one on my phone. I won't be hanging around long because it's a forty-five minute paddle home and I want to get back long before the sun sets. Not that it's shedding much light anyway."

Anderson put some water in the kettle and set it on the gas stove before clearing off some table space and pulling over a chair for his new guest. "Name's Frank, but mostly people just call me Anderson. How can I help?"

"I know, Mr. Anderson; your name precedes you, which is why I am here. Actually, I had tried to call the police first, but they seem pretty tied up this evening. All I got was their voicemail and my cell connection wasn't very good. So I came here – they tell me everyone comes to you when they have a lake problem."

"Please, call me anything but Mister Anderson. And yes, the police have other things on their minds today but – why do you need help? Why the police?"

"I think I found a body in the water."

Anderson didn't answer. He walked across to a cabinet beside the fridge, took out a small flask of brandy, took a small mug off its hook over the sink, poured in a couple of fingers from the flask, and filled the mug with the now-hot water from the kettle. This he delivered to his guest, who did not refuse it. "And what's your name, may I ask?"

"Marjorie. Marjorie Webster. My sister and I have a cottage on the little island off MacLean Point. And thank you; this will go down well."

"Ah... Now I know, exactly," Anderson nodded. "You moved out there a couple of summers ago, and I've probably passed you on the lake, but we've never met." He settled into a chair across from her and took a sip from his coffee cup. "I guess you should tell me what you think you have found, and where."

"I'm not really all that sure. I have a kayak, and less than an hour ago I was paddling slowly along the shore just east of town, watching the late afternoon birds come and go. Suddenly my paddle caught something – felt like a clump of weeds, but more solid. I didn't think anything about it as I pulled my paddle away, but then I thought..." she shuddered visibly, "I though I saw a face in the water."

"Geez. That'd be a shock to the system!" Anderson tried to sound somewhere between comforting and practical: "Are you sure? Was it right at the surface? Did you see it again?" The questions poured out a little too fast – in spite of his better judgement he was being more practical than comforting.

"No. I sort of looked around, not wanting to see it again but, well, you know. I had to try to focus a bit. All I was really able to do was paddle away a couple of hundred feet and try the phone. When that didn't work, I paddled straight into the village. Pulled my kayak up on your dock and ran up here."

Anderson got up and topped up his coffee. From a drawer in the kitchen he took out a beat-up pack of cigarettes and some matches and walked back to the table. "Hope you don't mind," he said.

"Not at all. Actually, could I have one too?"

He lit her cigarette, then his, before sitting down. Time to get practical, he thought. "With this overcast, it's going to be almost dark in less than an hour, and we should sort of retrace your route before you forget where you were when you saw... what you saw. Then we can try the police again with possibly better information. Is your sister home on the island?"

"Yes."

"Have you told her about this?"

"No, her cell must be off. We only have one charger and mine had just been plugged in when I left the house."

"Okay," said Anderson, carefully getting his thoughts organized. "We'll finish our coffee (and hot water) and go down to my boat, load up your kayak, and run along the shore until we get to where you think you found something. I can mark the spot with a float, as well as on the marine GPS, then quickly run you home to the island before it gets dark. Make sense?"

"Yes. Makes sense, and I would certainly appreciate the lift, and the company."

They sat in silence for a few moments. Anderson's mind started to fill with thoughts: Just outside the village; Anita gone for as much as three days; gotta get in touch with the cops – tonight; have to assume there will be a water search, no matter what, but oh God, how do we handle it with Georgina, and Fred, and everyone else?

"It's going to be a long night, Marjorie, but I'll try to keep the police from bothering you until tomorrow. If you're done with that brandy, we'd best be going."

She nodded, and gulped down the last mouthful. Anderson dumped his coffee into a travel mug, grabbed a jacket for himself and a blanket for Marjorie, guided her out the door and walked with her quickly down to the dock.

It didn't take long to fire up the main diesel and the small diesel generator he had installed a couple of months before. He was proud of that little "genset"; it gave him lots of household current for tools and lights when he was working for clients out on the islands, and carried some of the load from the boat's electronics. He checked the navigation lights and radar, loaded up the little kayak and strapped it down in the well deck with a couple of tarp straps. Within minutes he had cast off the mooring lines and was easing the boat out of the little harbour. He turned to his passenger: "Marjorie, there's no point in my filing a sail plan tonight because there's really nobody to receive it. However, I am going to call Arnold from the garage and tell him I'm out on the water and that I want to connect with him when I get back in. Okay?"

She nodded. "If you can reach him from out here."

There was nothing very modern about Anderson: old boats, old house, old engines, old machinery, old pick-up trucks. However, perhaps because he worked and lived alone,

Anderson did place a high value on communications technology, and he had equipped his boat with a cell-booster as well as good marine radio equipment and GPS. He had even installed an old citizen band two-way radio – even since the advent of cellphones, most of the island cottagers still used CB to talk together, especially with their sailing club. "No problem," he told Marjorie. "I have a cell booster."

Which he used, catching Arnold at home. "Hi there! Sorry to bother you but I have Marjorie Webster with me from the little island off MacLean Point, along with her kayak, and I'm giving her a lift home. I'll call you when I get back in; perhaps you could come by my place after. There's stuff we need to talk about tonight."

"Okay. Don't stay out there too long with those pretty ladies, Anderson. Dangerous ground!"

Anderson glanced at Marjorie. The cell system was on speaker, and she was chuckling at him. Obviously he had neither heard her chuckle nor even seen a smile since their introductions half an hour earlier, and the smile was nice to see. And yes, she was pretty. "Sorry about my friends. And my speakerphone," he added somewhat ruefully.

It didn't take the converted lobster boat long to retrace Marjorie's kayak route. When she told him they were getting close to where she thought she had seen the body, Anderson cut the throttle away back to just steerage way, and edged in closer to shore. The depth sounder was reading about seven feet when she said, "I wasn't any closer to shore than this, I'm pretty sure. And you see that rock outcrop with the funny tree on top, over there? I was pretty close to that when I stopped to try to call for help."

"So, a couple of hundred feet beyond?"

"Close as I remember. I was pretty spooked."

The lake bottom here was pretty rough, and the sounder was reading between five and eight feet. The launch drew two-and-a-half feet unloaded and flat, and bronze propellers do not get along well with granite; Anderson's eyes hardly left the sonar screen's bottom scan as they made a couple of passes.

"This is pretty shallow; we'll have to bring a skiff over here tomorrow," he mused to himself. To Marjorie, he said, "I always keep a little red float with an anchor attached; I'll turn and make one more pass, and when you think I'm close again I'll stop and throw it over. Then we can take you home."

She nodded, and stared unhappily at the shore – and the water – as he made the turn. After a couple of minutes, she said – almost shouted – "Here". Anderson took the transmission out of gear, stepped quickly out of the wheelhouse and threw the small anchor and the little red float – almost like a heavy balloon – overboard, anchor first. He returned to the wheel, carefully put the gearshift into forward, and edged offshore. He knew the lake well; once his depth sounder was registering about 12 feet he relaxed and pushed the throttle lever forward until the launch was making about eight knots.

He swung her nose southeast, and headed for what he (and only he, perhaps) called Ship Island because against the sunrise the silhouetted trees on the island looked like the rigging on a far-off ancient sailing ship. The rest of the trip was silent, each of them with their own thoughts. Anderson was glad to have his launch back on open, deep water and obviously Marjorie was just glad to leave behind that piece of shoreline, including what it may contain. They would both have things to deal with tomorrow, but tonight was, thankfully, over.

It didn't take them long to reach the island. Anderson knew there was a little bay with a dock and a boat shed on the south side, and he swung east to go around to the bay. "I'm going to signal your sister," he commented. "She can meet us at the dock. I trust it's deep enough to get the bow of this old tub up to the dock, or do we have to get you back into your kayak?" He levered off two long blasts of the horn as he rounded the end of the island; by now his navigation lights were showing brightly in the late dusk, so he knew Marjorie's sister would see them coming.

"We have an outboard tied up on the left side as we'll be

coming in," Marjorie responded. "There's at least four feet of water halfway down the dock on the right, so you should be okay. I'm sure Wendy will be down at the dock to help us in."

"Thanks – perfect." Anderson had already eased the throttle back and carefully approached the dock. Sure enough, he could see another person stepping up to meet them.

Between the two ladies, mooring lines were passed and tied to the rickety wharf. Introductions were made. Understandably, the probably younger and slightly plumper Wendy had been worried, probably very worried, so Marjorie kept the explanation to a minimum, just something about the foggy evening near the village and losing her bearings. More would come later. Anderson quickly took his leave, after receiving a gentle squeeze on the arm from Marjorie and one last flood of thank-yous from her sister. They cast off the lines for him; he backed away from the dock, turned out of the bay and back around the island, heading northwest toward the barely-visible lights of Spirit River.

***

Of course, he had known the night was not even close to being over. Anderson called Arnold when he was about fifteen minutes from the village, and suggested he warn Marion he was stealing him for a beer – at home, not at the pub.

When he pulled into his berth, he could see truck lights at the dock. Arnold was there to take his lines and help him tie up. Anderson made some quick notes in the log before he shut down the genset and the main engine, and tonight he did not forget to lock the wheelhouse and even put the padlock on the heavy security chain he sometimes used when he was away. Tonight he felt uneasy – not a feeling he normally entertained.

Arnold drove him up the block to the house. Once settled at the table with beers in hand, Anderson filled him in on his evening with the lady from the island, what she believed she had found, and what Anderson himself feared. "Somehow, I can't believe that – if indeed it was Anita – she would have surfaced so soon, but it is possible. What have you heard in town, and especially from the cops?"

"Almost nothing. Certainly nothing beyond speculation. I think pretty well everyone who knew her at all has been contacted, and at least informally questioned. With nothing to go on at all, and given the distances between where she was last seen and her home and friends around here, there is still no talk of a search."

"Well, what happened here tonight may well change everything." Anderson went on to speculations of his own: "Of course, this may have been a case of a nice lady with a big imagination having a bad experience with a clump of weeds, but she's awful level-headed, considering what she thinks she saw."

"Know what?" Arnold said slowly. "I think we need to reach the cops tonight, and get them going on a body search as soon as possible in the morning."

"How do we do that without lighting panic fires all over the place?"

Arnold nodded. "That's going to be tough, but we'd better start working on a plan, and doing it now. I know nothing at all about body searches but I bet they are tough enough to manage on land, let alone in the water."

"Okay," said Anderson. "Let's pull the trigger. It's almost ten o'clock; why don't you get the gendarmes on the phone... they always think I'm kinda weird (unless, of course they need to get out on the water when the weather's bad). They work away better with you tow-truck jockeys!"

Arnold sucked down a mouthful of beer and retrieved his phone from his jacket. "OPS" was on his speed-dial – there was no local police force and the Ontario Police Service served the communities in the area. A water search would probably wind up involving the Mounties and even perhaps the Coast Guard, but the OPS was where to start and he knew most of the officers and support staff anyway. Arnold and his tow-truck would likely be on their speed-dial too, and he hoped that at this time of night he would reach the local office and not be shunted off to a 911 dispatcher from lord-knows-where in the province.

He got lucky: Sergeant John MacLeod from Maple Falls picked up immediately. "Evening John, it's Arnold at Main Street Garage in Spirit River. I have some information that may tie in with the Antoine disappearance."

There was a pause. "Okay, I'll wait." Arnold looked up at Anderson and said, "He's put me on hold. I hate that!"

Anderson wandered over to the sink, cleaned out the coffee pot and started to brew a fresh pot while they waited. Just in case it would be a long wait, he popped open another couple of cans of "Blue" and brought them back to the table. "I thought this might be a long night. If we're gonna meet with those guys tonight – which we should - they can come here; probably not a great idea to arrive at the cop shop with a couple of beers under our belts."

"Hello? Yes, John," Arnold broke in. "I'm here at Frank Anderson's – yes, the boat guy – and he thinks there may be a body in the water just outside of town. Huh? Yeah, his instincts are pretty good about that stuff, but in this case it's from a third party. Why don't you talk to him..." and he handed the phone across the table.

"Hi Sergeant, Anderson here. Yeah, been a weird night so far. Yes, one of the cottagers was out kayaking around east of the village and thinks she snagged a body with her paddle. She paddled into town in a bit of a panic and wound up at my door. About 19:00 hours. Panic? No, I probably shouldn't have put it that way. Pretty calm actually – shock maybe. I gave her a warm brandy and water, then drove her out to where she thinks she saw this in my boat. Took her and her kayak back to her home after. Marked the spot with a buoy. Huh? Just a minute..."

Anderson took the phone from his ear and asked Arnold, "Did Anita ever hang around the docks or the beach? I don't think I ever saw her around there at all."

"Nah, I think she was more interested in fast cars and faster men. Even when she was a kid she never seemed much

17

interested in the lake."

"Sarge – did you get that? Yeah, it seems unlikely but you never know. And it also seems a little early for a body to rise. Huh? Sure, okay. Come on by. You know where I live? Yup, that's the place. See you in a few minutes."

Anderson clicked the phone off and handed it back to Arnold. "John's at the edge of the village in the patrol car – the local office number was forwarded to his cell and he's out driving around. He'll be here right away."

They polished off the beer cans and Anderson put them in a box by the kitchen waste bin before grabbing three coffee mugs. He filled two, set them on the table, and took some paper and a couple of pens from the desk before he sat down.

They didn't have long to wait; they could see the headlights as the Sergeant swung his cruiser around to the door. Actually, it wasn't a cop car at all – it was a nice new OPS-branded Escalade SUV. Arnold went to the door to welcome him in. "Nice ride, John. You're gonna have to give me more than two bits to cover my share! You two know each other?"

"You bet," said the Sergeant, sticking out a huge paw to shake hands. He was a big man – classic middle-aged cop with a few extra pounds but still looking like he could hold his own in the corners. "We had you take us out to the Johnson place a couple of years ago. A break-in, as I recall. And that was before I got my new stripes."

"I see the stripes, Sergeant John: congratulations!" Anderson took the paw and gave it a brief shake. "Coffee?"

"Please. Black. And guess what, this cop brings his own donuts and some to share!" He put the Tim Hortons box he had been carrying on the table. "And Frank, this is a really nice place – like a man-cave without the hockey posters. A person would never guess by looking at the outside, (no offense, but with the workshop and all!) I could settle right into a place like this."

"Thanks – and thanks for the donuts – I could use one!" Anderson said as he poured the coffee. "Supper was more like breakfast and seems like almost as long ago."

Munching down a couple of glazed donuts and slurping more coffee, Anderson gave the two men a more detailed account of the events earlier in the evening, while the sergeant wrote at length in his notebook. "That's about it," Anderson said when he got to the part about dropping Marjorie back home with her sister. "I called in Arnold, and here we are."

John put down his notebook, took another mouthful of coffee and said, "Any bright ideas, gentlemen, about where to go from here? I do know we can pull in a cadaver dog from Sarnia, but I'd kinda like to take a more low-key look first. Do you have any high-techie stuff we could use right away – I mean, in the morning?"

Anderson sat quiet for a moment. Then, "well, yes, I have a low-tech side scan sonar unit on the boat, but it really is pretty basic and I don't really have the right transducer to get the most out of it. If we're gonna go that route, there's a guy in Kingston who has a really good piece of kit and specializes in this kind of stuff. He ain't cheap, but he's good."

He paused. "Actually, I have in mind a really really low-tech approach to start with. The wind has been almost non-existent this evening, and the forecast says it will likely stay that way until later in the day tomorrow, when it will start blowing from the northwest – and offshore, which will not be a help. But, a few folks with rowboats and canoes could cover that whole area right up to the shore; if that body is sitting at the surface, which seems likely from what that lady told us, we might just get lucky if we did it right after first light. That's where I would start."

"We might have to wake some people up to make that happen," interjected Arnold. "It's getting late." He thought a moment, then, "Y'know, Anderson, the Protected Shorelines group has a couple of summer interns gettin' around with canoes and ATVs... I could make a call and ask 'em to help out. I'm sure they would be happy to take a break from water-sampling and frog-counting."

The sergeant thought for a moment. "I kinda hate getting

civilians involved in finding dead bodies, but I guess if I brought along a couple of our folks from the detachment – we do have two 3-man inflatable boats – and Frank, if you could bring your big boat and shadow us just off the shore, we could cover the area almost before anyone knew what we were doing. I could stay on the beach and look too, but mostly be there to answer questions if anyone curious shows up. Those interns of yours could help too, on an 'unofficial' basis. Arnold, you could be 'officially' in charge of your interns and work from the boat with Frank. Anderson – you're not saying much..."

Anderson had sat quietly through the discussion, but responded right away: "I like it. It's simple to make happen, and if we don't find anything, we haven't wasted very much time. Let's make some quick phone calls; Sergeant, dig up your guys to make sure they are available and Arnold, better track down those interns; there's just the slightest possibility they are over at the Inn, in which case you'd best keep the details out of the conversation. Just tell 'em to be at the dock with their canoes at, say, zero six hundred. Sorry... six o'clock; sun's up around five thirty."

It took less than twenty minutes for the two men to line up their personnel and equipment over their phones. The police officers were given a sense of what was going on, and the interns – who were indeed still at the Spirit Inn – didn't have a clue, but that was just as well. Anderson spent a little time finding a close-in satellite image of the whole search area and he colour-printed enough copies for all the expected search participants.

By the time they were done, the coffee pot was drained, the donuts had vanished and the men were tired. Arnold and the sergeant left for home, and Anderson rolled into bed with the latest copy of McLean's. He got about three paragraphs into the lead article before he drifted off to sleep with the bedside light still on.

05:00 JULY 13

Anderson's cellphone alarm went off at 05:00. On days when he didn't have early-morning plans he would just roll over and shut it off, but of course, not today. Dawn was breaking, still overcast but with pink sunrise streaks in the eastern sky. He rinsed out his thermos, travel mug and the coffee pot from last night and started another full pot. While coffee was brewing he made a quick breakfast out of a couple of pieces of toast with peanut butter, then filled his thermos and mug before heading out the door with the maps he had made last night for the team. This time he walked to the dock, assuming there would be lots of cop cars and other gear needing places to be parked close to the water.

As he stepped off the dock into the launch, he had a moment of thinking that he should have brought his little truck anyway, because it carried his diesel tank to re-fuel the boat. He unlocked the wheelhouse and grabbed the yardstick from its hook on the bulkhead behind the operator's seat and found a rag inside the engine room hatch. He opened the fuel pipe cover and dipped the tank; no worries about diesel: sixty percent full, and that would be lots for today's adventures. He wiped and replaced the measuring stick and noted the reading in the log, then used the same rag to check oil in the main engine and the genset.

He decided to leave the engines off until after people started to gather. He stashed his thermos by his seat and took the maps and his mug to the little map table on the port side of the wheelhouse, to the left of the three steps down into the cabin. In the process, he slopped some coffee onto the maps. He mumbled to himself as he snapped open the elegant aluminum briefcase that sat on the map table: "one of these days I am going to have to start actually carrying this damn thing." A couple of years earlier the folks who hung out at "The Zoo" had gotten together and given him the briefcase for Christmas, because he was legendary for always having his papers crumpled, greasy, and – covered in coffee. And he never had a pen. He had been touched by the gift, but somehow the case had never left the wheelhouse. "Maybe it's time I grew up and pretended I'm a big corporate CEO," he chuckled.

At that point, he remembered he had locked and chained the boat last night. As he was opening the lock and releasing the chain, a provincial police SUV pulled into the small parking area and swung around to place the trailer it was towing closer to the inner end of the dock. Two patrol officers got out and stepped around back to untie the two small inflatable boats that were rather haphazardly held on the trailer with small Canadian Tire ratchet straps. Anderson stepped off the boat onto the wharf: "Good mornin', folks. I'm Anderson, and I'm the first one here. Maybe bring those things over to the boat and we'll load 'em on deck... they're not the kind of outfit you want to row down the lake for half an hour before we even need 'em."

"Makes sense to me," said one, and with Anderson's help they quickly got the inflatables down and across the dock and into the well deck, making a third trip for oars, lifejackets, and personal gear. With that accomplished, all three stood together along the dock: "Hello sir, I'm Constable Andy Bathgate and this is Corporal Marie Beauchemin. She'll be our lead with the small boats; Sergeant MacLeod is right behind us with an ATV. He told us he would be staying along the shore to assist from there – and deal with the public. All of us will have radio contact."

Anderson shook hands with the officers and gave a brief outline of what was planned. He thought to himself that – in military or even police terms – this was hardly a carefully-planned exercise, but he hoped he came across as more-or-less organized.

If, so far, everyone seemed to know what they were doing, that illusion all fell apart in about a minute and a half when the PSP science interns arrived with the Program's beat-up old Ford 150 and a canoe piled on back and roped down with quarter-inch yellow poly rope. They quickly stepped out and headed to join those already on the dock. The driver was very tall, athletic, and very black, dressed in slacks, expensive sport shoes, an open-necked shirt and a Greenpeace ball cap. His passenger was short and blond, dressed in jeans that fit everywhere they touched, a Spirit Inn sweatshirt and long hair gathered up and stuffed through the strap on her plain ball cap. "So, what's all the excitement this morning?" she asked, eying the cops as though she had a joint stuck in her hatband.

Anderson, of course, knew them both. "Hi Cyndi, good morning Adumbi! Glad you could make it. Our uniformed friends here have a couple of inflatable rowboats with them, and together we have a bit of a search to do. Andy and Marie, please meet Cyndi Johansson and Adumbi Jakande. They are here as summer interns for the Protected Shorelines Program, so they are pretty familiar with observing the water from their canoe. Perhaps we can get that thing off the truck and tie it alongside the dock – on this side – and loaded up with the gear. Then we can gather back at the boat and go through the

23

search plan together... I see that Sergeant John is just joining us, along with Arnold from the garage and all of you know him."

The four younger folks headed for the old pick-up. Anderson chuckled to himself as he watched briefly; Constable Andy and Intern Cyndi were go get 'em types, immediately busy untying the canoe, turning it over and carrying it down to the water, while Corporal Marie and Senior Intern Adumbi were obviously slated for management positions, basically being helpful without doing much. Anderson waved at Arnold and the sergeant as he headed for the launch, where he stepped into the wheelhouse, fired up the engines and turned on the instruments and radios.

It was almost full daylight by now. There was no sign of yesterday's rain although there were still lingering clouds. And thankfully, no wind. "Morning guys," Anderson greeted Arnold and John who had unloaded themselves from Arnold's old pickup and joined him on the boat with – notably – a large Tim Hortons box. "Glad you live in Maple Falls and were able to pick up some breakfast rations for us troops."

"Yeah, but they're yesterday's, I'm afraid. I picked 'em up before closing last night 'cause I thought Timmy's might not be open so early this morning. Turns out I was wrong; I saw they were open when I drove up the highway but I already had these. Is what it is, I guess!"

"They'll work for me," said Arnold. "Thanks! Frank, have you had a chance to let everyone know what we're gonna do?"

"Nope. Actually, we haven't been here long enough, and in any case I kinda wanted you two here to remember whatever I left out. Which is mostly everything important except that it's Zero-Dark-Thirty on Thursday and I have lots of fuel onboard."

"Chicken-shit!" John teased him. "It was your idea, I seem to recall... Okay folks," he spoke loudly down the dock, "let's get together over here and make a plan."

The OPS officers and the young interns joined Arnold, Anderson and John, standing in the boat's well deck or perched on the wide gunwales. The sergeant continued:

"Folks, we're going to spend a couple of hours – along the east shore over there – looking for what we believe may be a body – a human body. Yesterday afternoon, a lady was along there with her kayak, had her paddle catch on something which disappeared under the water. Not a big deal except – she thinks she saw a body and particularly a face as it went under."

The lazily lighthearted mood suddenly went serious. In the case of the PSP interns, the mood became very serious; obviously this was not the kind of thing that had been written into their Program job descriptions – ever. The ever-polite and well-spoken Adumbi was the first to respond: "Sir, of course we are willing to help in any way, but for myself – and I am sure the same is true for Cyndi – I have absolutely no training to prepare me for this. The first time I was even out in a canoe was in May when we came here. How is such a thing done?"

"It's not a big deal," threw in Constable Andy, "you just paddle along and keep you eyes open."

The sergeant shot the young constable a hard look. "Actually, it is a big deal, in many important ways. You are right, it's all about keeping your eyes open, but there's more: things like this are upsetting for all of us, even for those of us who have done it before." Turning to the interns, he continued, "We are grateful you are here to help, and I assure you that not one of us will forget this morning, whether we find anything or not. It can be upsetting, and you will continue to experience the adrenaline rush that you feel right now. But it is, after all, just a process, and I'm going to ask Mr. Anderson to lay it out for us because – although three of us are police professionals, Mr. Anderson is the water guy and fully understands what we have to do for the next few hours." He smiled kindly to the interns, and then nodded to Anderson.

"Time to talk about things we can understand," Anderson thought to himself. "Hang on folks, let me get out some maps we printed off last night." He quickly stepped into the wheelhouse, scooped up the maps and most importantly the box of donuts John had brought.

He passed the box to the Corporal to distribute, and the maps to Arnold. "I have some hot coffee inside if anyone wants. Now, Arnold will give you each a map – nothing fancy but it gives you an idea where we are going. The location starts along the shore to the east and Cyndi and Adumbi can get there in about 20 minutes; I have seen them paddle and they do it well – and if the donuts are any help – fast. Arnold and I will be in this boat, and will carry Marie and Andy and their inflatables (which are slow) until we get to the general area where we will put them in the water and begin a search pattern, three little boats about ten feet apart starting very close to the beach. When we get to the end of the search area, you'll simply turn around and go back the other way, but a little further out from shore. And so on – we just repeat that process several times. Paddle slowly, eyes wide open like Andy says. The Sergeant will keep pace along the beach, and Arnold and I will stay well off away from you, but ready to help. John – I am hoping you brought enough handhelds for the three boats, for you, and for us – that's five? I can't pick up OPS radio signals from this old tub."

"Glad to hear it!" chuckled the Sergeant. "Yes, I have the radios... here..." and he unloaded the contents of a backpack he had brought and handed each person a small portable radio. "Mr. Anderson has pretty well covered it all, but there is one important thing I need to say: do not (I repeat, do not) touch anything you see. Stop paddling immediately, hold your position, wave your hands and call in on the radio."

"Okay," said Anderson. "If there are no questions, then it's time to get going as the sun is well above the horizon now. It's still nice and calm, but we want to finish before that changes. Adumbi and Cyndi – you start down the shore with your canoe first, then I'll get us off the dock and catch up. John, I assume you will drive down the shore road and unload that ATV somewhere?"

"No, I'll just unload it here and drive it down; it'll be quicker."

"Okay everyone, let's get at it. Take care and don't hesitate to call on that radio if you need anything." Anderson turned to clear his spring lines and asked Andy and Marie to get ready to cast off the bow and stern lines. He waited for Arnold to get back onboard after helping the Sergeant unload the ATV from his truck, looked to make sure the canoe was well out of the way, and called for the lines to be cast off. He pulled the launch away from the wharf and headed out of the harbour and along the shore behind the canoe. The OPS officers stood outside the wheelhouse gazing into the water as if already searching, while Arnold joined him in the wheelhouse.

***

Once well out of the harbour, he punched a course into the autopilot that would take the boat to the last waypoint he had set last night, well on the village side of what he supposed to be a search area, and set the throttle at a little less than half, moving them at about five knots toward the waypoint. "Arnold, got a smoke?"

"Early in the day for you ain't it?"

"Yeah, well, it's feeling like one of those days... thanks." He lit the cigarette thoughtfully, then asked, "I had been thinking I should let Marjorie – the lady from last night – know what we were up to, but I didn't want to involve her in this morning's adventure. Waddyathink... should I give her a call?"

"Hmm. Yeah, probably. And in any case, John's going to want to interview her, one way or the other, and he'll probably want to do that this morning, after this little search is over. I'd go ahead."

Anderson took out his cellphone and found the number she had given him last night. It rang twice: "Hello, Marjorie? It's Frank Anderson, the guy who gave you a lift home last night... yes, I did – and I hope you managed to get some sleep too. Mmm, ya, I can imagine it wasn't a great night. I'm calling because I wanted to keep you up to date. Right now, we're out with the OPS from Maple Falls, and three small boats covering the shoreline where you showed me last night. They thought that was the best way to start, and I know they will want to interview you, sooner than later. The boss' name is Sergeant John MacLeod, and he's a really good guy – Arnold and I have known him a long time. He even brought us donuts this morning! What? No, not to worry. We can do this preliminary look without getting you involved but – like I said – he will want to interview you. When I find out his timing, do you want me to give you another call and then bring him out to your place, or do you want to run in here with your outboard?"

There was a brief pause, then, "Okay, that'd be fine. I'll call you with a time and you and Wendy can run in and meet him at the village. At the dock, or at my place, or? Okay, my place it will be. I'll give you a shout."

He clicked off the phone and checked out the GPS chart. He punched off the autohelm and reduced speed a little; the canoe crew must be tiring because he was gaining on them. They were over half way there anyway. He turned to the police officers (who had joined Arnold and him in the wheelhouse) and explained, "That was the lady who started this whole thing by thinking her paddle had made contact with what might be a body. Your Sergeant has a whole bunch of notes from me, but as I told the woman, he'll probably want to visit with her himself, and pretty soon."

The Corporal had pulled out her notebook, but thought better of it and tucked it back into her uniform jacket. "Oh yes, I am sure he will, sooner than later is usually how that happens. I'm surprised he didn't go out and find her last night!"

"Well, I'm pretty sure he realized she wasn't going anywhere from her island in a fog in the middle of the night," Anderson said with a lopsided grin, which the Corporal did not see. Arnold did, and laughed out loud.

PETER KINGSMILL

06:25 JULY 12

In less than ten minutes the waypoint appeared on the screen and Anderson throttled back and told the officers to get their boats ready. Like all well-brought-up police personnel, they already had their lifejackets on. Anderson knew that was the proper thing to do, but hardly ever wore his own unless he was in a smaller boat, or alone in cold or rough weather, or when going back and forth to his barge. He also knew that statistics prove that his attitude was stupid, but he pretty much always ignored anything he considered to be bureaucratic crap. He remembered telling a Coast Guard boating safety meeting that the only reason they wanted everyone wearing brightly coloured lifejackets was to make corpses easier to find and save on search and recovery costs. It was not one of his shining moments; he did not make any friends with that one.

Anderson gave a couple of short blasts on the horn, and pulled the throttle into neutral; they were there. "Okay guys, here's where we begin. Put in your boats and get in once we've stopped. I've deliberately moved closer to shore, but this is as close as I plan to be – it gets shallow. You know the drill; pull into line perpendicular to the shore, and closer, and begin the first sweep. I'll give the same two shots on the horn when it's time to turn back the other way. You folks run the sweeps, keep the Sergeant and I informed on the radio. And – don't be too hard on those kids in the canoe; they are not having the

31

nice peaceful morning counting ducks that they had planned for."

Andy and Marie grinned at him, and nodded. "Okay, we're gone," and they climbed in and started rowing toward the canoe, which was by then about a hundred feet in toward the beach, opposite where the Sergeant sat waiting on his ATV.

Each sweep along the shore took a little less than half an hour. By the time they made the third turn, it was becoming a little frustrating for the small-boat bunch, and mildly tedious for Anderson. He had been all wired up for this since Marjorie came to his house last evening, and now he was coming down as his mind and muscles relaxed into the routine of "east for 25 minutes, west for 25 minutes". As his boat idled along at less than two knots, his thoughts began to drift.

Then, with a jolt that seemed almost physical, all the fears that had been eclipsed from his mind by the I-gotta-do-something part of his psyche, crashed into his consciousness like a blow to the stomach: *What if we find Anita out here? How do we cope with it? How do we tell Genevieve and all Anita's buddies. How do we deal with Fred? Anita's too young to be floating around drowned in a lake. Indeed, did she drown? Did she commit suicide? Was she murdered?*

Anderson called to Arnold, who had been propped against the edge of the wheelhouse roof staring shoreward through a big pair of US Navy submariner glasses he had picked up in a surplus store. "Hey, man. I'm kinda having a moment here, and it ain't a good one."

Arnold stepped into the wheelhouse, to be greeted by "What the hell do we do if we find Anita?" Arnold walked forward to the map table and looked across at Anderson. "I dunno. I've been assuming that's why we're doing this, and too focused to even think 'what if' or even wonder 'if not, what?' What are you thinking?"

"Don't know either. I just know that if this amounts to nothing, it's not over. The cops, I suppose, will have to deal with whether – beyond this morning – looking out here for Anita's body is even reasonable. Even as we're out here, there may be a rumour that she was seen in a bar in Toronto, or someone turns up with a Snapchat photo of her leaving a café in Kingston... both of which are, frankly, more likely than her floating around in a lake. There's just this feeling in my gut that maybe we jumped the gun on this."

Anderson took a quick look at the GPS, began a lazy one-eighty turn to go back west, and gave two quick blasts on the horn. Sergeant John came on the radio and said, "Last turn, last sweep ladies and gentlemen. I've only one visitor on foot so far – a couple of birders out for an early morning stroll; I was able to make them happy by saying we had lost some test equipment and were out trying to find it. And some guy came in close to the shore with a little car-topper boat and motor, pissed off because there was traffic out here and he wanted his fishing spot all to himself apparently. He putted back toward..."

The hand-held radios squawked, and a voice – Marie's – came across: "Sorry to break in Sarge, but I've got something here. Big. Can't tell what it is yet but I'm going to need help to figure it out."

Corporal Beauchemin was in the middle boat in the line, one of the police rowboats. Arnold and Anderson had seen her wave as soon as she came on the radio, and Anderson had immediately swung the bow of the launch toward shore. The small boats were only a couple of hundred yards away, so he left the throttle alone; they would close the distance soon enough. Arnold took the police handheld from the map table, keyed the talk button and broke in: "John, do you want to call in Andy on the other inflatable and have him row in and pick you up? If it's a body, I don't think any of us out here know how we should handle this as well as you do."

That decision had been made already; Andy was rowing to shore as fast as he could to pick up his boss. The PSP interns had stopped, of course, but had sensibly moved a good distance clear of Marie, her boat, and her newfound problem. Anderson swung the launch sideways as it neared Marie's boat, took the transmission out of gear, and let it drift very slowly until it stopped, about fifty feet off. By then, the constable and his sergeant had arrived and joined the group of eight who were staring at a lumpy brown object just barely showing at the surface. The sergeant picked up a small boathook from the inflatable he was riding in and used it to reach across the object. He pressed the hook end down on the opposite side from where he was sitting and gently pulled the object toward him, causing it to slowly turn over in the water.

None of them – not one – was prepared for what they saw next. Yes, it was indeed a corpse, but not that of a healthy young woman who had just drowned. It barely looked human, except that it obviously had arms and legs and was wearing what looked like a brown canvas parka. The face was a nightmare of torn flesh, exposed bone and wisps of clinging hair.

For a few moments no one said a word beyond a couple of horrified gasps from the interns in the canoe. The sergeant spoke first: "This one's been here awhile, and is certainly not our recently disappeared young woman. I won't speculate from here, but I know there was an elderly man from out of town who went missing early last spring; they found his car along the east shore about 10 miles up past MacLean Point."

Anderson spoke up next: "I think I can speak for most folks around town – including myself – that it is a huge relief that this is definitely not who we feared it might be a few hours ago."

Arnold was more to the point: "Anderson, why are you beatin' around the bush again? Everyone here knows we're talking about Anita and while this doesn't solve the missing Anita problem, it sure as hell is good that this is not her."

"Yeah, all of us out here on the lake know that, and are happy with this result," said the sergeant. "Maybe, though, we shouldn't talk too much about that. And of course I can't speculate who it might be until we get confirmation. I can publicly say – if anyone asks – that this is not Anita Antoine, and I will also be saying that the search was conducted in response to a report from a female resident to something she saw in the water last night, and no, it had nothing to do with the continuing search for Ms. Antoine."

Anderson had decided to bury his feelings in doing something useful, and had retrieved a couple of rolls of tie-down straps from a locker along the side of the launch's well deck. He pulled off the ratchets and motioned to the sergeant, tossing the straps over to the boat he was sitting in alongside the body. "John, let's call him Sam for now – I'm tired of talking about bodies. If a couple or three of you put these four straps around Sam, you should be able to roll him into your boat. Then we can tow the boat with Sam, and the other boat and the canoe, back to the village. In the meantime, you can make arrangements for the coroner to pick him up, and all these good folks can get back to what they normally do on Thursday mornings."

The sergeant smiled, and nodded. "Yup, let's just do that. Marie, and you folks with the canoe, take them around the other side of Frank's boat and arrange a couple of ropes to tow them with. Arnold, would you mind giving Constable Andy and I a hand getting Sam into this rowboat? We'll pull it – and Sam – over alongside the big boat so we have something to hang onto and steady ourselves."

And so it was done. Fortunately Sam had not been a very big man, so the loading went easily enough. Everyone got onboard the launch and Anderson began the slow haul back toward the village. The ATV was left on the beach, where Arnold could drive over with the sergeant and pick it up. Conversation onboard was sparse; nobody felt much like talking. Anderson had passed around some towels and alcohol wipes for anyone who wanted them, and between his thermos and the travel mugs and water jugs people had brought with them, everyone got something to drink.

The rest of the donuts, however, survived the forty-five minute trip home, untouched.

10:20 JULY 13

It was slow going. Anderson had to keep the speed down so the three little boats they were towing rode behind comfortably and didn't twist or tangle or – worse – flip over. On the way back to the village, Anderson explained briefly to the sergeant that Marjorie Webster would meet him at the village when they got back in, expecting to be interviewed about what she had seen the night before. "I don't suppose it's as urgent now that we know the body is not part of an immediate search, but I think she does want to talk with you. I'll call and let her know we'll be back in soon. She said she'd meet you at my place if that's okay."

The sergeant nodded. "That will be fine. Yes, I do have to talk to her, so I can fill in the blanks. I've called the coroner and obviously he says an autopsy will be necessary; if the ID proves out that it's the old boy I think it is, and the autopsy shows there's no sign of foul play, just maybe I can close the file on that old missing persons case and get it out of the way. So, thanks for setting things up with, ah, Ms. Webster?"

"Actually, there are two Ms. Websters out on that island... Marjorie has a sister Wendy, but she was home through last night's adventure." Anderson dug in his jacket pocket for his phone and placed a call to the island, and explained to Marjorie that, in fact, they had found a body in the water – the body of an older man from many months ago – and that the sergeant indeed wanted to chat with her about last night." He listened for a moment, said a quick goodbye, clicked off the phone and turned to the sergeant: "She's on her way in. They have a little outboard runabout they use to go back and forth; I expect she'll get to the dock not long after we get landed."

"That's good, thanks. Do you have a small tarp onboard? We're gonna want to cover up Sam until the coroner gets here."

Anderson nodded toward the locker in the well deck. "There's a blue eight-footer in there."

The sergeant spent some time with his officers, instructing them on what protocols needed to be followed when they got to the dock, as well as arranging with the corporal to go with Arnold and pick up the ATV from down the beach. For his part, Arnold spent much of the trip back to the village chatting with the interns, trying to put them at ease following what had been for them a rather traumatic morning. When Arnold came back into the wheelhouse, Anderson asked him how the kids were doing.

"Okay, I think. We owe them one – it's been a stressful morning, especially, it seems, for Adumbi who was kinda shook up. Cyndi, though, seems like a tough little chick; she pretty much shrugged the whole thing off."

"You gonna send 'em back to work this morning?"

"Absolutely. No point in them sitting around moping about it."

"Gack... you're a tough man, Mr. Jamieson."

"Ya think?" Arnold grinned at his friend, and they both chuckled. There had not been many laughs over the last day or two. "Oh, crap. I forgot to mention this morning that I had a call from Forbes last night. Sounds like a couple of the cottagers are pushing his buttons about getting that speaker in right away, and getting the TV and newspapers involved. Jeremy's having a fit and wanting me to call a meeting right away."

"Crap is right. Just what we need right now. These cottage guys seem to forget that they are on vacation out here but the rest of us have work to do and a community to take care of. You gonna do it?"

"I don't really have much choice. I called Flo at the Spirit Inn earlier this morning and she'll let us use their small meeting room tonight."

"Tonight? Geez, that's quick. Will you get anyone to come on such short notice?"

"Well, the way I see it is that it will have to be a special meeting anyway. It's Thursday, and tomorrow is the start of the weekend, and I'd just as soon not have all the city folks show up, jam the meeting and start trying to push us around. Quick meeting, small room, short agenda, and beer after. With things like this, most of the good stuff happens at the end – over the beer."

"Works for me." Anderson throttled the launch back even further as they approached the village's little harbour. They passed the gas dock at the marina, then the government wharf and then, about seventy-five yards further he pulled bow-first (and very slowly) into his dock at what was generally known as the "old industrial section". Anderson sometimes grumbled to himself that the only industry that happened there was him trying to keep the old docks from crumbling into the lake in piles of rotting wood and rocks, but he generally took the long view: the local – and provincial – governments pretty much left him alone. For his part, he kept it from falling apart and cleaned up after himself (and others).

Nobody hung around. The sergeant helped the PSP interns put their canoe and gear on their old truck, thanked them profusely for their help and sent them on their way, presumably to their next study area far around the lake. Arnold took the constable in his pickup to fetch the abandoned ATV, and Marie pulled the inflatables up on the beach, making sure Sam was properly covered with an official-looking OPS-issued yellow tarp to await his date with the coroner.

Anderson fussed about his boat, putting straps and ropes away, making logbook entries, and watching the lake for the little outboard he knew would be coming across from Ship Island. He caught himself wondering why that little outboard seemed so important; it was, after all, just another in a day full of loose ends. He did, he supposed, feel a little responsible for Marjorie and her involvement in this less-than-happy situation, even as he realized that she owed him for answering his doorbell, not the other way up. He did, however, admit to himself that he was looking forward to seeing her.

Which he did. About half an hour later, the little outboard appeared and pulled in at the foot of the government dock, where the island cottagers tied up when they came into the village to buy groceries and booze. Anderson could see the two women walk along the dock to the shore and make their way to a small grey hatchback in the public parking area. He waved at them, and Marjorie waved back and shouted, "be there in a minute". The car started up, backed out and drove up the road toward the shops; Marjorie turned and walked purposefully to the dock where Anderson was standing with Arnold – who had already returned from picking up the ATV - and the sergeant. "Hi Frank," she said. "Just sending my sister Wendy off to get gas before we head to Maple Falls on a Walmart run."

Anderson greeted her with a friendly smile and "good to

see you again". This is Sergeant John MacLeod from Maple Falls, and this is our friend and neighbour Arnold Jamieson. Arnold and Marion run the service station in town, and he's always giving me a hand with stuff."

The sergeant shook her hand and smiled. "Thank you for coming in to talk to me. I know it's an inconvenience and I appreciate it. I don't suppose this will take very long; Frank, could Ms. Webster and I just do our interview here on the boat, and then maybe walk up to your place? I need to stay here until the coroner gets here, although I could just brief Constable Beauchemin about how to handle it."

"No worries, that'll work fine. Make yourselves comfortable; Arnold and I will go up to the house and make some fresh coffee; we'll just wait for you there." Anderson and Arnold stepped off the dock and shook hands with the two police officers, who were sitting in the OPS vehicle with the doors open. "Thanks, Andy, thanks Marie. We're glad you're here to help our community with stuff like this!"

After the two men had turned and begun to walk up towards Anderson's house, Arnold punched him on the shoulder and said, "You running for Mayor or something? 'thank you for being here to help our community' my ass – that ain't what you said when you got that fine for pulling an overweight trailer with that little thing you call a truck!"

"No, I guess not. That cop was just a bitch, without even a sense of humour!"

"She was nice; I had to do a couple of accident scenes with her and she was great. It's you, ya miserable bugger; no wonder you haven't even got a girlfriend, let alone a wife!" Both men were laughing as they walked off the road to Anderson's front door.

"Actually, in another place, at another time, I had one of

those. It just didn't work out. At all."

When they got into the house, Anderson started to make some fresh coffee as he had promised while his friend settled at the table and ruffled through the classifieds in the Maple Falls weekly newspaper. "Hey," Anderson called across the room. "Is that meeting on for sure tonight?"

"I just talked to Marion about fifteen minutes ago; she reached most of the committee and they agreed to show up, so I guess we're on."

"Do you want me to make up one of those simple little agendas I usually do? I think it needs to be very short, like four items."

"Four items? Really? There's only one thing to discuss and it's about holding a public meeting with that idiot from Vancouver, or wherever."

"Yup. Four items: call to order, public meeting, adjourn, and beer."

"Yeah, okay, that'll work. Actually, maybe do it up exactly that way; perhaps a little humour will help keep it from getting too heavy." Arnold paused a long moment. "How do you actually feel about this public meeting idea? You don't usually say much at any of the committee meetings but folks look up to you, both sides. The cottagers think you actually know stuff, and even Jeremy calms down when you speak up. Am I wrong to be so negative about this? Should I rein in Jeremy a bit?"

Anderson finished pouring water into the coffee maker, turned it on, then went over and hunted for something on his desk. He found a couple of sheets of paper near the printer, and brought them to the table, laying them in front of Arnold. He sat down, saying nothing. The coffee maker snorted and snuffled across the room; other than that there was silence as Arnold read.

"Okay; that's pretty interesting. You spent some time in BC; does this ring true for you?"

"Well, that part of BC – the Chilcotin – really is cowboy country. It don't get any more redneck than that, and the good ol' boys eat university professors and TV glamour girls fresh-frozen for breakfast." He got up and walked over to the still-gurgling coffee pot, from which he stole two half-mugs of coffee and brought them back to the table. "But those good ol' boys had begun to think that maybe the problem was not the university professors, or the media, or – in their case – the Indigenous leaders, but maybe – just maybe – it was the mining companies that were pushing the development agenda and just making it look like the do-gooder side was causing all the trouble. So when the local committee got Horowitz to come out to a public meeting, things really started to change. Just for starters, they got the Globe & Mail and the three networks out there, and that was a huge help to their cause." He shrugged at Arnold and raised his eyebrows.

Arnold stared at him. "Okay, I've just learned more about you in seven minutes than I have in seven years. How come you don't tell us this stuff at our meetings?"

"Well, first, it's not my community. I mean, don't get me wrong; I've been welcomed here and it's where I really want to be. But I don't want to be a shit-disturber and especially not a shit-disturber from somewhere else. This kind of community activism just has to come from within the community, or it's just confused with all the other outsiders. There has to be buy-in at home for it to work."

Arnold suddenly stood up. "John and that lady friend of yours are almost here. We gotta continue this conversation later – but before the meeting. Don't forget, turkey!" He went to Anderson's door and opened it to John and Marjorie.

43

"Welcome to Frank's place. He couldn't wait for coffee so he left. That's some guy named Anderson over at the table."

The guy named Anderson stood up and grinned. "How do you like my new houseboy?" he asked. "As you can see, it's hard to get good help these days." Sergeant John and Marjorie grinned widely and shuffled the gravel off their feet. "Get any good spy stuff from the lady of the lake, John?"

"All I'll ever need to know," the sergeant responded. "Actually, the OPS owes all of you a big bucket of thanks for what you have pulled together, from Ms. Webster's powers of observation last night to all the stuff we did this morning."

"Wait 'til you see the bill," laughed Arnold. "Anderson even wants to bill Ms. Webster for disturbing the peace!"

"Yeah, we're pretty expensive around here," Anderson chuckled. "But a late lunch at the Zoo would more than cover it all; I'm starved!"

The sergeant laughed. "Sounds like a plan to me. If the Zoo won't take an OPS credit card, they'll sure as hell take my personal one! And we should go soon - but before we go, could we just chat together for a few minutes so I can make sure I have the continuity right in my notes?"

Anderson had already poured four coffees. Marjorie quietly made a point of sitting next to Anderson, and smiled at him quietly as she did so. She was grateful for his help, and his support, through this strange adventure and wanted to show it.

After a few clarifying questions, mostly about times and the order of events last night, the sergeant left for a few minutes to give some instructions to his staff. The coroner had finally arrived, and after a brief glance at the water-logged corpse he got the officers to help stuff Sam into a bag and load him into the back of his Dodge Caravan, and he rattled off up the road headed for Maple Falls. The officers, too, headed to

Maple Falls, towing the inflatables on their little trailer.

On the pretense of wanting to look at an outboard motor in Anderson's shop, Arnold went outside, leaving Anderson and Marjorie alone to catch each other up on the whole event. As with any two strangers who share a significant event, a bond had formed between them. She seemed pleased about that, and Anderson was nervous. He was a man who loved the ladies, but never got close except in midnight motel rooms. This lady, however, was not a motel room lady, and it was nowhere near midnight. And that made him more nervous.

PETER KINGSMILL

15:25 JULY 13

The late lunch had been pleasant and – predictably – busy. Arnold had called Marion and asked her to join them, leaving the garage in the hands of their very junior gas jockey (a half-way high school drop-out they were trying to help get through the last year, even if it took two). Marjorie had begged off, as she had promised her sister they would go shopping in Maple Falls after the session with the police was done. So, it was just Sergeant John, Arnold, Marion and Anderson who munched down the quiche-and-fries special of the day, but they had lots of curious visitors, all aware they had been out on a search in the water, and all comforted to know it was not Anita they had been looking for. That was the official line, of course, but all four knew that was shading the truth a little. Everyone in town knew that an elderly man had left his car and disappeared in the spring, but nobody knew the man himself; he was just an old man from "The Falls".

After lunch, and after John had retrieved his patrol car from Arnold and Marion's garage and headed back to his office at "The Falls", Arnold asked Marion to stick around and discuss the PSP special meeting that evening. He wanted Anderson to share his newfound perspective, and come to some conclusion about how to proceed. As the unwilling Chair of the PSP, Arnold leant heavily on his wife's practical outlook and understanding of the good people of Spirit River, where she could be elected Queen if such a thing were possible.

After she heard Anderson's comments, which Arnold almost had to pry out of him with a crowbar, she began: "Well, guys, maybe the time has come to make some changes about how we do things around here. How many committees and boards and clubs do we have around here that never really do anything they didn't do the year before, and the year before that, and so on. It's no wonder none of the kids stick around, or once they leave, ever come back. Even Gas-Jockey-George is frustrated by that; he'd like to do better than he does but he feels like a hamster in a wheel."

"George has no idea what a hamster is, or what it would do in a wheel," commented Arnold.

"Oh shut up Arnold, you know what I mean even if you and George never met a hamster!" Marion grinned across the table at him. "Anyway, guys, maybe it's time to bite the bullet and see if we can raise a little passion around this place. I, for one, am tired of people telling me they don't trust Robertson but are afraid to speak up because it's always about somebody's job."

Arnold sat for a long moment after she went silent. "Well, yeah, when you scratch the surface this is more about Robertson Mines than it is about university professors. So, you two, what do I do about Jeremy, who seems dead-set against getting this Horowitz in?"

Marion snorted. "Jeremy got superannuated by Robertson years ago, probably for being an old pain in the ass, but not because he was fighting them. He has no love for the company, and if he sees a little revenge built into this, he'll be good to go!"

"Woman, how do you know this stuff?" asked Arnold. "I think your parents were a phone book and an encyclopedia."

"Well, babe, while you're greasing wheel bearings, I'm talking and listening."

"Mostly listening, apparently," observed Anderson. "So, shall I print off a handful of copies of that article I found, and bring them along with the agenda tonight?"

"Might as well. Can't win a woman or a knife fight sleeping in the corner. Let's see if it flies."

They got up to leave, and Anderson noticed the ATV was still perched in the box of Arnold's pickup: "Say, did John forget to take that ATV back to The Falls?"

"Nah, he called me last night and asked if I had one to rent. I just told him no, but I have a demonstrator that I'd just bring along. I don't think he wore it out."

Anderson drove his old-model Colorado back to the dock and topped up the fuel in the launch from the slip tank he kept on the truck. He opened the engine hatch and checked fluids in the engines and the transmission, grabbed the left-over maps, mug, and thermos and stuffed them into his fancy and newly appreciated briefcase, checked the mooring lines, locked the wheelhouse, and drove home, all two hundred feet. When he got into his house, he emptied the briefcase and tidied up the cups on the table, putting them into the sink.

He opened the fridge and took out a small bottle of Pepsi. John had insisted that he and Arnold have a beer at lunch, even though he was wearing his uniform and couldn't join them. Anderson didn't want another beer before the meeting and had pretty well had it with coffee for the moment, so he opened the Pepsi. He didn't like the stuff anyway, but he absolutely hated drinking it from a bottle, so he poured it into a glass and went and sat down at his desk where he printed off several copies of the Globe & Mail article he had shown Arnold. He made up the agendas as he had promised, and settled down at the table to re-read the article.

He wanted to know exactly what he was talking about if they were going to have this item on the agenda, as he had a feeling he would have to be the person defending it. He then went back to his computer and Googled Robertson Mines, looking through their corporate information and at some of the commentaries and blogs that concerned the company. The financial wizards thought the company was a huge and still-rising star; the environmental commentators thought they were more like a black hole.

***

"Who knows," he sighed. It was time to go. He gathered the papers he had printed, got back in his truck and drove the half-mile west along Lakeshore Road to the Spirit Inn. It was still early, and the parking lot was pretty much empty. Anderson deliberately went in the lounge doors first and found Anita's mother Georgina wiping down tables. She looked up and smiled, "hey, stranger, how ya doin'? Haven't seen you for awhile – I suppose you're here for that meeting?"

"Yeah, hopefully it won't be a long one. Say, Georgina, as I'm sure you know, all of us have been worried sick about Anita. Any word from her yet, or any idea on where she might have gone?"

She put both hands on the table she had been cleaning and stood there a moment with her head down. Then she stood up straight and turned directly to face Anderson. Georgina was not a big woman anytime, but it seemed to Anderson that she had become even smaller. "Oh, Frank, I just don't know. I really don't know. There's lots of times she doesn't come home, but she stays in touch with her friends –

and even sometimes with me, by text usually so we don't argue. But this time, nothing. All I know is that she had been hanging out last week with the band working the Rock Pit in The Falls, but they're gone now – gone to Sarnia I think. The police were going to checked into them, but so far I've learned nothing." She wiped her hand across her right eye, and went on: "The whole thing is driving Fred crazy, 'cause there's nothing he can do about it – at least I can get out of the house and go to work in the evening. He's been very good this time. He's more worried than mad, and he's staying off the booze."

Two men had come into the lounge, and obviously had questions, probably about where the meeting was being held. Anderson took Georgina gently by the shoulders and gave her a short hug. "Is the meeting room open?" She nodded. "Thanks, Georgina. Folks are starting to arrive for the meeting so I guess I'd better go there with these guys. You take care, and say hi to Fred for me. And don't hesitate to call if any of us can help. We're all keeping our ears open."

***

Anderson introduced himself to the new arrivals, and led them through the small side door that led directly to the lobby and the small meeting room, which was in fact two main-floor hotel rooms joined together. Georgina (who did almost everything at the Inn except sign the cheques) had loaded up a 20-cup coffee urn on a small table in the corner, and set out some paper cups along with a jug of cream, a box of sugar cubes and some stir-sticks. The plain white walls were adorned with a calendar and some local photos – including his favourite, locally referred to as "The Crash of '69", when a bank manager, who commuted from his home on Toronto

Island to his cottage on Awan Lake in a small airplane, mis-timed his landing and flipped the floatplane upside down in the lake. The banker survived just fine, but his ego apparently didn't; he sold out that winter and hadn't been seen since.

It didn't take long for the room to fill up. Arnold and Marion were the next to arrive, and soon there were eighteen people crowded into a room set up for twelve. Arnold had invited the two PSP interns to join the meeting as observers (out of courtesy, but partly, he explained to Anderson, because if there was to be a public event later in the summer, they would likely need the interns to help with hosting it).

At 7:35, Arnold called the meeting to order. He handed around the agendas Anderson had prepared, and briefly explained the reason for the special meeting. He welcomed the ten or so visitors, and asked for everyone to introduce themselves around the table. He started with himself as PSP Local Chair, and went clockwise until it came back to Marion on his right, who simply jerked her left thumb in his direction and said, "I'm with him." Everyone knew Marion, and those who didn't, soon would.

One of the several people around the table who Anderson didn't know was an attractive young-ish blonde, in full make-up and hairdo and dressed in a business suit. She sort of looked familiar, and when she introduced herself as Wendy Webster from the cottage group, the light came on: he had just met her last night at the island. "So Wendy Webster is Marjorie Webster's little sister. Geez," he thought to himself, "she sure cleans up good. If she hadn't said her name I would never have picked her out; she bears almost no resemblance to the ponytailed little chick I met last night. Well, I guess it was dark."

"Okay folks, it's time to get at the business of the day,"

Arnold began. "First, though, Frank do you suppose Georgina could spare us a couple more chairs from the bar? I think we have brought in all the lobby chairs, but I guess we need a couple more." Anderson said "yup" and headed out the door and across the lobby. Arnold continued: "A couple of you have told me that we may have a unique opportunity to have the Protected Shorelines Program group host a public meeting here this summer. Dave Bradshaw is one of our cottage residents who works at Ryerson University, and he has a handle on this; Dave – would you start us off by telling us what you've found out and exactly what you have in mind?"

Marion began writing notes in a school exercise book, while a tall, slim young man at the other end of the table took a sip of coffee and began: "As I mentioned in the introductions, I'm an associate prof at Ryerson, and I get to travel to conferences in different provinces and even down into the States as part of my research. I was out at a limnology workshop in late April at Nanaimo, and had the privilege of spending some time talking with Dr. Sebastian Horowitz who was the keynote speaker. I'm sure many of you here tonight have seen Dr. Horowitz on television, where he is often being interviewed about the desperate state of Canada's – and the world's – water supply. Dr. Horowitz is actually a medical doctor – a specialist in pediatrics – but he has spent much of his career studying and writing about water. He has retired from his medical career and now he actually lives at Nanaimo, but he travels extensively, from deserts in northern Africa to the mountains of Nepal, and of course all over the States and Canada..."

He was briefly interrupted by a shuffle of chairs that Anderson was bringing in. Once everyone was seated he continued: "To make a long story short, he gets a lot of gigs hosting documentaries about water; he loves a camera and a microphone, so when the media calls, he answers. But more importantly, for us here at Awan Lake, when Horowitz calls the media, they answer him. When I told him about our group here, and the looming concerns about Robertson Mines, he told me that he would be happy to speak at a meeting here. I asked about cost, and he said he has a private foundation that pays his expenses except for flights, and his speaker's honorarium. He said it would be helpful if we could pick up the airfare. So, if we do the flights in and out, the whole cost to us would be perhaps $2500."

There was a short flurry of mostly whispered conversations around the room. "I've heard him on TV and he's such a self-important little bastard. He drives me crazy!" That was Jeremy Forbes who spoke up, not unexpectedly, and Arnold was ready for him.

"Thank-you, Dave. That's interesting information. I know that some in the room, and on our committee who are not here tonight, may feel this is the wrong time to have a high-profile event like you are proposing. Jeremy, you and I had talked a bit about it earlier this week; this would be a good time to get it all out on the table, so to give everyone a chance to speak up I'll go around the table again." Turning to the woman on his left, he asked, "Janette?"

And so it went around the table. Janette thought the speaker would be interesting to hear, but worried about the community's privacy with all the media showing up in town. Suzanne agreed with Jeremy's earlier comment, saying she thought the guy was a pompous little jerk and wanted nothing to do with him. The two interns were next, and protested gently that their roles were as observers, but Arnold pressed them for comments anyway; both were enthusiastic about the idea and offered to help set it up. Jeremy was polite enough to mutter, I've said all need to say," and shut up. Some of the other men around the table were cautiously favourable, wondering about costs, or logistics, or timing (should it be on a weekend to get more people?) When it was Wendy Webster's turn, and to Anderson's surprise, she said in a clear and confident voice that she wouldn't say anything because she was new to the community and didn't know enough about the Program.

Anderson was seated to Marion's right, so he would be almost the last person to comment. When it had gone around the table, he picked up the little stack of Globe & Mail reprints he had brought along and started to pass them around. "I asked our Chairman earlier if I could pass these around," he said, "and he agreed. We've heard an outline from David about who Dr. Horowitz is; this article gives an idea of the kind of impact he can have. Let's just read it to ourselves for a few minutes, then I have something to say."

There was a shuffling of paper, then silence. Marion made some notes from the article and was jotting them down in her notebook, and there were a couple of whispered exchanges down the table. After about four minutes, Anderson began:

"Those of you around the table who know me, know that I kinda stick to myself and spend a lot time on my boat, often out on the lake doing stuff for people, and usually alone. I'm not a person that likes to attract a lot of attention. But sometimes there is a time for that, and this may be the right time for this community." He took a big slug from his paper cup. "I'm sure most of us know that our local PSP Committee folks talk about more than just a few birds in the marshes around the lakeshore when we get together; we talk about everything to do with the quality of our lake whether it's about septic tanks, marker buoys, speed limits, the village's sewage lagoon, or the impact of the latest water toy of the season. All the things we see as threats. And anyone over ten years old with a pulse knows that Awan Lake could be under threat from mining activity, too, whether it's happening now or proposed to happen soon – or anytime. To be more specific, there is a huge threat from one of North America's biggest mining corporations – Robertson Mines – and its plans for a massive expansion of its ore refining capacity here that will almost certainly have a huge impact on our lake."

Everyone had looked up from the print-out he had circulated; he had their attention. "So now you know what I think I know, and frankly, I think that if we fail to get our concerns out in front of a much bigger audience as soon as possible, we may miss the only chance we'll get to save the future of our lake. I love this place and I don't want to see us miss any opportunity to save it. Going public with the help of Dr. Horowitz, love him or not, could give us that chance."

There was a short silence. "Thank-you, Frank," said Arnold. "You've certainly given us something to think about. I hadn't thought it all through before. Marion, I think you're the last one we haven't heard from. Any comments?"

Marion, apparently, was determined to be the strong silent type this evening: this time she jerked her right thumb in Anderson's direction and muttered, "like he said."

Arnold dreaded the next call: "Jeremy, I know you are not at all fond of this whole idea, but maybe you want to say more?"

Jeremy Forbes didn't answer right away, and when he did he spoke slowly: "I don't read much, and the only television I watch is hockey, so at this time of year that ain't much watchin'. But a couple of days ago I was talking to my favourite granddaughter, who's..."

Marion had evidently decided she had something to say: "Forbes, you old twit, you've only got one granddaughter. What are you talking about?" Jeremy was married to Marion's sister and their son had a daughter in her early teens, so the great aunt was having her moment.

"Arnold, tell your old lady to settle down," Jeremy barked. "Yes, she's my only granddaughter but if I had ten of 'em she'd still be my favourite. She's the only one around our place that makes any sense. Anyway, she's planning to go to college, which is usually where kids go away and never come back. But she asked me, "Grandpa, when I'm done college and want to come home, will our town and our lake still be here?" That kinda stopped me, y'know. Deep question from a special young lady. So... even if I hate nosy people and pushy experts and silly self-important news reporters, maybe we're gonna have to do something to make sure we keep what we got. So, yeah, Anderson, yeah, Arnold. maybe it's the right thing to do."

"Thanks for saying that, Jeremy." Arnold looked around the table at the others. "Any other thoughts out there? Haven't been many of us talking..."

Janette put her hand up and said, "Okay, you got me. Let's try it – we can put up with the busybodies for a few days." A few others nodded, and a couple said, "I'm in."

Marion nudged Arnold and suggested, "maybe we should get a count?"

Arnold held up his hand asking for quiet: "Okay folks, let's do a show of hands; all in favour of asking Dave to contact Dr. Horowitz and set up a public meeting, hopefully before mid-August?"

The response was positive, and unanimous except for the

interns and – to Anderson's surprise – Wendy Webster who, like the interns, did not vote either way.

***

It hadn't taken long for the meeting to be over. When Arnold went to adjourn, Marion broke in to remark that – once a date was confirmed for the proposed public meeting – the committee would need to put together some kind of special sub-group because there would be a helluva lot to do. And, she noted, someone need to make an estimate of how many people might show up, so they could figure out where to hold the damn thing. The community hall seemed an obvious place, but would it be big enough? Marion needn't have worried – there was a flood of hands offering to help and someone suggested they adjourn to the bar and talk about it.

As Anderson predicted, after the meeting adjourned almost everyone shuffled across the lobby from the meeting room and simply re-formed around a gathering of small round bar tables in the lounge. "Might as well have just held the whole damn meeting here," Anderson said as he settled into a more comfortable chair. He called to the bartender, "Nobody in at all tonight, Florence?"

"Nope, not since I've been here anyway. I figured I might as well sit here and give Georgina time to go home. She has enough on her mind these days and I figured she could use an evening at home." Florence was the lady who wrote the cheques. She had been the Inn's manager for years, a task she had taken on somewhat reluctantly for her brother who had bought the place in 2005 but continued to live in Ottawa where he had a federal government job. Apparently the Spirit Inn was to be his retirement Program.

Naturally, the chatter shifted to the missing Anita, a subject no one would have wanted to touch if Georgina had still been there. In that crowd of mostly cottagers, it was likely only a few knew Anita at all, but most had heard that a local girl had gone missing. The interns, though, who had made the Inn their home away from home most evenings, had gotten quite fond of her. "She was here most weekday evenings," Cyndi remarked, "but on the weekends she used to spend her nights at that club in Maple Falls. About a week ago, though, was the last I saw her; she was talking non-stop about a musician – bass player I think – with Amanita, the band playing at the club."

Adumbi's voice was unmistakable, with its African lilt and low British undertones. And he always sounded terribly polite and serious: "Yes, and after early Wednesday evening she left here and we haven't seen her since. We've been waiting to tease her about her new bass player but neither Cyndi nor I have seen her since then."

Marion was "Aunty Marion" to all the young girls in town and especially, of course, to her niece. "Well, I spent a little time on the phone this morning and I was actually able to track down the band that had been at The Falls. I talked to their lead guy – woke him up I think, around noon – and he said they had just had to hire another bass player because this guy never showed up Tuesday night. And no, he didn't remember Anita except he said his drummer told him that Albert (he pronounced like it was French) had been having some kind of trouble with a chick from Maple Falls. He didn't know anything more, or wasn't saying anyway. I told the cops, but I think they just filed that information. They're not as excited about this whole thing as they should be, in my mind."

"Where's the band playing now?" Anderson asked.

"Ottawa. Some hangout in ByWard Market."

"Oh, I thought somebody said they had gone to Sarnia. Well, if they're playing a club in ByWard Market, they're probably pretty good. Too good for that run down old rock joint in The Falls anyway. When was the last time Anita's buddies heard from her?"

"Monday evening, I guess. According to the police she texted some gal named Twyla in The Falls to say she was having a great time with someone new and that she would tell her all about it soon. That's it... Twyla has heard nothing since and nor has anyone else."

" That's not much to go on," said Anderson.

"Not a damn thing," said Marion. "I've told Georgina what I know, but there's no comfort in it. This must be awful for her."

The two interns had a few words between themselves, then stood up and said goodnight all around, smiling politely at everyone and thanking Arnold for letting them sit in on the meeting. Marion called to them when they reached the door, "Remember, I'll be calling you when we start planning this thing!"

"No worries, Mrs. Jamieson, no worries," replied Adumbi. "We're happy to help."

Jeremy was on his second double shot of bar whiskey. After they had gone out and the door had closed, he mumbled loudly enough for everyone to hear, "Nice way to go to school. Wish it was that way when I was young."

Arnold looked across at him: "Huh?"

"Well, Mister Cool and his cute little blond girlie and all."

Arnold chuckled: "You'd be surprised, old timer! I just learned the other day that Adumbi is gay and Cyndi is a lesbian, so I imagine there's not a lot of action going on there!"

Jeremy sat stunned, then made his second speech of the night: "Gays and lesbians shouldn't even be allowed to come here. You want to build our town but people like that don't even have children!"

About now, everyone in the room had ducked their heads in embarrassment. Again, it was Marion's turn: "That's just dumb, you old fart. For two or three generations now all the old folks like you have been telling all your kids and grandkids to get the hell out of Spirit River and move to Toronto or Vancouver because there's nothing to do here. You even said that back when you were mayor. What the hell do you care whether gay folks don't have kids? That's just stupid. That kind of thinking will make sure my niece never comes near Spirit River, ever again!"

Anderson laughed aloud and stood up: "Well put, Mrs. Jamieson! Forbes, the cops have been around all day and now you've got a skinful of whiskey; I'm gonna take you home so you don't add point zero eight to your troubles. Come on, we're leavin' before Marion takes another run at ya." Old Jeremy Forbes slammed his glass down on the table and went to say something... then thought better of it and got up, following Anderson unsteadily to the door and out into the parking lot.

Thankfully, Anderson thought, it was a short trip to the Forbes residence, but as he pulled up in the driveway Jeremy said quietly, "Thanks Anderson. Marion tells me I never shifted gears when the calendar turned from 1999 to 2000, and I guess she's right. The second whiskey didn't help... sorry for pissing people off."

"That's okay old timer. Tomorrow's another day," said Anderson. "Get a good night's sleep, and thanks for your support on the meeting stuff." Forbes mumbled something incoherent, shut the truck door and weaved up the driveway to his front door. Anderson waited for him to go in and shut the door, then reversed down the driveway and headed home. He considered it had been a long day, and the world could wait until he was good and ready for it tomorrow morning.

07:10 JULY 14

Anderson had hit the snooze button twice before he got up and headed for the coffee pot. He drained it, rinsed it out and prepared to brew another pot, making a mental note to buy another couple of tins of dark roast next time he went to Maple Falls. Anderson liked good food though he was not a fussy eater. But when it came to coffee, he was a fanatic: had to be fine grind dark roast, and fair trade coffee was a good way to go but the real stuff was hard to find in Maple Falls and very damn expensive and always whole bean. He told folks he was too lazy to grind his own.

When the coffee had brewed, he poured a cup, put on a light jacket and took it outside on the little open porch at his front door. The sun was already filtering through the line of trees along the shore to the east and over the top of a couple of ramshackle small sheds that blocked his view of the shore itself. Anderson went through the events of yesterday, arriving at the conclusion that it had really been just another day at Awan Lake and that he had work to do today.

One thing was puzzling him, though: just who were Marjorie and Wendy Webster, and in particular why had Wendy's responses at last night's meeting seemed somewhat out of place, over cautious perhaps. Indeed, why had she decided to show up at a special meeting at all, since neither of the women had shown any interest in the Protected Shorelines

Program before. "Well, one of these days I'll give Marjorie a call and maybe drop by their little island for a visit. Wouldn't mind seeing her again," he muttered to himself, putting his cup down by the door and heading down to the docks where his little trackhoe had been sitting on the barge since Wednesday morning when he had brought it back from the Jorgenson place.

A quick check around the docks satisfied Anderson that nothing had changed since yesterday evening. He started up the KX Series Kubota, slid the shore-end of the barge ramps onto the beach and backed the machine off onto the shore, where he turned it around and waddled it slowly along the road back to his shop. It was a nice day, so he parked it by the big door, turned off the engine, and headed back down to the barge. He spent twenty minutes unloading tools and leftovers from the Jorgenson job into the back of his truck.

On his way back to the shop, Arnold drove alongside in his own truck, and stopped. "Mornin' Frank! Got a few minutes?"

"You bet," Anderson grinned. "Needed a second cup anyway. Let me back this thing up to the shop and we'll go grab a cup."

The two men settled at the table with their coffee. "Shoot," said Anderson.

"Well, first, Marion says 'thank-you' for taking Jeremy home last night. I hope it went okay?"

"Oh yeah, no worries. He was well behaved. I think he had sort of embarrassed himself. He even thanked me!"

"Okay, that's good." Arnold paused a moment then continued: "Couple of things. First, I just got off the phone with – ah – LaChance (I forgot his first name) from the Feds at Environment. He's not the guy who normally comes to meet with us, but his immediate supervisor. Anyway, he told me we have to meet with him – Monday if at all possible but no later than Tuesday morning. He was pleasant enough, but obviously something serious is going on in his office and it has to do with the Awan Lake Protected Shoreline Program local committee." He stopped and looked across the table at Anderson: "So... how do you feel about a drive to Ottawa either Sunday night or early Monday morning? LaChance did say he will approve us taking the travel and hotel costs out of our expenses budget."

"Humph," Anderson growled, "it's not like we have nothing else to do with our lives except volunteer our time to a federal Program. And I don't really expect Marion will be thrilled with you going around the countryside meeting with bureaucrats and leaving her alone at the garage. However... I was wondering this morning if someone other than a cop might be able to get more information from the guys in that band about the bass player and Anita. I guess we could go take in some music on Monday night if the band is still in ByWard Market."

"I already told Marion about this. She had roughly the same reaction as you, but we didn't get to the Anita thing... not a bad idea. But, you're talking Monday night and some places close and some bands switch out over Sunday and a new band turns up Monday. Marion found out the club name. Why don't I call her and have her check it out? I expect she'll think it's a good idea."

"Go for it." Anderson got up and poured some more coffee. He did a little clean up around the kitchen sink while Arnold called Marion and explained what they were thinking.

It didn't take long. "Marion thinks you got a good idea, so she'll call and get more information. Let's hope there's someone at that bar this early in the morning. And," he said, "while we're waiting, let me fill you in on some of the talk at the Inn after you left. It seems things are heating up over at the proposed Robertson Mines expansion."

"I haven't been that far up the east shore for a while, and have no idea, except that I've seen a few more consultants in their pickups running around town. And Georgina told me a few weeks ago that the Inn's rooms are pretty well full most weeknights"

"Yeah, well, no surprise there I guess. Doctor Dave – Bradshaw, you know, the guy that was pushing the public meeting with Horowitz – says that he has heard from engineering profs at his university that Robertson has been hiring young engineers and technicians big-time – fresh out of school – since May, and they have them all working on their proposed Awan Lake expansion. Hold on..."

Arnold's cell went off with Beethoven's Fifth, which Anderson thought an odd ringtone for a guy whose taste in music was Waylon Jennings and Johnny Cash. "Hi Hon... huh? Sunday night? Damn. Well at least they're still there... you will? You are such a good women, must be why I married you. Yeah we'll behave."

He clicked off the phone and told Anderson that the band was playing through Sunday night but then was moving to a gig in Belleville, so if they were to catch them it would mean leaving Sunday around noon. Marion said she'd try to set them up with a hotel room close in, as they would need to get across to Gatineau for their meeting with Environment Canada on Monday morning. "At least we'll be able to drive home after that. I'll call that LaChance guy back and set the appointment up." He took his phone out of his pocket again, and looked up his early-morning caller.

A few minutes later he hung up and told Anderson the meeting was set for 9:30 Monday morning, at the Gatineau office building. "LaChance (Pierre, it turns out) was pleased at our quick response. And if it's okay with you we'll take Marion's Equinox. It's a lot easier on gas than that old Ford of mine, and anyway there's no place in Ottawa that I want to try and park a pickup with a long box. And I don't trust that old Colorado of yours – or those tires that have lasted you so well – you think!"

"Works real well for me," Anderson laughed. "So... the party starts at 13:00 hours on Sunday, right?"

"I don't know about you and your 13:00 hours, but I'll pick you up at 1:00, okay?"

"Perfect. And remind me to teach you how to tell time someday!"

Arnold went out to his pickup and headed home, leaving Anderson to spend the rest of the day unloading the tools and junk from his truck, installing the new parts on Mister Kubota and changing oil on both. He had fried himself yet another egg for lunch, but by early Friday evening he felt like something more like a real meal and took himself down to the Zoo, which was almost empty. He sat at his usual table, nursed a beer and ordered a very rare steak sandwich and fries with sliced tomatoes instead of soggy vegetables – even the Zoo couldn't make those things palatable.

07:45 JULY 15

Anderson's cell-alarm went off at 07:00 hours as usual. He punched the snooze button twice, shut the alarm off and finally got up half an hour later. He looked out the window as he headed for the bathroom and the shower: it was a beautiful-looking day, with no clouds to be seen and a light breeze from the west.

He took a nice long hot shower, as he always did if he had time, and this morning he had time. As he also often did, he thought of his father, who used to yell at him to get the hell out of the shower: *All you need is three minutes, and it's better for you if the last minute is cold water. You're wasting time and money on all that hot water!* But of course, his father had been a navy guy, and the younger Anderson had not. Bow, stern, port and starboard – and the 24-hour clock – along with a wealth of seamanship knowledge – had been passed down and become rooted in his soul, but not the part about short cold showers. Twenty minutes later he slithered out of the shower, towelled off, and dressed.

The coffee pot, of course had been put to work and the coffee was hot. He took a mug and went out to his porch. He didn't smoke a lot unless Arnold or another smoker was around but this morning he took a cigarette with him and sat back to think about his plans for the day. The waterfront by the docks was already busy with people launching their boats for a day's fishing or water-skiing. The lake got very busy on the weekends, and it had occurred to him that nobody would really notice if he took his launch for a nice slow cruise far up the east shore, past MacLean Point and south to where Robertson Mines had proposed to expand the small ore refinery the company had originally built several decades before Anderson ever came to the lake.

He had also been thinking about inviting some company along on this little adventure: Marjorie. Now he took his phone from his shirt pocket, found her number, and hit re-dial. After four rings, she picked up: "Hello?"

"Hi Marjorie, it's Frank Anderson. Good morning!" She seemed a little surprised, but somehow, pleased. Anderson continued, "Say, it's a perfect morning to be out on the lake and I was thinking about taking a morning cruise up the lake past your place. No big deal, but I thought you might enjoy coming along."

"Sounds like a great idea to me! Can I bring the coffee this time, and maybe a sandwich?"

"I sure won't say no to that! Someday it would be nice to go down the river to Maple Falls and have lunch in that nice little restaurant by the town dock, but that would be a longer trip, and I just kinda felt like going east instead of west. Could I pick you up in about forty-five minutes, or would you like more time?"

"Maybe give me an hour to make the coffee and find something fascinating to make sandwiches with."

"Perfect," Anderson replied. "I'll give you a couple of honks as I go around the island, like the other night, and pick you up at your little dock. And hey, the sandwiches don't have to be fascinating, y'know. I'm pretty easy to feed!"

Marjorie laughed brightly: "Okay, looking forward to it!"

Arnold is gonna tease the shit out of me about this, Anderson laughed to himself after he switched off. *But I have an excuse. I want to learn more about Wendy and why she had turned up at the meeting on Thursday night.*

He poured a second coffee into his travel mug and walked down to his boat, slipped the spring lines, started the main engine and genset and turned on the electronics. He stood on the dock for a few minutes, watching the traffic that was buzzing about the little harbour, and waved at people he thought he recognized, and some he had no clue. When his area seemed clear, he slipped the bow and stern lines, blew a long blast on the horn and moved very slowly off the dock. When the way seemed clear he headed straight out into the lake before speeding up, then pointed the bow in the general direction of MacLean Point and Ship Island, and moved the throttle forward until his GPS showed he was doing about eight knots. Anderson took out his second smoke, lit it and took a mouthful of coffee and settled in to enjoy the half-hour trip to his first destination: the Webster wharf on Ship Island. He loved moments like these: sunshine, a light wind, the diesels humming under his feet, and a place to go. It's why he lived here.

The thirty minutes went by too quickly, but as he gave two quick shots on the horn and swung around to the south side of the little island, he was indeed pleased to see his passenger perched on a small cooler near the end of the beat-up old dock. He nosed carefully into the wharf, reversed the engine and stopped alongside. Marjorie was ready... she had put on her small backpack, then handed across the cooler and a big thermos jug and then stepped across onto the boat as if she had done it all her life. Anderson put the engine back into gear and backed out into the little bay, then turned the launch around and headed southeast toward the far shore. "Good morning Marjorie," he said with a grin. "That was simple – looks like you've done that before!"

"Hi Frank. Not really, except with the little boat. This is going to be fun. Apart from the other night, I've never been on a boat this size, where I can actually lounge around and relax. Where did you say we are headed?"

Anderson pointed along the distant shore: "We'll cruise up that way until we get close to land a couple of miles up from the point, then follow the shoreline for awhile, up near where the big mining operation is. You can't really see it from here, but I'm sure you can see smoke and steam coming from there on most weekdays."

"Oh, sure, when we moved here Wendy told me that's Robertson Mines. I've never been up there – it's a bit far to paddle and anyway I prefer to go along the shore and poke around in the shallows and the little marshes and inlets from the streams. I'm not a very energetic kayaker, and not curious enough to zip around in the outboard – it's just our way to get to and from the village." She rummaged around on the well deck and unearthed the big thermos. "I see you brought a mug, so let me re-fill it and pour myself one. I noticed the other day that you took it black, but I brought sugar in case you like it. I do."

"That's great, and no, black is black, for me. On a cold – very cold – day, though, I've been known to add brandy and a bit of sugar." Anderson had the engine cranked up to about ten knots by now, and there were only distant small boats around so he clicked on the autohelm and let it do the driving while they sipped coffee and talked a bit about the events of Thursday morning. She did tell him that not until last night had she had a really sound sleep; the brief flash of that awful face as it turned under her paddle had stuck with her, and she expected the vision wouldn't completely go away for a long while.

As she was talking, she noticed that Anderson wasn't anywhere near the wheel. "Ah, Frank, you're, ah, not steering. And I've completely lost track of direction although I guess perhaps that's our island over there behind us."

"Yes, you're right on both counts – that is indeed your island back there, and we're still headed up the shore like I said. You been in an airliner, I'm sure, so you know they have autopilots? Well, this boat has an autopilot. Several ways to set it up, but the simple way is what I've done: you just aim where you want to go and push a button that tells it to keep going there. Electronics, a compass, GPS and little motors do the rest."

"That is so cool," she laughed, walking over and looking curiously at the switches and dials and screens. "That is so cool. Does it serve coffee and make music too?"

"Nope. That stuff takes up too much room. This outfit just steers so I can pour the coffee, and if I want music I just bring Arnold and Marion along. When they aren't shouting at each other or smooching, they actually play guitars and sing very well!"

"Really?" Marjorie asked. "Arnold so does not look like a musician to me, and if Marion is the woman who works in the Main Street Garage where Wendy told me Arnold works, she doesn't look like one either. They are both so very practical and rough-and-ready looking!"

Anderson chuckled: "Yes, indeed, they are, and if you like

73

country and old folk music, they make for good listening."
Anderson also saw his moment: "Say, as you probably know,
Wendy was at the same meeting I was at a couple of nights
ago. What does she do? Sorry, that's kind of rude. I should
have first asked what Marjorie does. I know nothing about you
at all except that you are brave, steady and cheerful."

"Hah," she smirked at him. "Brave, steady and cheerful
and not even pretty?"

Anderson could feel his face turn red, and his stomach
tighten ever so slightly: "In the words of our Prime Minister,
'this is 2017' and I never tell any woman I hardly know that she
is really pretty, even when she really is. Seems like it risks a
hard slap upside the face – or a lawsuit maybe!"

They both laughed, he a bit nervously and she with
pleasure. Marjorie began: "Okay, I'll take that as a compliment.
Let me fill you in on the girls from Webster Island."

"First, Wendy. Wendy is a writer, although she doesn't
call herself that anymore. She works for a small firm as a public
relations consultant with a bunch of corporate clients. And, in
fact, she doesn't hardly use her creative side as a writer at all
anymore; she manages PR stuff for her clients, and uses her
team of young beavers to do the creative work. She is making
herself filthy rich, but she is also a sweetheart, very generous,
and a wonderful sister." Marjorie paused a moment while
Anderson altered course to the south very slightly and re-
engaged the autohelm.

"Then there is her older sister Marjorie," she continued.
"Marjorie would like to be an artist, but she is disappointed in
herself. She does do contract work, fairly often, as a
commercial graphic artist, which she hates to admit. Even at
that, she works with pens and pencils and paints or acrylics,
and is not capable of working in the modern world of digital

art, computer graphics and the like. Marjorie is very lucky that her sister loves her, because she does not feel very worthy."

She paused. "Frank, I'm sorry. I sort of blurted all that out and I am sure it's not very fascinating."

Anderson had been listening intently, except for keeping one eye on a fast boat that was approaching from behind them on the starboard side. He put up his hand to Marjorie in a gesture that clearly said "wait a minute" and took control of the wheel back from the autohelm. "Don't know what this guy is up to," he said aloud. He held the launch on its course while the approaching motorboat overtook them, made a lazy half-circle to the left around the launch and shot back down the lake. The five or six passengers waved beer cans at him, and disappeared with the boat into its own spray, heading back the way they came.

"Okay, sorry about that. You never know what folks are up to." He set the autohelm on the previous course and clicked it on. "Actually, I am fascinated, absolutely, especially about the artist. I intend that we should spend a lot of time talking about the artist sister, but let's start briefly with the public relations sister. She came across at first like a bright and lively person, but she kinda kept her cards to herself, like she was sitting in at a poker game. She made no comment except that she was new to the area and didn't want to give any opinions and she sort of kept looking at me sideways."

"Funny you should say that. First thing Friday morning over breakfast she asked me what I really knew about 'that Anderson guy'. I allowed as how I really didn't know much except that you had been very kind to me and were sensible and obviously well-thought-of by the police and the other people involved. What more's a girl gonna say, I told her, after all I had only been around you for, like, two hours at most and

75

that was mostly in a boat looking for a dead body. She tried to grill me a little more, and I wondered if you had made a pass at her but that didn't fit with the little I already knew. I am still wondering what was going on in her head."

The launch was still about a half-mile offshore, but Anderson went to the wheel, shut down the autohelm, throttled back by about two knots, and set the sonar warning system to 25 feet. He knew the lake was – overall – very deep, as much as 250 feet and averaging over 75 feet, but the shorelines were rocky and while the paper chart didn't show any shallow areas along the east shore, he wasn't taking any chances. And, as he was not really very familiar with the east shore with its low rocky profile, he felt the twenty-five foot depth setting should give him plenty of warning at this speed.

Marjorie had been watching this process closely, so he took the time to explain it all carefully. By now, he had settled himself in the helmsman's seat behind the wheel and was keeping his eye on the GPS and sonar screens as well as the water surface as he edged the boat closer to shore, until they were less than a quarter mile off and running parallel to it. "I have a question for you," Marjorie said.

Here goes, he thought. "How can I help?" he asked.

"What is a knot, other than something you make in a rope? That doesn't sound like what you are talking about, though."

He chuckled, relieved: "Aha, a knot. Yes, the word 'knot' refers to more than just a thingy in a rope. In this case, it refers to speed: a nautical mile per hour. One knot is the same as just over one mile per hour, and just under two kilometers per hour. Heaven knows why, in this age of metric everything, we continue to have this unit in English-speaking countries, but there you go. Confuses everyone, don't feel badly!"

"So now I have a few questions for you," he continued. "They are about the artist sister."

"Okay, fair enough," she replied, "but first, I am looking at the instrument on top of your dashboard, and assuming it is a clock. It just clicked over eleven hundred – it now says eleven hundred and one. So, if it is a clock, does it start all over again at 1:00 pm, or does it do something different, like thirteen hundred, and so on?"

"You nailed it," Anderson chuckled. "Yep, it counts the hours in order all the way to 23:59, then goes back to four zeros and starts all over. That way there no duplicate hours in the day. It's called twenty-four hour, or often military, time. Actually the railways have always used it as well."

"So, like, twelve hundred hours is lunchtime in both languages? And since I'm starving, could we stop out here pretty soon and relax over lunch?"

"First, you are correct. 12:00 hours is lunchtime. Today, though, I would like to wait until we have cleared the area near Robertson Mines. This boat, with its size and design and dirty grey colour – to say nothing of a navigation mast full of aerials – looks kind of official, and I don't want any of Robertson's paranoid personnel thinking we're out here spying. If we slow down, they might wonder if there's more to us than weekenders out for a ride, and on top of that I want to take some photos, at least with my phone."

Marjorie was silent for a moment, then brightly piped up and said, "I think I can fix that." She went out onto the well deck and grabbed her backpack, which she took forward into the tiny cabin, closing the door behind her. In less that two minutes she popped back out of the cabin wearing a very attractive two-piece bathing suit over her very elegant frame. "If I go out on deck with this – she showed him a small but powerful looking camera – and lounge around the deck taking shots of seagulls and loons, they'll likely not give us another thought. And sometimes the birds might be between us and the shore."

"You're brilliant! That's a great idea. I'll speed up a little so it doesn't take too long to go by their facility. This is perfect..." he paused, and then almost under his breath: "And you may now officially forget what I didn't say earlier about your being pretty!"

She giggled at him, and asked when she should start. Anderson asked her to steady the wheel, took a pair of binoculars off the map table and scoured the shoreline. "I think now wouldn't be a bad idea. I can see the outline of some big buildings about a mile further and I thought I saw some orange markers in the water nearer shore, but just ahead. Yeah, Espionage Specialist and Artist Lady, let's go for it. Let me know if you see anything interesting through your lens, but don't keep it on the shore too long or too often."

She went out onto the well deck, and Anderson bumped the throttle up to about eleven knots, creating a substantially bigger bow-wave and wake which – just maybe, he thought – made it look more like they were just a happy couple out for a joyride. For her part, she wandered over the whole boat, taking snaps of occasional birds, the boat itself, Anderson through the wheelhouse window from the bow, and through the wheelhouse door from the stern. She put her cooler on the shore-side gunwale and took out a couple of beers she had brought, placing one in plain sight on the wheelhouse roof and took the other in to Anderson.

And every few snapshots, the camera lens swung to shore for less than five seconds. They travelled about twenty-five minutes like this until they were well past the buildings, then

Anderson changed course slowly to the west and out toward a big low-lying island about four miles away. After a few more minutes, he called, "Enough already! Let's actually open those beers and relax!"

Which they did. She was chuckling and giggling like a kid, and put him in the same mood. "Any birds? Seals? Tigers? Or are all the photos of my scrawny butt and bearded face?"

"Actually, everything except the seals and tigers, but yes, I got a whole bunch of orange – and maybe numbered – markers and some machinery on the beach. Some people in hardhats too, but too far away to see if they were paying any attention to us. But...this is an insanely expensive camera, and with Photoshop we should be able to get out some pretty good stuff."

"Wow, that's perfect. Thank you so much, for the photography and your imagination to set up the photo-shoot. Remind me to give you a hug when we get back. But now..." as he eased back the throttles until the launch was moving at about two knots and punched in the autohelm once again... "it's time for lunch. It wouldn't look well if you went boating with me, brought along the lunch, then I let you starve to death. Someone would be sure to notice!"

"Me, for one. I get super-grumpy when I'm hungry. And yes, I will remind you about the hug, Mister Anderson."

The roast-beef sandwiches, garden-fresh tomatoes and hard-boiled eggs disappeared almost as fast as the two bottles of beer, and the two sat out on deck for a long while talking about her struggles with learning her craft as a painter, and her challenges getting recognized for her work.

"I like painting pictures of rocks, and that's one of the reasons I convinced Wendy to come to Awan Lake. Trouble is, lots of other folks like painting rocks and scraggy trees on the

Laurentian Shield. I like detail; I was at a special exhibition in Banff while on a course there, recognizing an artist whose first name escapes me but the last name was Taylor. He painted the Canadian Rockies, and he saw them in ways I had not seen before. The level of detail was incredible, and I've always wanted to capture that with our northern Ontario rocks. Maybe someday before I die I'll get it right; if so, I'll die happy!"

By the time they had finished lunch and chatted for a while, they had almost reached a large, low island near the middle of the lake. It was about a half mile long, almost as wide and covered with a tangle of twisted little trees and scrub brush. It was uninhabited, but a few randomly-placed white signs along the shore identified it as a wildlife preserve, with no approach allowed during the spring, summer and early autumn. Anderson gave the island lots of space; he noticed that the depth readings had decreased as he got closer, so he took a wide turn around the south shore of the island before heading north toward Spirit River. Once clear of the island he increased the speed back to about eleven knots and settled in for what would be an hour-long run back to Marjorie's island.

***

It was about 14:00 hours and Anderson wanted to be home in lots of time to get ready to head to Ottawa with Arnold the next day. "I'm headed to Ottawa with Arnold tomorrow afternoon," he said to Marjorie, wondering how much he should tell her about why they were going. He left out the Anita component – it seemed a little silly out of context – but continued: "Every now and then we have to meet with the Feds about the Protected Shorelines Program. They have people they send out from time to time, but the funding agreement is with Environment Canada so once in awhile the bosses like to meet with the local committee executive, or in this case the committee chair and vice-chair. Kind of a pain in the ass 'cause it's a three-hour drive, but at least they pay for the gas, hotel room and dinner if we don't go crazy on the price!"

"I've been wondering about that Program," responded a very relaxed-looking Marjorie who had curled up on the navigator's seat behind the map table. "Those two young people who were out with you on Thursday – the ones with the canoe – I figured they must be part of it, right?"

"Yup, they are university-level summer students studying sustainable environmental management, with a focus on wetlands, lakes and wildlife. They refer to it as biodiversity management; the guy is a graduate student, chasing his Masters degree, and the gal is an undergrad in biology."

"What do they do?"

"Count frogs. Well, frogs and other critters."

"So what does the 'Program' do?"

"Long story, or short?"

"Well, I'd like to know more because that stuff interests me. Actually, I'm really curious because Wendy has no interest in birds or bees or frogs (or rocks, unfortunately) so the only thing she appreciates about the lake is that she gets some peace and quiet away from Toronto. And yet, this Program seems to have her all revved up. Yesterday – the morning after the meeting – she was all a-buzz on her cell phone and on the internet (she uses her iPhone as a 'hot-spot' so she can get internet on her laptop). But, she didn't really say anything to me about it, just said she was helping out a client."

Anderson pondered over that for a moment and decided

to answer Marjorie's curiosity before digging for more information about Wendy's clients: "Well, years ago – and several prime ministers ago – it seems the Feds decided to get out of environmental research and leave it to the private sector – mostly big non-profits – and over the years they have cut back on personnel – big time. Of course, there was still stuff that needed to happen – the environment was always prominent in public surveys even if people voted for jobs and tax-cuts at election time. So the Feds created some public-engagement programs so the government would at least be seen to support things like biodiversity. The Protected Shorelines Program, or PSP as we call it, is one of those. Basically it's a federal grant managed by local committees across Canada."

Anderson paused a moment, then: "I happen to think it's awfully heavy on public communications and youth education, and really low on research, but then I am not a biologist so I don't really know how it all washes down. I just know that we're pretty limited here about what our local committee can take on for Programs and – above all – what we can say in public. We have to crank out warm fuzzy brochures about the importance of the birds and bees to human health and happiness, and we get to employ some local folks on conservation Programs – like putting up signs on that island back there – and to bring in some interesting young folks as interns, like Cyndi and Adumbi. From a local feel-good perspective, it's worthwhile, I guess, and the interns we have had over each of the past four years do get to know, and maybe inspire, some of the young folks in the community. I am sure – in fact I know – that several young locals are in college or university now who likely wouldn't have gone there if it hadn't been for spending some time with the interns, whether on local Programs or even just after-hours at the Inn!"

Marjorie took in the information, and more as they chatted about the meeting and the upcoming event with the nearly-famous Dr. Horowitz. Then she laughed: "Maybe Wendy is all excited because she knows that what you really need is a public relations expert!"

They both laughed at that. Then Marjorie said, "Or maybe not." She got up from the navigator's chair, went to her backpack and took out her camera, which she fidgeted with for a moment then walked across the wheelhouse to Anderson and handed him the camera's memory card. "I want you to take this home, okay? Then, if it's alright with you, I'll come to your place with my laptop and we can have a good look at those photos I took, in private." She turned, put her camera into its case and replaced it in her backpack, then went back to her seat.

Anderson breathed a sigh of relief – he had been wondering about how to talk to Marjorie about his discomfort with her sister's recent behaviour, both at the meeting, and as described by Marjorie. He looked across at her with a smile and said, "Thank-you, and I look forward to going through these with you, soon. It'll have to wait until I'm back from Ottawa, though... maybe Tuesday or Wednesday."

"Perfect. I am looking forward to it myself."

Soon, Ship Island was only about a mile off and they could barely see the little dock and the cottage perched behind. Anderson left the autohelm switched on but pulled the throttle back to about half speed.

Again Marjorie stood up, walked across to him, then tapped him on the shoulder: "I'll take that hug now, if you don't mind."

Anderson stood up, embarrassed and showing it. He put

his arms around Marjorie, pulled her close and held her for a few moments, very relieved that she had changed back out of her elegant camouflage and was actually wearing clothes. Then he moved back and softly kissed her on the forehead. "Thank-you, Marjorie, for a perfect day, a delicious lunch, and some wonderful conversations."

He squeezed her shoulders gently and returned to the wheel and the guidance of his little ship, about which he felt a way more confident in his ability. By now they were just outside the bay, and could see that Wendy was walking down to meet the boat. And he and Marjorie both knew that it was for the better that her sister hadn't been a witness to that exchange of quiet affection.

14:30 JULY 16

Arnold and Anderson had been on the road for an hour and hadn't eaten any lunch, so when an A&W sign revealed itself on their side of the road, Arnold turned in and headed for the drive-thru. "I plan to have a good dinner on the federal government's dime," he said, but I do feel like a hamburger. Work for you?"

"Sure does. Maybe a junior burger with cheese, small fries and a small coffee," Anderson said and handed across a twenty.

Arnold doubled the order, moved forward, took the two bags and paid. "This will go down well. Did you even have breakfast?"

"Ya, actually I did have an eggo thing, but this will be good. Last night I made up for not much breakfast today: fried up a Salisbury steak (otherwise known as a big hamburger) and a couple of eggs and some onions. It was great. Of course I had a good lunch too: Marjorie brought along some great sandwiches, fresh tomatoes and even a couple of beers."

Arnold began to laugh. "Marion told me after the meeting on Thursday that sure enough you would be chasing after that pretty blonde that showed up, but I told her 'nah, Anderson likes her sister'. Hah, so you got her out on the boat didja? Might have known!"

"Yes, well, seemed like a good way to get to know her. But actually one of the things I wanted to find out was all about her sister. Wendy, it turns out, is a public relations executive with seriously big corporate clients. Between you and me for now, I have a sneaky feeling she is somehow connected to the Robertson bunch. And while we were out there, we cruised by the Robertson facility along the southeast shore, and got some photographs."

"Of what?"

"We don't really know, but Marjorie has a camera and telephoto lens from hell that she used, and she has Photoshop on her laptop, so we'll get a chance to see what her lens saw."

"Marion seems to think there's some weird stuff going on," Arnold replied. "She's usually the one that tells me I'm just paranoid about stuff, but this time even she thinks some things ain't the way they seem. And on another topic – talk about paranoid – she wants you and I to be careful when we go out to the bar tonight to talk to the band leader, in case he and his friends don't want people asking too many questions."

Anderson was silent for a moment or two. "I dunno, musicians aren't known for being conspiracy guys, unless maybe it's about drugs. Which, of course, could be involved with Anita's disappearance, but I don't see a connection with any other stuff." He paused again, then went on: "The other stuff sure has me a bit paranoid too, I have to admit, and even Marjorie seemed to be sensing the same thing, even though she really doesn't have a clue about all this stuff. I guess it's tied up around her sister's behaviour; they are normally very close but Marjorie seems to think something is different and that Wendy doesn't want to talk about it. Anyway, I trust Marjorie's perspective, even though I barely know her."

***

Two hours later, Arnold turned the little black SUV onto the Queensway headed east into Ottawa. "Where's our hotel, anyway?" asked Anderson.

"Day's Inn on Rideau, near the Market," said Arnold. "Marion says that since Parliament isn't in session in July, she had no trouble finding a reasonable hotel downtown, with parking, so we're within easy walking distance of the Market and easy to cross over to Gatineau for our appointment with the Feds."

He took the Nicholas Street exit off the Queensway, found King Edward Avenue and arrived at the Rideau Street intersection. As he turned right on to Rideau, he said to Anderson, "We're just a couple of blocks from our hotel, and we'll probably have to go around the block to get to it. I'm not one hundred percent sure this has been the most direct route here, but I kind of know it from coming downtown a few years ago."

"Could have fooled me," Anderson replied. "I might as well be in Spain for knowing where we are... hey – there, over on the left – Day's Inn. Ya nailed it!"

They did wind up circling the block to get into the hotel parking lot. Arnold took his briefcase full of PSP papers and an overnight bag, Anderson slung his worn-out old backpack over one shoulder, and they headed for the reception desk: "Hi there, reservations for Anderson and Jamieson?"

Anderson raised his eyebrows at Arnold: "Two rooms, yet... Marion must have been feeling generous!"

"She told me that for an extra eighty-five bucks she didn't want to have to hear you complaining about my snoring. She's got a good point, actually!"

"Cool. I kind of like my own room anyway – I'm kinda really used to living alone and not bothering anyone. That way

I can paddle around the room in the middle of the night if I get restless, and not worry about waking anyone up."

As they went up the elevator, Arnold suggested they head out to the Market area and find a pub near the nightclub where the band would be playing. "Marion gave me the name of the club (L'Hibou), and said the web reviews claimed they had good dinners, but it's too early to hang around there all night."

The rooms were not luxurious, but they were clean and comfortable. Both men put their bags in their rooms, washed up and headed toward the Market together. It didn't take long to find a pleasant little pub and settle into some beer and a bowl full of unshelled peanuts. The pub was fairly quiet – it was, after all, early on a Sunday evening – so Arnold and Anderson were able to plan how they would approach the band leader once they got to L'Hibou. Being good friends, they threw out a lot of ideas and ultimately decided to play it by ear. After polishing off another sixteen ounces of beer, they headed down the street to the club, looking forward to something more substantial than an A&W burger.

L'Hibou was "old-fashioned trendy", with an overdose of Great Big Sea blasting out of the house sound system. There were few people around, so service was immediate and friendly. "Menus, yes please, and two light local draught beers." Anderson asked if they had batter-fried owl, and Arnold called him a smartass; they settled on New York steaks, one medium and Anderson's very rare. The food took its time arriving, but was worth the wait, and the men took their time finishing their meal. By the time they were done, people were beginning to filter in for the entertainment. Anderson asked their server when the band usually showed up: "This outfit is usually here quite early," she said, "but they were actually here earlier this afternoon, cleaning up and getting ready to move out tonight.

While they were here they did some sound-checks, so they'll likely just come in time to start."

Anderson turned to Arnold and said quietly: "Damn. Seems like we missed that opportunity." Turning back to the server, he asked, "How have you liked them?"

"They're pretty good. A little more rocky than country, but that's pretty normal. And they were breaking in a new bass player this week, so they were a bit 'off' at first."

"Could you point out their leader to us when he comes in?"

"Sure. Better than that, I'll bring him over. His name is Xavier, and he's a good guy; had coffee with him after closing a couple of times."

"Thanks very much!"

About twenty minutes later, after a couple of shaggy young men had come in and settled in at a table between the side of the stage and the fire exit, a tall well-muscled guy with a shaved head and wearing a black tank-top joined them. True to her word, the server went over and spoke quietly to him, pointed in Arnold's and Anderson's direction, and accompanied him over to their table: "Hi," she said, "this is Xavier, Amanita's lead singer."

Arnold and Anderson stood up in greeting, introduced themselves and shook hands. Anderson thanked the server, and invited Xavier to join them at the table. "You talked to my wife Marion on the phone a couple of days ago," Arnold began. "She said to say hello and that she is very thankful for the information you gave her."

Xavier was visibly relieved: no drug cops or bill collectors this time. "Hey, there wasn't much to tell, really. You've come a long way looking for that girl – Anita? – and we haven't seen her since a week ago Thursday..."

"Thursday?" Arnold broke in. "We thought she'd been hanging out with your bass player right through the weekend."

"Either of you guys related to that chick?"

"Nope," said Anderson. "Daughter of a friend. And don't worry, we all know Anita had more than a normal person's share of, er, 'issues'. Really nice kid, but a pack of trouble."

Xavier relaxed and grinned: "Okay, well, then you already know she seemed a little flaky. Perfect match for Albert! So when she came in and talked to him all worried-like before the gig started on Thursday – then took off – we were all teasing him that she beat him to the "good bye" part of his love affair. Albert is a one-night-stand specialist, and we thought it was some kind of miracle that he had kept her around for three nights!"

"So you never saw her for the rest of the weekend?" Arnold asked.

"No, never did. And the gig at Maple Falls was over Saturday night, not like here, and we were packed and outta there by Tim Hortons breakfast time Sunday morning. Never saw her Friday or Saturday."

"Did Albert say anything at all about why she was so worked up?"

"Don't think he had a clue – he wasn't the brightest bulb in the pack anyway, even if he could play that Fender bass like a madman." Xavier paused a moment, then: "Wait a minute, he did say that she was going on about some older people coming and that she had to leave before they got there. We just assumed it was probably her folks or something. So I guess that wasn't it, or you wouldn't be here... and the guys are waving at me and I'm past starting time so I gotta go." He stood up.

Anderson, too, got quickly to his feet and shook hands:

"Thank-you, Xavier, you've been more help to us than you know. Much appreciated!"

"Welcome, man. Good luck! She may have been a bit of a nut, but she's an okay kid."

"We'll hang out here for your first set, anyway."

"Cool!"

After Xavier had gone back to the stage, Arnold leaned over to Anderson: "That puts the whole story on its ear, especially the timeline. Everyone assumed that she had been hanging out with that guy until at least Saturday night."

"Yeah, that means a 48-hour gap in the information we know. We have stuff to talk to the cops about when we get back... I'm glad we went with our gut and decided to call in here."

"I'm kinda thinking perhaps we should even call Sergeant John in the morning, and fill him in."

Amanita kicked into its first tune, and conversation became next to impossible. That was okay, though, because Xavier and his band were good at what they do. Anderson could tell the new bass player was still missing some shots and wasn't in perfect synch with the drummer sometimes, but all in all they were impressive and enjoyable. They even threw in a couple of original songs, which confused some of the small crowd but pleased Anderson. About half way through the first set, they stopped to tune a couple of instruments, and Arnold could see Xavier talking with the drummer. Before he called in the next tune, Xavier said over the mic: "This one's for our friends from Maple Falls. Please hang around after this set 'cause I got something to tell you..." and off they went with Great Big Sea's "The Night Pat Murphy Died".

When the set was done, Xavier made his way back to Arnold and Anderson. It took awhile – he and the band were popular and some folks in the club wanted to say hello, or high-five at least. Xavier pulled a chair out and perched on the edge. Throwing up his hands, he said, "Drummers. It's like sometimes they don't got ears! Dennis never heard any of the talk about Albert and that girl, apparently, 'cause just now he told me that just before we started playing that Thursday night, he was out back of the club smoking a joint and saw Albert's girl being led, or pushed, or something, into a big black truck. Dennis said it was like one of those SUVs from the show S.W.A.T."

"Crap." Anderson said. "That's a little scary. Drummer didn't see anything more?"

"Nah, he didn't say, but I expect he ducked inside pretty quick. He's not real fond of what might be a cop car when he has a little baggie in his pocket."

This time Arnold stood up and thanked him. "Like Frank here said, you've been more help that you can imagine. And – you guys are really fun to listen to. I hope you're never back in Maple Falls 'cause they don't deserve you, but if you are, or anywhere else close, we'll be coming to hear you." He smacked Anderson on the shoulder: "I have to get him out of here 'cause we have a meeting early tomorrow morning – nothing to do with Anita – but we gotta be there on time. Have a great night!"

"Take care guys, and again – good luck." Xavier turned and was gone.

Anderson drained his beer, stood up, and the two men walked out onto the street.

"Time for Timmys?"

09:00 JULY 17

Arnold and Anderson had finished off last night with a bed-time coffee and bagel at a small indie coffee shop in the Market, walked back to the hotel and slept soundly until their phones woke them up at 7:00 am, with time for a quick shower, bacon and eggs in the hotel eatery, check-out and the drive along Rideau to Wellington, then across the Ottawa River on the Portage Bridge and into Gatineau and the large office tower where they would meet Pierre LaChance.

As they drove, Anderson had dialled the OPS office in Maple Falls for Sergeant MacLeod and reached him on the second ring. Anderson explained where they were, and briefly described their conversation with Xavier at the nightclub, pointing out how his description of events messed up what they understood as the timeline for Anita's disappearance as well as the possible connection to a black SUV. The sergeant had been quiet for a moment, thanked him and asked how soon they would be driving home, so Anderson explained they had a business appointment in Gatineau over the next couple of hours and would be leaving for home immediately after. "If you could stop by the OPS office in Maple Falls on your way home, I would really appreciate it. I have an important matter to discuss about our friend Sam, along with this information as well," the sergeant had said, and Anderson said they would likely be at his office between 2:00 and 3:00 in the afternoon.

By now, Arnold had parked the Equinox in an underground lot a block from the government building and as they walked to the building and found the correct floor and office, they mulled over what the sergeant had said. "I assume they were able to ID the body – maybe it's not who they thought it was," Anderson mused. "It'll be interesting to hear more. Sergeant John certainly seemed interested in the Anita thing, too."

The office receptionist took down their names and disappeared momentarily, returning with a small pleasant-looking man in his early forties: "Good morning, gentlemen, and thank you for coming in so quickly. My name is Pierre LaChance, and I am Director of the Protected Shoreline Program programs, among others."

The men shook hands all around, and LaChance invited them along the corridor to a small meeting room, equipped with a table and chairs for six and a spectacular view of downtown Ottawa across the river. "Can I get you coffee?"

LaChance left them to gaze at the view, returning in a few moments with a small tray and three steaming cups. After an exchange of small talk, LaChance said, "Please, have a seat and I'll explain why I called you here."

"The office has heard reports – rumours, perhaps – of your PSP local committee possibly hosting a public meeting with a controversial speaker. If the reports are true, then you should know that there could be a conflict with the provisions of the Program agreement that deal with advocacy, which is not permitted under the agreement. I need to know what your committee is proposing, so we can make sure you are aware of those regulations. In short, local PSP committees must remain in compliance with all provisions of the agreement or they risk losing the program funding provided by the government, and – because of the reports we have received – I need assurance from your committee that it will not undertake any activity which could be construed as advocacy. It would be best for all of us if we can sort this out through yourselves, as representatives of the committee – Chair and Vice Chair I believe, that your committee will remain in compliance."

Arnold sat quietly for a few moments. "Yes," he began, "you are correct, I am Chair of the local committee and Frank here is the Vice Chair." He continued: "And I expect you are referring to a proposal by one of our committee members that we host a public meeting in the community which will feature Dr. Sebastian Horowitz as the main speaker. I have heard that Dr. Horowitz can be outspoken, but he is essentially an environmental scientist who focuses on water issues, so I would have thought this would be a good fit with the Protected Shorelines program and interesting to people in our community. I frankly don't see a problem, and I don't want to disappoint the folks on my committee, who are pretty enthusiastic about putting on the event. Frank, do you want to comment?"

Anderson resisted the temptation to shoot a withering look at his friend. "Yes, I think Arnold has expressed the situation pretty well. In fairness, some members of the committee were less than enthusiastic at first, but now they seem to be coming together around doing something to raise the profile of the PSP in the community. And, of course, any opportunity for a summer barbeque in the village always brings people together!"

"I'll be blunt," LaChance countered. "One would be naive to think that Sebastian Horowitz is anything less than an evangelist for the Greenpeace approach to any environmental issue he chooses. And yes, water is his most significant issue. And, I don't think either of you are the least bit naive, so you will understand when I tell you that the Department (and therefore the PSP Program managers) will almost certainly find the Awan Lake PSP out of compliance if it goes ahead with this event. The Awan Lake PSP has been well-regarded by the Department, so it is unlikely – not impossible but unlikely – that the Department would demand repayment of the federal contributions over the last three years since your local PSP committee was formed, but they will almost certainly feel forced to end the Awan Lake agreement going forward. And that would be unfortunate because of all the good things you have accomplished."

Time for the good-cop-bad-cop routine, Anderson thought to himself, *I'll be the bad cop:* "Okay, Pierre, I think we get the message, politely delivered but loud and clear. However, you know as well as I do that Arnold – as our Chair and a good one – can't sit here and make a commitment without taking the matter back to the committee. How soon do you need a response?"

"Well, I would appreciate being informed of your committee's decision, but we don't need a formal response to this informal discussion. Take it as a word to the wise, and as long as the Horowitz event doesn't happen, no harm no foul."

Anderson looked across at Arnold: "You okay with that, taking it to the committee?"

"Yes, that's fine," Arnold responded. "And Pierre, thanks for dealing with this at a personal level first. I will keep you in the loop as soon as the committee has met – probably later this week."

LaChance stood up. "Your understanding of the situation

is much appreciated." He paused, then: "This coffee is awful, and I suggest we wander down the street to Starbucks and I'll buy you a good cup. Does that sound like a plan?"

Arnold and Anderson glanced at one another. "Good plan. Lead the way!"

Starbucks was not far off. The conversation was light; Arnold mentioned that Annette Dubois had not been at the last couple of PSP local committee meetings and wondered if LaChance was replacing her as their Program supervisor. LaChance explained that no, that was not the case. Annette had been burning up some extra vacation hours she had accumulated, but that she was due back at work soon and would likely make the next regular meeting.

Once they had picked up their coffees and settled down at a tiny table by a window, LaChance again brought up the Awan Lake committee's Horowitz event plan, but with a stern warning that "this is strictly off the record." He continued quietly: "Two things, gentlemen. First, I sense you have both been around and understand how to read between the lines, and second, I personally think your committee is doing the right thing for Awan Lake. You need to understand that – right or wrong – government departments – like politicians – are influenced by other voices, particularly by powerful corporate voices."

LaChance paused a moment, then: "Your meeting about the event was last Thursday evening, right?"

"Yes," replied Arnold.

"So, by 8:30 Friday morning, my Director had received a couple of phone calls and by 9:30 he had called me into his office and told me to get together with you guys and rein you in. And there was no consultation – it was a directive. I think it doesn't take a genius to figure out that someone who was at your meeting has a direct pipeline to someone a way up in our department, or above, and whoever it is does not want to have media attention drawn to Awan Lake. Given the speed of the response, I suspect there is corporate money and process behind it – not just an ordinary lobby group."

After another pause, he continued: "So, I have some ideas about potential names, one in particular, but before I throw out a whole list I'd rather hear if you fellows have any ideas?"

Arnold and Anderson looked at one another. Anderson shrugged: "Well, yeah, I think we do. I have a sneaking hunch that Robertson Mines has future plans they are not sharing, and there is a potential for a lot of water use and mis-use there, depending on what they got in mind." Arnold nodded in agreement.

"Okay," LaChance replied. "We shall not mention that name again today, but that was where I was going, and I think the stewards of Awan Lake and its communities have legitimate concerns." Another pause. "And there is a way around this advocacy prohibition for federally-funded Programs. Scurry home and either find a local club or association to take on hosting the event or, alternatively, get a handful of people together to set up a separate committee – one or two people from the PSP committee could be members of that group, but you should have a majority of people not involved with the PSP. A new group could, for example, call itself 'The Friends of Awan Lake' and incorporate themselves as a non-profit association. Then you could host this event without risking losing the funding for the PSP. You will have to make sure it is – and looks – clean, and the PSP can't even be a sponsor of any part of it."

"That sounds like a perfect solution, actually," said Arnold. "Come to think of it, we already have a 'Board of

Trade' that is incorporated but doesn't ever do anything even though a few people meet every now and then and wish they could. This might give them something to bite on. I belong already... did you ever join Frank?"

"Nope, never did, but this would be the perfect time. And somehow, I imagine that would look a little cleaner than our starting a new association just for the one event. Anyway, I kinda like the idea of starting – eventually – a 'Friends of Awan Lake' association as a community group that could speak and operate freely. It might attract community involvement and corporate sponsorship more easily than the PSP committee, which is so... federal government!"

LaChance was smiling: "I figured I could count on you two guys to figure it out and do the right thing. I apologize that I have had to complicate your lives with bureaucratic BS, but that's the reality of where I work and what I do. And..." as he stood up to leave... "two things: it's best we don't leave here together so have another cup of coffee, and remember that we never had this conversation."

"No worries at all. We'll shake hands another time. Thank you, and we'll just sit for a while. I want a biscuit anyway." Anderson smiled, and turned away.

***

An hour later it was 11:30 and the little black Equinox was well on its way home. "We should be well on time to meet Sergeant John, even if we stop to pick up another burger. And talking about Sergeant John, I wonder what-all he wants to talk about?"

Arnold thought for a moment before responding. "I dunno. It seems like little Spirit River suddenly has a bunch of stuff happening, and not all of it is good. And you and I seem to be smack in the middle of all of it!"

"Keeps you from getting bored fixing tires and changing oil for all the little old ladies! Which reminds me, did you get those parts into that Honda and get her all fixed up?"

"Yeah, I got it done on Saturday morning while you were out floating around the lake with your new girlfriend. And picked up a couple of other little jobs too, coming in tomorrow. I don't imagine Marion's gonna let me out of her sight for awhile. I've been pretty much useless to her for the last four or five days. But anyway, yeah, I have no idea what's come up that Sergeant John wants to talk with us about. Doesn't seem like it's about Anita, so the only other thing I can think about is Sam. Maybe they've positively identified him."

"Could be. And perhaps there'll have to be an inquest or something, another time-waster for us just because we helped haul him out of the water."

"Yeah, don't really need that. Say, Frank, when are you going to get together with Marjorie and take a look at those photos?"

"I had been kinda thinking tonight, but I haven't been in touch. Anyway, that's a bit awkward because I don't want to send her back to the island in her little putt-putt in the dark so I'll have to pick her up and take her back with the launch. Maybe tomorrow morning would be better. And we still don't know where the rest of today is gonna take us. Yeah, I'll give her a call and set it up for tomorrow morning if she's available."

"I'll bet she's gonna be available, Prince Charming!"

"Shut-up, Jamieson!"

***

Arnold and Anderson rolled into Maple Falls at about 2:15. They hadn't stopped for lunch so they had called ahead from about 20 minutes out of town and told Sergeant John they'd meet him at the Flying J truck stop on the highway. The sergeant was already there, waiting alone at a window booth with his radio and cellphone on the table beside him. "How was the Nation's Capital?"

"It was okay. Listened to some good music, met some interesting people, had a great dinner last night and a decent sleep. Guess that's as good as can be expected."

"So you didn't let that sailor guy Anderson lead you astray?"

"Nah. He lives alone, so I asked him if he was celibate, and he told me he couldn't even give it away, let alone sell a bit."

Anderson joined the laughter, glared at his friend and the two civilians sat down and joined the cop. "Did that stuff we found out last night from Xavier – the band guy – lead anywhere yet?"

"Well, it sure as hell opened a big can of worms – a way more questions than answers. I got guys within a couple of hundred kilometers trying to identify all the big black SUVs they can find. Nothing yet. But, stuff is getting even more complicated. We got the autopsy results back, and all they did was throw a bloody big monkey wrench into the works."

Anderson: "So... what?"

"The autopsy shows that (a) Sam is not the old guy who was reported missing in the spring, (b) we so far haven't the faintest idea who the hell he is, and (c) he didn't drown. The cause of death was blunt force trauma – severe blunt force trauma, apparently one hard blow."

PETER KINGSMILL

16:00 JULY 17

"You gotta be kidding." Arnold was the first to speak. "Could whoever he is have fallen and hit his head on a rock or something? I just can't imagine anyone around here killing someone, especially an old guy."

"Well, he actually wasn't all that old a guy – the autopsy puts him at around fifty. And unlikely it was accidental or suicide; we have enough evidence of foul play to have already officially launched a homicide investigation."

"That'll set the fox among the chickens in our little town," said Anderson. "Arnold, you've been here all your life. Has there ever been a murder around Spirit River?"

"Well, there was a nasty thing maybe twenty years ago – A family of three moved in from Mississauga. They were staying in an old bus outside of town, on government land at the provincial campsite. Of course we all had the feeling they were kinda different. Anyway, guy killed his wife, kidnapped their little boy, then killed his son and himself out in the bush. Tragic, but folks suspected there were family issues there. Somehow, though, this is different. It feels threatening, like it ain't over. No explanation."

"So now what?" Anderson paused a moment. "You folks at Maple Falls cop shop suddenly have a pretty full plate: a young woman missing under what now seems like mysterious circumstances, the murder of an unknown man, and you still have an old guy missing and presumed drowned. Was the medical examiner able to tell when the murdered guy was killed?"

"Well, not very precisely at this point, since spring and over a month ago is as close as they're saying."

"Any leads at all?"

"No. Basically, everyone in Ontario is a potential suspect at this point, you guys included!"

Anderson laughed: "Well, I guess I'd be a prime suspect then, 'cause I'm always out on the lake. But for the record, it wasn't me. And I can vouch for Arnold... only time he gets out from under the hoist in his garage and onto the water he's with me, and I watch him real close!"

The sergeant joined the laughter, and then got serious. "Actually, guys, my imagination is beginning to run away with me perhaps, but I'm supposing that there may be some connections between those three cases – and some other stuff – so I'd like to stay in close touch and pick your collective brains on this. The Anita Antoine thing has me worried, especially with information you picked up from the musicians last night. And, I'd like you to tell me a little more about your meeting this morning. You seemed worried about it, and I sense it had something to do with your "shoreline" group. Is there something I should know?"

"Not likely any real connection there," Arnold responded. "The Environment department guys were just giving us a heads-up that our group shouldn't hold any public meetings that might be seen as... controversial. Just bureaucratic bullshit, really."

Anderson took his cellphone from his pocket. "Good thing you mentioned that. Reminded me that I should contact Marjorie about looking at those photos from the lake tomorrow morning."

The sergeant raised his eyebrows: "Photos?"

Anderson walked out to phone Marjorie while Arnold explained that Anderson and Ms. Webster had been out on the lake on Saturday and taken a bunch of photos over by the Robertson Mines property they wanted to look at together.

"Frank, which way does the current flow along the shore of the lake east of the village?" the sergeant asked Anderson when he returned from making his call.

"There isn't much current at all, really, but such as there is – east to west because the river flows downstream from where it leaves the lake west of the village."

"Arnold tells me you were out taking photos along the shore by the Robertson site. Could I take a look?"

"Of course... Marjorie's coming in to my place with her laptop and photo software in the morning. I'll put the coffee on – maybe around 10:00?"

"I can do that. And don't worry, yes I'll bring more damn donuts. That's all us cops are good for anyway, I'm told!"

"John, you don't think there could be a connection between that location and Floating Sam, do you? All we had thought about was that the Robertson bunch may be unhappy with our PSP group, and kinda wondering what they had up their sleeve over there."

The sergeant looked hard at Anderson, then across at Arnold: "That's why I asked about direction of the current flow... could a water-logged body have moved along the shore from away up there to where we found Sam. I do know that there are some trailers and shacks up there where mine and refinery workers have been staying – unofficially – for years. You catch my drift, so to speak?"

"Yeah. (And yes, that was a lousy pun, too.) Can you join

us in the morning Arnold?"

"I'll try to get away – depends on what work-orders are waiting for me at the garage. I might have to take a rain check."

Arnold pushed back his chair and stood up: "I used to think Marion had a corner on a big imagination mixed with being somewhat paranoid, but she can't hold a candle to you two," he laughed. "Anyway, I'd really like to get home before supper... I texted Marion and told her I'd be there. That okay with you guys?"

It was the sergeant's turn to laugh: "Comes with the territory! Thanks for coming in, both of you... I'll see you in the morning."

07:30 JULY 18

Morning came soon enough, and Anderson pulled himself out of bed a full half hour after he shut the alarm off. Yesterday had been a long one. Marion had asked him to stay for supper, but he politely declined, and after Arnold had dropped him off in front of his shop he had gone down to the dock and checked the launch and its mooring lines before going home.

***

His body had been feeling Sunday night's more-than-enough beer and Monday's more-than-enough flood of troublesome information. He wouldn't have admitted to anyone else, but he was feeling worn out, so there was no cooking supper. He had grabbed a bottle of peanut butter from the cupboard and some raspberry jam from the fridge and made a sandwich, which he took to his computer desk along with a double shot of dark rum, neat.

Time to learn some stuff, he had thought. Who controls Robertson Mines? Where is their head office? Who is their CEO? What is their track record? And, I wonder if Wendy Webster and her public relations firm show up on Google? At nine-thirty he had shut down the computer and the lights, taken a short (for him) shower and rolled himself into bed.

***

After frying a couple of strips of bacon and a pair of breakfast eggs, he fussed about the house tidying up. He washed the couple of days' accumulation of coffee cups, mugs and plates and removed a grey fuzzy thing that may have once been a tomato from the fridge, adding it to the week-old bag of garbage that he then put outside into the garbage pail, making a mental note that he needed to take that and some other stuff from the workshop and the boat to the landfill. Because he was a registered contractor and often collected garbage from island cottagers, the village gave him a landfill key – and a clipboard to keep a record of his comings and goings – so he didn't have to keep to the once-a-week schedule. The village's invoice, however, did come on schedule... once each month.

At 9:30 he started a new pot of coffee, took the notes he had made from last night's internet studies, and sat down at the newly-clean table to wait. He didn't have long.

He had heard what he thought was a boat motor in the harbour and looked out the door but couldn't see the marina docks. Ten minutes later, there was a tap on the door, which Marjorie then tentatively opened, stepped inside and said, "Good morning, Mister Anderson!"

"Good morning, Mademoiselle Webster," Anderson laughed as he went across and took her backpack and briefcase. "Just so you know, I'm now a world traveller who just returned from Ottawa and points beyond, like Gatineau Québec!"

"Woo hoo... no stopping you, is there! Glad to see you back, but mostly I just want a cup of that delicious coffee you make. And, you left me with a very short hug three days ago and I want another one."

Anderson could feel himself blush, but without hesitation – hell, with enthusiasm – he took a couple of steps across the room and gave her a warm squeeze. "I'm really glad to see you again, Marjorie," he said, "but I have bad news. You're gonna have to share me with the Ontario Police Service this morning."

"Really. So just exactly what did you and your sidekick Arnold get up to in the famed metropolis of Ottawa on Sunday night? Or Monday morning for that matter?"

"Well, you can chuckle all you want, but we actually learned a bunch of stuff and stayed out of trouble. But... Sergeant John is joining us to look at those dirty pictures you took on Saturday. He should be here any minute..."

He was interrupted by the crunch of gravel outside as the police cruiser pulled into the driveway. "And here he is, right on time! Good morning John, come on in!"

Marjorie grinned at him: "It's true, it's true! Third time I've ever talked to a policeman and twice now he's showed up with donuts! And here I thought people were just joking about cops hanging around in donut shops!"

"We are legend. And this time they're fresh, too," said the sergeant, putting the box on the table.

"And I'll have to find out sometime about the third occasion you talked to the police," Anderson chuckled.

"I was younger then."

"Ah, of course that explains all! Coffee coming up... I'll get the mugs. John, Marjorie only just got here, so perhaps you could fill her in on what we have all discovered over the past couple of days so she'll understand why her photographs may be of such interest all of a sudden."

"Certainly. And I'm sorry to barge in on you guys like this but, as Frank implies, there are things going on that have created a way more questions than we have answers."

Once they were comfortably settled at the table and

109

Anderson had brought the coffee and a handful of paper towels to deal with the fresh donuts, the sergeant began by telling Marjorie that the body ("Floating Sam" as Frank calls him) did not turn out to be who they thought it was, how the man had died, and the resulting homicide investigation. "So you see what I meant when I said we have more questions than answers. And, for what it's worth, he was more likely fifty than seventy, certainly not just an old guy like we thought. And – I forgot to tell Frank and Arnold yesterday – it was not just old raggedy clothes he was wearing, they just looked that way from sitting in the water so long. He was actually wearing fairly new Helly Hansen coveralls and boots – best in the business."

"And so you see..." Anderson said to Marjorie.

"I certainly do. Wow, that all changes things." She replied. "I suppose there's more?"

"I think there's a great deal more. I asked Frank about currents in the lake, and from the timeline, and our discussions, it is not unlikely that the new and improved Sam may have been carried by the current – albeit slowly – from further up the east side of the lake than we had been thinking before. After all, when we were thinking about the old guy, we were distracted by the fact that a missing older gentleman's car had been found relatively close to the village. But in fact, this guy could have been – and probably was – carried much farther. And that, folks, is why your photos may be even more useful than you thought."

"Well, I'm really a rather amateur photographer and I had no clue what we might be looking for but I guess it's time to take a look, don't you think, Frank?" She proceeded to uncork her laptop, put it on the table where all three could see, and asked for an extension cord to plug it in. Anderson pointed to a little brass screw-in cover plate on the floor under the table and said "I'll plug it in down there" while he went to a kitchen cupboard and retrieved the memory card she had given him Saturday. The sergeant watched with curiosity while he handed the card to Marjorie, then ducked under the table to plug the laptop into the flush-mount receptacle.

The system opened up over a hundred photograph files and Marjorie started to open them up individually. "You'll have to bear with me; not all of these are of the east shore. There are some of Frank's boat and some of Frank and I even tried a couple of timed selfies which hopefully didn't work. Ah ha... here we go with mostly shoreline shots. She opened each up full- screen and paused after each so all three of them had a chance to look them over thoroughly. About thirty photos in, Anderson asked her to zoom in as close as she could, and sure enough, there was what looked like a large orange bottle or jug just off the shore. "Can you re-name these or bookmark them somehow so we can pull them up later?"

"Good idea," said the sergeant. "One photo may mean nothing much, but a bunch of them might prove interesting." Marjorie repeated the process with every shoreline photo until they got to where Anderson had turned the launch west and headed to the middle of the lake. There turned out to be about twenty-five shots she re-named and placed in a separate folder before they took a short break to clear their eyes.

"I'm taking my coffee out into the sunshine and having a smoke," Anderson said.

"I'm in. I'm not good at staring for long periods at that little screen on the laptop."

"Bad boys and girls," said the sergeant. "But going outside on a nice day works for me!"

Once they were perched on lawn chairs on the porch, Anderson took a slurp of coffee and said, "most of those shots showed orange markers – buoys of some sort – anchored offshore – I can only guess because the telephoto lens distorts the distances, but it seems they are perhaps a hundred yards or so from shore and it appears they are widely spaced. But, I thought a few of the shots also showed buildings or vehicles in the background – back from the shore in the bush. And I'm not counting the two or three shots of the main refinery buildings. John, could they maybe be the shacks and trailers you talked about yesterday?"

"Makes sense to me, but I have to confess that – Sergeant or not – I have never been out that road. I guess that's now next on my 'to-do' list!"

"I saved out all the shots of the big buildings, and I noticed one photo showed what looked like a garage back from the shore. I didn't see a ramp but it could have been a boathouse. When we go back in we may want to look at that one a little closer."

"Not that there's anything suspicious about having a boathouse, but yes, I'd like to see it." The sergeant paused, then: "Could I ask to have copies of three or four of those shots on a flash drive? I can make out a receipt or a requisition slip if you would prefer."

Marjorie looked at Anderson, who shrugged: "That's entirely up to the photographer, I believe. Marjorie, you okay with that?"

"No problem here. I expect your people would like to have a record of who/what/when," Marjorie said to the sergeant. "As a sometime artist I am used to that sort of stuff, so I can make up a receipt with the photo identification stuff for each one, if that helps?"

"That'd be perfect. Let's go take another look."

***

"Now what, I wonder," Anderson mused aloud to Marjorie. After reviewing a number of the photos a second time, Marjorie had labelled nine of them and saved them on a second flash drive for the sergeant, who signed the receipt that Anderson had drawn up and printed, then taken his leave and driven off to continue his day, which he had admitted looked like it would be a long one.

"Now what, indeed. Frank, there is some stuff we need to talk about. I didn't want to get into discussions about conspiracy theories with Sergeant John, at least not until I had a chance to discuss some things with you."

"Yeah, me too. And I have a confession to make, a confession that goes along with a question." He refilled their coffee cups, offered her another smoke which she declined, lit his own and they settled back on the porch in the sunshine. Looking across the little harbour, the morning fog on the lake had cleared and it was a beautiful sunshiny day.

"My confession is embarrassing, really. I spent some time on the internet last night, and among other things, I found an outfit called Webster and Webster Public Relations. Wendy's name was prominent as the principal, but I have to ask: are you the other Webster?"

Marjorie laughed: "I never even thought about mentioning the name of sis' company... I guess I should've done that! The 'other' Webster was our dad, Walter. He had been a journalist for about twenty years but was laid off when Conrad Black shut down a bunch of newspapers back in the nineteen nineties and he decided to find a better way to make a buck in the PR business. Ten years ago Wendy joined him and they incorporated that name. Dad died three years ago, but Wendy carried on with the company and kept everything the same. Writing and marketing were never my thing, and as close as Wendy and I have been over the years I never got involved." She paused. "Actually, Wendy does give me pointers on how I should promote my artistic endeavours, but to her disappointment I am sure, I never follow through. Given the size of my savings account, maybe I should have!"

"Good to know, and thank you for clarifying that. It was none of my business, and really I shouldn't have been poking around your life without asking. I'm just trying to get my head around all these things that are happening and Wendy's odd responses at the meeting last week had me kinda curious."

"Well, funny you should mention that. I, too, have been wondering about my sister and the questions she's been asking about the village, the body search stuff, and – frankly – you (pun not intended). I think there is more to it than sisterly love worrying about who I might or might not be dating, and in fact she seems somewhat pushy about her questions. Something is worrying her, and at the same time she is being sort of cagey about all the emails and calls she is getting. She stops short of telling me they're none of my business, but it's like she feels that way."

"Did you mention our photography expedition on Saturday?"

"Heavens no!" Marjorie replied quickly. "I just told her we went out around that island bird sanctuary, but I didn't even get any pictures. And this morning she thinks I just came in to see if I could get a new memory card for my camera, and some milk. I did tell her I might see if I could find you for coffee, so she wouldn't figure she should come along to keep me company!"

"Makes sense – wise move," said Anderson. They both sat silently for a couple of minutes, as if there was more to say, but uncertain where to begin. Anderson began: "This whole thing is just... strange... and keeps getting more so." He filled Marjorie in on their discovery at the nightclub that Anita's disappearance might prove to have been some sort of kidnapping, or be mysterious anyway, and he outlined the discussions – both official and off-the-record – with the Environment official on Monday morning.

"Last night I actually started a little list," he continued. "It's like we are looking through the windshield at four seemingly unconnected things: a waterlogged murder victim, a young woman who has gone missing under mysterious circumstances, a development program by a company with a shaky environmental record (and a long reach into the federal government bureaucracy), and – frankly – the very distinct possibility that someone is trying to keep that development program out of the public eye, maybe explaining Wendy's behaviour which somehow seems out of character." Anderson paused again. "I dunno, have we all become screaming paranoids?"

"Where is Arnold in all this? He was with you in Ottawa, and I assume he has heard about the murder thing directly from John?"

"Yup, Arnold is up-to-date on all of it, except nothing specific about Wendy being somehow connected except a little shared puzzlement about the way she acted at the meeting. And Sergeant John knows nothing at all about Wendy, or the meeting. I have been waiting for you and I to talk first. Which reminds me... Arnold and the meeting... I hope he or Marion have been in touch with the Board of Trade folks this morning to see if they will host that public meeting with Horowitz. Once that is set up, then the OPS will need to be informed we are expecting to hold a public meeting in the village, and that it may attract a pretty big crowd. Cops like to know about that stuff. But they certainly don't need to know about Wendy or in fact, even about Robertson Mines. That they can figure out on their own."

"You know, Frank, I just feel terrible about this. I feel so torn between my sister (and perhaps her clients) and this wonderful lake and little village which is now almost my first home, not just a vacation place. And you. You are becoming a problem to me, because I like being around you. It's even fun being screaming paranoids together, but I do still feel torn."

That stopped Anderson dead in his tracks for a moment. He looked long and hard at Marjorie before speaking: "Two things. First, I am honoured by your trust and very happy that we share a growing connection with each other. It's not something that I am used to – the connection bit – so forgive me if I seem awkward. Trust isn't easy for me either, and that's part of the second thing: normally I would keep things to myself and not easily share information. But back to the paranoia thing, we – I anyway – have been avoiding an important thing about Wendy. I have no real reason to believe that she is involved at all with this stuff. She may have been having a grumpy moment, or just been shy, at the meeting the other night. And at home with you, it is possible she is just worried about some unrelated work stuff and worrying about her sister at the same time. So it seems unfair – especially for you – not to be able to share the things we are thinking with a friend and sister. And – even if she is somehow connected to this stuff, and if it's bad I expect that deep down inside she is family and would dump her client if you could show that her client was up to bad stuff."

Marjorie put her head to one side and looked at him hard. "I hope so. I really do. I have trusted her for many years about many things, and have never been let down, even though she was always a whole bunch more aggressive than I am. Are you suggesting we should talk to her about all this? I guess that way we'd learn right away if she's even remotely aware."

"I've always preferred to sort out the good from the bad, and then make sure the good things are on my side of the river. And I surely don't want to screw up your relationship. We also have to remember that you, and I, and Arnold, are just bystanders in all of this. It's really not our battle, so I think, if you're game, let's simply go talk to her before we take all these suspicions with us down the rabbit hole. It's weird enough down there already. Let's start by driving up to the Zoo and I'll buy us lunch."

***

Ten years ago, the Zoo had been pretty much a hamburger joint with things like pork chops for lunch specials. A young couple from Ottawa inherited a (very) small fortune and bought out the ageing owners; he had been a line chef in a chain restaurant, and wanted to do something better, so while they only barely refreshed the interior they kept it clean and neat. The burgers and fries were tastier, and in the summer tourist and cottager season he began to serve quiche specials at lunch. They were good, and popular, and now he offered a wide variety year around, which the locals devoured and talked about to anyone who'd listen.

Anderson and Marjorie ordered a ham quiche with fries, and wolfed it down with a half-draft each. Half way through, Marion joined them for a sandwich and Coke; she smiled warmly when introduced to Marjorie, nodded wisely to Anderson and said, "Your reputation precedes you!" to Marjorie.

"I hope that's a good thing," Marjorie chuckled.

"It is. Very." Turning to Anderson, she told him that Arnold had been on the phone first thing and lined up the Board of Trade committee members, who were only too happy to host the public event – and the fundraiser bar afterward – so long as they didn't have to pay for the guest speaker. And now Arnold was catching up on work, so stay the hell out of the garage please until after supper.

"No worries, Marion – thanks! I'll go out to Tony Barker's place and see if I'll have any luck getting him to dredge up a sponsor. And I guess one of us should ask Dave Bradshaw if he was able to nail down Horowitz, and if he got an idea of what it would cost to get him here."

"All done," said Marion. "David called this morning and gave me a date too – August 10 (a Thursday) and the cost will be a maximum of $3000, including flights, car rental and one night in a hotel in Toronto."

"Wow, that was quick. Thanks! Did you tell Dave about the change in hosting organization?"

"Nope... figured I'd leave that to you. Or Arnold. Or maybe both of you in case he bitches too hard!"

"Nah, I don't suppose. He wouldn't have survived at the university this long if he didn't understand the politics of that kind of stuff."

Anderson stepped out into the sunshine to answer a couple of messages from people wanting work done at their cottages, while Marion and Marjorie chatted away like old friends. They shared a love of growing good things to eat in the garden, and a frustration of never having the time to do it properly. With Marion, it was work. With Marjorie, it was that planting time at her city home was before she came to the lake, and harvest was before she got back home. And growing anything but a pot full of chives was impossible on that rocky little island she shared with her sister.

When Anderson came back in, he paid the tab and returned to the table, saying he supposed they should be getting out to the island, and that he wanted to visit Tony Barker on his way home. As they left, Marion called out, "Marjorie, next time you're in, I'll have some lettuce for you. It's the only damn thing that's growing – like a weed – and if you don't help me out I'll have to buy a rabbit!"

PETER KINGSMILL

14:00 JULY 18

They chose to take Anderson's launch, as the wind had freshened since morning and was raising a noticeable chop out of the northwest, although the day was warm under an almost cloudless sky. The thirty-seven foot launch barely noticed the waves, but Marjorie's little fourteen-foot outboard runabout would have kicked up enough spray to make for a wet ride. Anderson had turned on the ship-to-ship radio as usual, and had clicked it over to the marine weather forecast, learning that a cool front was moving in this evening which would bring some showers by morning. Out of habit he flipped the radio back to the call channel, not because he expected any calls from the very few boats on the lake that used radios, but because the marina at Spirit River had equipped its half-dozen rental houseboats with them, so there were, in fact, other ears within reach.

Marjorie was happily standing outside the wheelhouse with one hand on the roof, facing to her right and apparently drinking in the wind. Anderson, though, was less comfortable, worrying that meeting Wendy and bringing her up-to-date on recent events could yield some uncomfortable moments in the next couple of hours. He kept those thoughts to himself, but he did ask Marjorie if Wendy would be worried to see them in the launch rather than the little outboard.

"Actually, I'm surprised she hasn't called me already to tell me about the waves and suggest I come and get you! When it comes to boating, she is nervous as a cat when there is any more than a ripple on the lake."

" I had thought maybe we should tow the outboard behind and take it to the island, but if it gets any rougher than it is now, that has its own set of problems. Tell me, how do you ever convince the poor girl to come to the island with you, if she's so nervous about the water?"

Marjorie chuckled: "If truth be told, it was her idea, and she probably wouldn't even have come to Awan Lake if I hadn't agreed. She relies on me to take care of all the wet stuff. She doesn't even swim unless it's, like, flat calm, 45 degrees in the shade, and no shade!"

"Why then?"

"She yearns for the peace and quiet she can find at the island. Of course, she needed to have all the internet and cellphone connections so that she can keep in touch with her office, but she usually only allows herself less than an hour a day for that stuff, then she turns it all off. Period."

Anderson began a lazy turn to go east of the island so he could nose into the little bay and the dock with the bow into the wind. He gave his usual two short blasts on the horn as he went past where the cottage sat along the island's south shore, and noticed that most of the south-facing roof was covered with solar panels. "Ah ha," he said. "That's cool, you ladies are making your own power!"

"Sure are... all the comforts of home! We do have a small generator in case we need to top up the batteries in cloudy weather, but usually we generate enough from that roof to keep our refrigerator working – it's just a little one the same size as the ones they put in campers, but it keeps the milk cold and the lettuce fresh. That, a couple of lights in the late evening and keeping the phones, laptops and a radio charged is all we use it for. We love it, and it wasn't even all that expensive. The folks at the marina are selling the equipment for a store in the city, and they installed it too."

"Could I get you to put the fenders over the side as we come in? Since your boat isn't at the dock, I'll pull along our starboard side like I do in town, and the wind – such as there is in here, it's pretty sheltered – will keep her quiet alongside instead of pulling unevenly on the ropes. Thanks!"

Wendy had heard the horn and already walked the hundred yards across the island from the cottage. As she approached, Anderson could see she had suddenly recognized Marjorie on the deck, and given her a big wave and a grin. "Hi Sis. Wondered who was arriving at the dock with the Queen Mary, then remembered the boat from last week. And you must be Frank... maybe now we can actually be introduced properly!"

By now Marjorie had looped the bow and stern lines over the posts that anchored the dock, so Anderson stepped off the boat and held out his hand: "Hi Wendy! I guess we sort of met twice... once very quickly here when I dropped off Marjorie and her kayak last week, and again at that meeting at the Spirit Inn – you remember, the Protected Shorelines committee. Nice to finally shake hands!"

Anderson checked the mooring lines with his eyes only, nodded thanks to Marjorie, and the three of them took only moments to cross the island on a rough path that had been hacked out of underbrush. "I've spent most of the day lying around on the porch swing reading, and was just wishing I had an excuse to have a glass of wine. Now I have one... you two will join me I hope?"

Marjorie grinned at Anderson: "Should have warned you we didn't have any beer."

"No worries at all. And nice to see you are at least drinking a civilized wine made in Ontario. All the folks in the village ever drink is some god-awful pink fizzy stuff from California, and the cottagers all seem to pickle themselves in imported stuff!"

It was Wendy's turn to smile: "Actually, I used to be an imported wine buff, but the winery from Niagara that produced this stuff is a client of mine, and they keep dropping cases of the stuff on us. Now, I really like it!"

With glasses of wine in hand, and seated comfortably on the little veranda, in the sun and out of the wind, Anderson pondered how to begin the discussion he knew they had to have. Seemed a shame to ruin the moment, somehow, but he thought he'd start with the PSP meeting.

"You were pretty quiet at the meeting on Thursday," he began. "I hope we didn't come across too disorganized. We can be pretty hillbilly when we get together, and there is almost never a well-planned agenda!"

"No, it seemed to me that you all seemed to know what you needed to do. And, I've always noticed in small groups – especially small communities – there's always a wise and well-organized woman who keeps everyone in line... Miriam or... sorry, I forgot her name."

"You'd be talking about Marion. Yeah, she does that. She and her husband Arnold have a way about them, for sure. Everybody in town appreciates what they do, which is cool."

"That must have been her I talked with at lunch. Hey Sis, we're going to have some fresh garden lettuce next time I go to town!"

"That would be so good!" said Wendy. "On the subject of California wine, I can handle that but I hate going to a store in Ontario and have to buy California lettuce in July. It infuriates me!"

Anderson began to relax. *I like these people. I like the way they think, and I like that they are close to each other. Maybe I should just dive right in.* "Wendy," he said thoughtfully, "I need to ask you a question, which is none of my business except it's related to that meeting. Marjorie has told me you are a public relations specialist, and I am wondering if you have any government departments – or corporate clients like Robertson Mines – as clients?"

Wendy looked at him steadily and never even blinked. But she did take a quick sip of wine. Marjorie chose that moment to take Wendy's cigarettes off the table, offer them around and take one herself, which she lit and sat back down, looking out at the lake. Anderson lit Wendy's cigarette, thanked her and lit his own, then continued quickly, "Reason I ask is that we had to go to Ottawa for an emergency meeting on Monday, and the government department – Environment – knew about the meeting and what it was about." He forced a laugh: "In my experience with government departments, they never ever move that fast!"

"Hmm. No – and yes. Much as I would like to, I don't have any government clients at all, or even government agencies except for a couple of provincial ones in the secondary education field. But, Robertson Mines' Canadian Division office in Toronto is a client."

You could have cut the silence with a knife. All eyes were turned to the lake, and no one looked at each other. *Crap. Now where does this go,* Anderson wondered.

It was Wendy who broke the silence: "Well, some of that was me, and now I feel terrible about it. Before the meeting was even over, I recognized there could be a public relations nightmare for my client, so I called my primary contact – a senior Robertson official – from the parking lot before leaving for home. And I didn't hang around because I had the little boat and I wanted to get home before dark... boats aren't my thing. But the next day was full of emails and calls about that public meeting, expecting me to be prepared in case it all blew up. Marjorie, Frank... this is awful. Really awful."

Marjorie put her head down, and remained silent. "Wendy," Anderson said quietly, "please don't feel badly about your part in this. You had a responsibility to your client and you did what you had to do." He paused. "You had no way of knowing where this might lead, but now is a turning point. There is information on both sides of this issue that have huge implications, and now there are decisions to be made and – in seaman's language, there are courses to be set."

"Thank goodness for white grapes and Ontario tobacco." Wendy walked to the little table by the porch door, poured herself a second glass of Chardonnay, sat down and lit a fresh smoke from the one she was finishing. "Actually, thank wineries and tobacco growers a lot, because not only do I have wine and cigarettes, but one of the wineries – and the tobacco growers association – are both clients of mine. Now I am beginning to wonder about what I'm doing in this business at all. I feel like an information slut – wine is a curse for many people and families, tobacco is never good for anyone, and all along, deep down inside, I have felt that Robertson had inexcusably bad business ethics, especially when it comes to the environment."

Her voice raised and her eyes moistened. "Damn it, I'm supposed to earn my living making excuses and keeping these companies looking good regardless of all the bad stuff. Shit!"

Marjorie stood up, walked over and sat down beside her sister. She smoothed back Wendy's hair and sat with her a few moments, letting a hand rest on her shoulder. Anderson felt acutely embarrassed. He was not a debater at heart: he got no pleasure from putting people on the spot, let alone making someone cry. And a woman especially. "I apologize, to both of you," he said slowly. "I didn't mean to barge into your lives with our local problems, and I confess I don't really know what's happening at all. It just seems like a bunch of weird stuff."

Wendy pulled her self together almost instantly; just as quickly, Anderson recognized that she was a person who was used to taking charge of a situation and dealing with it. "Frank. there is absolutely no need for an apology. Emotions aside – and I have some – we are dealing with the real world here and like you said, decisions have to be made, and I'm the one who has to make them. And in this case, I need to talk with Marjorie for awhile, not because she is part of my business (which she isn't) but because she's my best friend."

Marjorie glanced across at Anderson, and said to Wendy: "This sounds flaky, sis, but the timing is actually pretty good. Frank has an appointment at Tony Barker's place this afternoon so he has to go right away anyway. That will give us a chance to talk."

Wendy looked up in alarm: "There's no way I want to wreck your afternoon, you two. But – Frank – would you come back and join us for supper later?"

Anderson got to his feet. "If that works for both of you, I'd love that. I need a couple of hours anyway – perhaps about 6:30?"

"Perfect. I hope you like New York steak – so happens we have a package of three I picked up Monday in Maple Falls. Marj... take Frank to the dock and be nice to him for heaven's sake, but then come back. I do need to talk to my little sis..."

Marjorie and Frank walked back across to the bay and out on the dock. The wind was, if anything, a little stronger but the launch sat happily leaning on her fenders. Anderson got onboard and started the engines, then came back out of the wheelhouse to take in the dock lines.

"I'll let go the lines. Frank..." she walked over to him and took both of his hands in hers. "Frank, this is such an awkward thing for you, and I feel so badly that we've got you tangled in the Webster Web, so to speak. It's not like you don't have a lot of other stuff to worry about. Two things (as you are fond of saying): first, please please come back for supper, and second, if she does what I think she's going to do (quit her client) can I fill Wendy in on all the other stuff that's going on, so it all makes more sense to her? We could use her skills, I expect."

"Of course... you be the judge of what and when. And you bet I'll be back for supper!"Anderson leaned forward and delivered a very quick kiss on her forehead, turned, and disappeared into the wheelhouse.

***

It was a forty-five minute trip to Tony Barker's place. The launch bucked and splashed its way into the headwind until things smoothed out a little in the lee of a gathering of islands south of the marshes where the lake empties into the Spirit River. Anderson radioed to the marina where he was, and that he would possibly not get back to his dock tonight but not to worry unless he called, and warned that mid-lake was pretty rough for the small fishing boats they rented, except maybe along the northwest shore. He then used his cellphone to call Arnold, also saying the he might not be back at the dock tonight and not to worry and that he was on his way to the

Barker place to see if he would help find three grand to sponsor the Horowitz event. He also filled in Arnold on the conversation – likely to be continued in the evening – with Marjorie's sister.

Arnold had news too. Sergeant John had dropped by midway through the afternoon to say that he had taken a drive up the county road that served mostly as the Robertson Mines access. He told Arnold that – if we were looking for big new black SUVs, there were several up there; not SUVs exactly but full-sized pickups, new and black, with colour-coordinated and factory-supplied tops over the truck-boxes. He said they had small white numbers stencilled on the left side of the tailgate and were almost certainly associated with Robertson as there were a couple in the company yard. And, there were a few others parked in the worker accommodations area where the trailers and cabins were scattered about. He had stopped to talk to a couple of people and showed them Anita's photo, but no one, apparently, knew her. Sergeant John said he found the whole situation curious, at least.

"Could we get together tomorrow morning?" Arnold asked.

"Of course. Do you want to meet at the Zoo for coffee, or do you want to come by my place so we can talk?"

"Your place at ten-thirty sounds good. Quieter. Have a nice visit with your sweetie!"

"Shut-up!"

Arnold had chuckled and hung up. A few minutes later, Anderson had cut the throttle back on the launch as he passed between two closely-placed islands and approached a third with a red-roofed, green-sided boathouse which opened to a slip between two old but well maintained rock-filled wooden docks. He gave the traditional two short horn signals, flipped the fenders over the side and manoeuvred the launch alongside the upwind dock, using reverse to almost stop. As the boat slid past a mooring cleat, he flipped a spring-line over it and went back to the wheel to put the controls to forward with the engine idling, keeping the boat snugged temporarily against the dock.

The first sign of life was a large and boisterous golden lab, which was barking menacingly until Anderson shouted "Oh shut up, Ben!" The barking changed instantly to an excited whine and Ben bounded over for a pat and a scratch behind the ears. Anderson had spent the best part of three weeks with Tony and Jean (and Ben) this season, re-doing the foundations under the Barker's very attractive but very old summer home. Three generations of Jean's family had spent all their summers in that house, and it had a feeling of dignity and quiet wealth. No new money here. And it was an almost universal tradition among the island cottagers that people arriving by boat would signal their arrival, and wait at the dock until the host showed up. Presumably this prevented surprise interruptions of outdoor – but private – clothing-optional activities.

Tony came down the path to the boathouse, fully-dressed as always. Tony was an accountant, a very wealthy accountant, and a very dignified wealthy accountant. He was also an honourable and friendly man, who specialized in corporate ethics, the subject of two books he had written. The most recent one – published last winter – focused on corporations and the environment, a subject about which he was passionate and had chatted at length about as he hung around helping with the foundations. None of this had been lost on Anderson when he suggested to Arnold that he would approach this man about sponsorships for the public meeting.

"Hi Frank! It's good to see you..." as they shook hands

and Tony picked up the bow line to tie down the launch. "I have a nice new bottle of very old scotch that I've been waiting to open. Let's go up to the house."

"Sounds very good to me!" Anderson cleated down the stern mooring, put the transmission in neutral, shut down the engines and followed Barker's tall lean figure up the well-groomed path.

Jean welcomed Anderson at the door and embarrassed him with a friendly hug. She was the bubbly one of the pair, a lively sixty-five-ish lady with greying hair tied back in a ponytail. "We've talked lots about you, and the wonderful job you did to set the old place up for another hundred years."

Anderson smiled at her and said he was looking forward to seeing how the new concrete held out over the first winter. "I'm damn certain we did it right, but time always tells!"

Barker had produced an elegant squat bottle with a block-printed multi-coloured label and a couple of glasses. "Let's take this out on the porch... can't bear to sit inside even if it's a little windy. How was the trip from the village?"

"A bit bumpy – I came across the lake from the Webster place on that island near MacLean Point, so it was a little bumpier than coming from town. I wouldn't be surprised if there was a Small Craft Warning out, but I haven't checked the radio for a couple of hours.

"I heard that the wind is supposed to be gone this evening and that rain is moving in for a couple of days. Anyway, Frank, how can I help you? I knew when you called that something must be up."

Anderson paused. "Well, I'm not really sure where to begin. This has to do with some of your specialties, actually: corporate ethics, environment, government regulation, public participation and governance... lots of good stuff!"

"Good grief, man," Barker chuckled, "that sounds like me wondering where to start my next book! Can you narrow down where to begin a bit more closely than that?"

"Yeah, eeny meeny miny mo! I'll start with the environment. I expect you have heard of the Protected Shorelines Program, a federally funded research and conservation program. A local committee – of which I am a member – applied for a Program for Awan Lake a few years ago, and it has been pretty successful, I guess, certainly in the sense that people are more aware that the lake is a special place for the community, and that water is an important resource that needs caring for. And, we've been able to hire a couple of grad students each summer to do some research and help run the project. The project has been pretty low-key so far, but we are hearing voices – particularly from Dave Bradshaw – you know, the guy with that little cottage along the mainland shore north of here who's a prof at Ryerson – he is concerned about a proposed expansion over at Robertson Mines. I guess their refinery process uses a great deal of water, which is then contaminated and discharged who-knows-where."

Anderson hesitated a brief moment, and received a quick nod to continue from his host: "Anyway, Bradshaw suggested to the committee at a special meeting last week that we should hold a public meeting, and that we should bring in a certain Dr. Sebastian Horowitz as the speaker."

"Hah!" Barker interrupted. "Bradshaw is aiming high. Horowitz is a very high-profile speaker, and yes, he's passionate about water. He is also a bit of a scoundrel, but he's on the side of the angels in this regard. Does Bradshaw think he can get him down here from his roost on Vancouver Island?"

"Apparently Horowitz offered directly to Bradshaw that

he would come here if we could reimburse him for flights and accommodation. There was some reluctance from the locals present, who for any number of reasons also think he is... a scoundrel, to use your word. Some of them were less polite. But, obviously the idea of contaminating the lake doesn't please anyone, and they agreed we could put up with a couple of days of chaos in our quiet little village if it would draw public attention to the issue."

Barker's wife had joined them, sipping on a mug of tea while the men sipped on their scotch. She was obviously deeply interested is what Anderson had been talking about.

Anderson continued: "This, Tony, is where I need to cut to the chase, so to speak. I told the committee that I would visit you to see if you know of a company or agency that might sponsor the three grand we figure we need. The PSP group, we have just been told in no uncertain terms, cannot undertake advocacy, let alone sponsor it from federal funds."

Barker was quick to respond: "I am almost certain my publisher would do that."

"Tony, it was not my intention to put you on the spot. I was only wondering if you could point me at some organization where you might be able to put in a recommendation on our behalf."

"As I said, I am almost certain my publisher would do that. Why don't we ask her: Jean, would you plunk down three thousand bucks to hear Dr. Horowitz without having to drive to the 'wet coast' and get on that ferry again?"

"I most certainly would, gentlemen," said Jean. "Consider it done, with pleasure, as long as you'll get us a good seat!"

Anderson was stunned. He had dreaded this afternoon, mostly because he hated fundraising and saw himself as the world's number one lousy salesman. "Geesh. I don't know what to say, except, of course, thank-you. Thank-you from me, for making this moment so easy, and on behalf of the committee for coming to their support."

"I can write you a cheque right now, if that'll help?"

"Hmm. That's a whole other thing. You will recall a few minutes ago I said the PSP committee can't be involved with this. So Arnold Jamieson, the committee chairman, has gone and asked the few remaining members of the village Board of Trade if they would put on the event, and when we last talked that was looking positive but I need to make sure they even still have a bank account. I will let you know as soon as I know, if that's okay?"

"Of course," nodded Jean.

Anderson continued: "My apologies for the confusion. We went to Ottawa Monday morning for an 'emergency' meeting with Environment, whose minions had apparently learned on Friday morning about our Thursday evening meeting. The gentleman in Gatineau made it very clear that we could not do this through the committee. I have to say we found it very interesting that the government had learned about our plans within ten hours, and most of those hours were when normal people sleep!"

"I can see, Mr. Anderson, that you are going to have to read my husband's latest book," Jean laughed. "It won't comfort you at all, but at least you'll no longer be taken by surprise. This kind of stuff goes on all the time."

Anderson politely declined a second scotch, saying he had promised to get back to the Webster place in time for dinner.

"The Webster place – that's such a tiny little island!" said Barker. "Are they getting you to do some work over there?"

"Well, no, it's more of a social call; Marjorie Webster helped us out with some stuff a few days ago, and I agreed to have dinner with her and her sister Wendy."

"I understand Wendy is a pretty high-profile public relations consultant. Apparently she teamed up with her father, and kept going after he died. Very successfully, I believe."

Barker's wife continued the thread: "That's what I hear, too, and her sister Marjorie is an accomplished but little-known multi-media artist, mostly a painter. I have met her at an exhibition, and she is a sweetheart to talk to."

"Thank you very much for your help," Anderson continued. "I'll be in touch as soon as I know next steps." Turning directly to Jean, he said, "Yes, she is," and headed out the door and down the path to the boathouse and his launch. The Lady Barker smiled at him as he left.

***

The launch rolled slightly in the following waves. As the afternoon was fading, so was the wind, so by the time he got back to the little island the waves were smoothing out and there was just a slight silvery grey swell as the sun started to sink below a cloud bank growing in the west. Anderson called Arnold again to tell him about the sponsorship and that he needed the organization's full name for the cheque, assuming the old Board of Trade still had a bank account. His friend was impressed and thankful, and they agreed Arnold should call Dave Bradshaw and let him know the sponsorship was in the bag, but not to tell him the source at the moment because Anderson didn't know exactly how the Barkers wanted it listed.

He then called Marjorie to let her know he was about twenty-five minutes out from their island, and he pushed the launch a little faster because he realized he was a bit later than he had hoped. It would be seven-thirty before he got there.

08:00 JULY 19

Anderson was up, had enjoyed a quick breakfast with Marjorie and her sister and was heading back to the village on a cool, rainy but calm morning, and Awan Lake was living up to its name this morning, Anderson reflected ("Awan" is the Ojibwe word for "foggy").

The previous evening had been interesting – and surprisingly relaxing. By the time he had returned from the Barker's island, a new bottle of wine was open and poured and the barbeque was hot. The two sisters were in good spirits, as if all the trauma of the earlier afternoon had never happened. They had been busy solving the problem (a bit dramatically, Anderson thought): Wendy had written and sent an email letter to Robertson Mines withdrawing from her contract with them, stating a conflict of interest. There had been a flurry of calls on her cellphone, but she politely and skillfully held her ground... it was over, no details necessary.

Dinner had included new potatoes from the farmers' market in Spirit River, dressed with chives from what Wendy jokingly called the world's smallest spice garden (the island was basically a rocky outcrop surrounded by water, and just to grow the chives and a couple of other spices they had to import two bags of topsoil from the Co-op in the village). And the steaks were delicious. While they ate and sipped wine, Anderson and Marjorie had filled Wendy in on the events of the last week. She had listened carefully, and volunteered to help out with promoting the Horowitz event. She had also told them that while her own professional ethics would prevent her from talking directly about what she had been told by her former client, this was the beginning of a new day, and from now forward, everything she could find out about Robertson Mines and possible government influence was fair game.

They had chatted until late in the evening, and Wendy had taken herself off to bed. Anderson stretched himself out on the large sofa in the tiny living room-kitchen, and was just drifting off to sleep when he was joined by a very cuddly-looking Marjorie with a blanket and a pillow. "Hope you don't mind," she said. "I often fall asleep here myself." She had given him a quick kiss on the cheek, snuggled up close and dropped off to sleep.

***

Anderson smiled to himself as he throttled back to enter the harbour. He reflected that yesterday had been full of surprises, and that Marjorie was the most surprising of all. Once at the dock and tied up, he shut down the main engine and genset and used the yard-stick to dip the fuel tank: it read half a tank, so he walked up the road, checked the house and shop, grabbed his truck keys and drove to the Spirit River Co-op to fill his slip-tank with diesel and two litres of diesel-spec synthetic oil. He visited with the attendant for a few minutes, talking about the rain and fog, and observing a large new pickup which had stopped in for fuel. It was a crewcab, black, with a black cap. And it had numbers stencilled in white on the tailgate.

"Nice truck," he remarked to the attendant.

"Yup, Robertson Mines must have got a better lease deal and changed over their fleet. There's a bunch of these now – used to have white ones. I wouldn't want a black truck... they look dusty – or muddy – all the time, especially on gravel roads like the one to their yard."

Anderson charged up his diesel, the motor oil, and a pack of smokes and drove back down to the dock to re-fuel the boat. At about ten-fifteen, he took his truck home, made a pot of coffee, and sat down to wait for Arnold. He didn't have long.

"Howdy, stranger! I expect you had a busy day – and night – yesterday!"

"Well, yeah, kind of. But I behaved myself, in case that's what you were thinking."

"Never even occurred to me that you wouldn't behave. Just a matter of how well you behaved," chuckled Arnold. "But hey, pretty cool about that three grand sponsorship. I have all the details from Marion." He handed a piece of paper across the table, managing to spill some coffee on it. "Geesh, sorry. Can you still read it?"

"No worries, it's still clear enough. What's this about a tax receipt?"

"Marion says that the Spirit River Board of Trade still has federal charitable tax status, kind of left over from the nineties when it was active. And, they still have a bank account, with a couple hundred dollars in it. So she can issue the sponsor a tax receipt for donations, which is always a nice touch. Say, who is the sponsor, anyway? Barker himself?"

"Well, sort of," and he explained yesterday afternoon's visit to the Barker cottage and the conversation. "I think she told me she calls her company 'Awan Lake Publishing

Corporation' and she uses it to publish Tony's books. Who knew!"

"Yeah, I'm sure no one around town knows it. Likely just some little guy in a registry office in Toronto! Before I forget, I called Professor Dave as you suggested and he is tickled. He was going to confirm the date with Horowitz last night."

"Good. I'll get in touch with Jean Barker and give her the name for the cheque, and the tax thingy information. They come into town often enough, although I recall they have a little outboard and sometimes take a shortcut to the shore across the mouth of the river and have a little property with a garage on it where they lock up their car. Says it saved him a pile of time with that big old antique boat he has when he used to go to Ottawa twice a week. Nice to have money! But, if they're not coming in I can go out and pick up the cheque."

"Shouldn't be a problem anyway. They get their mail at our post office in town." He went over and helped himself to Anderson's coffee pot, pouring some in both cups. "Let's talk a bit about what Sergeant John had to say about that overgrown campsite out at the Robertson plant. John's a cop; he looks like one and just to prove it he wears a uniform and drives a cop car. Not the best way to get information from a bunch of hillbillies. I've been thinking, if a couple of old mechanics in a beat-up half-ton went out there, they might learn something. Ya think?"

"Sure do, makes all kind of sense. Can you spare the time? I can, but I don't have a line-up in front of my shop every morning wanting something fixed!"

"Not really, but looks like we're into this for better or worse. And Marion gets it, too. She's already starting to call you and me 'The Hardy Boys'!"

Anderson snorted a laugh: "Okay, and I am assuming you

mean, like, now, this afternoon?"

"My granddad was a horse-logger, and as he used to say, 'never say whoa in a bad place'. Might as well get it over with... we can take my truck – it may be muddy out there and it has four-wheel drive. And it's plain – no sign on the side. Your little truck has a picture of a muskrat or something on it!"

"Okay... a hamburger at the Zoo first, before the lunch crowd, and we're gone! Anyway, it's not a muskrat, it's a beaver with a shovel and a toolbox."

"Whatever. I gotta go to the garage and gas up first, so I'll meet you at the Zoo. Order me the hardcore special, not the quiche."

***

It was about a twenty-five mile drive from Spirit River village to the Robertson Mines location, and as Arnold had pointed out, it was "just a county road" and not one in good shape. The rain had let up, but the road was still pretty gooey. "See those survey stakes along the edge of the road allowance? Somebody has big plans to fix this up, and I don't suppose the county is springing for all of it," Anderson observed.

"Guess that explains the surveyors' trucks that have been hanging around the last few weeks. Staying at the Inn, I think. Mind you, the county contracts out all its survey work too. I stopped by the village office first thing this morning to see if they had a county map – one with land ownership and sub-divisions marked on it. All Freda had was one that's about ten years old, but it did show a provincial campsite adjacent to a good-sized block of land – maybe 60 acres – running between the campsite and the mine property, east of the road and along the shore. Owner at that time was a Gerald Giordano."

"Well, that's not a name that I've heard of," said Anderson. "I expect he owned that land before I moved here fifteen years ago... is it an old name in the community?"

"Not that I've heard of. Have to ask Marion, our walking encyclopedia, for the history and I expect someone who's good on the internet could get the name of the current landowner through the province."

There was little traffic this afternoon, just a couple of older cars and one black pickup going the opposite way. No one passed them headed south. A few miles later they saw a few rough trails leaving the country road in the general direction of the lake, which they had only seen glimpses of since they had turned south off the secondary highway. Another mile on, they slowed down as a larger and more travelled road took off to the right. There was a battered sign on the corner: *Provincial Campsite*. "Y'know," Arnold said as he turned onto the road, "now I remember this. Our dad used to bring us up here when I was a kid. We'd camp out for the night and fish. And, I think he used to hunt up here in the fall, but I never went with him for that. Occasionally he'd bring back a side of moose, but mostly it was a drinking party for the good ol' boys."

"I've been on a few of those when I lived out west for a few years. Didn't enjoy it much, but friends are friends and ya do what ya gotta do so you don't piss 'em off. Most times I volunteered to cook and clean up for them... then they were really happy!"

"I didn't know that you cooked," Arnold snickered.

"Hey, how hard is pancakes in the morning and burnt grey T-Bone steaks with boiled spuds in the evening? Remember, whiskey fixes anything! They treated me well – shared their whisky and always gave me a good share of meat when we got back. Actually, the only deer I ever shot was while I was doing dishes at the camp after they left to go hunting in the morning. Had him all dressed out and hanging up in a tree by the time they got back in the afternoon... I was the only guy who got lucky that day!"

By now they had passed a number of shacks, ancient old truck campers and trailers scattered throughout the campground. "Boy, some of those old trailers have been here a long time," Arnold observed. "Check out the license plates – there are several here from fifteen or twenty years ago, and most of them still look like folks use them pretty regularly." The road curved through the trees for a mile or more, then swung back toward the main road. They turned south again, and less than a quarter mile along there was a much newer sign that said *Robertson Mines Staff Accommodation* and a second sign that said *Please Stop at the Office.*

The office was very small – really just a log-sided cabin with one door, a window, and a nice new black pickup parked outside. Behind the office, maybe a hundred feet away, was a large double-wide mobile home, that looked like it had been there a long time and seen better days. Once, there had been some landscaping done, but now the yard was populated by some older cars, motorcycles, four-wheelers and – of course – a large and unpleasant-looking dog, running loose. "Guess we're gonna follow directions and stop here," said Arnold as he pulled in and stopped. "Don't want to start by making enemies... I hope that dog recognizes our good intentions!"

By the time they got out of Arnold's truck, the door to the office had opened to reveal a giant of a man in his sixties, wearing dirty grey bib overalls, green barn boots and a T-shirt. He was shaved bald and his face was scarred with a badly-set broken nose: "Something I can do for you?" The dog had slunk off behind the building and laid down.

"Hello. Not really, just passing by. My name's Arnold, and my dad used to bring me up here fishing when I was a kid – long time ago as you can tell! I just wanted to show my neighbour Frank around a little. We live in Spirit River."

"I know. You run the garage on Main Street. Can't say as I know the other guy... Frank you say?"

Anderson thought to himself that he definitely did not want to meet the man who broke that nose. He could see this was a man who knew lots, shared nothing, and liked it that way. "Yup, I'm Frank and I do building and renovations around town and out at the cottages."

"Lot's of stuff going on out here? I'd heard there was a bunch of construction planned, and we sure see lots of trucks going through town." Arnold paused a split second: "Surveyors and consultants, looks like, and the road is pretty well all staked."

"They don't tell me their plans, and all questions are to go to head office. They don't like folks snooping around out here, and they pay me to shut up and keep strangers out. We have workers staying here but they gotta do their socializing somewhere else, not here. Makes it easier to keep things quiet in the camp."

It was Anderson's turn: "Ah... sorry, I forget your name..."

"I didn't tell you. They call me Gerald."

"Thanks Gerald, nice to meet you. I was gonna ask what they do for women – are there families staying out here too?"

"We have some couples, maybe a couple little kids too. There are some girls work in the office at the plant, but they mostly come in from Maple Falls. The guys mostly keep to themselves, if that's what you're asking."

"Sorry, I don't want to pry into your business, we're just out for a drive. I'd heard a while ago there was a couple of girls in town who used to party out here, but maybe they moved away or settled down somewhere else. No big deal."

"It's a free country, but this is a dry camp – no booze. Guys work their shifts, that's it. If they want to drink or screw they go to town. I run a tight ship, that's what I'm paid for."

"Makes sense to me. Can we drive through and take a look on our way out?"

"Like I said, it's a free country. But it's my country, so don't stop anywhere. The drive through will take you less than five minutes, and I wouldn't want to have to come looking for you." Gerald whistled to his dog, turned and went back inside the office shack. There was no goodbye.

Anderson and Arnold got back in the pickup and took the road past the mobile home and past a series of small cottages, arranged like a parody of a suburban housing development. Most of the cottages had vehicles parked outside, many had small aluminum boats and motors on trailers or ATVs on the driveways beside the buildings. Anderson counted about thirty cottages, and there was an obviously new loop with more under construction. There were a couple of work-crews framing one cottage and roofing another.

They slowly rounded the loop and headed back to the entrance. Neither man saw any point in engaging Gerald in further conversation, and the dog was a whole other thing. "Gerald and that dog deserve each other," Arnold observed as he gave a quick honk beside the office and they drove out on the main road which would take them by the Robertson Mines refinery. "Now that he sees we are going to the company yard, do you suppose he phones ahead to let them know?"

"Maybe, but I doubt it. Did you see those two cameras on

the light pole by his driveway? One pointed each way along the main road... someone else is watching us, not him. Gerald is rough and tough, I'm sure, but the folks watching those cameras probably have guns instead of a big dog!"

Less than half a mile farther, the county road detoured to the left and the company access road went straight to a gate that would take them through a high chain-link fence. Or, it would take them through the gate if it was open, which it wasn't. As they drove up a woman in uniform stepped out of the gate house and waited for them to stop.

"Good morning, gentlemen. Do you have an appointment with one of our staff?"

"Nope," said Arnold. "We're just tourists, passing through." Noticing that she looked hard at both of them, and at the old truck, he chuckled loud enough that she could hear: "Yeah, as tourists go, we're pretty local! Just drove up from home in Spirit River 'cause it's a lousy day and we were bored!"

The gate lady relaxed, and smiled a little. "Okay, now I know you – you fixed a tire for me a month or two ago. I live in town in one of the rental units."

"Tire's still holding up, I hope?" She nodded. "I don't suppose you are going to let us through that gate unless we have a note from the Pope, or the Prime Minister maybe..."

She laughed: "Not even the Pope, let alone the Prime Minister! Sorry, I'm given a list at the beginning of each shift and that's who gets in."

"Hey, no worries. We really are playing tourist today – just driving around. We'll get out of your hair and leave you to your Sudoku!"

Anderson leaned across toward the driver's window and asked, "Say, you're from town... do you know a gal named Anita?"

She dipped her eyes for an instant, then replied, "Yes, I do, sort of. I mean, I don't know her well. We met at the Inn after work a couple of times. She used to hang out with one of the steam engineers that works out here. One day she said she... ah... was busy falling in love with a rock and roll musician, so I guess Hassam (the guy who works here) was out of the picture. Haven't seen her since."

"Hassam still working here?"

"Oh yeah, every day. Checked him in this morning. Never got to know him, though. They have rules here about 'fraternising in the workplace'. Seems friendly, but he's not my kind of guy anyway."

"Thanks, nice gate lady. We'll leave you alone... if someone's watching that camera up there, they'll think you're goofing off!"

"Never thought of that," she said, glancing up. "Maybe they will," she laughed as Arnold started to back up. "Bye now!" Arnold backed the truck around and headed back down the county road toward the village. They road in silence for a few minutes, then Anderson was the first to speak:

"Well, that was definitely interesting. The mystery of who was driving the big black SUV that the stoned drummer saw outside the bar in Maple Falls is likely solved, anyway."

"Yup... and I can imagine Sergeant John will be pleased to hear about it. I have a feeling that Hassam guy was not about to let his cute little chicky run away with a rock 'n' roll bass player."

"And I want to know more about handsome Gerald at the campsite. I could be imagining things, but I have a hunch we'll find that it's the same Gerald whose name was on that old map – Geronimo, or whatever?"

"Giordano," said Arnold. "Yeah, good point. Not sure

how that ties in along with all the other bits and pieces we're trying to put together, but it might take us somewhere."

"Well, if the lovely Gerald used to own that piece of ground, Robertson would almost certainly want to buy it. Back in the day, they may have cut him a deal that included money along with a lifetime promise that he could live there. That could have turned him from being Lord of the Empty Swamp into the Emperor of the East Shore, with a personal budget and now, a job that really does give him power over his little kingdom. Too crazy?"

"When you put it that way, not at all crazy. Well, you're crazy, but that theory actually makes sense!"

"I always like it when you admit I'm a genius."

"I wouldn't go quite that far!"

17:00 JULY 19

On the ride back from Robertson Mines, Anderson had phoned the sergeant at the OPS office but the call went to voicemail. After a couple of tries he called the sergeant's cellphone, and he had picked up immediately. He was tied up in an interview, but he agreed they should meet as soon as they got back to the village, since he was already there. Again, it would be at Anderson's place because, as the sergeant put it, "nobody ever goes there except sailors, mechanics, and cops, and there ain't many of those around!"

Arnold pulled up at the Zoo so Anderson could pick up his own truck while he went to check in with Marion. By the time Anderson had driven down to his own place, the sergeant was already there, police radio squawking while he made notes and talked on his cellphone. Anderson waved at him and went into the house to make coffee, which he dearly needed since they had forgotten to take anything to drink on their trip up the east shore road.

When the sergeant came in, Anderson said, "you could have just walked on in, John, instead of sitting scrunched up in that little mini-cruiser they buy you these days."

"Thanks, Frank, next time. But I needed the radio, too. There's some guy flipped over in the ditch the other side of The Falls, and it seems like Marie and Andy have it under control but Marie just wanted to make sure she was doing all

149

the right things."

"Anyone hurt?"

"Banged up, maybe a broken arm, but the ambulance has come and gone and the tow truck is there now. My crew has been handling it fine... Marie has had a few "firsts" as a corporal this last week or two, but it's good for her. Now, what's this you were telling me about black trucks and drummers?"

Anderson filled him in briefly and closed with, "I have to remind myself that while our conversation with the drummer – or more accurately the band leader Xavier – took place in Ottawa, what the drummer saw had actually taken place in The Falls a few days earlier. Anyway, finding out that some guy who was courting Anita works at Robertson Mines and drives a big black truck lines up perfectly with what the drummer says that he saw."

The sergeant laughed. "So, to old drummer Jones it looked like a U.S. Drug Enforcement Agency truck because he watches too much TV and was half stoned. To the rest of us it's just, well... a company truck. And now I have a definite lead, for which I am very grateful to you guys. I hesitate to commend civilians for doing investigative work but believe me, I couldn't have gotten anywhere with anything over the last week without both of you. And yes, I know that as a cop I was getting nowhere out at the Robertson camp."

By now, Arnold had joined them: "I have to say, I'm not a chicken-shit kind of guy, but I'd as soon not have to visit that Gerald guy again for awhile. And yes, Anderson, he is indeed Gerald Giordano, the guy who used to own that property. They found a newer map at the town office and left the information with Marion."

"What's this?" asked the sergeant.

"Living proof that Anderson can be a conspiracy theorist and still not be wrong. Tell John your theory, Frank."

Some people talk with their hands. Anderson liked using a pencil and a piece of paper instead. He grabbed one of each from his desk and scrawled a rough map of the east shore, showing the sergeant the adjoining locations of the old provincial campsite, the Robertson site, and the land in between. "And now, it seems to me that Giordano has a hell of a lot of control of what goes on over a big stretch of the east shore. Not that he is in real control over the land, but I would be surprised if the Robertson bunch really care what he does there. He provides them with a sort of no-man's-land buffer and keeps strangers away."

"My turn for conspiracies," Arnold chimed in. "You could even get rid of a body over there and no one would ever know."

The sergeant suddenly sat forward: "Damn it, I knew I had forgotten something. We had a call in this morning from someone who lives near the county line road where it crosses the Spirit River, about halfway to The Falls. They found a rather new leather jacket in the water yesterday afternoon and wanted us to know. I sent Andy and the other corporal out to pick it up and try to identify exactly where it was found, and they were almost out there when the accident call came in. I'll have to call those folks and tell them we won't be there until the morning."

Arnold said quietly, "I really hope it doesn't belong to a small female who is missing. That would not be good at all. I haven't seen Fred and Georgina since last week, and I hate to think how they're doing."

"Yes, that would not be a good thing for them," said the sergeant. "Actually I called on them around three o'clock today

– before I came here – just to see how they were doing and if they had heard from any of Anita's friends. Mum and Dad are doing quite well – better than I expected to find. Fred has really buckled down and is supporting Georgina, and laying off the booze. Of course, tears are still coming easy to both of them and they have no answers. And... obviously I didn't talk about jackets in rivers, but I did go over with them again what she had on when they last saw her. Georgina remembered she had a cellphone photo of her wearing her favourite jacket, which I got her to text to me. That will be useful when we pick up the jacket."

The sergeant stood: "Y'know, I could even pick it up now if I hustle out of here. It's on my way home, sort of. I'll radio Andy, and if they haven't got there yet, I'll call to make sure they're home and go myself. Thank you guys again. I owe you a lot of donuts!"

"No worries!" After the sergeant left, Arnold also said he'd better be going back to his garage and then home.

"And I've got a bunch of messages to answer, a quote to send out and some calls to make," said Anderson. "I've been pretty much ignoring the real world these last few days!"

***

Anderson had spent a couple of hours at his desk catching up, and decided that supper should be a pub-burger. He was planning to call Marjorie later, but wanted a chance to sit alone and sort out his thoughts so he got into his quarter-ton and drove out to the Spirit Inn.

The Inn was half full, but the only people he recognized were Georgina and her boss, Florence, who saw him come in and signalled "beer?" from behind the bar. He sent a Trump salute to her and chose a small table in the corner near the bar.

When Anderson had moved to the village fifteen years earlier, Florence considered him to be just a crazy young guy who came into town with a great big boat that you couldn't water-ski behind. They got along well enough over the years, and now he was fifty, she was sixty-five, and the age difference didn't seem so huge to her. "Here ya go, Frank. I got a couple of cases of that Saskatchewan beer in the green case you like so much, so this isn't Export, it's Great Western. Hope you plan to spend some time in here over the next few weeks 'cause nobody else will drink it!"

They both laughed and he thanked her. "Guess that's why it's so hard to get. Thanks for remembering and ordering it in!"

"You look wore out... been a busy few days?"

"Yeah, Arnold and I have been chasing around about a bunch of stuff. I imagine you know about us pulling that body from the lake last week."

"Yes, and I can only imagine how not fun that was. It would have driven me over the edge. Good for you guys for helping out... and, Mr. Anderson, I have also heard rumours that you might have a sweetie! I'll only tell you once, but I'm a little jealous, sir. And... I am also happy for you!"

"Well, I have to admit that Marjorie – Marjorie Webster is her name – and I have been seeing a lot of one another over the last week, but only time will tell if it's going anywhere. Circumstances can push people together, and after the dust settles it's all over and you can see it wasn't really there in the first place. This time, though, I have to confess that I hope there's more to it... we'll see."

"I'll cross my fingers for you, Frank. One thing I do know for sure is that romance is harder to put together as you get older." She paused. "I assume you're not here this early

153

planning to drink everyone under the table. What can I get you to eat?"

"Antonio in the kitchen? Good, I'll get a rare hamburger and fries with sliced tomatoes, as usual. Thank you, Flo!"

He turned his chair so he could watch the TV screen. Ottawa was playing the Lions in Vancouver, and the Red Blacks were ahead in the second quarter. He reflected that he was now a Red Black fan, although he had spent several years cheering for the Lions when he lived out west.

When Flo came with his supper, he asked her how Georgina was doing. "Aw, geez, poor Georgina, she's going through hell. I offered her time off, with pay, but she refused, saying she needed something to keep her from going nuts. The only good thing – if that's possible when your kid is missing – is that she and Fred have become incredibly close. He has really gotten his act together and stood close by Georgina. Things don't always happen that way, especially with guys who are boozers, but in this case, yes, it did happen."

"I'm not a guy who does much praying, but really, I pray for them. Fred's a good guy at heart and a really hard worker when he's off the bottle, and of course Georgina's a sweetie. Don't know how Anita turned out to be such a basket case, actually."

"Hmm, I dunno, Frank. I've gotten to know her over the years, especially with Georgina working here. I've kind of been a cross between a granny and an aunty to her. She's bright as hell and has a heart of gold, but unfortunately the emotions of a six-year-old. Always trying to find herself... it's kind of ironic, of course I always hoped she'd find herself before she was lost – really lost."

Anderson's cell started to beep, so he took it out of his pocket and had a look. It was Sergeant MacLeod. "I'm sorry,

Flo... I gotta take this." He got up and stepped into the parking lot: "Hello Sergeant."

"Bad news. The jacket matches the photo, and we can tell it's only been in the water a short time. It was picked up out of the water along the shore about a quarter mile downstream of the County Line Bridge. We'll need complete tests of course, but I am certain enough of the match to order an official search. Assuming you can travel the length of the river from the lake to The Falls, and have clearance under the bridge, I'd like to hire you and your boat."

"Crap. I mean – of course – but... crap anyway. This is so not good news. Okay, when do we start and where do you want me to be – I assume by the bridge, but when?" He paused... "Tomorrow at ten? Yup, I can do that. You'll bring those inflatables? Good. Are you bringing in special tech gear yet – hi-res sonar – or do you just want me to keep my cheapie sidescan on for now? Okay. We can do that. How are you fixed for personnel... you'll want two in each inflatable and I'll need two – one observer on deck and one on the sonar. Okay, I'll figure it out. See you in the morning," and he clicked off, walked to his truck and called the bar. "Flo, can you just keep my tab? I gotta go. Yeah, I promise I'll come back! Thanks Flo."

And he clicked off again, started up his truck and headed for home, thinking how pleased he was that he had fueled up the launch this morning and checked all the fluids. When he got to the house, he sat for a moment with his ever-present sheet of paper and a pen, and considered: *I need to call Arnold, and I need – and want – to call Marjorie. Where do I start...*

He called Marjorie. She said that she and Wendy had spent a really pleasant day, mostly inside out of the rain, visiting together like it seems they hadn't in years. He told her that he and Arnold had taken an interesting trip up the east shore on the country road, and he had lots to talk about, but he had a problem. He filled her in quickly, touching only the high spots, then asked the big question: "Are you game to join us on this search? It'll be an early start in the morning, and I'll need to find a deck observer between now and tomorrow. Not you, because I'd love to have you watching the sonar screen, since you have an obvious skill with screen images."

A quick silence, then she responded: "Of course. Two questions... does the sonar unit have a computer interface? Yes? Fine, because that screen on top of your dashboard is pretty damn small so I'll also bring my laptop. Second, can I bring Wendy to help? She'll feel really secure on your big boat, and on the river you're never far from shore anyway. I only say this 'cause she is a really focused person who looks for every detail in everything. Trust me, I know," she chuckled, "everything!"

"That would be really great, if Wendy's okay with it."

"Perfect," she said, "what time can you pick us up – remember our little runabout is still at the marina! Seven? Great, see you then. Hugs!"

Anderson smiled broadly to himself. He really did admire that lady, game to do anything and always good-natured! And, she had solved his next problem; he clicked on his phone and called Arnold.

"Hi Marion, how's it going? Yup, we did indeed have an interesting day. Uh huh, I would not be unhappy if I never saw that sucker again. I'll bet there's a lot of history out there, and not much of it good! Yes, I would." There was a pause.

"Hi Arnold. Sorry to bug you again but guess what: we have another emergency. We'll keep it obviously off the record for now, but we have another search for a possible body in the morning..." and he filled his friend in on his call from the sergeant.

After sharing the details, Anderson said, "I have my boat fully crewed by Marjorie and her sister – and probably John – partly because both are good at staring at images on computer screens, and partly because I can't bear to drag you out of that shop for another day. Well, actually, that's not the only reason: we'll have a bunch of boats going down a narrow river and cop cars and trucks all over the place. I'd rather have you and your towtruck and a mess of chains on shore, along with a guy who knows what to do when the going gets tough. Make sense? Cool. Keep your cellphone no more than two feet away, all day! Thanks man, g'night!"

07:00 JULY 20

It was exactly seven when Anderson gave two hits on the horn and swung around the island. As he approached the dilapidated wharf, he could see Marjorie and Wendy coming across the island with extra jackets and small backpacks. As the launch came to a stop along the dock, both women stepped across the six-inch gap and onto the well deck. "Good morning Frank!"

He already had the engine in reverse and was backing away from the dock. "Good morning ladies, I don't usually make a habit of inviting my friends on ghoulish adventures like this, but welcome onboard!"

"Don't listen to a word he says, Wendy," responded Marjorie. "Remember, this is what we were doing the first time we met!"

"Maybe so, but you will also recall that you supplied the corpse that time!"

"Fair enough!" she laughed, and walked into the wheelhouse and planted a kiss firmly on his lips. "Now, I've got my laptop and enough cables and adapters here to start an electronics store. Let me get started while you explain to Wendy what we're going to do, why, and how. I'll listen when I'm not staring at this thing in stunned silence. And, there's a big coffee jug in my pack but I see you brought along one too – big surprise – so I'll get us started on yours."

The boat was now headed southwest, to a low spot on the

far shore just west of the village. What was usually the low hum of the main diesel became a persistent growl as Anderson pushed the throttle almost to full speed. "Sorry about the noise. I have to make up a bit of time because once we get into the river we have to cut back to less than six knots (that's about ten klicks)."

Wendy had been standing close to the wheelhouse, getting a "feel" for the boat. She walked into the house and smiled, "This is pretty cool, Frank. I can see why Marj has such confidence – in you and the boat. Away nicer than bouncing around in that yammering little outboard!"

"It'll be much nicer once we're in the river, and when we get to the bridge and start the search, we'll be going only slightly faster than the current, so the boat'll be dead still. And that's a good thing, because I want you to be up there (he pointed through the windscreen at the forward deck with the small railing) searching the water surface ahead. There'll be a police sergeant with us I expect, and he'll spell you off. Anyway, don't go forward yet. It's a bit unnerving up there because of the illusion of the speed we're going, It's only about twelve knots but it seems a way faster and less steady up there!"

"Marj, I feel dumb here. What's a 'knot'?"

"Like miles-an-hour, but different. I'll explain later!"

"Okay. Now tell me what magic you have going on with that laptop."

"I think I've found the right cables to hook it up," said Marjorie. "Frank, where can I plug in the laptop?"

"There's household current in that receptacle port side of the companionway to the cabin. Sorry, left of the door to the steps." He reached forward to some larger switches under the dash and flipped one up. "There, that should be good to go."

"Thanks. Anyway, Wen, this computer is now hooked up to an instrument over by the wheel that measures depth, I understand. In a second, I should be able to read it... yes!... now I have it over here on the table, so I can watch through a much bigger screen without having to crowd Frank. Which would be fun for me but maybe not a great thing for this project. Frank, what else does this thing do and why is depth so important?"

"It's more than a depth sounder. If I set it up differently over here on the instrument itself, it becomes what's called "side-scan sonar". Instead of beaming radar-like signals straight down to measure, basically, depth only, it sends them almost a hundred and eighty degrees from side to side, which shows all the things on the bottom (and sides of a narrow river like this) as we pass over on the surface. You can actually see shapes of rocks, bridge piers, bicycles, outboard engines and – maybe – bodies."

"Wow, that is really cool. Is it reading now? I just see a bunch of squiggles and lines that don't seem to make much sense,"

"It won't make much sense at this speed and depth, although the depth information itself is pretty accurate. It's like photo resolution, in a way... the slower we go, the more signals cross the bottom and the higher the resolution – and the easier it is to pick out shapes."

By now, they were nearing the marshes that stretched from the group of islands where the Barkers lived, to the north shore. There were navigation buoys marking the entrance to the river and as they passed through the first set of buoys – red on the left and black on the right – he slowly brought the throttle back until the GPS showed six knots as their forward speed. The engine resumed its more peaceful hum, the waves pushed up by the launch reduced to a bit more than a ripple, and the marsh and river entrance closed in on them.

Pretty soon the river was more like a rough canal, fifty to a hundred feet wide at this point although it narrowed more downstream. The waterway was navigable for small boats until it reached Maple Falls. There, the water went over a small dam and spread out into more marshes and next reach of the river below.

"Holy cow," said Wendy, who had been standing silently on the well deck for the last fifteen minutes, "This is a bird-watcher's paradise. Who knew we had stuff like this in Ontario, or Canada for that matter. I feel like Katharine Hepburn in the African Queen - that movie with Humphrey Bogart!"

"It's not all as rough and overgrown as this. When we get downriver of the County Line Bridge and closer to Maple Falls, we'll start to pass some fields along the side, and the wildlife begins to look more like Holstein cows. But that's pretty too. Marjorie, I had promised on Saturday that we'd come down here someday soon for lunch at the locks in The Falls. I am really sorry, this was not exactly the relaxing voyage I was thinking of at the time!"

"Hey, this is fun, so far anyway. And, I think I am beginning to understand what I'm looking at on this screen, although stuff still goes by pretty fast."

According to the GPS, about an hour after entering the river they were about a quarter-mile upstream of the County Line Bridge, so Anderson cut the throttle back again, adjusting the speed until he barely had steerage way. He guessed the current was running at just over one knot, but even at idle the boat was moving forward at about two and a half knots. He was relieved that the day was calm, so the launch wasn't being pushed around by wind and steering was relatively easy.

They rounded a small curve in the river and there in front of them was the bridge. It was just a flat concrete affair with no superstructure, set on two piers with about thirty feet between them, so there was ample room for boats to pass under smooth conditions. Ahead on the right bank he could see the small concrete dock running about fifty feet along the shore; he knew that there was enough depth there to tie up the launch, but there was a cluster of small boats already there: two inflatables and an aluminum car-top fishing boat. In hopes that the people gathered on the dock would understand what he needed, he gave five very short blasts on the horn, put the transmission in reverse to slow and stop the launch – and waited.

There was a brief lull in activity on the dock then – as if a light bulb had turned on, two uniformed cops scrambled to pull the inflatables out of the way while a couple of others moved the fishing boat to the downstream end. Anderson told his two passengers to pick up the bow and stern lines and be ready to tie down the boat, and then he carefully manoeuvred the launch so that it came to a dead stop along the dock. The women jumped onto the dock and found a flurry of willing hands were there to take the ropes and tie them around the flat-topped pieces of pipe cast into the concrete that served as mooring bollards.

Anderson looked at the knots they were using and said to himself *Oh well, we won't be here long* and stepped ashore. He nodded at the owners of the willing hands and thanked them, then turned to his passengers with a smile and said "thank you ladies, that was perfect!"

By now the sergeant had already come up to where he stood, so Anderson introduced Wendy and said that she and Marjorie would form his observation crew going downstream.

"We didn't have time to talk about this last night, but you are welcome to ride with us where you can be on a more stable platform for communications, and high enough off the water to watch what is going on. Is your team and gear all here yet?"

"Just waiting for the diver to bring down her kit, but the boat people are all here and ready to go."

"Diver? The OPS has a diver out of Maple Falls?"

The sergeant chuckled at his surprise: "But of course! We always have everything and everyone we need, stored in the garage! Actually, when I filed the search plan last night and asked for a dive team to be on standby, they said they had a lady on contract who only lived about an hour away. So, since I have a dive-master ticket from years ago, and we would only be working in shallow water, we don't need a second diver as long as she has an extra kit for me – which is what they are bringing down now. And you, my good friend, can stand in as the third hand!" He paused. "And oh yeah, I forgot to ask: can the diver and all the gear join us onboard?"

"Of course. Load 'em up! Sergeant, I need to talk a bit about process, here. There's not a lot of current – about one knot – but I need to maintain steerageway so our minimum speed will be over two knots. Your inflatables, however, can – and should – go much slower than that. I don't want to go ahead of them, because the prop may churn up the water and any mud down there, so I'm suggesting your inflatables go first, and we'll follow once they are well downstream. When we catch up, we'll just stop and hold our position again, and so on. Your folks won't need to worry about us, and just focus on the search. Sound okay?"

"Sounds sensible to me. And... could we step into your wheelhouse for a moment? There's something we need to discuss."

Marjorie and Wendy discretely stepped away from the wheelhouse area and Anderson led the sergeant in. "What's up?"

"Last night, I was going through a folder – like a little flat wallet – that I found zipped into an inside pocket in that jacket. And I noticed something strange: some bills (about twenty-five bucks), miscellaneous ID including an out-of-date debit card, but no drivers license or any other cards. To me, it seems that perhaps it was left in there deliberately: enough information to identify a person who may have owned the jacket, but no pieces of ID that could be quickly checked out. And, a little money to make it look like an accident and not like a mugging. Long and short of it is that I don't think Anita's body is in this river. Someone just wants us to think so."

He paused. "But that's just me, and we must go ahead with the search anyway, so nasty guy that I am, I locked the wallet into my safe, and told my staff about what was in the wallet but nothing about what wasn't. I want them to remain entirely focused on this search. However, I wanted you to know, in advance. You are, after all, unofficially part of my management team!"

"Okay, I get it. Makes sense. These searches are a crapshoot at best, anyway, but most of these folks are young and eager, so might as well have them focused on the possibilities! I'll let you gather and instruct the team, and we can get started." They left the wheelhouse and the sergeant introduced Monica the diver, who had now assembled the two sets of gear on the launch's well deck. The sergeant gathered the team on the dock beside the boat and ran through the procedure as Anderson had suggested, then sent them to work.

In less than ten minutes, the inflatables were headed downstream, guided this time by paddles and drifting about thirty feet apart down the river. Anderson checked the engine gauges and instruments and also made sure Marjorie's laptop was properly receiving the side-scan signal. He then took the sergeant to the small deck in the stern that included the engine hatch, and took the lashings off the "lunch hook" anchor he had placed there this morning. He explained that it had about fifty feet of line attached, fastened to a cleat on the gunwale, and would be deployed if they needed to stop the boat facing downstream. Then he took Wendy forward with a lifejacket and a heavy canvas-covered cushion, placed the cushion on top of the main anchor, and sat her there between the pulpit railings. "As I explained earlier, this is where you watch from. Stay comfortable and focused, but don't stare. If you feel at all motion-sick, just call for someone to come and give you a break. Thanks Wendy!"

Then he poured some coffee and waited until the inflatables were well downstream but still in sight. "Okay, gang, let's cast off and get going!" Anderson put the transmission in reverse enough to take the pressure off the mooring lines, and when they were safely onboard he gently oozed the boat backwards and out into mid-stream until they faced directly between the bridge piers. Then he let the boat slide along under the bridge at minimal speed.

"Wow," called Marjorie from where she sat staring at her laptop. "Those bridge piers just went by as clear as a bell, and I can see what must be the river banks on either side. This is so cool!"

Monica had joined them in the wheelhouse and was looking over Marjorie's shoulder at the screen. "I've seen lots worse side-scan images than these from professional-grade equipment. The only advice I have to offer is to look for anomalies, not what you have already seen. Seems like your head builds up a library of images – like 'that's a rock, that's a bigger rock, that's another rock' – then suddenly something comes along and you go, 'shit, that's not a rock!' Those are the anomalies that are worth re-visiting."

"Hey sarge," Anderson called out, "whose fishing boat was that at the dock? I thought someone from the team was going to follow us."

"No idea at all. It was there when we got here. Guy must have gone for fuel or something... it looked like it had been used this morning. He had it tied to the dock with a bunch of little chain like you'd use to tie up a Chihuahua."

After about twenty minutes, they were catching up to the inflatables, so Anderson drifted the boat in neutral, then reversed and stopped and held the launch against the following current, switching back and forth to stay more or less in centre stream. "My screen is going nuts!" called Marjorie.

"No worries, it'll straighten out once we start moving again." He called forward through the opened windscreen, "Wendy, how are you doing up there?"

"I'm just fine. So far I've seen two bicycles under water by the shore and far too many plastic bags, but that's all."

"Feeling okay?"

"Yes, it's all good. Thanks for asking!"

And so it went. After five cycles of "catch up, stop and hold position, then follow" the sergeant suggested they take a break. Anderson agreed, suggesting the sergeant radio ahead and let them know to come to a stop next time the boat caught up, and they'd stop for coffee.

This time, when they caught up Anderson had sent the sergeant to the stern anchor and when the boat was drifting in neutral he signalled to put the anchor over the stern. There was a splash, then a few feet further along they could feel the

167

anchor tug at the boat, skid along a little, and stop. "Okay, coffee time folks," he said, and they watched as the two small-boat crews paddled back up to the launch and tied on. "Catch anything folks?"

"Nothing. Well, not nothing I guess. Bicycles, garbage, a couple of empty fence-wire reels. That's about it."

"Trouble with body searches," ventured Monica, " is that no news isn't good news even if it should be. Finding a dead person is what the mission is, but that goes against all my intuition even if it's my job!"

"Boy, do I ever get that!" said Wendy. "It just seems surreal!"

***

The rest of the morning went along much the same. Close to noon, The sergeant received a call from the one constable left at the office, who had been instructed to do some research about Hassam the steam engineer at Robertson Mines. According to what he had learned so far, Hassam lives in an apartment building in Maple Falls and commutes to work, usually in a company truck but he also has a not-very-new grey Toyota Camry. The sergeant told his constable to find out from the Robertson human resource office about his shifts from ten days ago and for the next couple of days.

"Anderson, let's do a lunch stop next time. All I brought along was a couple of pizzas – not very appetizing cold – and an armful of Subs, which will probably be better. It'll have to do!"

"Just so happens Frank has a little microwave in the cabin," chimed in Marjorie from inside the wheelhouse.

"Geez, you sure know how to rough it, Anderson,"

responded the sergeant. "That's great – it'll help make the pizzas a touch more appetizing!"

"He even has a tiny little wood stove in there too. He takes good care of himself, apparently!"

"Laugh all you like folks. Not every day I'm out working up the lake is a gorgeous day in July! Hmm... Okay, I see the gang ahead, so get ready with that anchor again."

***

Half way through the second cycle after they'd had lunch, the sergeant's radio crackled. "Constable Bathgate here. We have a dead calf in the water, south side of the river."

"Ask him how far off the shore," said Anderson.

The sergeant repeated the question into the radio. "Close. About three or four feet, looks like. It's just at the surface, bloated and two legs are down, probably touching the bottom."

"Thanks," said Anderson. "Marjorie, we'll let you know when we're passing it. Might give you an opportunity to see what a similar-sized corpse looks like on the side-scan."

"Lovely."

Anderson chuckled.

***

As they approached what would likely be the second to last reach of the river into Maple Falls, the sergeant, Anderson, and Monica the diver all agreed that they were now far beyond where a drowned person could have reached in two weeks. The jacket had actually been found in the water about one hundred yards downstream from the bridge where they had started this morning, but the folks who picked it up said it had been snagged in some fallen branches.

"So, do we call it off now and figure out how we are all going to get home?" Anderson asked.

"At first I was thinking we would pull into the dock at Maple Falls, have the on-duty constable pick up the inflatables and four officers, then come back for the diving gear plus Monica and I, and take us back to the bridge to pick up my SUV. And Anderson and crew could just cruise home, hopefully arriving in time for a late supper." He paused. "Does that work for you, Frank?"

"Well, anything works as long as I don't have to do this river in the dark! I guess the only thing that has me thinking a bit is the media. We can do whatever we like at the dock in Spirit River and the only folks that know about it is the family of beavers that live on the point. At Maple Falls, however, the comings and goings of cops, cop cars and a big grey boat with aerials all over it will ensure that there is at least one TV camera there within twenty minutes. Is that a good thing, or a bad thing? If it's a bad thing, I can turn this outfit around at the next stop, get everyone on board, put a line on the boats and get back to the bridge in about an hour, maybe less. And you'd only have to have your constable send out one car."

The sergeant paused – a long pause, then said: "The media are going to be all over us soon anyway, I expect. From my unit's point of view, it might as well happen when they can show some footage of us actually doing something, and since the head of the unit – the sergeant, which is me – serves as on-site communications officer this far out of Toronto, I'm easy with that. Anderson, you have something in mind?"

"Yeah. Do Anita's parents know what's going on today? I'd hate to have Fred and Georgina learn from the evening news that the police are out scouring the river for their kid."

"Yes they do. I called them last night and told them."

"Then, I just had a thought for you: on the foredeck of this boat is a highly qualified professional public relations consultant. It might serve us well to ask her opinion about how to handle this – certainly how I should handle it if a reporter insists on talking to the boat skipper. And... we're now catching up to the boats, so we need to figure this out soon."

"Excellent suggestion. I'll radio the guys to stop and come back to the boat. So, Marjorie's sister is a PR expert, is she?"

"Yup. Her company is based out of Toronto and handles big corporate clients. Knows her stuff!"

The sergeant nodded, then radioed his team and went to the stern anchor for what would likely be the last time today. In just over ten minutes, the launch was stopped mid-stream, the boat crews were tying their lines to the quarter cleats, and the sergeant had gone forward to talk to Wendy. When they both came back to the well deck, the sergeant leaned against the wheelhouse and called all nine people together. "Okay, here's what's gonna go down: our skipper and our diver have a way more experience than I have when it comes to looking for things in the water, and both agree that we are now well beyond the reasonable search area. I agree too and incidentally, we found evidence late last night that the jacket may have been deliberately tampered with to set searchers off-track. We'll shut down the search here, and thank you all for your work today, although I guess it's not really over yet.

" I would like to point out that this is an amazing little boat you are working with today, not least because of its useful technology but also because of its crew. Most of you know Mr. Anderson – or just Anderson as he likes to be called, and by now you have met the Webster sisters, who are Anderson's guests and assistants today. Marjorie Webster is a digital graphics professional, and she has been staring at the sonar screen for the last six hours. Her sister Wendy is a highly qualified public relations professional and I've just been talking to her because it is almost certain we will be found at the Maple Falls dock by at least one television crew. So, I am asking Wendy to give us our marching orders for our arrival there. Wendy? They're all yours."

Marjorie had moved over to stand beside Anderson, and had taken his hand, which she continued to hold while Wendy began speaking, in a firm and practiced tone that belied her relaxed pony-tailed appearance:

"Thanks Sergeant MacLeod. I am pretty sure everyone here hates having media around, having to stand right, be dressed right, and – God forbid – say the right things. However, I want you to think of the media today as your new found best friends. It's simple, really. First, don't change your clothes. You've been working all day, getting sunburned, tired and wet. That's good – that's what people pay you for and they are pleased to see you take your tasks seriously. Second, let's make this little grey ship with the forest of whiskers and funny-looking things on top look like part of the British navy. Well, maybe not, but let's arrange everything as neatly as possible. If there are two of something, make sure they are lined up nicely. If you are going to deflate your boats, wrap them up in their cases. And so on.

"Now, if we are approached by reporters or camera operators, there are two – and only two – spokespersons for this operation: your Sergeant, and Mr. Anderson. And Mr. Anderson is a separate spokesman from the police because he and his vessel are contracted by the OPS for this operation, and as such he is a private individual. So if you are not those two people, cheerfully say nothing except 'You'll have to ask the sergeant' or 'You'll have to ask Mr. Anderson, he's the skipper.' Be polite, be relaxed, get on with your tasks when not being spoken to, and smile a lot. That's all – just relax and enjoy it! You too, Sergeant!"

Anderson beckoned Wendy, Marjorie and Sergeant John to follow him into the wheelhouse. "John, I am asking Wendy to remain in the wheelhouse when the media are around. Wendy may have a conflict of interest with a client that could be triggered if she winds up on camera, let alone being interviewed. She can explain later at a later date. And Marjorie, would you feel more comfortable in the wheelhouse with Wendy?"

"I don't mind being back and forth. It'll confuse 'em!"

"Fair enough. Works for you Wendy?"

"Yes, and thank you. I didn't want to chicken out, but staying out of range is a good decision, and the one I would have recommended to a client. One more thing, and this one's for you, Sergeant John. You have a pretty photogenic team and bunch of kit assembled here, and you have a story to tell that is valuable not only to your unit and the OPS as a whole, but also to the friends and family of the missing girl. I would suggest that we actually leak our arrival at the dock to the media, to make damn sure they turn up! I know it sounds off base, but I can tell you that communications officers in the RCMP and the Toronto police and many other departments do this kind of thing all the time. It's all about controlling the story, and the message."

The sergeant glanced at Anderson, then back to Wendy, then across at Marjorie and back to Wendy. Anderson chuckled: "Any time you're done making the rounds, Sergeant!"

"You took me totally by surprise. 'Totally!' as my teenaged daughter would say. But you know, that just ain't a bad idea. How, though, do you create a leak like that?"

"You just said you have a teenaged daughter?"

"Yup."

"She have a cell phone?"

"Duh."

"So text her to say you're coming into the dock with a fancy big boat at around four-thirty and if she wants she can text a few of her friends to come down and take a look. She might even meet a TV personality (if they show up from the TV station) and the boat crew will buy them a milkshake."

The sergeant snorted and shook his head in disbelief: "Here goes my badge!" And he began to text.

"Apparently Wendy is the evil Webster sister. I, Marjorie, on the other hand, am the kind and gentle one."

Anderson laughed at them both, gave Marjorie a squeeze on the shoulder and began to tidy up his boat.

***

It worked. An hour later, when the launch chugged into Maple Falls, turned into the current and pulled alongside the dock, they were being captured by a TV camera from the sidewalk up the hill behind the dock. On the dock itself stood three attractive 17-year-olds. "That's amazing, simply amazing," said the sergeant to no one in particular as the boat finished docking.

***

The lone TV reporter had been engaged and professional, spent a long time talking with the sergeant and asked Anderson a few questions about his vessel and side-scan sonar. The girls went for milkshakes and to pick up the two hot pizzas and some cans of Pepsi that Anderson had ordered for the almost three-hour run home.

The trip back upriver was uneventful. By the time they passed under the bridge, the police cruiser, Monica-the-diver's car, and the fishing boat were long gone. Sergeant John had called to say he watched the news – said it was a good report – and yes, he had called Fred and Georgina beforehand and affirmed that the team had not found Anita, and that was a positive sign.

Anderson had also received a call from Arnold just after the early evening news, saying that Marion had heard from Georgina before supper that the search turned up nothing. "That was an impressive newscast, Anderson. Somehow they even made you look like a sensible kind of guy. What the hell did you do with the Webster girls?"

"Hid 'em in the cabin, of course. I'll explain in the morning. Poor Georgina is going to have a difficult time in the bar tonight... there'll be a pile of questions from folks who saw the news."

Just after eight-thirty, Anderson pulled the launch into the Websters' dock. Wendy recommended wine, so they crossed to the cottage, sipped on a glass of wine, and had a relaxed couple of smokes. After about half an hour, Anderson stood up, thanked the sisters at length for all their help, and said he had best get home.

"If you don't mind, I'll keep you company. Then I'll be able to bring the outboard back so we're not stranded out here," Marjorie joked. "You okay alone, sis?"

"Yes, I'll be just fine. Despite the ghoulish overtones, this has been one of the best days I've had for years. Time to relax, time to think, things to do a little outside my comfort zone – it just doesn't get any better. And hey, I was even able to ply my trade! Take care of yourselves, you two. See you tomorrow."

By now it was almost completely dark and though it was clear there was no moon, and no wind. The lake surface was like a sheet of black glass, and ahead Anderson and Marjorie could see clearly enough the lights of Spirit River and – nothing else except the glow of the red and green navigation lights and the reflection on the deck of the forward steaming light from the navigation mast. A half-hour after leaving the island, Anderson brought the boat into the little harbour at dead-slow speed, turned on his forward spotlight, found his dock and slithered alongside. Marjorie was ready with the bow line, and he tied down the stern and spring lines.

They stood looking at one another for a moment and Anderson said, "I'm going to simply shut her down, lock her up and let's go home. I am really beat, and I'll bet you are too."

Ten minutes later, they stepped into his house. He turned on a wall light by the kitchen and looked around to see if everything was as he had left it sixteen hours ago. Out of habit, he picked up the coffee pot from the table. "Whoa." Marjorie walked up and took the pot from him, setting it back on the table. She turned to face him, took both his hands and said, "There is nothing more I want at this moment than to curl up beside you and sleep. For a long time. Is that okay with you?"

Anderson leaned forward and gave her a very gentle kiss. They walked together to his bed, pulled up a blanket, curled together and slept.

06:45 JULY 21

Anderson woke up to the smell of frying bacon.

He rolled out from under the blanket and stood up to see Marjorie standing in the kitchen area, fiddling with the toaster and a carton of eggs. "I really think that waking up to the smell of bacon cooking and a pretty lady cooking it is as close to heaven as I'll likely ever get!"

"Hah!" she laughed. "You just spent the night sleeping with me and all you can say is that the smell of frying bacon is the closest thing to heaven?"

" 'Sleep' was the operative word, as I recall. I am assuming I behaved?"

"Don't remember. I was asleep at the time."

"Well, we're a fine pair," Anderson chuckled. He walked up behind Marjorie, took her shoulders gently and planted a warm kiss on the top of her head: "You scare me. Well, actually, I think I scare me. But I do know that I like the feeling."

"So do I. How do you like your fried eggs?"

"Fried."

"This promises to be a productive day, I can just tell.

They'll be sunny side up unless you squawk."

"Perfect!" Anderson went to a drawer, took out some cutlery and placed it on the table, then poured fresh mugs of coffee for them both. He went to the refrigerator and took out a bottle of orange juice, looked at the best-before date, and dumped it down the sink. He then took a can of concentrate out of the freezer and made up a fresh batch and set it, too, on the table with two glasses.

Marjorie joined him at the table with two plates of fried eggs on toast with bacon. After a couple of mouthfuls, she said quietly: "I have to go back to Toronto on Sunday."

Anderson stopped in mid-mouthful and looked across at her: "Not an emergency I hope?"

"No. Routine. I really don't want to go, but it is what it is. Wendy needs to spend some time with her staff at her office, and now of course she has some new issues on the table. And I go back and pretend to fix up the garden and clean the house. We usually go in on Sundays – early enough to beat the rush – and try to be back here Wednesday or Thursday night."

"I am only just getting to know Marjorie-from-the-island, but I have really no idea about the rest of your life. Do you have a condo or apartment in the city?"

"No, Wendy and I share our folks' old house in Scarborough, and I have my studio there. It's a quick commute into the city for Wendy – we're a short walk from the GO Train – and I only go into the downtown area for exhibitions and occasionally research at the ROM or the Art Gallery. We love the house, but it needs a lot of fixing, which is usually my thing but now that we have the island both of us refuse to spend our summers hammering nails and painting."

"Have the Webster sisters ever married?"

"Wondered when you'd ask!" she laughed as she finished

her last piece of toast and bacon. "Wendy – no. Some love affairs, but they were always short and sweet. Not even so sure they were all sweet, even, but in any case, she worked so closely with our dad I think she felt one grumpy male in her life was enough!"

"And Marjorie?"

"Yes, I did have a brief and really unsuccessful marriage. He was a university level athlete – a skier – whose name was Tom. We met at the bottom of a ski lift at Blue Mountain near Collingwood and were on our first date by the time we got off the chairlift at the top. We had lots of fun for a couple of years before I realized that there were a lot of ski-lifts in Canada and he pretty much found another date at each one. We parted on good terms, and we still have coffee about once a year when he comes to Toronto. He has long-since settled down in the Okanagan in BC, where he is a phys-ed teacher and has three blond blue-eyed kids!"

"Miss him?"

"What's to miss?" she laughed, "wasn't ever any substance to our relationship anyway."

"You're saying it started off at the bottom and went downhill from there?"

"Ha Ha, funny man! But, yes, it was a weird relationship right from the start. I grew up thinking that love and marriage was supposed to involve at least a little passion. There was none, so I guess the good news is that there was no hatred, either." She paused a moment, then: "So, that's enough about the life and times of Marjorie Webster. How about the mysterious Mr. Anderson?"

"One wedding, one divorce, three years and one son in between there somewhere. Genette had a degree in French literature and taught at a small high school. We met at a resort town in southern Québec where I was a 20-year-old kid working as a gas-jockey at the local marina and sailing club. Just after our son was born she fell in love with an older man who was 'more in her social station' as she used to put it, so we split up. We amicably traded my responsibility to our son with her desire to never see me again. And that`s the way it stayed. I took off to chase my fortune on the west coast, and we have never been in touch since. I do know that my son started work as an accountant in Denver, Colorado, a couple of years ago, but that`s all. I don`t feel good about our estrangement, but I am pretty certain that his life worked out for the better that way."

"That's sad," said Marjorie.

"Maybe. It would make a good country and western song, but I don't sing."

"Any girlfriends?"

"Are you asking if I have been celibate? No. But I have tended to avoid lingering affairs."

"So, can I see you again next week when we get back?"

"I certainly hope so. Hell, we haven't even had an affair yet, let alone a lingering one!" Anderson laughed and smiled at her: "Just kidding. I really like you, and that's why I said earlier that I scare me!"

Anderson's phone went off. He rolled his eyes at her and muttered, "Oh crap, and I forgot to plug it in." He went and retrieved it from his bedside table and answered on the fourth ring: "Anderson here."

It was Sergeant MacLeod, calling to tell him that he had sent an officer to Hassam's apartment yesterday evening but there was no sign of him, so he sent the constable along with Corporal Beauchemin out to Robertson Mines a few minutes ago. The sergeant also gave Anderson a heads-up to expect a call from one of the Ottawa newspapers about yesterday's search. It seems they were asking questions about why Anderson's equipment was involved in the investigation; he had just told them Anderson was a contractor engaged because of the side-scan technology that his vessel carried, and was not a regular part of policing out of the OPS offices at Maple Falls.

After they hung up, Marjorie was already cleaning dishes after breakfast, so Anderson went over to the kitchen to wipe up and put things away. He was explaining the sergeant's call when the phone rang again. This time it was a freelance reporter from Ottawa, who quizzed him at length – and repetitively – about how Anderson was involved with the search for a body. He explained what he did for a living and why his equipment might be considered of value to the OPS, but he gave no indication that he knew anything about the people or circumstances surrounding the search or the people involved. "The folks at OPS simply asked me to bring my equipment on the job, but they didn't supply any information about why the person was missing, or who the person was," he repeated several times, thinking to himself that he was actually being perfectly truthful because it had been he (and originally Marjorie) who had informed the police in the first place.

Eventually the reporter thanked him and hung up. "Geez," he said to Marjorie, "I have no idea how Wendy puts up with people like that. I wish she had been here!"

"Yeah, she bitches all the time about reporters who are trying to make a name for themselves rather than report the facts. Sounded like you did okay, though!"

It was going to be a busy morning, it seemed. No sooner had Marjorie spoken than a small UPS cargo van pulled into his driveway. "What the hell..."Anderson said, then: "Oh yeah, right..." and he went outside to greet the courier. A few moments later he arrived with a large, obviously heavy, cardboard box which he placed carefully on the floor just inside the door.

"Rabbits?" asked Marjorie.

"Nope, but close. Radar."

"Are you trapping speeders on Main Street in Spirit River or taking up flying?"

"Boats use radar too," he replied. "Every now and then, Awan Lake lives up to its name, and I get stuck at the dock for a couple of days because of the fog. That's not a huge problem 'cause I'm never in that much of a hurry, but I have had times out on the lake when the fog came in without much warning and I had a hell of a time getting back to the village. These units are pretty expensive, but I got a really good deal on this one online – it incorporates GPS and radar signals into one image on the same screen."

"Why is it so big? There'll be no room on your dashboard for that!"

"No, the screen and controls are quite small, it's the antenna that is so big – and it goes on top of the wheelhouse on the navigation mast. And installing it will give me a chance to speak with Anita's father, Fred, who is a really good welder. I can weld steel – badly – but I am hopeless with aluminum. Fred, on the other hand, is quite good at it." He added, "Shall we try for a second cup of coffee and a smoke out on the porch?"

They had taken their mugs and had barely settled in the morning sun on his porch when up the driveway came Arnold. "Marjorie, apparently the only way you and I are going to be able to talk together is to get back in the boat and get out in the middle of the lake! Good morning Arnold... coffee?"

"Please. Hi Marjorie." He smiled warmly at her and said,

"I hate to break up this scene of domestic bliss, you two, but there's all kind of weird stuff going on."

"We've hardly had a chance to say good morning to each other, let alone share any domestic bliss! Frank's phone keeps ringing and a courier has been here already. 'Oy' as my Ukrainian aunt used to say. This gets to be a busy little not-so-peaceful place, it seems!"

Anderson arrived back on the porch with a coffee for Arnold. "Here ya go. What's new in your world?"

"Well, some of it is expected of course, ever since you guys splashed away down the river yesterday and that television crew found you in The Falls. You and Sergeant John are local heroes – King Arthur and Sir Lancelot, and that big canoe of yours is the mighty steed that charges around doing wonderful things! And of course, less fortunately, the Anita thing is back at the top of everyone's mind."

"Sir Lancelot, eh?" And they haven't even met my Guinevere yet. Like I said, we kept Marjorie – and Wendy – in the cabin during all that."

"You can hide 'em all you like, but everyone is talking about Anderson and that Webster girl! All very complimentary, though, Marjorie!"

"Don't ya just love small towns," Anderson grunted. "Shifting topics only so slightly, have you heard anything more about the Robertson Mines thing and our Italian friend Gerald? John told me half an hour ago that he just sent a couple of officers out there this morning, looking for that Hassam guy."

"Well, not exactly, but we have a problem that is likely related to that. First, as you know, the date and place are set for the Horowitz event, and Marion put up some notices around town yesterday morning. Late last night, after we talked, Adumbi and Cyndi came to the house, tired, wet, and scared shitless. They had been up the east shore at that marsh south of MacLean Point, doing a bird survey, and when they started to paddle back to their truck, a motorboat came whipping along the shore from the south and buzzed them. Not just once on the way by… they circled around two or three times and dumped their canoe with their wake, then they buzzed them in the water. Didn't try to hit them, they said, but came really close, then they took off south again."

"What kind of boat?"

"One of those big bass-boats is my guess, and they said it had no license number on the front. They described it as low and kinda beat up, aluminum, with two big engines on the back. Two guys in it, wearing peaked caps pulled down too low to see their faces clearly."

"Must have scared the crap out of the kids," Anderson said. "Are they okay?"

"Yes, but they lost all their equipment – laptops and software, cameras, and their personal gear including their phones. Just lucky they were wearing their lifejackets. And, I'm afraid we may be losing them as our PSP interns. They told me – didn't ask me, told me – they were leaving for their homes this morning and taking today, the weekend of course, and Monday off, and they'd be in touch by phone Monday or Tuesday morning. I'll tell you, they were some shook-up."

Anderson started to speak, but Arnold broke in: "Oh ya, and there's something else. Cyndi said something about 'with what happened to Anita, and now this, I'm not sure I can come back.' I asked what Anita had to do with this, and she said, like, didn't we know that she was running a Facebook page – a 'group' I think she called it – about birds and wildlife and the sanctuary island and a bunch of environmental stuff including the PSP. Guess she had a bunch of followers, too, from all over, not just here. Like, who knew! That's not one of the first things I'd have thought Anita was into, although Marion disagreed with me – said Anita had talked about it with her a couple of months ago but asked her to keep it quiet locally because she didn't want to be teased by the bar crowd, or even her parents."

"Man, you are just full of good news this morning, ain't ya! This stuff makes our little baby conspiracy theories seem kind of tame!"

"So, do you guys think Robertson Mines is behind all of this?" asked Marjorie. "If so, this sounds like really heavy-duty and dangerous stuff. I'm not defending that outfit for a moment, but it doesn't seem logical that they would have staff running around in boats scaring university students counting birds with binoculars, or disappearing some unknown young girl who has a Facebook page." She paused. "Tell you what – Frank, can I use your desktop to see if I can find that Facebook page?"

"Absolutely – that's a great idea!"

" So, Arnold, where the hell do we go from here? Do we talk with the sergeant right away, or let it slide for now and do some other digging, or what?"

Arnold paused for a long moment. "I think we have a pretty good under-the-radar thing going with John. Maybe we should talk to him, without forcing his hand. We can probably look into some stuff that he can't, at least not without raising some hell at headquarters."

"I agree. I think there is a connection between all this stuff – Anita, the interns being scared off, and even the Horowitz thing and what LaChance said at Starbucks in Gatineau. And my gut tells me the connection, somehow, is at the Robertson Swamp."

"Robertson Swamp?"

"Well, yeah, that's my pet name for it. You know, that land around the old provincial park. Here, give me your coffee cup."

Anderson went into the house to refill the coffees. Marjorie looked up from the computer: "Hey, that was easy. Pretty sure I've found it. There's a public group on Facebook called 'Save Awan Lake' and it's run by someone who calls herself "Foggy Swamp Girl". Lots of people post on it – it has several hundred followers – but the Swamp Girl herself hasn't posted on it for almost two weeks."

"Wow, that was quick – tell Arnold and I'll bring another cup." He filled their cups, put on another pot, grabbed his smokes and went back outside to hear Arnold asking Marjorie what people have been posting about.

"It's probably worth spending more time on the page, looking for topics, patterns and names and connections of people who post. I'll go back in and check it out a little more. And I think Wendy – who is really good at watching social media – might help us too. Any way, I need to call her and say hello this morning... she's probably wondering where I am."

"I somehow doubt she's that naive that she doesn't know where you are," Arnold chuckled.

Marjorie blushed and grinned. "Hush up, dirty old man!" and headed back to the computer and her cellphone.

Arnold dialled his phone: "Sergeant – it's Arnold in Spirit River. Are you anywhere close? We need to talk to you down at the Anderson conference centre – a lot of heavy shit this morning. Twenty minutes? We'll be here."

"Anderson Conference Centre... has a nice ring to it! Feels like it anyway," Anderson chuckled. "Say, I know Fred has hunted and trapped all around Awan Lake. I wonder what he knows about Robertson Swamp?"

"Right on, hadn't thought much of it but now that you mention it, I'm pretty sure he even used to have a registered trapline over that way. We should talk to him, although I hate to bug him and Georgina with more stuff to worry about."

"Well, it so happens that I could use him to weld some aluminum for me today sometime. I've got to put a radar antenna bracket on my navigation mast... the radar unit just came in this morning. So, while he's welding I can just drift questions into the conversation without tipping him off to the latest bad news."

"That'd be perfect."

"Okay, I'll call him now, and try to set it up for maybe two o'clock this afternoon. I'll have to look at the instructions and installation drawings before he gets here."

Anderson found Fred and Georgina's number on his phone, and called: "Fred, it's Anderson. I hate to bother you, but could I get you to come over and weld some aluminum for me? It's not a very big job, but I sure as hell can't do it as well as you can. Bring it over? Well, no, I'd have to tow the boat over – it's already kind of attached to the boat. Cool. I'm tied up for the morning, but how about two o'clock? No, don't worry about chasing down acetylene – I have my torch here, but you'll need some rods, or whatever you call what you use for aluminum. And if you have some medium heavy two-inch angle, even scrap, that would be useful too, maybe four to six feet. See you then. Thanks!"

Anderson was just hanging up when Marjorie came out, took a cigarette and lit it. "Okay, guys, we're on a roll here. There are a significant number of comments about Robertson Mines, and a whole whack of related stuff. I phoned Wendy and told her what we had found, and she said she has a program she uses with algorithms that allow here to search keywords in Facebook and other social media, without letting them know who's looking. She'll dredge the site and tell us what she finds."

" 'Algorithms' – what the heck is an algorithm anyway," asked Arnold. "Sounds like an alligator doing a line dance."

"A series of linked math equations that do what you want them to do, as far as I know," Anderson replied. "Marjorie, I expect you can do better than that?"

"Dancing alligators may be closer than you think. Computer scientists and mathematicians could probably spend an hour giving you a better answer than that, but for what we're talking about, Frank's answer is close."

***

The sergeant was ten minutes late, didn't have any donuts, and was begging for a cup of coffee. "Hi Arnold. I had told you I sent a patrol unit out to Robertson Mines to look for Hassam? Well, Marie and her partner just arrived there a few minutes ago. I expect we'll know pretty soon what kind of reception they get."

"Your coffee, sir. Fresh pot. We've been sucking it back pretty good this morning."

"Thanks Frank, and hi, Marjorie. So... what's up this morning? I'm starting to dread coming near any of you folks... as you mentioned before, more questions than answers!"

Arnold began with the interns' run-in with the motorboat. The sergeant's notepad appeared when Arnold was halfway through. When Arnold was done, the sergeant turned to Anderson and asked, "You're the marine expert, any charges there that I could lay without witnesses other than the interns themselves?"

"Getting charges against recreational boaters to stick is damn near impossible. If the interns are correct, there were no registration numbers on the boat, so that charge would stick if you can find the boat. If the kids will testify, you might get dangerous operation of a motor vessel to stick. I say 'might' for good reason. Usually that only sticks if there is a witnessed collision. To me, it's attempted murder, but I don't think you'll ever find a judge who thinks it's more than a prank."

"Okay. Thank-you. We all know this is a serious occurrence, not the least because of the harassment of workers on the federal dime, if not directly on payroll. The biggest thing to consider at the moment is the 'understory' – the extreme intimidation, and why." He looked up from his notepad: "And you had more?"

Arnold described what he had learned from one of the interns about the Facebook page that Anita was running, and Marjorie filled in with what she observed once she found the page on the internet.

"So again, it's who and why. I get the pattern... it all appears to be connected with Robertson Mines. But of course at the moment it's all conjecture and circumstantial."

He closed his notebook and stood up: "Marjorie, I really appreciate you and Wendy continuing the research on that Facebook page. That may add some direct information about local goings-on." Stepping off the porch, he said, "Thank you all. I have to go back to The Falls... we're two folks short today because I've got them scheduled for the weekend evenings, of course, and oddly they don't like working 24-7. I'll let you know as soon as I hear from Marie out at Robertson Mines." He got into his cruiser and disappeared up the road.

Arnold, too, got up to leave, but Anderson stopped him: "Arnold, I'd like to know more about that old provincial park location south of Robertson Swamp. Do you happen to remember if it was sold or shut down, because it doesn't seem to be open, or even maintained."

"No, I have no idea except that nobody – locals or tourists – ever seem to mention it anymore – not for years. I haven't seen any conservation officers around either, except in hunting season of course, or out on the highway checking fishing boats on trailers with too many fish onboard. And they shut down the provincial office in The Falls years ago, so there's nobody to ask except by phoning Toronto."

"Well, it just so happens that I have to be in the city for a couple of days next week," said Marjorie, "and instead of being bored out of my head, I could trot down to the main provincial offices and poke around. Would that help?"

Both men turned and stared at her. "Would you be willing to do that, Marjorie? It could be a huge help," said Anderson.

"Sure, like I say, it'll keep me from being bored silly."

"Thanks very much, Marj," Arnold said as he walked to his truck. "That would be great!"

After he was gone, Anderson and Marjorie sat finishing their coffee for a few minutes, going over the morning's discussions together. "Damn, I forgot to tell John – and Arnold too, I think – about the reporter's call. I guess it's not all that exciting anyway."

"Not yet," was Marjorie's response. "Depends on what she writes!"

"Yeah, good point. I don't hold out much hope!"

"Frank, if I wandered down to the marina and picked up our outboard, could I take it over to your dock and have you look at the gearshift? It seems to sort of work – well, that's silly, it does work, but not as smoothly as it used to. It sticks, and sometimes jams when you try to get it into neutral."

"Absolutely. I'll head down there in a few minutes and meet you. Bring it around inside the dock, opposite the launch."

"Doesn't your boat have a name?"

Anderson chuckled. "Never has, which is strange I guess because every other boat I ever had, no matter how small, I gave a name."

"Where did it come from? I don't suppose it was built here."

"East coast. Bought her already partially converted from a real fishing boat – lobsters – into a tourist boat. Did some of the basic work down there – replaced the engine, transmission and drive, fixed up the decks, all that stuff because they had good boat builders there who gave me advice and sometimes a hand. When I found this place at Awan Lake, I got her lifted onto a big transport truck and moved her out here to finish her off. I'm still finishing her, but that's okay... I enjoy it."

"To you, the boat is a "she"?"

"Traditionally, boats all used to be referred to as feminine, even ugly big tug boats. To me, they – like women – are all attractive, especially when they do what they promise to do if you treat them – and the wind and waves – with respect."

"Hmm. We'll talk more about this, I think, but if you're going to help me with my little outboard... which we call Polly... and then you have to get ready to talk to Anita's father, we'd better get going. Don't forget to take your radar thingy."

"Right, and also load my acetylene torch onto my truck, which I almost forgot." He walked to her and kissed her, first on the forehead, and then – ever so timidly – on the lips. "See you in a few minutes!"

Marjorie looked into his eyes for fifteen seconds, reached out her right hand and tapped his nose with her finger, smiled at him thoughtfully, and turned and walked down the road toward the marina.

***

As Anderson had suspected, the shift lever mechanism on the Webster sisters' runabout simply needed taking apart, cleaning, and applying some graphite grease. He took the little boat for a quick spin out of the harbour and back and pronounced Polly "healed". Together they took the welding equipment off his truck and put it on the dock beside the wheelhouse, and then took the box with the radar unit into the wheelhouse and unpacked it so the antenna would be ready for Fred to install.

"It's just after noon," Marjorie said. "If you'll drive, I'll buy you a quiche at the Zoo, then I think I'll head back to the island. Wendy and I need to spend some time getting ready to take off Sunday morning."

"Lunch would be great; still lots of time 'til Fred gets here, so if we're back in an hour or so that'll be perfect." Anderson paused. "Not sure how great your 'taking off' feels... it's an awful lot of fun having you around."

"I know. Of course, there's all this mystery stuff that's sort of fun to be part of, but you're a big part of why I've had a pretty special week."

14:45 JULY 21

Fred Antoine had already spent half an hour measuring, cutting and fitting a heavy extension to accommodate the radar antenna onto the navigation mast on Anderson's launch.

"Anderson, got a smoke? I'm about ready to do the last welds but you'd better take one last look to make sure I've got it where you want."

Anderson brought him a cigarette and a mug of coffee he had heated in the boat's microwave. After taking a quick look at the work Fred had been doing, he nodded and sat down on the edge of wheelhouse roof.

"Looks just fine to me, Fred. Your welds always hold and you've thought out the strut placement just right, I think. All you need to do is finish it up, we'll drill some holes and bolt the antenna on, then I can spend a bunch of time sorting out the wiring."

Anderson paused, then changed the subject: "Say, Fred, you've trapped and hunted all around the lake – and away beyond – do you know whatever came of that provincial park south of MacLean Point? Arnold and I took a drive out to Robertson Mines the other day, and it looks like the province totally gave up on that."

"Oh hell yeah, that campsite – it never really was a park – has been abandoned by the province for years. They used to hire old Giordano to take care of it since he had the property just south along the lake to the mine. I guess he sold that to the mine, but seems like he still lives there."

"Doesn't sound like you're too fond of old Gerald?"

"Hell no. He's even more of an asshole than his father was, who had owned the place long before I was even born. I have a trapline around MacLean Point, north of there, but it never included the provincial campsite land, and I have always stayed well away from all of that mess. I think there have always been squatters camped out there, and I wouldn't be surprised if Giordano still collects money from them. That'd be just like the old jerk. Anita told me she went partying up there a couple of times, and I told her to stay clear, but she was never one to take any advice from her old man. Probably too much like me to pay attention."

"How long ago was that?

"Couple of summers ago, I think. Maybe even last year." Antoine paused a moment and stared off onto the lake. "This is rough, Frank. Rough on Georgina of course but rough on me too. I hope to hell Anita turns up soon, but I'm beginning to lose hope. I know she's been pretty wild, but she was never out of touch with her mum for this long."

"Can't imagine what you're going through. As you know, there was a scare a couple of days ago when they found her jacket and we went looking for her down the river, but Sergeant MacLeod seems to think that the jacket was left deliberately to make people think she was in the river, so I guess that's the good news, as far as it goes."

"Yes, MacLeod has told me all that you and Arnold have been doing to help, and believe me we are very grateful. I guess there's even a couple of cottage women who have been helping out too."

"Yes, the Webster sisters from that little island off MacLean Point. They have been a big help."

"Thank them for us, please. Well, I'd better get this thing attached. Can you hold it for me until I get it tacked in a couple of places?"

"Yup." Anderson did just that, then his phone rang just as he was getting down from the wheelhouse roof. He stepped off onto the dock and went to his truck before picking up: "Hey, Arnold, I've just been helping Fred finish off the welding for my fancy new radar antenna. Stuff to talk about. What's up?"

"Lots," Arnold told him. "First, the two cops that the sergeant sent up to Robertson Mines had no trouble getting access, and they did talk to Hassam as well as the company's human resources people. I guess they hired the guy without checking his paperwork very closely, so after a few radio-calls, it turns out he is classified as an international student but does not have permission to work in Canada. Hassam says he does have papers and that they are at his apartment in The Falls. The company was not fond of the idea of having the police take him away mid-shift, so the cops agreed they would meet him at his apartment after work tonight and he would produce his papers."

"That sounds a little weird," Anderson said into the phone. "I guess even Canadian cops are friendly, but that seems extra-special friendly."

Arnold continued: "I guess the officers have all been told to avoid any immigration incidents unless a crime is being committed. Anyway, I guess they'll have a chance to interview him about Anita this evening, too. It doesn't stop there, though; on their way back, just a couple miles north of Robertson Mines, they stopped an old beater of a car with two guys in it – and a pocketful each of oxycodone. The cops seized the drugs, parked the car off the road, arrested the guys and they're now headed back to The Falls – should almost be there by now."

"Geesh. Just gets better and better, don't it!" Anderson chuckled. "Not sure how much that has to do with a missing woman, and Hassam, but it'll certainly tie up Sergeant John's office for a little while. Are we likely gonna hear more later today?"

"Yup. Sergeant John says he'll call us once he talks with Hassam. Probably about seven or eight tonight."

"Okay, keep in touch. I'm not going anywhere for the rest of the day. Just talked with Fred and learned a little bit more about the land out at Robertson Swamp, but nothing very exciting – kind of what we expected about Giordano: all around jerk! Talk to you later," and Anderson hung up.

It took Fred Antoine twenty minutes to finish his welding and it took another half-hour to attach the antenna. Anderson wrapped the cables and attached them temporarily to the mast, and gave Fred a cheque for two hundred dollars for his time and the materials he had brought. Over the years Fred always asked for cash, and Anderson always gave him a cheque instead, to make sure that Georgina would see at least some of it before Fred drank it up. This time, Fred did not protest. He simply thanked Anderson warmly, and left.

Anderson suddenly felt tired. He went into the boat's cabin and retrieved a pint bottle of brandy from a locker under one of the two berths, sat down at the table in the wheelhouse and poured a healthy three fingers into an empty coffee mug. He sipped slowly, running the events of the day through his mind, especially the lingering kiss he had shared with Marjorie before she left in her little boat en route to her island. That memory made him smile a little, but his mind was busy trying to make sense of the events today, and over the last nine days.

He took some squared paper from his briefcase and started to make a day-by-day list. He wound up having to re-do it twice to get the timelines correct, then he drew a rough map of the lake, the Spirit River as far as Maple Falls, and the area roads and highways, numbering locations and tying the locations to his list. In reality, it wasn't very complicated, but seeing it laid out on paper seemed to make more sense of it.

Three cigarettes and an empty mug later, however, and he didn't feel like he had made any real progress. No one thread seemed to link together all the items on his list. It was obvious something was going on out on the east shore north of Robertson Mines, but somehow none of that was clearly linked with Anita's disappearance. There was a probable link between Robertson Mines and the planned event with Dr. Horowitz (and therefore with Wendy) and there was maybe a tenuous link between that and Anita's Facebook page, but nothing pointed to her disappearance unless one took paranoia to extreme. If the sergeant was correct, the location – and condition – of Anita's recovered jacket pointed to either a kidnapping (which seemed unlikely) or possibly a deliberate attempt on her part to keep from being found.

That last point led to a question: Why? So Anderson made a second list, this time a list of unanswered questions instead of barely-connected events. Why would Anita not want to be found? If she had faked her drowning in the river, was she acting alone, or with someone (more likely)? If so, who? And why had the interns in their canoe been assaulted on the east shore?

PETER KINGSMILL

Around and around the questions and speculations went, and by 18:00 hours Anderson put his stuff away, locked up the boat and headed for the Spirit Inn. He needed a steak sandwich.

***

Anderson drove around to the Spirit River Inn to have his steak sandwich, but it would not be a peaceful time. It was Friday evening, of course, and he had just been all over the news on television and – it turned out – in the press as well. The place was at least three-quarters full, so Flo was behind the bar and Georgina was serving. When she got to his table, Anderson looked up at her and smiled, shaking his head slowly: "I would love a beer and a rare steak sandwich with fries, but it looks like I should have got here earlier when it was quiet. How are you holding up?"

"Then you'd have had to come about two hours ago," she replied. "Lots of these folks come every Friday evening from the mine for a few drinks on their way home. And I'm doing okay but lots of people – especially the locals of course – want to talk and no one has any answers – just questions. Fred told me he was out at your boat today doing some welding. Thanks for giving him something to do. He's having a tougher time than I am, I think."

"Well, thank Fred at being really good at what he does. It was perfect. Say, who are those three guys over by the door?"

"They all work at the mine. One of them – the dark-complected one with the beard – used to hang out here with Anita but since she went missing I haven't seen him until tonight. Haven't had a chance to talk to him, but I catch him looking at me every now and then. I've wondered if he knows

198

something, or maybe he's just embarrassed. His English is a little shaky, I remember."

Anderson hesitated a moment, then asked, "Did Anita introduce him to you?"

"Yes, maybe a month ago. Strange relationship – I didn't think he was a boyfriend, but whenever they were here together they'd talk and talk, very serious like. And it wasn't often that anyone ever joined them, except a couple of her friends from the village, and they wouldn't stay at the table long before they'd drift off to join others or play pool. So... steak sandwich rare and fries, and a can of that green beer Flo gets in for you?"

"You bet, please!" After she took his order and left the table, Anderson contemplated briefly whether he should contact the sergeant. After all, he was meant to be producing his work papers this evening. But then thought better of it. *Maybe I can get into a conversation with him and learn more.*

When Georgina returned with his green beer can and a glass, he asked her, "Did that guy with the beard ever visit with our PSP interns Adumbi and Cyndi?"

"Yes, lots... I'd forgotten about that. And they would sit with Anita and him quite often."

"Could you do me a favour and ask him if he'd come over and talk to me for a minute? You can tell him I'm with the PSP project, and a friend of those two. Tell him it's about the big public meeting that's coming up."

"Sure thing... I'll just deliver this tray of beer and go ask him."

Anderson sat wondering what kind of a stir this would cause, and if being asked would chase the guy – Hassam he assumed – out of the bar. He watched Georgina cross the lounge to the table, carrying a tray of empties, and speak to the

199

bearded young man, motioning to where Anderson sat. All three men looked across, but the one with the beard shrugged politely and nodded. He got up and approached Anderson, who stood up and put out his hand.

"Hi, my name is Frank Anderson, and I wanted to ask you about Adumbi and Cyndi who work on our conservation project."

"I am Hassam. Hassam Khoury. I don't know those two people very much. How can I help you, sir?"

"I am on the committee that Adumbi and Cyndi work for here, and I like them. And, I'm worried about them. Would you join me for a few minutes? I'll order another beer."

"I will sit down, but nothing to drink please. Maybe a soft drink."

"Coke?" Anderson signalled Georgina and gave her the order. "Hassam, Arnold got a call today from Cyndi, and she told us that they'd had a bad scare out on the lake yesterday. She also said they were headed home early for the weekend. Did they mention anything to you about what happened? It sounded kind of scary to me and I'm worried for them."

Georgina arrived with a glass of ginger ale, complete with ice, a straw, and a section of lemon. She smiled and put it down in front of Hassam: "You'll have to forgive my friend Frank. He's not used to ordering for people who don't drink beer, but I have noticed that you always drink ginger ale with ice!"

Hassam looked nervously across at Anderson, then laughed nervously. "Thank you Madam. Thank you very much!"

Anderson laughed, then grinned: "That's why she's the best server in Ontario! Forgive me for assuming just Coke... sorry Hassam!"

The tension between them vanished, and Hassam laughed. "Sometimes I wish I had been brought up differently and could have a beer. So many good friends in Canada like it, but I have also seen things not go well when there is too much beer, so Allah says not, and I don't." He paused a moment, then added: "I talked to Adumbi last night when they were going, and he was almost as scared as the girl – Cyndi. He tell me that men on the lake tried to kill them, and that they lost all their expensive equipment."

"Did they have any idea who, or why?"

Hassam paused again, longer this time, and looked around to make sure nobody was listening. He dropped his voice: "Sometimes we talk about bad things coming to the lake, and powerful people with evil plans to destroy the water and the birds and the fish."

"Adumbi and Cyndi work to save the environment. Did they talk about this?"

"Yes," Hassam said very quietly.

I might as well be hung for a sheep as a lamb, thought Anderson. "I hear Anita has a very good Facebook page about saving the lake. Did you ever see it, or talk about it with her?"

If Hassam could have turned white from fear, he would have. His eyes widened and he looked around, finally taking a quick swallow from his glass and standing up. "I am sorry Mr. Anderson, but I have to go now. I cannot talk any more." He reached into his pocket and took out a five dollar bill, which he placed on the table before leaving. He waved quickly to the men he had been sitting with, and went straight out the door into the parking lot.

Anderson sat back and watched Hassam as he left. Less than a minute passed before the two men he had been sitting with stood up and followed him out the door, leaving full drinks on their table. Georgina was arriving at his table with his supper, but he waved her back saying "I'll be right back" and went out the side door through the lobby and then into the parking lot, just in time to see a black pickup following a grey car out onto the road toward the westbound highway access.

Now it was time to call the cops. Anderson stepped back into the lobby and called the sergeant at his cellphone number, which was answered on the second ring: "John, it's Anderson. Hassam is in a small grey car westbound in a hurry on the highway to Maple Falls from Spirit River. He's scared, and he's being followed close behind by a black half-ton with a Robertson Mines number on the back. No, didn't catch the number or the plates. Okay, call me back later."

Anderson avoided the lounge, and went through to the kitchen from the lobby. Staying out of sight of the bar patrons, he called to Flo from the kitchen: "Flo – please ask Georgina to clean off my table and pretend she never saw me leave. My supper's gonna have to wait. I'll tell you everything later. Thanks!"

He retraced his steps to the lobby, then into the parking lot and over to his truck. He started it up and headed down the road to the highway.

About five minutes later, he saw a single headlight coming down the highway toward him. It was going very fast when it went by headed east, and it belonged to the right-hand side of a black half-ton. Anderson felt his heart trip and his stomach contract as it shot by; he stomped on the accelerator until the little quarter-ton started to float over the bumps. After about four kilometers he slowed down by about half and started to watch the right-hand shoulder.

Some broken glass and red plastic on the highway in front of him caught his eye. He pulled on his flashers and slowed almost to a crawl, searching the side of the highway. Suddenly, there it was: Hassam's grey Accord was on its side across the ditch with the roof wrapped around a tree. Anderson stopped the truck, jumped out and ran to the car, calling frantically to Hassam. When he reached the car he tried the driver's door but it was jammed shut. The passenger door was no better; he was going to need help, and he could smell gas. He ran back to his truck and grabbed the two fire extinguishers it carried and the small flashlight and adjustable wrench he kept in the left door. Knowing the police were on their way and he would soon have help, he knew the biggest danger in the meantime would be fire.

He went to the engine hood and was able to get it open about half way. He felt around for the battery and sprayed a half-extinguisher of dry chemical on it, then used the wrench to take off one battery lead which he tucked out of the way. It wasn't a perfect fix, but he hoped it would prevent a spark that could set the whole thing on fire. Until help arrived, it was all he could do. The front window was smashed, and with his flashlight he could see that Hassam was wedged down on the front seat and unconscious. Anderson hoped it wasn't worse than that. He called the sergeant's number again, said where he was, and told him to send an ambulance, a fire truck, a rescue unit with the "jaws of life" and a tow truck in case they needed it to put the car back on its wheels to get Hassam out.

Anderson waited beside the car with the extinguishers, talking all the time to Hassam and hoping it provided some comfort if he was on the edge of consciousness. There was now some Friday evening traffic on the highway, and cars were stopping along the shoulder. A few folks gathered and offered to help, but there was little they could do until help arrived. It felt like an hour, but it was less than ten minutes until the first police SUV arrived with the sergeant onboard, wearing blue jeans. A couple of minutes later a police cruiser arrived with two officers. One constable had extensive paramedic training and he went about assessing what could be done to assist Hassam while they waited for the equipment to arrive.

Anderson took the sergeant to where the glass and plastic was scattered on the highway about fifty metres back from the crash, and explained that he had seen the black truck speeding back toward Spirit River with only one headlight, so he assumed it had struck the Honda from behind on the left side and forced it off the road, breaking its right headlight as well as the car's left tail light. No traffic had passed since the crash, so all the pieces were still there and the officers quickly took photos and put out some traffic cones to protect the area.

The van with the rescue equipment from Spirit River was the first vehicle to arrive, with a couple of volunteer firemen, followed by the village's small fire truck and a big enough crew of men and women to direct what little traffic there was. Arnold came shortly after with his old towtruck, and then the ambulance from Maple Falls. Within half an hour, the car was gently pulled back on its wheels, the door was cut off and the roof cut and folded back so they could get Hassam stabilized, out of the car and loaded onto a stretcher and into the ambulance. He was alive, but mostly unconscious; Anderson stayed with him until the ambulance left.

It was almost dark by now. Arnold came over to him, along with the sergeant. "I ain't even gonna ask how the hell this all started and how you got involved, but I guess you'll tell me someday," said Arnold.

"I was going to say that you may as well hang out with me," chuckled the sergeant, "cause he's gonna have to give me the whole story right away. However, I need you to take that car to the Falls and put it into the compound, inside the garage. And Frank, you did many things this evening that all saved a man's life, and just saying thank-you doesn't seem like enough but it's all I can manage at the moment. Hang tough here, we'll talk shortly."

He paused and looked around the scene for a moment. "Arnold, I don't know your fire crew, but would you thank them and send them back to the village as soon as you have the car out of the ditch and ready to tow. Please tell them for me that they did a great job tonight and that I'll be in touch tomorrow." He called over his Corporal and asked her to finish collecting the broken pieces from the highway: "Wear rubber gloves, Marie, and put the stuff in evidence bags and seal them. This is not just an accident. Until further notice this is a crime scene. Once you've taken more pictures and cleaned up, send one car back out on patrol and you head back to the office for now. Drop Constable Bathgate off at the hospital to keep an eye on Mr. Khoury, but don't start to question him if he comes to. Just call my cell and let me know when he does. I'm going to get Mr. Anderson back home so he can wash up, and I will be interviewing him. Are you okay to drive Frank? Good. I'll follow you home."

***

Forty-five minutes later, Anderson had washed off the dirt, some blood, gasoline and dry chemical powder, changed his clothes and was sitting at his table with the sergeant and a hot cup of coffee. The sergeant had his notebook out, and waited while Anderson sent a text to Marjorie saying he'd had a weird evening and would call her in an hour or so.

"Maybe you should start at the beginning, whenever that was," said the sergeant. "First, give me the straight-up facts so

I can get them down. Of course we will get into the speculation afterward... we both know there's more to this than a traffic accident."

Anderson described the hour and a half that started in the bar, leading up to the crash and the arrival of the police. He even included the part about missing his steak sandwich. The sergeant asked for a description of the two men at Hassam's table, but Anderson wasn't very helpful: "fairly big, white, forties, short hair, dressed in jeans and work shirts".

The sergeant filled several pages in his notebook as Anderson talked, then put the notebook back in his jacket and said, "Okay, let's get to the real stuff. I know there's lots more to tell."

"Yes, there is, but I have a personal thing to talk about that is gnawing away at my gut. I just have this uncomfortable feeling that I somehow caused this to happen by getting Hassam to talk to me. I have this feeling it could have indirectly been my fault that the guy is in serious condition in a hospital."

"You didn't say anything to the men at all?"

"No. I ignored them. But Hassam kept looking around at them. I do have a feeling those guys were planning trouble for him anyway. I assume, given the truck they were driving, they all knew each other from working at the mine, or they wouldn't have been there in the bar together, especially since Georgina said Hassam hadn't been there for a couple of weeks. And while she knew Hassam, it seems she didn't know the other two. Guess we'd have to ask her that."

"And I will." The sergeant was silent for a moment, then: "What are your instincts telling you? What I see is that you knew something was amiss from your conversation with Hassam, but you wisely held back so as not to force a confrontation, which happened anyway and there was nothing you could have done differently to prevent it. Like I said earlier, you probably saved the guy's life, tonight or possibly in the future. Someone wants him gone, either by scaring the crap out of him (like with your project interns, or even Anita possibly) or more permanently which almost happened two hours ago."

It was Anderson's turn to be silent. He got up and refilled their coffee cups, then sat down and looked hard at the sergeant. "Something is bugging me. I've been around a little, and have dealt with working men like myself and with big corporations as sort of a task-specific consultant. There's something about all of this that is... well, clumsy. I'm not suggesting that Robertson Mines is above using scare tactics to chase away people they don't like, or even arranging murder once in awhile, but successful global corporations are usually better at it than this. They deal in government lobbying, public relations like with Wendy, and lawsuits. They don't like to get their hands dirty, so while all this may suit their agenda I have a feeling there's something else going on. Is that too crazy?"

"No. I left my smokes at home, can I bum one of yours?" He took one and Anderson passed him his lighter. "I think you're dead-on. The bosses out at the mine likely know a bit about what's going on but like you I don't think they know how weird it's getting. It's kinda like someone is using Robertson as a cover, the environmentalists are providing a distraction, and that same someone has a quite different agenda. Don't know what it is yet."

"Well, like Deep Throat said in the American Watergate incident, 'follow the money'. And, like Watergate, it's almost certainly illegal. Only thing is... we don't know who, and we don't know what."

"Tonight is the first time we have hard evidence of a crime. The old boy we found in the lake – we don't know yet. Anita really is missing but she could be in California with another musician for all we really know. The incident out on the lake with your interns and the motorboat is unproveable as a crime unless we know more. It's all about what we don't know, but somehow, they all seem connected." When he finished speaking, the sergeant stood up. "I still have a long night ahead of me, and you need to at least fry yourself an egg or – you could go back out to the Inn and reclaim your steak sandwich!"

"Think I'll give that a miss tonight, thanks. Just can't warm up to the idea of a Friday night bar and a whole bunch of questions. That egg will work fine!"

08:00 JULY 22

Anderson's phone woke him up – just the alarm, so he rolled over and grabbed another rather restless hour before getting up. Last night after the sergeant left, he called Marjorie and gave her a shortened version of what had happened. She was concerned – very – and told him to be extra careful. "Lock your shop and house doors tonight... those guys may still be getting around and may have recognized you and want to cause more trouble." She said she was coming in first thing after breakfast in the morning and would come straight to his place. After they said good night, he decided to take her advice and started by walking down to the dock and making sure the wheelhouse and engine room were securely locked. He put the mooring chains and locks on: *I may not be paranoid, but that doesn't mean they're not out to get me,* he had thought to himself.

He turned on the Maple Falls radio station, made a pot of coffee and checked out the weather forecast on the computer. The weather promised that fog and light drizzle would settle in for the region early Sunday morning, and the radio news talked about a single-car accident near Spirit River, with the lone occupant taken to hospital where he was listed in serious condition. Nothing more.

Anderson sat for a while drinking his coffee and reading the radar installation manual. Today would be a good time to get it working, he considered – perhaps he could try it out Sunday! The sergeant called at about 09:00 and said the doctors had put Hassam into an induced coma until they could figure out how badly his head had been injured. He also had a few broken ribs and a broken right leg, but there were no apparent internal injuries; the doctors had debated moving him to Toronto, but decided to leave him at Maple Falls Hospital. In turn, the sergeant had placed a 24-hour guard on his room because he considered him still under threat. He had also called for the crime scene investigation team and a couple of extra constables to handle the hospital guard duties.

Anderson was out in his workshop gathering some tools, wire and parts to help with the radar installation when he saw Marjorie walking up the path. He felt a rush of appreciation, first for how pretty she looked but mostly that she was here at all. He met her on the driveway with a big un-self-conscious kiss and a long hug. Then he realized he had been holding a grease gun and she was now wearing some of it; they laughed together and headed for the coffee pot. "You only really like me for my dark roast coffee," he teased as they went inside.

And at that moment, of course, up the driveway came Arnold. They stood in the doorway waiting for him, hand in hand and laughing together. When Arnold got to where they stood, there was no teasing today. He gave Marjorie's arm a gentle squeeze as he walked in the door. "Good morning folks... glad to see you Marjorie! Hopefully you've come to baby-sit our resident community hero and keep him out of trouble. Well, to keep him out of more trouble than he's already in."

Anderson chuckled: "Like that, is it? What have I done

now?"

"Nothing yet today, far as I can tell, but you sure opened a hornets' nest last night, and the hornets are still buzzing this morning. Did Flo get a-hold of you?"

"Nope, not yet, and I've had my phone on all the time."

"Well, I'm not clear how things started yesterday, but it seems you wanted to talk to that Hassam guy, who was seated with two other guys from the mine, then you all left and we know what happened after that. Anyway, Flo wanted to let you know that one of the other guys from that table came back into the bar around eleven o'clock and was asking questions about who you were, where you lived, and so on. And this morning, before Flo called me, a couple of big guys came by the garage and asked where I'd taken... 'that car that was in the accident last night' was how he put it. I told him that I usually took wrecks to the OPS compound. Then he asked if the guy in the car was hurt. I said I figured so 'cause the ambulance came and took him away. Then they left. Oh, and before you ask because I know you're gonna... they were driving a big old 3/4 ton 4X4 beater, white."

"Coffee?" Marjorie arrived at the table with a steaming mug. She was laughing: "What's with our friend Mr. Anderson here? Does trouble always follow him or does he always start it?"

"For sure he'd bring bad luck to a good huntin' dog, near as I can tell!"

"Come on guys, must be the company I keep," said Anderson. "I'm just a frustrated old sailor who was forced into slavery as a carpenter when I was a child."

"Marj, was that your sister Wendy I just saw in the nice little grey Toyota hybrid headed uptown?" asked Arnold.

"Yes it was. She and I came in from the island together,

and she's taking a room for tonight at that little bed and breakfast on King Edward Street." Anderson was looking at her in surprise. "I haven't had a chance to tell Frank yet, but I'm hoping I can have a corner of that nice long couch over there."

"Aha," said Anderson. "I can tell that you must have listened to tomorrow morning's weather forecast. Under some circumstances, I do have to admit that I just love fog!" He paused. "But that doesn't sound helpful for tomorrow morning when you head out to Toronto."

"I wouldn't worry," put in Arnold. "Once you're a few klicks away from the lake – maybe twenty klicks – the fog almost always disappears. The Indigenous folks didn't call this Awan Lake for nothing!"

"On the subject of fog, Arnold, is someone around the garage today? I want to get my radar installed and I may need some fuses 'n stuff. I can try the Co-op but they always have that stuff packed one-at-a-time in enough bubble pack for the whole damn car."

"Yep, Jim's there, and I'm around. Marion is at home trying to catch up on garden work. And, I'd better get going. I need to service the winch-brake on that old wrecker of mine... kept slipping while I was hauling that car last night. See you later folks!" Then he stuck his head back in the door and called out, "Marj, don't forget when you get back from the city that Marion has some garden stuff for you and Wendy," and then he was gone.

"Peace. For a moment anyway. Would you mind giving me a hand wiring up the radar? It goes much easier if there's someone to help string all the wires. I never did get around to breakfast, but maybe we can go for a quiche at the Zoo. Would Wendy want to join us?"

"She's gone to The Falls to help out with that children's fair they have on Saturday afternoons. She pitches in every now and then in the summer. So we can take as long as we like at the boat and yes, quiche does sound good because my breakfast was pretty light. One muffin only lasts so long."

As they were taking the bits and pieces to the boat, Anderson said, "Pretty cool that Wendy helps out at the children's fair. She doesn't even have kids of her own."

"I do tease her about it, accusing her of fulfilling her frustrated maternal instinct (like I should talk!) But yes, she does the same kind of stuff in the winter in Scarborough. Even I help out there too, teaching kids art classes. We have fun at it."

They spent the first half-hour clamping the antenna cables to the mast and threading them through the rubber grommet that protected and water-proofed other wires from the mast through the wheelhouse roof. At one point Marjorie said, "You have a really cute sign with a picture of a beaver with a toolbox on your truck door. Why don't you call your boat '*The Beaver*'?"

"Hmm. Well, there was a sign painter who hung around here about five years ago who did up that drawing and showed it to me. I bought it to help him out, of course, and I thought of naming the boat too, but it seemed silly at the time."

"Not at all silly. And hey, it's nice and gender-neutral!" she chuckled.

"There are boy and girl beavers, y'know!"

"Can you tell the difference?"

"Ah... no. I could say something about the boy beaver having the tool kit, but I'd likely get smacked!"

"You would indeed," she laughed. "But think about it. After all, male or female they are most definitely working

213

critters that get around in the water. Just slightly different tool kits."

They laughed – a lot – and grabbed a quick coffee from the thermos before putting the radar unit with its screen on the dashboard inside, and connecting wires. Just before noon, they headed for the Zoo and lunch.

***

As they were walking from the truck to the restaurant door, they met up with Marion. "Hi you two, am I ever glad to see you. Now I don't have to have lunch alone!"

"Arnold said you were gardening today," said Anderson.

"Yeah, I am, which is why I'm having lunch here. And the old man had to go out to the cottage subdivision at Muskrat Lake to pick up a car to be fixed, so I'm all alone!"

"Marion, you are never alone," he teased her. "And yes please join us."

The Zoo was almost empty. They sat near the window and were instantly brought two coffees. The server smiled brightly at Marjorie and said, "I know what those two drink, Ma'am, but for you I haven't had the pleasure yet. What can I get you?"

"I'm going to be difficult and have a glass of root beer, if you have some."

"Sure do! And Mr. Anderson, I have been hearing tales about you... and Arnold too, Marion. And quite a night last night, too!"

"Well, you can't always believe what you hear, y'know!"

From across the room, a middle-aged man in jeans and a scruffy cowboy hat shouted, "I've been hearing tales about you too, Anderson, and just in case you were wondering, I don't like what I hear."

214

"Well, like I just said, you can't always believe what you hear. What seems to be the problem?"

"You and that damn conservation project getting too big for your boots. Gone too far this year, what with the people you hire and now this anti-development protest you are running. Just burning up tax dollars with things we don't want."

"Well, it ain't tax dollars being used for that event coming up. The government made sure of that. And anyway, what's wrong with the people we hire?"

"We need lots of jobs for the good people that the Robertson expansion project is gonna have, and we don't need jobs for university-educated fags and lezzies who count birds."

"Well, you are free to have your opinion, of course, even if I don't agree with you about any of it. Perhaps you should come to the meeting and speak up there... today we're just trying to have lunch."

Sam, the owner of the Zoo, had been cooking in the back but he had been listening in. He was big, and now he was mad. He stormed out of the kitchen, went to the man's table and grabbed his plate of half-eaten hamburger and his coffee cup and glared at him: "You will leave my restaurant, now, and you are not welcome back here."

The man slammed his fist on the table and swept the glass of water onto the floor, where it broke. Anderson pushed back his chair, stood up and headed across the floor to join Sam at the table. The man stood up and made for the door: "I hate all you pricks," he yelled as he went out. "I got friends and I'm gonna make sure we get you all kicked out of our community." He got into an old white crewcab 4x4, slammed the door, and spun his tires away from the curb.

"Okay then, now we can have lunch. Sam... thanks for

standing up!"

"You too Anderson. That jerk comes here every now and then and he's always looking for an argument. Hopefully that's the last I'll see of him."

Anderson sat down and looked at Marjorie, who had a mildly surprised look on her face. "Well, that's a side of Spirit River I hadn't seen," she said.

Marion was quick to answer, with a laugh: "That's not a side of Spirit River, honey. He's the place where they put the hose when they give the world an enema."

They chuckled a little over that, although Marjorie was looking thoughtful. Lunch came, and was delicious as usual, and they chatted about the sisters' upcoming trip to Toronto. To Marion, Spirit River was where their home was, and the Toronto trip was just an outing and a chance to do some shopping. To Anderson, it would be an unfortunate break in a new part of his life.

To Marjorie, it was a worry.

***

Back at the boat, Anderson and Marjorie worked for another hour getting the radar unit hooked up. He turned the unit on, and gave a happy "All Right!" when the antenna started to turn and the screen came to life. "Now to adjust," he said, and Marjorie begged out for a few minutes, going back to the house to use the washroom.

Anderson's phone rang. It was the sergeant, and he sounded very serious. "Can I drop by?"

"Absolutely, John, anytime. I know you're meant to be good at finding things and people, but if you let me know when, I'll try to be there!"

"Ten minutes, at your place."

"Actually, Marjorie and I are at the boat, making the radar work, I hope. Is that okay?"

"Yes. I'll see you there. And I'll bring donuts!"

"Cool. Marjorie will love you forever. See you soon!"

Marjorie had just come back onboard, and she rolled her eyes: "More visitors?"

"Just the sergeant. He wants to talk, and he sounds serious. Well, he's usually pretty serious, but this time he sounds very serious."

"Actually, I'm glad he's coming. I have questions for him. Meantime, is Miz Radar working?"

"How do you know it's 'Miz' Radar?"

"'Cause it goes around and around and sounds pretty fussy."

"I will definitely remember you said that!" Anyway, I've tried all the ranges and they seem to work fine but I'm really not sure what to expect. The only ones I've looked at before were ancient and had no bells and whistles at all. This one is away more complex inside and apparently a lot less complex to use. It also displays GPS at the same time – I'd like to take the boat out and see how the two functions work together. Anyway, can't do it now 'cause John is coming over. And he's bringing donuts... I said you'd be happy."

"Indeed I will! When did he say he'd be here?"

"Now. There he is pulling up to the end of the dock."

The sergeant arrived with a half-box of donuts and a thermos full of coffee. He greeted them both warmly, and passed around the goodies. "How's the new radar working? Impressive antenna going 'round and 'round up there!"

" I think I have it doing what it expects to do, now I have to figure out what it is that I expect it to do, and how to get it done. Let's sit outside. I think from the sound of your voice on the phone, I'm gonna need a smoke!"

They spread themselves around the well deck and settled in. "Okay, folks. It's this way, and I don't know how it got this way: Frank Anderson is one of the most unassuming men I've ever known, but somehow, right now it suddenly seems he has a target on his back."

Marjorie sat stone-faced. Anderson bristled a little: "Geez, how the hell did that happen? Surely that idiot we saw at lunch hasn't started a war already!"

"Henry Mistraika? Okay, we'll start there and work backward. I've just come from Arnold's place, and was talking to him and Marion both. She mentioned your brief luncheon meeting with some guy whose name she didn't know but when she described his truck it checked out with the one Arnold saw early this morning. Arnold had phoned me his plate number so I was able to get a name, and after a few phone calls my office crew was able to identify him as a back-to-the-land American immigrant from Michigan who moved here some thirty years ago and lives on a few acres of land about forty klicks southeast of the village, not very far from Robertson Mines. You've heard of the phrase 'blood and soil'? Yeah, he's one of those guys. Self-styled Nazi... not good. Off the record, he has been seen in the company of that Giordano fellow you mentioned, who is supposedly in charge of Robertson Mines 'accommodation camp'."

"I hear that phrase "blood and soil" and it makes my frickin' blood boil," said Anderson.

"Well, he and another guy we don't know yet were the ones checking things out with Arnold, of course and also with the bar staff at the Inn last night. The other guy is younger, it seems, and probably works at Robertson's. There is likely a third guy involved because I don't think Mistraika was in the bar when you were. Now, let's talk about Hassam for a moment. As you know, I have him under guard at the hospital, and he does seem to be getting stronger although they still have him knocked out. But when he came to for a few moments very early this morning (before they knocked him out) he asked for two names: Anita, and Mr. Anderson. You're not as pretty as Anita, Frank, but you must have made quite an impression in the few minutes you talked to him!"

It was Anderson's turn to sit stone-faced, and Marjorie spoke up: "It's about trust, John. I don't have Wendy's way with words, but I think the word I mean is "empathy"... I don't know him nearly as much as I'd like, but from my perspective Frank is a walking definition of the word. Frank, it seems unfair to talk about you while you're sitting there – or behind your back for that matter, but we do need to understand why Hassam – and others – reach out to you and I think that's why."

"I would agree. And as a cop, of course I must protect Frank, but right now I also need him, both for his empathy 'cause we need to probe Hassam's mind when he is able, and for his uncanny way of sensing what may be happening around us. So, Frank, I don't have the right to put you under guard in a hospital but I would like you to take steps to remain safe. I haven't even mentioned that you are my friend. And anyway, who would run this boat if we need it?"

"Arnold probably knows these people better than any of us... what does he say?"

"He wants John to lock you up in a safe place," said Marjorie. "Marion called me when I was up at your house just now, and they are frantic – which is why she called me. I think you were still there, John?"

"Yes. I confess I was. And she said she was going to call

and I didn't say no. Sorry, Frank."

Anderson took a long deep breath... and lit a smoke. "Okay. This whole affair is like a freaky big spider that has taken on a life of its own and managed to suck us all into its web. As a person who likes to stay a long way away from involvement, I would normally be looking for a way out, but I have also just discovered new friendships, emotions I didn't know I had, and a sense that every now and then standing up and being counted is a good thing. And I confess that in a weird way, I'm having fun."

"So where do we go from here? I have no great urge to be shot, or even have the crap beat out of me by ugly men, but I am not sure if that's on the cards anyway, as long as I live my life in a normal way until we get to the bottom of this. After all, I am pretty sure I'm not the main target... there are other agendas out there. What do you – both – suggest?"

"I think I know what Marjorie might say at the moment, but I'll start. I agree that nobody is going to come after you in broad daylight, or when you are with friends, or working. I would worry mostly about your boat and your house at the moment, both of which I can put under guard for now and no one will ever know except you. I do think this is not going to last forever, but it may take some time. Marjorie?"

"I was going to suggest that Frank spend the nights at our island, but these folks have boats too, so I like your suggestion better. I'm glad you have access to staff, otherwise we'd all have to take turns sitting up at night with a baseball bat. I do know that under the present circumstances I am not going to Toronto this week."

The sergeant got up and looked at Anderson. "There will be a plain clothes and armed officer hanging around your house and the dock 24-7 beginning at about 18:00 hrs tonight.

He (or she) will introduce themselves to you each day, and if the neighbours ask what the hell, just say that you have someone doing some work on your stuff. It would be best if you did not lock the boat cabin or the house and shop, so they can go in and out during the times you are not there. I hope that's okay, Frank?"

Anderson got up and shook his hand. "Sure. And thank you for your concern. And don't forget to keep me in the loop – I'll try to pull my weight!"

"You always do. See you both later – Marjorie, please say hello to Wendy for me, and if you do go to Toronto, take care down there. It may seem like it's safer in the city than out here in the sticks, but really... it's not. We only have a few idiots out here... in the city they have bunches! Glad I ain't a city cop."

And with that, the sergeant was gone. Anderson walked over to Marjorie and took both her hands. "I'm awfully fond of you, and it will take some time for me to get used to someone who matters and who actually worries about me. And I feel suddenly very weary. Could I suggest we shut down this boat and the radar project and go to the house and a good glass of wine? Notice I said 'good glass of wine' not 'glass of good wine', but it'll have to do."

She smiled and kissed him gently. "Let's."

***

Wendy had joined them at the house at about five o'clock, importing with her a (warm) cooler full of Chinese and Thai food. "Hope you like Asian food. Marjorie and I do and there's a place in Maple Falls that does it well for take-out. I figured you folks would be just as happy to eat in this evening... I expect it's been a long day. And is that wine I see over there? Love those kids, but a glass or two of wine looks like the perfect antidote!"

Anderson grinned: "Hi Wendy, yes, indeed I love Thai food especially, but Chinese too if it ain't too weird. Got to watch out what you order in Vancouver or you get floating turtles and stuff! And yes, wine, but I'm going to head uptown and get some more. We just about killed off this bottle."

"Give me your keys, Sis, and I'll go get it. You two haven't even had a chance to get to know each other."

Anderson poured a glass for Wendy and they sat down at the table. He told her a little about the day, and last night, and warned her that they would be interrupted at some point by his new prison guard. Wendy laughed appropriately, but suddenly turned serious: "I am so glad. Marjorie is my strength, and always seems so calm and strong, but she was up most of last night worrying about you, and sounds like things got even worse today. Marj was ready to kidnap you and take you with us to the city, although she knew that wasn't in the cards. She adores you, you know that don't you?"

Anderson sat quiet for a moment. "Yes, Wendy, I guess I can sense that. I've never known anyone such a short time that somehow feels like a lifetime. She fills my thoughts, something that has totally taken me by surprise. Marjorie is very special."

"Yes, she is, and I am all at once thrilled for her and jealous of you... we have always been very close – not lovers, just very close – and now I have to share her. But she deserves this, and you're a pretty good guy so I think we'll all get along!"

"I forgot to tell you, Wendy, that good old sergeant John said especially to say hi. You must have made an impression on him the other day... I think he was blown away by the "communications" exercise at Maple Falls. Kept muttering about how the hell come the OPS can't get someone like you!"

"Yes, he's a pretty cool guy. Not at all what I expected

from a senior cop. And his daughter was a hoot... she sure loves her dad. Reminds me a bit of the way I was with my dad. What's his wife like?"

"He doesn't have one of those. I think she died several years ago. He hasn't talked about it, but then really, I hardly know him. In a short time, though, he has become a good friend."

Marjorie drove up and joined them with a couple of bottles of wine. The three of them stuffed themselves on the food and drained one of the bottles of wine over the next couple of hours. Anderson took some time to greet the OPS officer at 18:00 as promised, introduced him to the sisters, showed him around the shop and then walked with him down to the boat. They decided he should park his unmarked SUV by the shop, facing the dock so he had a place to sit when he wasn't walking around and could still see any activity or strange lights at the dock.

Wendy left at about eight o'clock and drove back to the B&B. Marjorie looked at him coyly – a look he hadn't seen from her – and said, "you don't have a nice big sofa like we do at the island, so let's take a glass of wine and go to bed, okay?"

Anderson could feel himself blush. "That sounds like a good idea. A wonderful idea, actually." She headed into the corner of the big room that served as his bedroom, and began to fuss with blankets and pillows while he opened the second bottle and poured two glasses. He locked the main door and the one to the shop and turned off all the lights except the bathroom light in the opposite corner, and carried the two glasses over to the bed. Marjorie had puffed up the pillows and was sitting on the side of the bed. He put a glass on the lone bedside table on his side and leaned across on one knee to hand her a glass. While he was at it, he kissed the top of her

223

head gently and then turned to sit down against the pillows. She took a sip and handed her glass back to him and put up one finger, touching his nose then her lips. With both hands free she got up, unzipped and slid off her jeans, then knelt on the bed facing him and unpinned her hair, letting it fall onto her shoulders. She motioned for a sip of wine, gave him back the glass and unbuttoned her blouse which she wriggled out of and dropped to the floor. She pulled the blanket over her legs and faced him full on again and took the wine glass. She motioned to him, whispered "your turn," and took another sip.

Anderson was speechless, but he got the message. He stood up, kicked off his shoes and socks, undid and stepped out of his blue jeans and took off his buttoned shirt. He stopped for a moment at the T-shirt... then stripped it off over his head and sat down on the bed beside her, pulling part of the blanket up to his thighs. Marjorie looked openly – and admiringly – at his chest and shoulders, then reached up with one hand and unclipped her bra, shrugging it off her shoulders. One strap caught, and Anderson leaned toward her and guided it off her arm. As he brought his hand back he let it caress her right breast gently, then leaned down and kissed the nipple. She gasped slightly and held his head close with her free hand.

Anderson was shaking like a leaf, all over. He sat up on his knees, took her wine glass, and put it by his on the table. "Later" he mumbled, and took Marjorie's head in both hands, kissing her forehead, cheeks and neck and finally full on her lips. That's when the lightning began to flash; she opened her lips to his, grabbed him around the shoulders and squirmed her body around under him. When her breasts pressed against his chest, it was as if he blacked out, awakening briefly in short agonizing moments of ecstasy.

The only thing he remembered next morning was falling asleep with his mouth at her breast like a baby, and she was stroking his hair.

07:00 JULY 23

Anderson woke suddenly to the beeping of his cell phone alarm across the room on the dining table. He crawled out of bed, had a funny feeling someone was watching him, and looked back at the bed. A mess of blond hair on the pillow, a pair of sleepy eyes and a sweet smile greeted him. "Damn," he said. "I'm sorry, I obviously forgot to shut it off." He quickly crossed to the table and shut off the alarm before returning to the bed, where he leaned over and kissed Marjorie on the nose, eyes and forehead.

"Wondered when you'd wake up," she said. "I've been lying here watching you snooze ever since I heard the changing of the guard outside."

""Police? Oh, geesh, I'd forgotten all about our new burglar alarm system! Wonder what time that was."

"Six o'clock, according to the clock on the wall over there."

"I am so sorry." He stretched out beside her and started to nuzzle into her neck: "Sleeping in would have been so much nicer. I might even get to know you a bit this morning!"

She sighed and kissed him on the nose. "Someday soon, someday soon, my very special friend, but in about fifteen minutes Wendy is going to show up and spirit me away to the big city. She probably wouldn't be shocked to find her sister pinned to the bed by a naked man, but I just have a feeling that

Mr. Anderson might feel a tiny bit embarrassed!"

"Oh crap," Anderson sputtered, and rolled out of bed again. "That's another thing I forgot about this morning," he said as he scrambled into his shorts, T-shirt and jeans and sat down again to pull on his socks and shoes. "I have forgotten pretty well everything except that somehow, I think last night was the most special time I can ever remember... or sort of remember anyway. It was like a lightning storm in a warm fog, and no, it was you, not the wine."

Marjorie was tucking herself back into bra, blouse and jeans. "It's been a very long time for a number of things – most things actually – but I don't ever recall being compared to lightning and fog. Strangely though, Mr. Anderson, I think I understand you." She wiggled across the bed on her knees and grabbed him from behind, kissing his neck and right ear. "I am really glad I met you."

Anderson turned and gently put his hand on her cheek and kissed her. "Yes, so am I. Coffee?" He got up and headed for the kitchen area. Before starting on the coffee pot, which was still where she had placed it on the table eight hours ago, he glanced out the window. It was drizzling rain, and a light fog was whisping across the harbour and the docks. "Not the best day for driving. Sure you have to go?"

"Better get it over with for the next few weeks," Marjorie replied. "As you pointed out, the fog won't be too bad once we get away from the lake, and if we have to be driving instead of enjoying the lake in the sunshine, a little rain won't bother."

"Be careful, please." He saw Wendy's car come around the corner of the shop: "Here she comes, as promised, right on seven-thirty. We're gonna want breakfast, so I'll start some bacon. while the coffee brews."

"Wendy told me last night she was going to buy us

breakfast," Marjorie said, "but a decent cup of coffee would go down well first."

"Well, good morning lovebirds," chirped Wendy as she tapped on the door and came in. "Surprised to see you up and around! Say, that's the same SUV that was here last night when I left. Is the same cop still here? Makes for a long shift!"

"No, the day-shift arrived in a police cruiser and they traded vehicles," said Marjorie. "Reminds me, is the tank full?"

"Yes, I gassed it up at Frank's friend's garage yesterday. His wife was teasing me about owning a hybrid and putting her out of business."

"Yeah, that'd be Marion," Anderson laughed. "She's an equal-opportunity tease – she gets everyone about something and she names people: I'll bet you are now called 'that hybrid lady from the island'!"

"Maybe she's right. Our grandmother was Ukrainian. Does that make us hybrids?"

"Of course," interjected Marjorie. "We're Irish girls with Ukrainian roots driving a Japanese car in Canada."

"Better not tell that idiot blood-and-soil guy who was in the Zoo the other day," said Anderson. "He'll try to get you deported to Mexico or something!"

"You be careful of him this week," said Marjorie. "He and his buddies worry me."

They had a quick coffee and left for the Zoo and breakfast. Marjorie rode with Anderson in his truck; the sisters planned to leave directly from the restaurant. Sam welcomed them happily – especially happily because they were his first customers this morning. Anderson asked him if he had seen "that idiot old guy" again; Sam replied that he had indeed seen his truck go by several times the day before, but he had not come back to the restaurant.

Anderson and the Webster sisters chattered away their breakfast, talking about the drive ahead, which routes they took, and other small talk which did not address the thoughts that lurked in their minds. Wendy asked Marjorie if she had given Anderson the keys to their place; she said "Dammit, I forgot" and fished a set of keys out of her small backpack that passed as a purse. "This is the main door key, and these two are padlock keys for the shed and for Polly," she said as she handed the keys to Anderson. "There's never been any reason to check the place, but just in case – or if you need to go there, here they are. And while we're at it, I know you have my telephone number but – Wendy – you should maybe trade numbers with Frank, too."

Soon enough, the sisters got up and prepared to leave. True to her word, Wendy went to pay Sam for the breakfast, and as Anderson and Marjorie walked outside onto the restaurant's covered porch, he felt his cell phone vibrate in his shirt pocket. He took it out and hit the "decline" option, sending the caller to voicemail. "Got things to do before I answer that," he said as he took Marjorie in his arms. "Like this..." and they shared a long kiss.

A very long kiss; they were still at it when Wendy came out the door. "Come on, you two, and no, Marjorie, you can't take him with you 'cause he might get lost in Scarborough. And Frank, it's only three days and we'll be back!"

Marjorie delivered one little kiss and a fingertip on Anderson's nose as she got into the car. "Don't be sad, and mostly take care. Please."

"And you two be safe... if the fog turns into pea soup, remember to put on your four-way flashers until it gets better. Phone me when you get there!"

Anderson got into his truck and out of the gentle but cold rain before checking his phone. The call had been from the OPS detachment in The Falls, and the message was from the sergeant saying to call back asap, which he did: "Hi John, the girls are just leaving for Toronto and I was just saying goodbye. What's up?"

"Where are you? Not at your place, I assume?"

"We went to the Zoo for bacon and eggs."

"That explains it... our constable on duty just called in and said you were gone. It seems like a boat came into the area by your dock and let off a couple of gunshots before turning back and disappearing into the fog. Our constable says she even got a warning shot off as the boat turned away. I told her to wait back near your house until help arrived, and I'm on my way now."

"Crap. I'm in my truck headed down there right now."

"Check in with Jennifer – Constable Jennifer Schwartz – when you get there, and maybe stay clear of the dock until I get there. Which will take a little longer than usual with this fog, and I'm running dark – no flashers or siren – because I don't want to get people all fussed up."

"Okay, see you soon." Anderson jammed his truck into gear and took off down to the harbour, thanking his lucky stars that the sisters had already left. When he got to his place, he could see that the SUV had been moved and was closer to the dock, with the police officer standing outside staring towards the lake. He pulled alongside and got out: "Good morning, Constable Jennifer, I'm Frank Anderson and your sergeant has already let me know roughly what happened. You're okay, I assume?"

"Good morning Mr. Anderson! I saw you leave earlier

with the ladies. Yes, I'm okay, but a little nerved up. I sorta figured this would be a sleeper of a job and we'd be bored to death, but I guess that's not the case!"

"Nope, we seem to find ways to make life exciting around here sometimes, I'm afraid," as he shook her hand. "Would you tell me what happened?"

"I was sitting in the truck out of the rain, and while I was pouring some tea out of my thermos I glanced up at the docks and saw a boat going by your boat. I grabbed my binoculars (and spilt my tea) and took a look through them just as I heard two shots. There were two people in the boat, and the one who wasn't driving had a rifle in his hands. I grabbed the microphone for the loud hailer and yelled "stop, police", pulled out my sidearm and fired one shot into the air over top of their boat. They turned and accelerated away from the dock and I fired one more time, this time at the boat. I hope I don't catch shit for that."

"I doubt it," said Anderson. "Can you describe the boat at all? I know it was a ways off, and the fog is closing in, but anything you can tell me would be useful."

"Well, I know a little bit about boats – my family was big time into fishing and I took a couple of the OPS courses about them, but honest, I didn't see much. The boat was the same colour as the fog – grey – probably aluminum, and it was pretty big – over twenty feet long anyway. It was an open boat, and it had two big outboards... when they left the area they had them revved up and just screaming!"

"Any idea which way they went?"

"Well, couldn't see anything – they disappeared into the fog right away – but I listened until I couldn't hear them anymore. The fog and rain muffled the sound too, so it was confusing, but I think they went that way..." and she pointed east.

"That figures. Thank-you! And here comes your boss... good morning John!"

"Morning, folks... Frank, Constable Schwartz. Man, that fog's pretty thick up on the highway. At least down here I can see your boat. Been down there already?"

"Nope," replied Anderson. "I was trying to behave myself and wait until we're all here. No worries, though, your Constable filled me in on what happened. Okay if I go take a look?"

"Sure, we can all walk down. This isn't wartime – yet – so I don't suppose there's another gang waiting to get into your house. Wait a sec..." and he went to his cruiser and took out a small fishing tackle box with "OPS" stencilled on it. "Jennifer – we're pretty informal around Frank here – maybe you can tell me what happened too? Just quickly - I assume you've had a chance to make some notes?"

"Yes, Sergeant, I have" and she gave him a quick version of events as they walked to the dock. Anderson stepped on first, looked around the well deck and then walked around the port side of the wheelhouse.

"Okay, there's a bullet hole through the side of the wheelhouse wall, and – oh yeah, crap... one of the small windows in the forward cabin has been shot through. From the looks of it, both shots went through to the inside so we'll have to see what more damage they did once they got in there," and he came back to the well deck and unlocked the wheelhouse door. He stopped outside and waved the officers to go ahead of him. "I don't want to mess up any evidence so I'll watch you from behind. That one that came into the wheelhouse likely went just behind the swivel seat at the wheel."

The sergeant walked into the wheelhouse, took a quick look around, then poked his head into the forward cabin before calling out, "okay, you both can come in. There's nothing to see on the floor, so the more sets of eyes down here the better. And I forgot my flashlight... you got one?"

Anderson opened a small locker beside the swivel seat and pulled out two flashlights. "Here folks, enjoy!"

"Thanks." The sergeant opened his fishing tackle box and took out some gloves and small zip-lock bags. "Oh, and here's another flashlight too. Duh."

"I wondered – thought you were planning on doing some fishing while you were down here," said Anderson.

"Nope," chuckled the sergeant. "Evidence gathering stuff."

Anderson had been looking around the starboard side of wheelhouse: "Here's where I think one bullet ended up, right in the side of the seat. Glad I wasn't sitting there!"

The sergeant walked over and examined a messy hole in the fibreglass where the seat back met the seat itself, then looked around on the floor with his flashlight: "And here it is!" He took out a small pocket knife and scooped the battered bullet into a bag which he closed, and wrote on with a marker. "Happily, not much damage there, except through the side of the cabin."

"Nothing some faring compound and paint won't fix," said Anderson. "For now I'll close the hole on the outside with some duct tape. Let's see what damage was done in the forward cabin."

The bullet had shattered one of the three small glass windows, and after some poking around in the cabin the constable found where it had become imbedded in a large coffee tin. They emptied the coffee gently into a small cooking pot until they found the bullet, which was in better shape than the first one. "That was no .22 they were using," said the sergeant. "At least a .308 – fairly heavy rifle, anyway. They'll tell us more back at the lab."

Anderson taped over the hole with a small piece of tape, then did his best to close off the small window in the forward cabin. "I'll come back down later with a piece of light plywood or aluminum, just to keep the rain and spray out until I can get a piece of glass cut. I think it's time for coffee, don't you?"

The other two agreed. The sergeant took some photographs, inside and outside, and then a couple from the dock and from back up the road. There was still some lukewarm coffee in the pot, which Anderson poured apologetically, and then set up a fresh pot and turned it on.

"I think," he began, "that we are being warned – intimidated would be a better word maybe. That's three times now – probably the same boat that came here this morning was the one that dumped the interns' canoe last week, and then there's the truck that ran Hassam off the road. In none of those three times was there any attempt to finish the job. The folks who dumped the canoe could easily have run down and killed Cyndi and Adumbi. The guys who came here today could have unloaded a lot more shells into the boat, and with a rifle that heavy they could have aimed at the waterline and several shots down there would have done a helluva lot of damage. And that black truck on Friday night didn't hang around to make sure Hassam was dead – they just took off."

"And I think you're mostly right," said the sergeant, "but I think there's more to the Hassam situation. He's had two or three would-be visitors at the hospital. Of course, the officers on duty turned them all away. Two guys – rough-looking, white, thirties – and one woman. Jennifer, you were the one posted guard when the woman came last night. I've read your report, of course, but maybe you can tell us your impression of that event?"

"Sure. It was after midnight, and a young-ish woman came looking to see the subject. She was very polite but a bit pushy, and was openly disappointed when she left. She seemed sad... I wished I could have let her in to see him."

Anderson was listening intently. "Jen, can you describe her for me?"

"Yes, she was pretty, in her early twenties, long black hair tied back, wearing black jeans, a black company jacket – you know, the kind with a logo on front pocket. She didn't look to me like she was very healthy."

Anderson looked across at the sergeant, who was suddenly very attentive and asked "what race"?

"Well, we're being trained not to profile, but I would guess she had native – Indigenous – blood in her background."

"Shit!" said the sergeant. Anderson nodded: "Anita."

"Who?" asked the Constable.

"Of course," said the sergeant. "Anita is a young woman who has been missing for a couple of weeks, Jennifer, and you wouldn't make the connection because you've been pulled in from outside the detachment to give us a hand here. And, we have reason to believe that she and Hassam – the patient in a coma – were close friends. And yes, she is Métis. Her folks live in the village here."

"I am so sorry I didn't catch on... and now she's gone!"

"Jennifer, there is no reasonable way you could have known. And, course, we are not at all sure, really, that might have been someone else. But there will be some happy folks here – all over town, she was well-liked – if it was her and if we can locate her."

"And keep her safe," said Anderson. "We're not sure where she fits in this whole picture, but she, too, has been threatened."

"Constable," said the sergeant, "would you please bring the evidence toolbox to my cruiser and bring back my briefcase?"

"Certainly, Sir." After she had gone out the door, the sergeant turned to Anderson: "Two quick questions. One... do you have a rifle? Sorry, that's silly: don't answer that. Yes, you do – a rifle and a shotgun – I already know 'cause I looked you up a couple of weeks ago before we started to work together. Second question, do you have any ammo here today, and may we take your shotgun with us on the boat?"

"Of course," said Anderson. Then he looked sideways a little sheepishly: "It's already there, actually, over the starboard berth, loaded, in a blanket."

"I didn't hear that, of course. Okay, third question, is that radar of yours working?"

"Yes. I haven't done any sea-tests with it, but it appears to work correctly."

"Then can you and I take a quick trip this morning, along the east shore where the interns got their canoe dumped and then beyond Robertson Mines? It occurs to me that the fog gives us an opportunity to scope out stuff along the shore, a little closer than you and Marjorie got a week ago. Just maybe we could spot that boat that came here, if they got careless because of the fog."

"Absolutely. I have lots of fuel onboard, but no coffee; I'll make some."

"Good. And I'll ask my constable to nip uptown to pick up some hamburgers for us all. She'll be staying here, but she might appreciate some real food! At that point the constable came in the door. "Thank you, Jennifer." He rustled around in the big aluminum briefcase and found a couple of sheets of printed paper. "This is the form we have to fill out every time we discharge a firearm. You're gonna be hanging out here all day, so you might as well save some time and fill it in and sign it. Just tell it like it happened; I will approve your shots. And another thing – Frank and I are going out with his boat along the east shore in the general direction you pointed out, just in case we can find that boat." He took out a billfold and handed her a twenty. "Now this is a favour, not an order, but would you please go uptown to that restaurant on Main Street and pick up hamburgers and fries for all three of us? I imagine you brought lunch, but I'm willing to bet it's a cold lunch!"

"Absolutely sir. Thank-you, I'll be right back. With cheese, everyone? Perfect!"

"Nice lady," Anderson remarked.

"Seems to be. I've only just met her yesterday, but she seems eager and smart."

"I'm going out to my shop to cut a piece of roofing to fit that window and something better than duct tape to stick it on with. I'll be right back."

***

The corporal returned in about twenty minutes with the burgers, and the men took theirs and a coffee thermos down to the boat. Anderson fired up the diesel and the genset, turned on and checked the navigation instruments including the new radar, and unlocked the mooring chains. By now, the sergeant knew the drill and cast off the spring, bow and stern lines. "Normally," said Anderson, "I would blow the horn to leave the dock, and periodically as we travel in the fog, but under the circumstances that seems counterproductive. To use your words, we'll run dark and silent. The new radar should make that a lot safer, but we will still want to keep our eyes sharp – maybe sling those binoculars over there around your neck in case there's something you need to look at." They began to munch down their hamburgers.

They were only about five minutes and three-quarters of a hamburger out of the harbour when the sergeant's cell phone rang. It was apparently his office calling... he mostly listened, then said "how about tomorrow morning" then said "Okay, I'm actually out on the lake with Mr. Anderson, looking for some possible evidence. We'll be back in a couple of hours. No, try my cell, I'll see if I can hook into his booster. If you can't get me by voice, send me a text message. Okay, bye," and he rang off.

"So that's interesting," he said to Anderson. "Seems like the doctors have taken Hassam out of his coma and he's come to, sort of. They figure he'll be okay to talk to in the morning. Can you make it into The Falls tomorrow? I actually would like you to be the first one to talk to him, because yours was the last name he spoke (apart from Anita) when they put him under."

"Sure, I can do that. I need to go to The Falls anyway to order a new piece of glass, it seems, and I also need to pick up some groceries. I try to buy most of what I eat here in the village, but some stuff – like coffee – I have to get there." He paused. "And another thing, is there a good sign shop in The Falls that makes that vinyl lettering that you can put on trucks?"

"Yes there is, near the edge of town. They do printing and stuff as well. Figure you need a sign saying "don't shoot at my damn boat?"

"Well, it's a long story but I'll keep it short. I have this boat, see, and I've never given it a name. And I know this lady, see, and she thinks it should be called '*The Beaver*' and I am inclined to agree. Thought I might surprise her!"

The sergeant burst out laughing. "Well, well, Mr. Anderson. You do have it bad, don't you! Can't say that I blame you, though... Marjorie and her sister seem like pretty special people. And given the picture on the side of your pick-up, '*The Beaver*' seems like a pretty good name. And it's gender neutral, though 'beaver' may have other implications in there somewhere."

Anderson was laughing. "You're the second-to-last person I know who might worry about a gender-neutral name for a boat!"

"I have a teenaged daughter, remember? She's always finding things like that to worry about! And I suppose Arnold is the last guy you think might worry about a gender-neutral boat?"

"Nope, Marion."

"Tell you what I'll do," said the sergeant. "When we get back to your place, you print out exactly how you want that lettering for *The Beaver*, and I'll take it over to the shop first thing in the morning. I'll apply a little charm, so they'll have it ready for you to pick up when you're in town to go shopping and talking to Hassam.

Soon they were nearing the Webster sisters' island, and it showed up distinctly on the radar, in perfect agreement with the GPS. To the east of the island they could clearly distinguish the form of MacLean Point. Anderson set the sonar depth alarm to fifteen feet, and turned the boat to leave Maclean Point to port.

"Does it look like you're going to arrest Hassam?"

"I may not have a lot of choice if he wants to stay alive.

And there is the business about working outside the terms of his student visa so we have a reason. But for now he's safe enough under guard in the hospital."

Soon the GPS was showing they were less than a quarter mile from land, so Anderson throttled back to about four knots and turned so they were running parallel to the shore. The shoreline was still visually hidden in the fog, and the depth reading was over 50 feet, so he edged the boat closer and re-set the radar range to one mile. He re-set the sonar unit to show side-scan to get a better look at the shape of the bottom, particularly to port, closer to shore; the depth reading stayed at just under 50 feet. "Watch closely for a visual on the shoreline," he said to the sergeant. I think we can safely get to where we can watch it through the glasses... I don't suppose those folks we're looking for have a lot of sophisticated warning equipment. So far they seem a little bit hillbilly in the technology and strategy departments. Anyway, one hard turn to starboard and a burst of diesel power and we'll be out of sight in the fog anyway."

As they went along the shore, Anderson edged even closer until it was clearly visible. The sonar still showed over 40 feet and the bottom showed lumpy but fairly even on both sides. "John, if you slide open the window over the map table, you'll be able to kneel on the seat and rest your arms and the binoculars on the window sill. It'll be a lot more comfortable and steadier."

About twenty minutes later, the sergeant's voice interrupted the low hum of the engine: "There's a roadway coming down to the shoreline, and what looks like a little boat pulled up on the beach."

"That's likely where the interns launch their canoe. In a couple of minutes you should see the beach change into a marsh, and the landscape will look lower. I'm also getting a tiny blip about fifteen degrees off the bow... maybe start checking that out every half-minute. I think it may be one of the buoys we saw when I was out here with Marjorie."

"Okay, there's the marsh you talked about... and... there is a round white thing in the water, ahead but about half-way to shore. Whoa, that was a shotgun – three shots – slightly behind us maybe. Nothing to see, though."

"I'll bet it's some good old boys hunting a duck dinner out of season," laughed Anderson. "Anyway, shotgun pellets won't reach us out here."

"I think you're right... I hear dogs barking like they're all excited about something! How far from here is the old provincial park?"

"Pretty close, I think. There should be more roads coming down shortly."

Fifteen minutes later, the sergeant said in a stage whisper, "There – just ahead is a road coming down and a much bigger boat pulled part way onto the shore. Yes, that's the one both the interns and Jennifer described, I'm almost positive. There's a truck right in front of it, backed down. And another one, facing the lake! I'll take the wheel while you take a look!"

They quickly changed places, so Anderson could see through the glasses: "Yup, looks like the same one! And a couple of them have started looking our way... crap, they're trying to push out the boat. Here, you watch and I'll drive." Anderson crossed the wheelhouse and got in behind the wheel. He pushed and held the button on the GPS to set a waypoint for future use, swung the boat hard to starboard and pushed the throttle to full speed, so he was headed as fast as possible straight off shore. As he did so, he caught a glimpse of another tiny blip on the radar screen, almost straight ahead. He veered further to starboard and stared out the windscreen. In about thirty seconds it loomed up out of the fog and skated slowly by them – another marker buoy, this one with a number on it that he couldn't make out. "Come on fog, I want more fog!" he muttered.

The sergeant had moved from the wheelhouse window to the door to the stern, where he stood leaning against the doorjamb with the binoculars glued to the shore. Soon he let the binoculars hang from his neck and turned back into the cabin. He instinctively checked his sidearm, then crossed to the bench and picked up his carbine which he had brought from the cruiser. He checked it over, stood it against the wall by the door and came over to Anderson. The diesel engine was screaming at full speed so he had to yell: "I lost sight of the boat in the fog – seems they were only just off shore. Can you see them on the radar?"

Anderson pointed to the bottom of the screen. "The boat is that blip there, and it doesn't seem to be moving," he yelled. "I think we've probably lost 'em. I hope to hell." The fog thinned out a little ahead of them, then thickened up again. Anderson throttled back to half speed, ran that way for a minute, then took it down to idle. The blip seemed to be getting further away, then again became part of the shore behind them.

"Hate to tell you this, but they fired some shots a few minutes ago – could hardly hear them over the engine, but they were rifle shots – big rifle shots – and I think I heard one that must have hit the water nearby and ricocheted – I'm guessing just ahead of us. Didn't bother to tell you because you were concentrating on what you were doing, and there was nothing we could do any differently except get the hell out of there!"

Anderson rolled his eyes at the sergeant and said, "I don't

think they're even in the least bit friendly on this shore. Not even a bit!" He turned north about 30 degrees and put the throttle forward to just over half, and took the GPS back a couple of screens until he could see the village. He adjusted his course to miss the little island that had recently become so friendly for him and headed for home. It was 14:20 hours, still very foggy (thank goodness) and the drizzle had changed to rain. "Let's have some of that coffee." And he pulled the throttle back to about four knots so they could relax a little.

Both men sat in silence for a few minutes, sipping their coffee. "Y'know, Anderson," began the sergeant, "seems like the more we find out the less they connect. In my mind there is no way that Robertson Mines would even dream of approving this type of crap. Don't know what they might countenance in Africa or South America, but in Canada or the USA? No, almost certainly not. So the way I see it, there is another agenda that we – and they - aren't yet aware of. You touched on this when we talked a few days ago. Now that we know where the bad boys hang out, we need to find out why. Even assholes don't start raising hell like this unless they have something to gain."

"Or to protect, maybe?" said Anderson after a pause.

"Good point. Hmm... Tell me, how do you suppose Hassam, and Anita if she's alive as it now seems, and maybe the interns and that public event (and Anita's webpage) connect together?"

"Maybe through Robertson Mines and they don't even know it. As I talked about earlier, they're used to dealing with public protest and government influence, and may be totally unaware that things are going on totally beneath their radar. But – they could be kind of like a catalyst for the explosions happening around them."

"From what we cops cynically observe, crime is usually about drugs, sex, and immigration. And power – which may be related to all of those things but is a strong enough motive all on its own."

They batted these thoughts around until they arrived back at the village and landed at the dock. They had no sooner landed when it was Anderson's phone that rang. It was Arnold, who said he had just had a call from Cyndi and that she and Adumbi were coming in the next morning and needed to talk. Anderson told him he was with the sergeant, and to hang out by his phone – he'd call him right back. "John, that was Arnold, and our PSP interns are coming in the morning and want to have a meeting. I've half a mind to tell them to meet us in The Falls where it's relatively safe from prying eyes and ears. We need to extract some information from them about Hassam and Anita, and maybe more. And at the moment they should maybe stay in The Falls anyway. Make sense to you? We'll buy them motel rooms for a couple of nights until we get a handle on this."

"Yes it does." He called Arnold back and asked him to call Cyndi back and set up to meet at Timmys in The Falls around 09:00. They locked up the boat and walked back to the house, where Corporal Jen was still waiting. "Only one person came by," she announced. "Said his name was Arnold and that he'd call you later."

"Thanks Jen," said Anderson, "he actually just called and everything's good. Thanks for babysitting the place – I'm very grateful!"

"We found that boat," the sergeant told her, "and those folks certainly didn't want to be found. We'll be paying them a more official visit in the next few days. When the officer taking over your shift turns up this evening, you can fill him in, of course, so he is warned, but don't be too full of details. And Frank, I'd better be going – I'll be in touch later this afternoon or evening, but before I go, would you make up the template for that sign lettering you want?"

"Sure will," and Anderson went into the house and fired up his computer. He wrote:

Heavy outdoor vinyl, black, 4 inches high, Helvetica bold   or   similar,   3   copies: THE   BEAVER and   one   copy,   3   inches   high AWAN LAKE

He printed it out and handed it to the sergeant who grinned: "Cool!" then got into his cruiser and headed up the road. Anderson went back into the house, took a beer out of the fridge, called Arnold, and told him to come over and join him: "We have things to talk about. Really? That sounds good, I'll be over in half an hour – thank you!"

Steaks and beer over at Arnold and Marion's house felt like a really good idea this afternoon.

06:30 JULY 24

Anderson punched the "off" button on his cellphone alarm and swung his feet out from under the sheets onto the floor. He rubbed his eyes and gazed around his one-room castle which, he noticed, was in need of some clean-up, or at least some re-organizing. Last night's barbecued steak and beer with Arnold and Marion had been just what he needed: a chance to touch base with his usual – rather more normal – existence.

And, while such things were somewhat new to him, a lengthy phone call with Marjorie had been comforting too. He did not share with her the events of Sunday morning, save to say that he had taken the sergeant out for a run along the east shore up to Robertson Mines and back in the fog, trying out his new radar toy. Marjorie said the fog had thinned out and disappeared within half an hour's drive from Spirit River, but the showers and cloudy skies had lasted all the way into Toronto.

He stood up and paddled in bare feet across the varnished floor to the south window overlooking the docks; he could see Constable Jen had arrived for the day-shift and was standing beside her cruiser having a smoke. His launch was in place at the dock, the fog had lifted and the sun was struggling to shine through a partially overcast sky. A light breeze had blown in from the west and would soon cooperate with the sun to dry the soggy grass and the dripping pine trees that sparsely lined the road. Given the rather hectic and unusual turn of events over the past week, today looked strikingly normal: time for a shower, a cup of coffee while tidying up a bit, and getting on the road in time to pick up Arnold and make it to Tim Hortons in Maple Falls for 09:00 and the first appointment of the day – meeting with Cyndi and Adumbi.

***

The PSP interns were already into their coffee and bagels when Arnold and Anderson arrived and bought their coffee – dark roast for Anderson and regular for Arnold, who started the conversation: "Hi gang," he said as the two men wedged into the two empty seats at the interns' table. "Hope you had a more peaceful weekend than your canoe adventure last week!"

The interns smiled thinly and nodded. "Yes, it was good to get away," Cyndi said quietly and paused for a long moment. "Mr. Jamieson, and Mr. Anderson, we don't feel we can go back to work anymore. We are biology students and technicians, studying birds and frogs as a summer job and shouldn't have to deal with criminals trying to drown us when we are doing field work." Adumbi remained staring deep into his coffee mug, obviously a little shy about being as outspoken as his Canadian-born colleague.

"No worries about that," said Anderson. "We – and the police – are very aware of the danger and nobody will be going into the field until we get this sorted out. However, as Arnold will explain, the community needs a lot of help getting ready for the event with Dr. Horowitz, and it's all work you can do in the village. We will set you up in an unused office at Arnold's garage, where his wife Marion can keep an eye on things... she's kind of the boss of that event anyway. Arnold, can you explain a bit more?"

Adumbi had finished his research into the bottom of his coffee mug and was listening intently as Arnold began: "Yes, Marion really does need help with everything to do with the event... lining up volunteers and sponsors, making sure the hall is set up and figuring out a sound system, making and distributing posters, and so on. And Cyndi, I also expect you will need some computer-time to record and report on your summer field work anyway?"

Cyndi had brightened up considerably, but still had a question: "Don't you think all these bad things – Hassam being run off the road, and those guys attacking us in the canoe – are related to the public meeting and Robertson Mines trying to shut it down?"

"No," said Anderson. "We – including the police – are all convinced that these things are not related at all. And that reminds me, we need to ask you both some questions about Hassam and Anita. I will be talking with Hassam later this morning – he is out of his coma now and he wants to talk to me before he talks to the police... I think it has to do with Anita. Please tell us how close they were – Hassam and Anita – and if it was a dating thing or friendship?"

"Hassam adored Anita, but so far it was just friendship," Cyndi began. "Anita is – well, she is Anita, you know, and always bouncing from boyfriend to boyfriend and back again. The thing that drew them together as buddies was her love of the lake and the old cultures – before the Europeans came to settle here. She was kind of like a spaced-out hippie, if you know what I mean, and Hassam was drawn into her vision somehow."

"Was she knowledgeable, or just passionate?" asked Anderson.

"Both. She was both," chimed in Adumbi. "Hassam (he is actually here to do graduate studies like me) told me that Anita was amazing – reading and doing research online and asking questions all the time, except when she was in the bar or at a party somewhere. And of course she has this Facebook group for Awan Lake – calls herself 'Foggy Swamp Girl' I think."

"Did they do pot or other drugs than booze?"

"Not at all," Adumbi continued, while Cyndi nodded in agreement from time to time. "Hassam, of course, is Muslim and takes it seriously (and doesn't drink liquor either). And even Anita, she loves being at the bar or at parties, but actually she doesn't drink very much as far as I can tell. She talks about sweetgrass ceremonies and spirits, and if she smokes a little marijuana it wouldn't surprise me, but I have not seen it."

"My wife Marion always tells me not to believe all the village gossip about Anita," Arnold put in. "I guess she's right – people don't really understand her at all."

"Yes, she's pretty special," added Cyndi rather wistfully. "I hope she is somewhere safe."

"Do you think she's in trouble? Or dead?"

"In trouble – probably. Dead – I don't think so. I hope not." Cyndi added: "Apart from Hassam and a few locals, some of the people she hung out with were pretty scary."

"How so?" asked Anderson.

"Big. Like bikers, but better dressed. Dark-skinned – not like Adumbi here – like Indians. I guess we're supposed to call them Indigenous. I guess some of them were quite good looking, but scary."

"Hmm. Interesting," said Arnold. "Thanks for the input, folks. You've been a big help. So if you're okay with carrying on as we talked about, I'll let Marion know you're headed over to see her, and she'll get you set up. Make sure you get her to fill you in on plans for the event, and take some time to look around and make a written plan, with location drawings and so on to plan sound systems, parking and security. We have a kind of a committee, but frankly they need all the help they can get! Marion will introduce you to the volunteers whenever they turn up."

After they left the coffee shop, Arnold took Anderson's pick-up to head out to the auto-parts stores at the edge of town, and Anderson walked the half-block to the police detachment, where he joined the sergeant, chatted a few moments about the interns and what he had learned, then rode with the sergeant in his cruiser to the hospital.

Hassam was in a room opposite the nursing station on the top – third – floor. The sergeant spoke briefly to a uniformed officer hanging around the hallway, and introduced him to Anderson. "Constable Marchand here says there have been no incidents over the last two shifts, and that Mr. Khoury seems to be conscious but only responds to the nurses' and doctors' questions with barely audible yes or no answers. I'll wait out here out of sight for now. Learn what you can, and see if you can get him to trust the police – or me anyway. You may have to explain that he is under guard for his own safety, not because he is under arrest. Although, of course, that may have to happen because of his student visa, but I hope not."

Anderson nodded, and went into the room and closed the door behind him. "Hello Hassam, this is Frank Anderson," he said quietly, standing just inside the door. He looked at the patient: he was a mess. Hassam's head and upper body appeared to have taken most of the punishment: his head had been shaved and bandaged and he was in a complex-looking neck brace. Tubes were everywhere, and his bed was surrounded by a battery of monitoring instruments. Strikingly, it seemed, Hassam's eyes were open, and his gaze bored across the intervening space directly at Anderson.

He crossed the room to the badly injured man's left side, and reached out to cover Hassam's uncovered left hand with his own. "Hassam, I'd be lying if I didn't tell you that you look like crap, but you look better than when I saw you the other night. You're going to need a new car, but I'm awfully glad to see you!"

Hassam smiled, ever so slightly: "I am pleased you are here." It was almost a whisper. It was almost inaudible.

"Do you know who did this to you?"

"No."

"The truck was from Robertson Mines. Was it someone you work with?"

"No. Not them. Other men drive those trucks."

"Were they the men you had been sitting with?"

"Yes."

"But you don't know them. Where do they come from?"

"Near. Near there I think."

"Where is Anita? I am worried about her."

"Not know."

"Hassam, you cannot help her from your hospital bed, and I am a friend of her family and want to help. And I can help. Will you tell me who I can talk to?"

Hassam said nothing, and closed his eyes. The silence was broken only by the beeping of the monitors for almost a minute, then: "Grandfather. Crazy man. He take her with him."

"Thank you, Hassam. Did she want to go with him?"

"Yes. Anita trusted crazy man her grandfather."

"Are the same men who hurt you wanting to hurt Anita?"

"Yes."

"I have a friend, a policeman, who I know and trust. He has made sure you are under guard here, all day and all night, in case those men come to kill you. They have now tried two times. His name is John, and he is the top policeman here. Can I bring him in and introduce you to him? Him you can trust."

Again, he sat silently with his eyes closed, then: "Yes."

Anderson went to the door and motioned for the sergeant. Together they approached the bed, where the eyes remained closed. "Hassam, this is Sergeant John MacLeod. I just call him John. He is on our side – your side, Anita's side, my side."

The eyes flickered open and stared long at the sergeant's face, then back to Anderson before closing. "Yes."

The duty nurse whisked into the room, glanced at her patient and the monitors and motioned the two men to leave. "He is coming along well, all things considered, but it doesn't take much to tire him, and now you have him worn right out. Maybe tomorrow again, but not before."

They thanked her and left. As they walked down the hall, Anderson fiddled some wires out from underneath his jacket, took the little recorder out of his pocket, and handed it to the sergeant. "Here ya go, John. It's not like it was a long and complicated conversation, but I did learn some stuff."

"I'll take it to the office and have one of the civvy staff transcribe it. Meantime, we can talk about it while I drive you over to the sign shop where they have the beaver things ready."

"Man, that's quick! How'd you do that?"

"We take care of him sometimes. No big deal."

About seven minutes later they were leaving the sign shop with a roll of vinyl-cut signs, complete with their application paper and ready to go. Anderson had reached for his credit card, but the store owner told him it was paid for "by our friendly cop who's waiting for you outside". When he asked the sergeant about it, he simply explained that the launch's name had been scratched up while they were doing police work on the river and they were just repairing the damage. "Cheap at twice the price," the sergeant chuckled.

"Okay, then I'll buy you lunch. It's just before noon, so drive us to your favourite café and I'll text Arnold to join us. He's out somewhere with my truck buying parts."

After they had settled into a booth in the restaurant, Anderson told the sergeant, "We need to find a crazy man, also known as grandfather. That's where Anita is, apparently, but I don't even want to speculate about who it might be without Arnold, who I am willing to bet may at least have a clue. The other important thing I learned is that – in Hassam's words – 'other men' drive those black trucks, and that it is really unlikely that Robertson Mines is even aware of what is going on."

Arnold arrived, and announced that he was really impressed with Anderson's little truck because he had driven all over Maple Falls and it hadn't stalled even once. They looked over the menu and discovered that the Monday Luncheon Special was liver and onions, so they ordered three open Denver sandwiches with fries and coffee and settled down to talk.

Anderson began by asking Arnold if the words 'grandfather' and 'crazy man' meant anything to him, especially with reference to something Anita might have said. Arnold paused a moment, then lit up: "Yes. Yes, it does connect. I'd have to ask Marion to make sure but I think it goes like this: Marion is Anita's aunty, because Marion is the sister of Georgina, Anita's mum. Anita's dad, Fred Antoine, is the son of a weird old guy they call Willy (Crazy Man) Antoine, and his mother was Juanita – I believe her last name may have been Rodriguez."

Arnold paused, held up a finger, and thought awhile: "As I remember, Willy, or Crazy Man, was born on a Reserve a long way southeast of the lake near the headwaters of the Spirit River, but he and his wife couldn't get along on The Rez so he took a land-grant along the river, maybe fifteen miles upstream from the lake. He's kind of a hermit... maybe the moniker "Crazy Man" explains that."

"Okay," said Anderson. "That's where Anita is. Makes perfect sense. How do I get in touch with Willy?"

"I gather you are suggesting that we don't simply requisition a chopper and go up there and get her?" the sergeant chimed in.

"Nope," said Anderson. "John – and Arnold – I think there is still much more to be learned about all of this, and it will come together better if we operate under the radar (so to speak). I think we can assume Anita is safe at the moment, so there's nothing to be gained by charging in with the cavalry. Arnold, can you ask Marion how we might reach out and talk with Willy? I'll bet he comes to town once in awhile."

"Yes, he does come in once or twice a year. He has a really old but classy little guide skiff he uses – you know, the cedar-strip double-enders with a one-lung engine in the middle? I've seen it. Anyway, let me give Marion a call and see if there is a way to make contact. I have a hunch that what we used to call the 'moccasin telegraph' still operates. It's a bit mysterious but when it works... it works!" He grabbed his phone off the table and headed outside.

"Travelling with you guys is quickly becoming the most interesting part of my career," chuckled the sergeant. "Some day I'll write the book!"

Anderson and the sergeant were halfway through their omelette when Arnold returned. "Well," he said, "Marion informs me that Anita's dad Fred hasn't spoken with old Willy for over twenty years – ever since his mum died – so that channel is cut off and the same goes for Georgina. However, there is a cousin – when you start talking about the Rez, there's always a cousin, it seems – and this cousin can probably reach him. Marion says she'll try to set something up for Willy to meet with Frank. Apparently Anderson here is considered a neutral and respected character in that world. Ordinary people like John MacLeod and Arnold Jamieson might think that passing strange, but there you go!"

"Okay," said Anderson, "so now we wait."

"When it comes to the other world my good wife sometimes touches, I don't think you'll be waiting long. Marion has, hmm... she has ways."

The sergeant just shook his head. "Keep in touch, Frank. Close touch, and if you have a meet set up, let me know by telephone to my cell – not voicemail – to keep it off the record for now. Having said that, give me as many details as you can share, including especially coordinates if you're out on the lake. As long as we're in communication, I'm fine with all this, but if we lose touch, then I will call in the cavalry, as you put it. If there's more to this than families playing silly-buggers, as I suspect there is, I don't want to lose you, Frank, so please take care!"

Lunch was over, and they parted company outside the restaurant. The little truck headed back to the village with Arnold and his car-parts and Anderson and his Beaver signs. "Hey Arnold, I had forgotten all about the Horowitz event until you mentioned it this morning. Has a date been set, or did

I forget that too?"

"It's been set and changed a couple of times, but now I think it's set in stone for Sunday evening, August 13th. And for your information, we got the cheque from Jean Barker – much appreciated – and Dave Bradshaw dredged up another grand from some outreach fund through his university, so we will be able to host the whole affair without the old Board of Trade losing its shirt. Folks are actually pretty excited now, even old Jeremy!"

"Hopefully all this other stuff will be over by then and we can just enjoy it. I know Marjorie and Wendy will be more than happy to peel potatoes or flip hamburgers to help out."

Arnold chuckled: "We all know about you and one of the Webster sisters, but I sense that Sergeant MacLeod has a soft spot for Wendy!"

"Yeah, I wondered about that. The other evening Wendy was asking about him, too."

***

After dropping off Arnold and his supplies at the garage, and topping off his slip-tank with diesel at the Co-op, Anderson headed down to the boat dock, stopping at the police cruiser long enough to visit a few moments and have a cigarette with Constable Jen, who had enjoyed an uneventful – and boring – day. He drove onto the dock, unlocked the wheelhouse and prepared to top off the boat's fuel tanks. He carefully unrolled the new sign lettering he and the sergeant had picked up in the morning, and smiled wistfully at the neat letters, thinking mostly how surprised Marjorie was going to be when she saw them.

He took clean rags, scrubbed and dried the starboard-side bow and applied "THE BEAVER" about a foot below the deck line. He had to use his little row boat to get at the opposite side and the stern, where he added "AWAN LAKE" under the name. It all took less than an hour, but he was having fun. And he had to admit to himself, it looked pretty cool! He then finished re-fueling, measured the engine fluids and checked out all the instruments before driving back up to his house, where he spend another hour finishing off the house cleaning he had started in the morning. While he was at it, he noticed that some groceries were getting short, as well as his beer supply, so he headed up to Main Street to pick up the essentials: butter, bacon, beer, bread, plus eggs and some fresh tomatoes.

When everything was safely home and stowed away, it was about 17:00 hours, and he figured that he might as well head up to the Spirit River Inn and settle up for the steak sandwich he never ate last week, order another one, and eat it this time.

Flo was holding down the fort alone. "Well, howdy stranger!" she greeted him. "Last time you were here you raised all kinds of hell. What you got in mind for this evening?"

"Oh, just the usual. One wrecked Toyota topped off with a green beer and a steak sandwich." He sat at a table close to the bar and apologized for walking out on his meal last week. "Turned into a long night – several long nights, actually. I'll bet that accident was the main topic of your weekend's conversation!"

"Sure was. And of course, you were the hero of record, saving his life and all that!"

"I didn't really do anything. You have no idea how frustrating it is to have some poor guy wedged in a mess of crumpled steel and have no way of getting him out. I was able to talk with him for a few moments today... he is not in good shape, but he is alive. Seems like a really good guy."

"He was popular here. Folks respected him, ginger ale and all. So, were you serious – steak san with fries and green beer?"

"Yup. Thanks Flo! Say, how is Georgina doing?"

"She's still upset and terribly worried, of course, but she's hanging in. She is really grateful with Fred, who it seems has basically devoted himself to being loving and helpful. He brings her to work, will have a coffee and visit a little while, then come back and pick her up when her shift is done. Total turn-around there!"

"Cool. Very cool. She deserves that."

This time he almost finished his steak before his cellphone rang. It was the sergeant:

"Hi John, just finishing supper. What's up?"

"It's not good. Actually, it's terrible. Hassam is dead."

"What the hell? I know the nurse said we wore him out, but not that bad surely!"

"He was murdered. One of my officers took a bullet and is in critical condition. One of the assassins is dead. Two nurses, one security guard and a doctor are injured, and a random car burned and exploded, injuring a couple of bystanders."

"Shit. How did it go down?"

"Close as we can put it together right now – and this only happened about forty-five minutes ago – apparently they set fire to a random car two blocks away, to distract the police. Five minutes later they lit a fire in the laundry chute at the opposite end of the hospital from Hassam's room, and fired a couple of shots down a stairwell. The constable on duty left his post to help, and one assassin forced the ward door and shot Hassam in the head. On his way out, the guy shoved the nurses and the doctor down the stairs and shot the security guard in the stomach before going down the stairs and out onto the street, where he was shot and killed by one of our officers, but not before he took a bullet in the neck."

"How many assassins?"

"Near as we can figure, three on the ground and maybe a driver, because the two that weren't killed disappeared very quickly."

"Crap. You're okay?"

"Never knew it was going on until it was over. I was having a shower at home."

"I don't mean to make light of it, but this one is bound for the ten o'clock news, isn't it. And will attract a whole bunch of attention upstairs in your department."

"Yes. Call Marjorie. And Arnold too, please. And keep your head down, stay out of sight, and don't go anywhere. I am doubling your guard, because you were the last to talk with Hassam and I expect one of these guys could know about that. Weird thing is, I don't have any idea what he knew or did that would bring this on. A random push off the side of the road is clumsy, but this is really serious stuff."

"I'm at the Inn, but I'm headed home now."

"Good. Again, don't go anywhere."

"Better idea maybe. Why don't I just get into my boat and go offshore outside the harbour? That'll free up two of your staff, which you are now officially short of. You and I can keep in touch on the phone."

There was a pause. "Yeah, good idea. I'll tell the officer on duty to wait until you clear the harbour, and to leave you a police radio and charger. Might be handy."

"Good. Going there now. Take care, my friend!" And he clicked off the phone.

Flo was staring at him wide-eyed: "Only heard your half

of that, but it doesn't sound nice at all."

"Not nice at all. Bad, shoot-up in Maple Falls." He handed her three twenties: "Here's for tonight's burger and beer, plus for the one I never ate. Gotta go!"

PETER KINGSMILL

19:15 JULY 24

Anderson was cruising dead slow about kilometer away from his dock, still headed due south away from the village. He had grabbed a can of coffee, a dozen eggs, a package of bacon, an extra lighter and a couple of packs of smokes from the house and locked it before taking the radio and charger from the police officer who had been briefed a few moments earlier. He was now smoking one of the cigarettes, sipping on a beer and trying to clear his head.

First things first. Gotta call Marjorie. He took out his phone, clicked on the booster and dialled. "Marjorie? It's Frank."

"Hello lover, you okay? It's early!"

"Yep, I'm fine. I am sitting quietly out on the lake, sipping a beer and preparing to watch a beautiful sunset. All good with you?"

"Yes, of course. But it's not all good with you, I can tell from your voice. What's up?"

"Ah ha, yes, you know me too well. I'm glad I reached you before you see the television news, so here goes: about two hours ago, Hassam was killed in his hospital bed by someone who can only be called an assassin." The gasp from Marjorie was plainly audible, but he went on: "That shooter was shot and killed by a cop, who himself was critically wounded. Two other men were working with the shooter, providing distractions down the street and in the hospital, where a security guard, two nurses and a doctor were injured as well. John is fine (he was in the shower at home when it all went down). I had just seen him and visited Hassam in the morning."

The silence at the other end of the phone call was deafening. "You there?" he asked.

"Yes I'm here, and as usual I am in the wrong place. I should be there with you."

"Much as I would love that, I am most happy that you are in the big bad city right now and not in peaceful Spirit River. I'm pretty safe out here on the water in my little boat, which is where John and I figured I should be to stay safe and thereby release two cops to help out in Maple Falls. Besides, I have beer, coffee, cigarettes and bacon... how bad could it be!"

"John is really okay? I want to tell Wendy but that'll be the first thing she asks."

"Yes, he really is. The man has nerves of steel, but he's gonna be one busy cat these next few days. Hey, we may have found a way to connect to Anita, who we are pretty sure is alive and safe. I am supposed to meet her grandfather shortly – he lives away out in the sticks south of here, and we think that's where she is. And – related subject – did you find out anything about that old park land by Robertson Mines? That may well be relevant."

"Almost forgot. Yes, I did. The province shut down that park over twenty years ago and leased it to two guys: Gerald Giordano and Henry Mistraika. Isn't Henry that jerk who tried to assault the owner of the Zoo when we were having breakfast?"

"Wow, yes it is. And Arnold and I had already met with Giordano a week earlier."

"Another interesting thing: I must have been wearing the right clothes because I was able to get the resident bureaucrat to show me the record of who actually made the lease payments... all of them were made by a numbered company. Wendy was able to pull some strings and discover who that company is: it's owned by the Robertson Group, which in turn is a majority shareholder of Robertson Mines."

"Boy, you *and* Wendy must have been wearing the right clothes to get all that info... sure you were wearing a bra? That's amazing, and it's a huge help. A lot of things are beginning to make sense all of a sudden." He paused: "Crap. Arnold's calling. I guess I should take it."

"Yes you need to. Mr. Anderson, I think I am falling in love with you, so please take care."

"Ms. Webster, I know I am falling in love with you. I will be careful."

Anderson stabbed at the buttons on the phone but dropped the call. He had called Arnold's number earlier but it had gone to voicemail so he asked for a call back. He dialled again and Marion picked up: "Frank, is that you?"

"Hi Marion, yes it is. You got my message?"

"Yes, we did – just now. I have some news for you..."

"Yeah, I have some for you too, but you go first."

"Okay, Crazy Man Willy will meet you. That's the good news. The bad news is that he wants to meet you just after dawn tomorrow morning, right off the west end of the wildlife preserve island in the middle of the freakin' lake. Does that make any sense?"

"On a day like this, oddly, it does. I'll be there. I'll be really happy if he comes alone."

"He will – and he asked the same: 'Tell that Anderson guy to come alone' is what he told me. So what's your news?"

"You obviously haven't had your TV on for the evening news. This news is all bad: Hassam was shot and killed in hospital. The shooter was killed by a cop, who in turn is hanging on by a thin thread in hospital. Several others were hurt, but Sergeant John was not hurt... it was he who called me."

"Shit. This is crazy. Too crazy. Here, tell Arnold, who's staring at me like I gave birth to a spotted calf."

"Hey Frank, Arnold here. Whazzup?"

Anderson repeated what he told Marion, but added that he was now sitting in the middle of the lake to free up a couple of cops. "At least I'll have a head start on meeting Crazy Man Willy at dawn!"

"Are you armed?"

"Yeah, shotgun of course and I even brought along my old bolt-action .308. But I have a feeling I could have ten of those and still be out-gunned. We're dealing with some serious dudes here. No point going into a shoot-out with an empty net."

"Some day I'll explain how hockey works, my friend. Got beer?"

"Yup."

"Cool. Take care out there. I'll make some phone calls..."

"Hold it – got stuff to tell you from Marjorie about that provincial park." He filled Arnold in on what they had learned.

"Marion's right. This is all crazy. But y'know, what the girls just found out starts to make sense. Like I said, I will make some phone calls and call you back later."

They both clicked off, and Anderson called the sergeant to tell him what he had learned and where he was going. It took two tries to get past the voicemail and talk to the sergeant directly... he was a busy man this evening and the conversation was short: the key points were Big Island, Willy, and dawn.

Anderson had put the launch on autohelm, but he checked the radar and looked around the slowly darkening horizon with his binoculars before going into the forward cabin to make some coffee. The genset bucked slightly when he turned on the coffee maker and he smiled to himself: *I have a hammer-drill that draws less power than that damn coffee maker!*

He decided to plug in his cellphone too, then stepped out on deck and gazed around the lake again. The sun was a ball above the western shore, creating a brilliant red and gold stripe above the far-off trees. By now the launch was just south of Ship Island where the Webster sisters had their cottage, and for a brief moment looking at it shot a pang of loneliness through his chest. He retreated to the wheelhouse, where he set a waypoint at the west end of the big wildlife refuge island on the GPS. He then set the autohelm to make for the waypoint and watched the south shore as the launch adjusted course slightly to the west and held.

By then the coffee was ready, so he poured a cup, took a cigarette out of the pack on the wheelhouse table, and went on deck to watch the sun go down. The lake was dead calm and looked like molten metal under the sun's slowly-fading light. The diesels purred beneath his feet, and he could hear the bow wave lap the side of the boat under her new name: *The Beaver.* He smiled.

After awhile, he went back to the instruments by the wheel, decreasing the radar range to three miles and setting an audible alarm to alert him of any vessel within that radius. He also set the sonar alarm to ten metres, and his cellphone timer to two hours. Finally he grabbed a sleeping bag, pillow and mattress from the forward cabin and put them on the wheelhouse floor, took one last look around the horizon, stretched out under the open sleeping bag, and went to sleep.

His sleep was far from restful. Normally a sound sleeper who seldom dreamed, tonight Anderson's mind was very busy. There were glimpses of Hassam, and Anita, and Marjorie. He saw flashes of light and heard gunfire and men cursing. He awoke twice before the timer went off, and jumped up each time to scan the empty horizon and check his position. When the timer went off, he re-set it for two more hours.

And so it continued for six hours, when he got up to see a faint glint of light on the eastern horizon. He poured a cup of lukewarm coffee, put it in the microwave and bundled his bedding back into the forward cabin before checking the GPS for his position. He reckoned he had five miles to go to the waypoint where he expected to make contact with Crazy Man Willy, so he eased the throttle up until the launch was making five knots. The lake was still calm and the launch had held her course well, so he left her on autohelm without adjustment and re-set the radar to five miles. As he expected, the low profile of Big Island showed up at the edge of the screen. He took his warmed-over coffee and a cigarette out on deck and watched the eastern sky. With the increased speed, the gentle lap of the bow-wave had become a sizzle of bubbles along the boat's sides, reflecting green in the starboard navigation light. Today would dawn bright, he thought, and he expected the wind to rise slightly with the sun. He considered it wouldn't hurt to turn on the weather channel on the marine radio, which shortly confirmed his estimate. It would be a beautiful warm late-July day with few clouds and little wind. *Perfect for wakeboarding behind Crazy Man Willy's guide skiff*, he chuckled to himself.

By the time he was less than a mile from his waypoint, the sun was just on the horizon and Big Island was showing at about mid-screen on the radar. He set the range back to one mile, wondering if he might pick out the skiff although he doubted it: the skiff was a wooden boat with no superstructure, and it rose a metre or less above the waterline... not a good radar target. Looking out the wheelhouse window, Big Island was soon clearly visible directly to port, so he reduced speed back to steerageway only, took his binoculars, and went out on deck and up the ladder to the wheelhouse roof, where he steadied himself against the navigation mast and scanned the waters between the launch and the island.

He didn't have long to wait. After fewer than ten minutes, he was able to pick out a small boat coming off the shore and headed toward him. He came down from his perch on the roof, went to the wheel, switched off the autohelm, turned the launch toward the shore and added a couple of knots to her speed. When he was a couple of hundred yards from the skiff, he pulled the diesel back to idle, put the transmission into neutral and went out on deck. The lone figure on the skiff gave a short wave, and Anderson waved back. He could hear the heartbeat throb of the single cylinder engine as the skiff approached and slowed down. The operator shut the engine off and made a quick turn to port... and the skiff slithered gracefully alongside. "Anderson?" a rough old voice asked.

"Yes Willy," Anderson answered, and leaned over the gunwale to pick up the bow mooring line, which he made fast to a bollard amidships. "Welcome," he said, and stretched out a hand to help his visitor out of the skiff and up onto the deck.

The man was probably quite elderly, but he was strong and able. His silver hair was pulled back from a sun-etched face and tied in a ponytail. *He is a strikingly handsome old man... I'll bet he had to beat the ladies off with a stick not so many years ago,* Anderson thought to himself.

"Coffee? I'll make a fresh batch."

"Coffee would be good," and he followed Anderson to the wheelhouse door.

"You spend a lot of time on that boat with sandpaper and varnish. She looks lovely."

"Have to do something in April. Re-built the whole boat once, and the engine twice. I bring the boat into my house every spring... I see you have a house like that."

"Sort of. Haven't had my boat inside though. You've been to my house?"

"Before you came. I bought wood and parts from old man Daoust. Sometimes I would work for him and learn things."

"I wish I had known him. He was a very fine craftsman... too few of them left."

"Every age has its good men. I hear that Jamieson and Anderson are good men too."

"Arnold? Certainly one of the best. You know him?"

"Of course. He married my son's wife's sister. Where I live, we call that a cousin. Keeps it simple."

"Well, Willy, Arnold is the finest friend you can imagine and he feels like a brother to me, but I am flattered you say my name in the same sentence as his."

"If I didn't know that to be true, I would not be here today. We have things to talk about more than old boats. Let me bum a smoke from you, and we will sit and drink coffee and talk."

"That would be good. Sit here at the table... the cigarettes are there and the coffee is almost done. I will drop my anchor here (there is thirty-five feet of water underneath us) so I can shut off the engines. It's too peaceful out here to be so noisy."

Willy settled at the navigation table and gazed around the wheelhouse. He heard the splash and rattle of chain as

Anderson let go the anchor and chain from the foredeck, then quietly watched Anderson as he returned to the wheelhouse, put the transmission in reverse and gently pulled back on the chain until he could feel the anchor catch on the bottom. He turned off a number of switches, including the big diesel and the genset, poured their coffees and sat down opposite Willy. The sensation of peace was palpable.

"I have only two grandchildren," Willy began. "I think you know Anita. Her grandmother's spirit keeps her safe. There is also my grandson Juan, and his spirit cannot reach him. Nobody you know around here knows Juan. Even in the daytime, his spirit is in darkness."

"I know Anita, and the more I have learned about her, the more I know she is a special person. And what you have just said tells me that she is like your wife, who I have heard was also a very special person. Did they know each other?"

"My wife Juanita died two years after Anita was born, but I believe she breathed all of her spirit into Anita when she passed."

"And what about Juan?"

"Juanita and I had one son together – you know him as Anita's father Fred. Juanita had her first son – Miguel – four years before we met. He was not a happy boy, and he did not like our home. He left when he was sixteen and went back to California to his father's family. He never settled down there, but he did get a girl pregnant. She and Miguel were killed in a car accident almost thirty years ago and the baby – Juan – grew up with Miguel's father's family. Three years ago, Juan showed up here. He said he was 'finding his roots' but really, he was finding routes – spelled r-o-u-t-e-s. He was only interested in finding pathways to move drugs from California – and Mexico – to markets on the streets in Canada. Since he has been here, he has made bad people worse and good people die."

"Do you see him?"

"Not often – he stays away. If he were not Juanita's blood, I would simply kill him and that would be the end. But Juanita – while never a church person – held dear in her heart this idea that no one is beyond redemption. That is not my way, but the memory in my heart and soul of the spirit of the finest person I have ever known prevents me from doing what I know is the right thing."

"Where did you get the "Crazy Man" title?" Anderson got up and checked out the windows (and on the GPS) to make sure they had not been drifting while they were talking, then topped up their coffees and lit another smoke.

Willy was smiling, a little wistfully. "Well, it sure wasn't because I played a tough game of hockey," he laughed. "I met Juanita at an outdoor folk-music concert in Toronto – I think it was maybe Ian and Sylvia, or even Pete Seeger. We fell in love the first night, and I brought her home to the Rez, away south of here by the provincial park. I was just an Indian kid with grade eight from a residential school, and it wasn't until we got up here that I realized that this beautiful white chick with the gentle soul, who shared my love of music, also had a degree in biology from California and was trying to finish a masters in sociology in Toronto. My mother thought she was okay, but just a passing affair until I settled down with one of the ladies on the reserve. Juanita intimidated my father with her notions about gender equality, and my older brother and his friends tried to hit on her the second night we were there. And worst of all were the Elders (and their women) who felt threatened by her education. So we moved away – a long way away – within a month. We squatted on the land where I live up the river and built a home and a way of life. She was eventually able to buy the land from the government, under a special grant program for American immigrants."

"Cool," chuckled Anderson, "now, back to the Crazy Man thing?"

Willy laughed: "That's what my family and friends called me when we moved away."

"You don't speak like a man who has a bad grade eight education and lived in the bush all his life."

"Juanita spent a lot of time teaching me everything she knew from university. Not just telling me about it – teaching me. Then we went on reading and talking and debating and arguing and making love. I may be Crazy Man Antoine, but I am the luckiest man in the world to have had all that."

Anderson got up from the table, put his hand on the old man's shoulder and gave it a slight squeeze. The sun seemed suddenly very bright in his eyes, so he turned away to start the genset. "It's nine o'clock. Time for some bacon and eggs, my friend. After that will be time enough to talk more about Juan."

***

Willy went out onto the afterdeck to check his skiff and to have a pee. The wind, while still light, had freshened enough that he decided to untie his mooring line from the side of the launch and re-attached it to a towing bollard on the afterdeck, so the skiff streamed out straight behind the launch. When he rejoined Anderson in the cabin, the smell of frying bacon filled the air with promise.

"Willy, you mentioned earlier that Juan maybe made bad people worse and good people dead. Can I ask you about some of the bad people around here? I know there are some... we got shot at last week, and the same people (I think) tried to run down a couple of summer students out doing field work in a canoe. We had been thinking about something to do with Robertson Mines, but now we're not at all sure. And there's more to tell since then, but let's start there."

"Maybe blame the sixties. I may be the only Canadian Indian hippie to have gone off-grid in the forests of Awan Lake with a beautiful American chick, but there were dozens of American whites who came here and settled back then. They came here as idealists, singing Pete Seeger songs, smoking a little weed and cutting their shins with their axes while their women made the world's worst all-grain bread. God, you could have built three-storey buildings with that stuff, and rainproof too! But for most of them, soon their allowance money runs out and the winters get cold and they head back to the cities – in Canada if they were draft dodgers, or back to their homes in the great old USA."

"Not all of them, though..."

"No. Some did okay and were good neighbours, raised their families, and so on. Others, though, saw opportunities to make money with raising or importing drugs, or getting into dealing in stolen property, or whatever. The leftie idealism went out the window, and it was like the wild west – every man for himself. That's kinda what goes on around here, anyway, and that is exactly the bunch that Juan has tied up with. He's big and strong and charming when he wants to be and is seen as a big-time drug lord from California and Mexico. And our locals may be rough and nasty, but Juan is brutal. He scares the shit out of everyone, but he makes them a little money, you know, and keeps them drooling for more. Last I'd heard, he's put together a small army – well, maybe more accurately a "security force" for his operations."

"How do you think he stays under the radar?"

"Friends in medium-high places. Folks who don't mind

turning a blind eye if they can pick up some extra coin. I don't think Juan has a huge operation, so likely he stays away from the really heavy hitters. For now."

"What's the operation? He's not simply flogging cocaine to the cottage-owners on Awan Lake..."

"Near as I have it figured out, packages are dropped from airplanes, mostly at night. They are recovered by two-or-three-person teams and stored out of sight (and away from people and roads) for a few weeks to ensure there are no authorities in the loop. Then they are repackaged and moved to the market, using cars, trucks, pleasure boats, snowmobiles. Nothing very complicated for equipment, but the planning is pretty sophisticated. And the enforcement of secrecy is, as I said, brutal."

The bacon and eggs were ready, as was a fresh pot of coffee, so the two men settled back down at the table. "I'm gonna ask you a tough question, Willy, but I don't want to wreck your breakfast."

"Nothing ever stands in the way of enjoying bacon and eggs. But I know what you are going to ask, and the answer is why I am here eating your food and drinking your coffee in the middle of an empty lake. Yes, Anita got tied up very briefly with Juan, and yes, she is safely under my care and no, nobody knows about it except a Syrian student named Hassam. Even her girlfriends or her mother or my son – her father – don't know. She's my sweetheart grandkid, but I literally had to break her two cellphones on a rock with a hammer."

"Thank you. So she met a charming handsome man a little older than she is, with a similar ethnic background, and started to have a fling before the warning bells went off in her head, and she broke it off. And things started to get rough... is she – or he – aware of their shared background?"

"No, but I imagine he doesn't like being shut down by women, probably thinks she knows too much, and thinks her other friends may have connections in his neighbourhood. That is why Hassam became an issue."

"Well, I guess I have news you don't want to hear: Hassam is dead. He was killed yesterday afternoon by an assassin's bullet while he lay under guard in a hospital bed in Maple Falls."

"Crap."

"That's exactly what I said. Same spelling and everything. But my question is, what did Hassam know – or do – that would make a minor drug lord put together a carefully-planned three-man assassination team to take down a Syrian student already at death's door in a regional hospital in rural Ontario Canada?"

Both men were silent, except for the scrape of forks finishing off breakfast. "I think," said Willy, "that between Anita and Hassam, they had possibly disconnected information from their own networks of workers and locals that could lead back to Juan and his operation. Anita has already told me she knows about a drug operation going on in the area, and wonders if Juan was part of it."

"Did she know Hassam had been in a car crash that looked suspicious, and was under guard in the hospital?"

"Yes, and no. She knew he had been hurt, and she knew Mr. Anderson had probably saved his life, but the rest, I don't think so. She is going to be terribly sad and very angry with this news."

"May I ask how you have her protected right now?"

"Of course. Juanita and I had built a tiny cottage at a small lake (sort of a hidden inlet from the river) about a mile from our house and outbuildings. It is now completely overgrown and hidden – I had never been there since Juanita died – but this seemed like the right time and the right reason, so I took her there, along with three big boxes of books from Juanita's library. And, since I still have family and friends in my original community, I contacted them and asked for three well-armed and tough FBIs for a few weeks to help out a family member. They were there the next morning. Tell ya, I sure don't want to argue with them!"

"FBIs?"

"You haven't heard that expression? 'Fucking Big Indians'. Not politically correct maybe, but if they don't care I'm sure I don't!"

"How did they get there? If they can get there, maybe Juan can."

"They put a shiny new jet-boat into the lake at the boat launch beside your dock. To you – if you saw them – they looked like just another three yahoos out for a day on the lake. Two big guys and one hefty chick, and a case of beer!"

Anderson paused and giggled: "That's cool. That's really cool!" He picked up the plates, wiped them off and went out and rinsed them in the lake before drying them and putting them away. He also rinsed the coffee cups, refilled them and said, "let's take our smokes and go sit in the sun. It's nice out there. Take the coffees and I'll grab a couple of deck chairs from the hatch."

"Let's talk about people: friends and allies, jerks and creeps, and enemy targets. Maybe I should write 'em down... I'll get a clipboard and a pen." Anderson returned from the wheelhouse with a clipboard and made three columns. "Let's start with enemy targets: unfortunately we have to start with your grandson Juan."

"Yes we do. And also unfortunately I don't know who are

his contacts up the chain."

"Okay, let's put OPS Sergeant John MacLeod on the friends and allies side. I have learned I can trust him and he sees the big picture. I've been working with him on this ever since Anita disappeared from the village."

"Yes, I have been told he is a good cop, tough and fair – and intelligent."

"And of course Arnold and Marion, and Fred and Georgina. Not sure if we want Fred and Georgina in on the rough stuff under the circumstances, but we can trust them." Anderson paused. "What do we do with people like Giordano and Mistraika?"

"Gerald and Henry? Both should have been drowned at birth and saved everyone a lot of trouble. They make lots of noise but they're strictly bottom feeders. Juan might use them for cannon-fodder but I don't think he'd even trust them for that. And we can't trust them either... maybe put them in the 'jerks and creeps' column."

"I'm going to put the Webster sisters (from that little island southeast of the village) in the Friends column. I have a particular reason not to want them in danger, but they are being extremely useful doing some research for us, and they are a hundred percent trustworthy. For example, just last night they were on the phone from Toronto and had just found out that Giordano and Mistraika were the registered lessees of that former provincial campground north of Robertson Mines, but that the Robertson Group actually pays the lease. Now that means something, I'm pretty sure!"

"Whoa, Frankie... whoa! We just about slid right by that and suddenly I see connections. I know that the one or two times I ever talked to Juan a couple of years ago he mentioned being down to see friends at Robertson Mines. And, I'll bet if you look it up on the internet you'll see that Robertson has mines in Mexico – and maybe others in South America. I wonder if his upstream connection is through someone there? He may just be a manager and enforcer, not a business owner!"

"Well, sure as hell they'll disavow any connection at head office. I wonder if they have any record of shady operations. I could ask Wendy Webster to check – she used to work there as a public relations executive."

"Hold it," Willy spoke up suddenly. "We're going fishing. I'll get the rods." and he jumped up and went for the mooring line to his skiff. Plane coming!"

"Got it!" Anderson re-arranged the deck chairs along the starboard side and went in for the beer cooler and binoculars. In less than a minute they were both sitting with a beer in one hand and a fishing rod between their knees with the lines out. It was only then that Anderson saw a two-engine plane about a mile west, headed right over them. He had his cellphone out and sitting on the deck locker, camera ready to go. "Good eye, Willy!"

An instrument in the cabin started to beep. Anderson swung around to look, then remembered: "Geez. No worries, hadn't remembered to turn off the radar's warning signal. Nice to see it works!"

As the airplane flew overhead, maybe 700 feet off the water, the two men looked up and waved. The pilot dipped his wingtips and flew on in a straight line toward Big Island, which was a half-mile east. Willy grabbed the binoculars and followed the plane, while Anderson flipped through the shots on his cellphone to make sure he had a good clear picture. "There," shouted Willy. "There... that's got to be one of their planes because he just opened the door and dumped out eight or ten sacks. Did you get a photo?"

"Yeah, not great though. We'll have to see what a lab can do with it. I didn't want to make it too obvious that I was taking pictures! Keep an eye on that thing 'til it's out of sight, then we'll talk about next steps, you and I."

"Uh huh. If he turns around and goes back, we'd better keep fishing. I think we must have fooled them though, otherwise they wouldn't have waggled their wings and then made the drop."

It was most definitely cigarette time, and since the beer was now out, they opened up a couple of those too and tried to relax. They watched as the airplane flew on over the east shore, then turned north and was soon out of sight.

Anderson was the first to speak. "It's mid-morning, almost ten. We have people to talk to and a bunch of information to get, and even with the booster I need to be six or eight miles closer to the Spirit River tower to get cell and internet service. I need to call Marjorie and Wendy – mostly Wendy I think – in Toronto to dig a little further into the Robertson Group and their holdings in Mexico and California, and I need to get to them before too long because they are planning to leave the city in the morning tomorrow to come back here. And, we need to involve John – Sergeant MacLeod. I would be happier if you could meet him and we could talk together – maybe with Arnold too. Do you have to get back home or can you reach them and say you're staying away another day? My place is yours."

"I can try from here with my mostly-portable ham radio. If that don't want to work, I'll have to wait until we get cell coverage."

"So that's the famous Moccasin Telegraph – ham radio?"

Well, it's sometimes more complicated than that. If I have to use the phone, I call my youngest brother on the Rez, and he radios in to my place where I have a powerful radio and a big antenna. That's how Marion gets to me, but she'll never tell you that. I'd do it through Fred, but much as I love my son I can't trust the alcohol thing."

"He's been a lot better since Anita went missing."

"So Marion tells me. I hope it holds. I'll get the radio from my boat and maybe I'll power it from your main battery and put the Yagi antenna up on your roof. I have a clamp."

Anderson did some cleaning up around the boat, checked engine oil levels and started the genset while the not-so-crazy man set up his radio, pointed the antenna southeast in the general direction of his home and started his call procedures. He received a response within less than a minute, and launched into a hurried conversation in a language Anderson didn't understand. He signed off and shut the radio down: "Okay, Anderson. Everything's fine at home and they won't expect me back until tomorrow. I did tell them to keep a 24-hour watch on the radio in case we need to tell them something."

"That was Ojibwe, I assume?"

"Yes. Sort of... my people talk a different dialect, but yes, basically Ojibwe."

"Much as I enjoy your company, I don't think we should travel back to the village together in case someone turns that plane around for another look. You could go straight in, and I'll swing west and go back through the cottage islands by the mouth of the river."

"Good. I'll walk uptown for coffee and listen to the gossip until you get in. Let's trade cellphone numbers."

"You're saying that little skiff is faster than my big diesel?"

"Oh yeah. You named it right – *The Beaver*. Big and slow. The skiff is like an otter, especially since I bored out the cylinder and added a couple of inches to the prop."

"Crazy Man is well-named too, apparently! Okay, I'll start my puny little diesel and pull the anchor. Might as well get going. I'll start by calling the Websters once I get cell service, then I'll call the sergeant and set up a meeting somewhere – away from prying eyes."

"Need help with the anchor?"

"Electric winch."

"Geesh. Okay, I'll get untied and started. And Anderson – Frank – thank you."

"No worries." Anderson went into the wheelhouse, started the main engine and eased the transmission into forward for about fifteen seconds to take the pressure off the chain before he went forward to tend the winch. He glanced over at the skiff, where Willy had settled down in the middle of the double-ended boat, behind the engine. He fiddled with a couple of valves and a big switch, then gave the big open flywheel a big flip. It bounced forward, then back, then caught... there was a little puff of blue smoke from the exhaust pipe below the waterline, and the sleek little boat took off toward the village.

The anchor chain flaked into the under-deck locker until the ring at the top of the anchor itself appeared over the bow. Anderson toggled the switch a few times to settle the hook into its chocks, screwed down the dog that kept it in place, and returned to the wheel. Within a few moments he had set a course for Barker's Island on the GPS and autohelm, and *The Beaver* was travelling northwest at just over ten knots.

***

After a half-hour, Anderson made sure the cell booster was on and checked the signal strength on his phone: four bars. He dialled Marjorie. "Hello? Marjorie? It's me."

"I know it's you, silly, and I'm sure glad to hear from you. I tried your number an hour ago and you didn't pick up."

"I'm way out on the lake. It was like being written into a spy movie; we met at dawn at the end of that big island you and I passed. Crazy Man Willy is an extraordinary old man, tougher than nails, bright as hell and speaks like a grumpy old university professor. We need as many answers as we can get in the shortest possible time about the Robinson Group – especially what holdings the company has in Mexico and California. It seems that all the bad stuff here is all about drugs, pure and simple. Probably all the action is under the radar of Robertson's senior management, but there are likely some fairly senior linkages to what's going on. And it would appear that California and or Mexico is the source."

"Wendy's here – we are packing to leave tomorrow as planned. I'll talk to her right away and get back to you as soon as she learns more. Will you be within reach?"

"Yes, I'm on my way back to the village. Lots of things to pull together today, specially with sergeant John and Willy. And, well... I'll just be really glad to see you back here!"

"Me too. Stay safe... and I'll call you when we learn something, or not."

They switched off. Anderson placed the next call to the sergeant, which went to voicemail immediately: "Hey, it's Anderson. Hope you're okay. Call me ASAP." After a three-sixty sweep of the horizon with the glasses, Anderson put on a fresh pot of coffee and cleaned up in the forward cabin. He had sent the rest of the first pack of cigarettes with Willy, so he dug out the second pack from the groceries he had brought onboard yesterday and took it to the shelf beside the wheel, where he fished out a smoke and lit it. *I'm gonna have to quit playing cop and get back to real work. I've sucked back more cigarettes in the last week than I usually do in a month!*

He called Arnold. "Hi, it's Frank. How's everything in town?"

"Crazy, and not good. People are talking about nothing else but the Maple Falls Assassination, as they are calling it on the news. The nurse that was hurt – broke her leg – lives here – Lucy Forbes, Jeremy's youngest daughter. The cop that is on life support is Marie Beauchemin, the corporal who patrolled here just about every day. Folks loved her. Lots of the younger folk knew Hassam, and especially Cyndi and Adumbi who are terrified. We've put them up at the house. The sergeant called once this morning to see if I had heard from you – he couldn't get through on your phone. He's up to his ass in senior inspectors and crime scene experts from Toronto. How's your world? That reminds me, I drove by your place last night and locked the doors, dummy. Hope you've got keys! Drove by this morning too, looks okay."

"Thanks man. I thought about locking up but forgot. So I met up with Crazy Man Willy, who's about as crazy as a fox and a really good guy – and a big help. This is all about drugs, and he knows a lot of stuff that I'm pretty sure John and his bunch know about, so we need to meet. I'm an hour – maybe an hour and a half – out and Willy is headed to the marina by a slightly different route. I've got Marjorie and Wendy digging around for some stuff in Toronto – more about Robertson Mines – some of their personnel may actually be tied into this. Can you get free to join us somehow, somewhere, later on? Something has to be pulled together or way more people are going to get hurt."

"Yep. My phone's on and the truck's running. Just let me know."

"Maybe don't tell anyone anything yet. I hate secrets but they're safer when they are kept. Take care!"

A couple of miles ahead, Anderson could now see the cluster of small, low islands near the mouth of the Spirit River. He adjusted the autohelm to pass west of them so he could swing back around between the islands and the marsh before heading back to the village. It was 13:00 hours.

***

At 13:21, the sergeant called. He briefly filled Anderson in on the situation in Maples Falls, along with the news that Marie was still in a coma and had been airlifted to an Ottawa hospital. There was pain in the sergeant's voice that Anderson had neither heard before nor expected to hear. It had all gone down under his watch, she was his second-in-command, and he had been in the damn shower. "Were you able to learn anything from the grandfather, Frank?"

"Actually, yes. A helluva lot. I'm almost certain this is all about drugs – international stuff – and I think we have solid information about the source, the top end of the distribution chain – including airplanes, boats and trucks, the name of the regional kingpin, and probably some of the local soldiers. The grandfather and I will be arriving at the village in separate boats but at roughly the same time in just over an hour. If you can spring it, let's get together, and I think your top dog should come with you."

"Okay, I'll grab him and stuff him into my car and get to your dock at 15:30. I can fill him in on why I have kidnapped him on the way out here. He's a really good guy, but I expect he'll be a bit surprised about my team of SMEs."

"SMEs? I've heard about FBIs... what are SMEs?"

"Pronounced 'smee' and stands for 'Subject Matter Experts'."

"Yeah, I guess that's pretty much what we are. See you at 15:30 John... take care, my friend and bring donuts, dammit... I'm starved and I bet Willy will be too!"

He called Arnold. "Three-thirty at the dock. John and his senior investigator, plus Willy. Maybe get Marion to drop you off so there isn't a big bunch of extra vehicles to attract attention."

"Better than that. I'll drop off Marion and she can join you for the discussions while I mind the store for a change. She is closer to Willy, Anita and the Indian – Indigenous – bunch than I am, and as you said the other day, she always knows... stuff."

"Okay my friend. Probably a good call. Thanks. Later!"

By now Anderson was threading *The Beaver* through cottage islands. As he passed Barker's island, he could see Tony fiddling around at his boathouse and wharf, and bumped his horn a couple of times. Tony looked up and waved. A few minutes later the launch passed the east end of the marshes and was headed east toward the village. The afternoon was bright and very warm, so he was not surprised to see a couple of boats come out of the channel through the marsh. He assumed they had come upriver from The Falls... one was a high-powered wakeboard boat with two couples onboard, and the other was a high-powered fishing boat, with a small trolling motor and a couple of big Mercs cranked right up and probably pushing 300 horsepower and two men onboard. The boats were a couple of hundred yards apart, and sped by as if the launch was standing still. The occupants of both boats waved – it was that kind of afternoon.

It was 14:45 when he got to the harbour, and he had to wait a few moments for a young couple with a sailboat to sort themselves out and get out of his way so he could land safely.

The marina had it's own small-boat launch around the little point of land that split the bay in two, but these folks had put their boat in at the public launch beside his dock. They waved at him as they glided by: it was a perfect afternoon for a pleasant but not too rough sail.

Anderson shut down both engines and dipped his fuel tanks before checking the engine oils. He had lots of fuel for whatever they would do for the rest of today, but he made a mental note to re-fuel first thing in the morning. He made written notes in the boat's log book – in more detail than usual, making sure to log the times when he met up with Willy and his boat, anchored offshore, as well as the fly-over this morning and his route home. He went into the forward cabin and made sure his shotgun and rifle were safely stowed and out of sight under blankets, and that the boxes of shells were in a small locker on the opposite side. *No point in pissing off a senior cop I haven't even met yet.*

While he waited for his odd mixture of guests, Anderson poured a cup of lukewarm coffee, sat down in the wheelhouse, and emailed himself all the photos he had taken over the last few days, and in particular the two snapshots of the airplane. He played a little on his smartphone screen with the best of the airplane photos, and thought it possible that he – or someone in the police lab – might be able to read the identification numbers. And any airplane expert could easily tell the make and type of plane.

Of course, he thought, he hadn't seen or heard Willy arrive. He looked up suddenly to see him standing on the dock beside the wheelhouse. "Hey, Willy, you made it. Come onboard; I'm just waiting for the gang.

"Yup, saw you come in. I have a boathouse slip over there and had to pull some other guy's boat out of there before

I could tie up. So, you been making phone calls... who is in the gang?"

"The sergeant, John MacLeod. Marion, and MacLeod's senior inspector. And you and I."

"You work fast."

"That's not all – I have the Webster girls digging up stuff about the Robertson empire."

"I know all about you and the Webster girls. Like I said, you work fast!" And he gave a wide grin.

"Geez, nothing is sacred around here," Anderson laughed.

Willy looked out onto the lake and paused. "Love is sacred." Turning back to Anderson he said, "So have you made coffee for your guests? I'm pretty dry."

"Good idea. We have been promised donuts, too. I told John to bring lots."

Anderson started the genset, and had just finished pouring the water over the coffee and turning the maker on when a somewhat dusty-looking police cruiser pulled up to the end of the dock. The sergeant got out of the driver's seat and walked along the dock with a shorter, stocky man, also in uniform, and Anderson went out on the dock to greet them. "Hello again, John. You bring a guest..."

"Frank, this is Superintendent George Daniels. He is the man in charge of all major crimes investigations, and boy have we ever had a major crime, as you know."

"Good to meet you, Superintendent," said Anderson as he shook the big man's hand.

They had arrived at the boat, and the sergeant stepped onboard immediately and went to Willy. "Mr. Antoine, I'm John MacLeod and we have met before, a couple of years ago. It is good to see you again."

The Superintendent had stopped on the dock, and was looking over the launch from one end to the other. He nodded, as if to himself, and turned to Anderson: "Permission to come aboard, Mr. Anderson?"

"Permission granted sir, with pleasure, and welcome!"

The two men joined Crazy Man and the sergeant, who introduced Willy to the Superintendent. "I told you, George, that I was thoroughly impressed with our SMEs and it just gets better: Willy is a wise and honoured man, well-connected in the First Nation community."

"Well, our SME team is almost complete," Anderson said, looking down the dock. "Here come Arnold and Marion Jamieson. Arnold is dropping Marion off with us... she is the wisdom of this village community and beyond. Knows everybody, not only where they were born but also, I expect, where they were conceived."

"Damn, I forgot the donuts," the sergeant said as he jumped off the boat and headed back to the cruiser. "I'll be right back," and he waved at Arnold and Marion as he went by. Anderson finished off the introductions, then Arnold shook hands, smiled at Willy and squeezed Anderson's shoulder as he left to go back to his truck.

***

Anderson put the coffee pot and some cups on the navigation table and fired up the main engine. He went out on deck and was watching a couple of little fishing boats and a family runabout that were moving around between the dock and open water. The Superintendent came to him and said quietly, "I'll slip your lines as you direct, if you want to take the wheel."

"Much appreciated. We'll start with the stern, on my call.

I'll twist the boat a little, then call the bow." He went back to the wheel, blew a long blast on the horn and checked again to see if there were any boats beside him, then bellowed out the window, "Let go the stern!" In two seconds the rope was lying in the well-deck, and the Superintendent was walking quickly to where the bow line was cleated to the dock, took off a couple of wraps and waited. Anderson put the transmission in forward and spun the wheel clockwise. The rounded bow pulled in toward the dock and the stern started to move out. Anderson put the transmission back into neutral and centered the wheel before calling out, "Let go the bow. All aboard!"

When the Superintendent was back on the boat, Anderson took the launch away from the dock in reverse, straightened her around and gently edged her out into the lake. The sergeant turned to his boss and said, "You've done this kind of stuff before, haven't you!"

"Five years in the Coast Guard out in B.C. Still miss it. And you have a good boat and captain here... I couldn't resist showing off!"

Anderson took the launch about a quarter-mile offshore away from the pleasure boats, turned east toward Ship Island, throttled down to a couple of knots and punched in the autohelm. "Okay, we'd better start sharing some information, try to fill in some blanks or at least learn what more we need to know, and then figure out what's next to do. Willy, you have a lot of really important stuff to start off with, so why don't you start..."

And he did, explaining all about Juan, how he was involved through Anita with Hassam and some of the bad guys out along the east shore. He emphasized the Mexican or Californian connection through Juan, the angry brutality of the young man, and the probable Robertson connection. A conversation that took a couple of hours this morning took less than fifteen minutes. When he was done, Anderson said he had the Webster sisters digging this afternoon for information about the Robertson Group. He pointed out that the company was, in fact, paying the lease on the property on the east shore, and told whose names were on the lease, as the sisters had discovered yesterday.

And Willy talked about the airplane. Anderson showed the officers his cellphone with the photo, and they immediately asked him to email it to an address in Ottawa the Superintendent provided. As Anderson was emailing, the Superintendent was on the phone to the photo lab. Anderson's phone had no sooner finished sending the photo when it rang. It was Wendy.

"Hi Frank, got some info for you."

"Hi Wendy, I have John and his Superintendent out here on the boat with me, along with Arnold's wife Marion and Willy Antoine. Can I put you on speakerphone?" He throttled back the engine to make it easier to hear and called the gang into the wheelhouse. "Okay, fire away Wendy!"

"Okay, the Robertson Group has an office in San Diego, and several operations in western Mexico, in the mountains. There are some news reports of Mexican staff involvement in the drug trade over the last four or five years, but the reports appear unverified and appear to have stopped a year ago when the reporter – an American – was killed in a car accident. There have been no arrests or charges, at least in the US. I have bushels of paper and links for you, which we will bring with us tomorrow unless you need something scanned and emailed tonight. I raised some eyebrows at the Robertson office when I asked a bunch of questions, but even though they are mad at me, they know I am always a curious kind of a cat so I didn't get grilled."

"Thank you Wendy," said John. "Drive carefully you two, and hope to see you soon. That is invaluable information, and I want to take you out for dinner when things settle down. Anderson?"

"Bye Wendy, and many many thanks. Tell Marjorie I'll give her a call later tonight." He clicked off the phone, and turned to the sergeant. "See what I mean? There's too much there to be coincidence. I'm not so very sure how big an operation this is, or how high up the food chain Juan really is."

"High enough to plan a successful assassination in a very public place and not even let us capture a live suspect," chimed in the Superintendent. "And at least in our country, the concern is rippling all the way to the PMO. The yanks don't seem as concerned as they should be, so they may not care if our kids are frying their brains on this stuff, but I sure as hell do."

"Amen," said Marion.

"Okay folks," said Anderson, "that looks like all the info we're gonna get today. Superintendent, do you have a drug investigation group to call in, or does this start to touch the Mounties, or...?"

"We do have a team, but when it gets across borders – east, west or south – we need to work with the RCMP. I called our guys in Toronto half an hour ago and told them not to go home until I called, which I am going to do right now. I expect a couple of officers from both departments will fly in to Maple Falls in the morning." And he walked outside and along the deck forward of the wheelhouse to make his call. He waved the sergeant to go with him. Willy and Marion sat deep in conversation outside the wheelhouse, and Anderson noticed that by now they were close to Ship Island, so he decided to make a pass around it before they headed back to the village. He took the speed up to about four knots, turned a few degrees to port to miss the island and re-set the autohelm. He found his stash of cigarettes, went outside and offered them to Willy and Marion, lit them and one for himself and returned to the wheelhouse and his remaining half-cup of coffee.

He had barely started the turn around the south side of the island when the two police officers came back and joined him by the wheel. Sensing that they wanted to talk, he throttled back down again, looked up and said, "Gentlemen?"

"Captain Anderson, I am going to sound very official for a moment. I need to officially commission this vessel and her captain for officially sanctioned support during a crime investigation. The owner of the vessel will receive our standard day-rate for vessels of this size. Are you the sole owner?"

"Yes, I am."

"Good. Are you willing to lease this vessel as I just outlined?"

"Yes, I am."

"Good. There's more. If you are willing, I am officially appointing you as an Auxiliary Sergeant in the OPS Auxiliary. You will have similar powers of a police officer during the length of this engagement. I need to do this in case we have other members and forces working with us and I need Sergeant MacLeod here to be able to set the correct chain of command as far as the operation of this vessel. Do you agree?"

Anderson looked over at the sergeant, who shrugged and smiled somewhat thinly. Anderson looked back at the Superintendent: "Yes, I agree."

"Thank you, Sergeant Anderson."

He called Willy and Marion in from the deck, and explained what he had just arranged. "And now, one last thing which I should have said earlier. My name is George. That's John, this is Frank and that's Willy and there's Marion. Let's just call each other by those names except in front of the media, which we will all avoid as much as possible. As the senior officer on location, for now, I handle the media anyway, and that's the only bunch I want to call me Superintendent. And in public, this is still Captain Anderson, a Sergeant in the police auxiliary."

As he made his last turn before heading the boat back to the village, they were a good distance away from the little bay where the sisters docked their little outboard, and where it would have normally been, there was a much bigger boat. "John," he yelled, "grab the binoculars and check out that boat in the bay. I think it's the same one that shot at us!"

Everyone, including Superintendent George, was staring off to starboard while John peered through the glasses. "Almost sure that's it."

"Whoever it is, they are trespassing and probably stealing Wendy's and Marjorie's stuff," said Marion. "Shouldn't we pay them a visit? Couple of uniforms onboard should probably scare them off."

"Not a chance. I have a small shotgun and a bolt-action rifle on board and only a handful of shells. You guys aren't even carrying side arms, and those idiots almost certainly have big guns if they are involved with the same group we're chasing and I think they are. Willy says those two yahoos – Mistraika and Giordano or their little buddies – are very likely involved with Juan even if they are only bottom feeders. I think we should motor casually by and head on home."

"Yup. Captain's right. We'll live to fight another day. Let's go back to the dock." Anderson held his course and speed for a few more minutes, then sped up to eight knots and pointed

The Beaver home.

As he pushed the throttle up, a cellphone rang. This time it was the Superintendent's: "Daniels here. Yes Corporal. You did get some numbers? Owned by who? Really! Okay, thanks. E-mail me the report right away. Thanks. G'night." He turned to Willy. "Your airplane from this morning is owned by Robertson Logistics, part of the Robertson Group obviously. It's registered in the US. It's definitely time to tell the boys and girls at head office to call in the RCMP. I'll set that in motion right now." And he started stabbing buttons.

It was becoming dusk, and Anderson flipped on the navigation lights and checked the radar, setting it back to one mile radius. He was kind of enjoying his new toy, but he knew there was no more looking everywhere but forward... there were likely a number of small boats out there headed for the marina, or back out to the cottages, and the radar wouldn't pick up half of them. Twenty minutes later, he slid *The Beaver* alongside her dock, where Super George helped him tie her down. They put out spring lines for the night and locked the chains. Anderson opened a beer for each of his passengers, who sat around on the gunwales and talked about tonight – and tomorrow. "If one of you will give us a lift," said Marion, "I'll take Willy home so that he can visit with Arnold and get a decent night's sleep that isn't on the bottom of a boat."

"Done," said the sergeant. "I've ordered up two patrol cars to cruise the streets tonight, from your house Marion (where you have the two interns who are material witnesses, as well as Willy) and down to the dock and back again. Frank, I want you to go back to your house and get a good night's sleep, because I'll be waking you up really early in the morning. Breakfast is at the Zoo at 06:00. Maybe by then we'll have the beginning of a plan, and we will start assembling resources, like personnel and equipment."

"Works for me," said Anderson. "Just one thing, though. Not much point in taking action unless we know how – and where – we can nail the boss – Juan. We have no idea where he's hanging out."

"Exactly. But we may be closer to answering that by morning. I have some undercover guys working around – at John's suggestion – between the Robertson property and Maple Falls. They are doing the land stuff. Tomorrow, Frank and a team will lead the water stuff, and I've ordered in an unmarked but very fast boat that should be here early in the morning, with her armed crew. On the subject of armed crews, there will be two on this boat in the morning, and our new Sergeant Captain Anderson will have a sidearm and shells before we leave tonight."

The Superintendent continued: "The Plan, if you can call it that, is to flush Juan out before he can do something worse or – more likely – leave. If we wait around, he'll decide he's better off to find a way out. We have to force his hand, but we have closed all the small landing fields and the larger airports are notified. They all have his picture. Let's get started – with a good night's sleep, although it'll be short enough."

They walked to the patrol car where the sergeant handed Anderson a sidearm and a box of ammunition. "Keep this with you tonight, then maybe stash by your controls in the wheelhouse in the morning." He was dropped off at his door, and yes, he did have the keys.

He went in, turned on the lights, opened a second beer and sat at his table with a cigarette. His house felt friendly, even though he knew the relaxation would be short-lived. He dialled Marjorie, wondering if her voice would quiet the hollow feeling in his stomach and the slight headache at his temples.

05:30 JULY 26

Anderson rolled out of bed and shut off the alarm. He had slept well, although he was aware of the comings and goings of the police patrols during the night. Most times, that would be annoying, but last night it was almost as comforting as the ticking of a favourite clock. The phone call with Marjorie had also been comforting but of course he didn't give out a lot of details – he mentioned that a top cop was in town and had "officially" requisitioned the use of the boat today as they continued their investigation out on the lake. He asked her to stop by Arnold's garage and talk to Marion before they went out to their cottage, and of course to give him a call when they got there.

He dressed quickly and went out to his truck, where he stashed the P229 Sig Sauer and the 9mm shells under the seat on the passenger side, and shoved some rags and a couple of tools and an empty windshield washer jug over top before he drove up to the Zoo to meet the sergeant for breakfast. He had taken handgun courses when he lived in British Columbia, but he was not particularly keen on them: he knew this one was an efficient killing machine, but he had never visualized wanting to have one, never mind use it. He had read somewhere that if

297

there is a gun on a wall at the beginning of a story, it will be fired before the story's over. He hoped the story that would unfold today would be an exception to the rule.

The sergeant was already at the Zoo drinking coffee, along with two other officers in Tac vests. "Constable Bathgate and Corporal Ajay, this is Auxiliary Sergeant Anderson, who is our boat captain today. Andy, you are already familiar with Frank."

"My pleasure," said Anderson. "Yes, Andy has been out with us a couple of times in the last month, and welcome, Corporal...ah... Ajay?"

"Just 'Ajay', sir. My first name is hard to pronounce, so I never use it!"

Sam brought over another coffee for Anderson and some cutlery. "The usual?" he asked Anderson.

"Please. You're up early, Sam, even for you!"

"I had this little phone call from John last night, warning me of an early morning invasion of strange men in blue uniforms. Is this all of them, Sergeant?"

"Nope. I expect three more cars in about twenty minutes, with probably two officers in each, so six more people, plus Arnold."

Anderson chuckled aloud. "I assume that 'undercover' is not today's buzzword?"

"Nope, just the opposite. Today is a wide-open response, with maximum visibility. A very fast speedboat with two well-armed officers will be going straight to the boat launch by 07:00, and we will have two choppers and one fixed-wing in the air over and around the lake by 08:00. Every road around the lake will be road-blocked and we have an undercover detail watching that two-engine plane where it sits outside an industrial hangar at the airport in Ottawa. We want to force the suspect to come out of his hidey hole and into the open, somewhere."

"And 'command central' is... where?" asked Anderson.

"The on-location command is your boat, and we have brought the mother of all police radios to install onboard and plug-in to your power system. I am in charge of the field operations on and around the lake, and back at Maple Falls we have the local office staff helping Superintendent Daniels and an RCMP Inspector, who are in overall command. This is planned as a joint operation, but the Mounties have deferred to our personnel and command structure, particularly out here. Daniels is jealous – he'd like to be out on your boat instead, but there are also a number of officers who will be making house calls on individuals we have identified as persons of interest, and that needs coordination and real-time intelligence analysis. We're the blunt end of the stick out here."

Anderson thought for a moment before replying. "So the plan... is to make as many bad guys as possible jump into the lake, and then we go fishing?"

"Yeah, that's one way to put it! I also forgot to tell you that I am dropping off a handheld radio with Arnold. I asked him to stay home with Marion and Willy and the interns. I don't foresee trouble there, but as we talked about yesterday they are all material witnesses. I've left the police patrol working the village until were done, and at least now Arnold can contact them by radio. Anyway, sorry about that – I commandeered your buddy and lead hand I suspect."

"No worries, good call I think. I have to head down to the dock and transfer some diesel from my slip-tank into the boat. Won't take long, but I'll swallow down my breakfast and get going. I'm just hoping you brought donuts!"

"And coffee, and Sam here is making the boat crew

sandwiches."

"You didn't sleep much last night, did you!"

"Time to catch up later. Couldn't have slept more than a couple of hours anyway... something about planning a high-profile operation under the watchful eyes of senior cops from two different forces, just doesn't make for a peaceful sleep!"

Anderson left to fuel up just as the other three police vehicles arrived – one SUV and two half-tons. He waved and bellowed "Sergeant's inside" then drove down the street to *The Beaver*, passing one of the night-patrol cars returning from the dock.

By the time the sergeant and his team had arrived just after 07:00, the launch was re-fueled, the mooring chain as unlocked and the spring-lines slipped, and the engines were running. Anderson had loaded the P229 and stowed it in the small waterproof Pelican case under the helm console where he kept the launch's papers and his tickets. Ajay and Andy struggled aboard with a bunch of radio gear including a small antenna tower that they assembled with a handful of bolts and strapped to the port side of the wheelhouse. In less than ten minutes they had the unit tarp-strapped to the top of the navigation table, plugged in, powered up and had made contact with the office in Maple Falls.

The last things on board were a couple of Colt carbines and ammunition, and most important of all: coffee buckets and donuts from Timmy's and sandwiches from the Zoo. "Ready to get underway, Frank?" asked the sergeant.

"Anytime, Sergeant. Andy, would you please let go the bow and stern mooring lines, and we'll get this show on the road. Where do you want us to go, and how fast, Sergeant? You're the guy with the plan."

"I'd like us to be off the east shore about opposite

Robertson Mines by 08:00... can we do that?"

"Yup, I'll have to crank her up pretty good, but yes, we'll be close. Are those guys with the speedboat coming soon?"

"It's a Seaswirl, they tell me – pretty good little boats. I'll call in and find out. I want them between our position and that big island where Willy saw that plane drop those sacks. We should be in sight of each other that way?"

"Yup."

Anderson took the launch clear of the village harbour and pushed the throttle up past twelve knots. The 225 hp Volvo diesel growled happily but noisily. The day had dawned bright and sunny, but today there was a stiff breeze rising out of the west so once they were out in the open there was enough chop that *The Beaver* rolled a little as she headed to pass east of the Webster sister's island then south along the east shore.

***

At 08:00 hours, traffic on the police radio suddenly went from occasional short conversations to an intense series of radio calls to and from police cars and the office at The Falls, and with the airborne units. The speedboat had been launched at 07:45 and was already well underway across the lake.

"Sergeant, I can see Robertson Mines up ahead and we're about a mile offshore. We won't get right opposite for ten or fifteen minutes... do you want me to keep going at this speed or cut back a little. We are actually about opposite that marsh and landing place where we got shot at."

"Maybe cut back to half speed. We're getting tossed around on the waves a bit and we should start scanning the shore more closely."

"I can quiet that roll quite a lot by cutting speed back and putting the bow into the wind so she takes the waves head-on.

Just tell me when."

"Keep going for awhile. That Seaswirl will be having a bouncy ride out there but I imagine he's still going full speed. My guess is he should be getting into position in about twenty minutes. And the choppers should be approaching each other inshore from north and south and cross at 08:30. Ajay... can you ask the office where that airplane is? It's a thing we chartered and I have no idea what it is or what it can do – just the pilot and our observer onboard."

"Okay if I try to reach the Seaswirl on marine radio?" asked Anderson. "Or are they running silent."

"They'll be running silent, in case the bad guys have radios too."

Anderson could see Ajay was looking agitated all of a sudden, and he motioned the sergeant over to his radio and handed him his earphones. There was still too much engine noise in the wheelhouse to hear what was going on, but in a couple of minutes the sergeant handed back the headset and came across to the wheel. "Fuckin' screw up already. The pilot managed to get tipped over by the wind on take-off and planted the damn airplane into a swamp, upside down. I guess both he and our observer are banged up pretty good but alive... and now we no longer have eyes in the air and won't have for an hour or more until we make new arrangements. That is definitely not a good thing, and I don't want to pull the choppers off their routes inside the shore or we will lose the pressure there."

"Well, we're okay out here for now. Do you want to get that other boat to make a circle of the island close-in on the off-chance someone is trying to get at those sacks?"

"Yeah, I'll call 'em. Maybe cut back and head upwind like you suggested, trying not to go too far offshore and we'll hold position for now." The sergeant told the other constable to settle down in the stern and sweep the shoreline with binoculars, then went and called the Seaswirl.

That wound up being a three-way conversation, because the sergeant had to reach the boat through the command office in The Falls. Anderson could only hear one side of the conversation but understood that the boat was going to make a full-speed revolution of the island. The wind had continued to freshen, but the launch now rode the waves bow-on relatively quietly with only the occasional splash over the bow which didn't even make it to the wheelhouse window. Anderson set the autopilot long enough to leave the wheel, grab two sticky things from the donut box and re-fill his coffee before coming back to the wheel and re-taking control as the boat fought with the autohelm and wandered back and forth against the waves. There was no choice – he had to be on the wheel if they were going to hold a steady course into the wind. And he hadn't been back there long before he noticed out of the corner of his eye that Andy had suddenly put down the binoculars, stood up and run to the gunwale and thrown up over the side of the boat. "John, take the wheel for a moment please?" and he darted down the steps into the forward cabin and returned with a bottle of pills. "Andy, grab two of these and chew on them. Don't use the binoculars for awhile – just look at the horizon to steady your stomach." He brought the binoculars back to the sergeant and reclaimed the wheel. "A little sea-sick. He'll get over it, poor guy. I wonder how Ajay's doing, head down in the cabin fiddling with the radio."

"Seems to be happy as a clam. Guess he's getting a call... and sounds like I'd better hear. Ajay... put it on speaker, it's quiet enough in here now."

It was the Seaswirl, direct this time. "We have a boat on

the northeast side of this island and are pulling in to take a look. Big old aluminum boat, two big engines. Don't see anybody around."

"Seaswirl from MacLeod, Seaswirl from MacLeod: pull back. Do not engage. I repeat, pull back and do not engage."

"Message received, we are turning away and withdrawing to one kilometer. Should we hold position and observe or continue around the island?"

The sergeant paused and glanced at Anderson momentarily then keyed the microphone: "Hold position and observe. Report any activity at all, immediately. I repeat, observe and report any activity immediately. The subjects are almost certainly armed with heavy rifles."

"Roger that. We will hold position and observe and report."

Anderson looked hard at the sergeant: "Now I know why you wanted that airplane up there. We're just screwed out here 'cause if we can't see we can't help. I'm willing to bet that old boat has enough speed to outrun the Seaswirl, and worse... if those idiots on shore decide to try and run down your police boat, they could do it and are probably better armed. And those guys are dumb enough to try... I hardly think they're the brain-trust of Juan's operation."

"Good point. Think I'll call the shop and talk with the Supe. I think we should spring a chopper free from the shore-side operation for at least long enough to have a look over here." The sergeant paused: "Your cell booster work out here?"

"On a good day, maybe. This ain't a good day, but here, try it with my phone."

The sergeant took Anderson's phone, stabbed at the dial pad and got through. He talked with the Superintendent for over a minute, then clicked off. "One of the choppers is on the way. And, the folks in Ottawa just arrested two men – the pilot and one other – as they prepared to get that Robertson Logistics plane onto the runway. Neither one of them is our guy Juan. However, they're both in for a long morning of questioning and the dogs are now working the plane over for drugs."

Two minutes later they could see a helicopter flying low off the shoreline and headed in their direction. Within a couple of minutes the EC135 overflew the launch, and the rapid thud of the blades seemed to fill the air. It did not pause: it veered to the southwest and aimed for the island, flying fast and steady at less than 500 feet above the water. The Gravol had apparently worked on Constable Andy, since he was now leaning against the wheelhouse with the binoculars and was following the chopper. Anderson was still holding the launch's bow into the waves and was doing his best to hold a position midway from Robertson Mines and the island.

Big Island was little more than a flat rocky outcrop overgrown with scrub brush. It was just over a mile long and perhaps a quarter-mile wide. The chopper approached the island from downwind end and flew slowly west along its length. Even without binoculars, Anderson could see the chopper turn, circle around and approach the island again about a third of the way along.

Ajay called from the radio that the chopper was reporting people working at something in the middle of the island and was turning for a closer look. Anderson looked across at the sergeant: "Let's hope they're not dumb enough to try and shoot down your whirlybird." It was exactly 2.5 seconds before Ajay yelled, "Shots fired, shots fired. They're shooting at the chopper!" They could see the helicopter turn abruptly toward them and appear to lose altitude. "Pilot's hit... still in control. Gonna ditch... calling mayday, he's gonna ditch!"

Instinctively Anderson slammed the throttle forward and swung the bow southwest toward the place where he had last seen the helicopter as it began one lazy spiral then disappeared. The sergeant yelled at his radioman: "Ajay... tell the Seaswirl to come around the east end of the island as fast as they can to pick up the chopper crew... we're going to be at least twenty minutes getting there." He went to one of the duffel bags they had brought onboard and fished out a bulletproof vest which he handed to Anderson. "Better put this on, Frank. And is your sidearm handy?"

Anderson pointed down at the Pelican case and nodded. "Yup, and loaded. Don't think I could hit the broad side of a barn in this chop, though. It's kind of bouncy out here! I think we should prepare to bring the chopper crew onboard here... your little boat will be there first to pick them up but we have more room. We can get out of the waves under the lee of the island to do the transfer." The launch was travelling about thirty degrees off the wind and was taking spray over the starboard bow, along with the occasional burst of solid water that sluiced across the foredeck and ran off over the side ahead of the wheelhouse.

The sergeant told Ajay and Andy to break out their carbines, load them, and put extra ammo clips in their Tac vests. Anderson pointed out the lockers on the afterdeck and suggested they get out a couple of lengths of rope. As usual, all three officers had put on police-issued lifejackets when they boarded, but he suggested they get out two or three more and put them out of the wind in the wheelhouse, in case they needed to use them during the transfer.

***

There would be no transfer. Twelve minutes later they were still over a mile away from where the chopper had hit the water, and they could see the Seaswirl had cut close – too close apparently – around the end of the island and was heading to the chopper when Ajay yelled from his station at the radio "Shots fired, shot's fired... it's our boat." There was a pause, then: "The shots are coming from the island and they were returning fire... now they are trying to get further away from the shooters... one officer may be down."

A couple of minutes later, Constable Andy called from outside the wheelhouse where he stood trying to steady his binoculars: "The boat seems to have stopped moving."

The marine radio beside Anderson suddenly crackled to life: "Mayday Mayday Mayday, police vessel 1042 at Awan Lake is on fire and crew of two is abandoning ship. I repeat, we are getting off the boat..." and went silent. Anderson keyed the microphone and replied they were about a mile off to the northeast and would be there soon – but there was no further response.

"Yeah, they're sure as hell on fire now!" yelled Andy. "Can't tell if they got off. Still too far away and too rough to see clearly."

"Sarge, the guys at command are wondering what the hell's going on out here. You'd maybe better talk to them," said Ajay as he got up and handed over the headset.

"MacLeod here. We have one Seaswirl burning after receiving gunfire, and I think the crew got off okay. The chopper is still visible upside down in the water a half-mile from the Seaswirl. We're going as fast as possible but we're working against pretty big waves and are still a few minutes from the boat... nope, we'll call you if we need the other

307

chopper for rescue but for now get him out here to keep track of the suspects. They are either on the island or in their boat by now. And tell him to stay 'way the hell up in the sky 'cause these guys may be stupid but they shoot big guns and they shoot 'em often. And, I do expect injuries so get a medevac underway ASAP. I'll call it off if we don't need it... okay, thanks. I'll put Corporal Ajay back on."

Anderson was having his own private little conversation – a debate – with himself: *Upwind, downwind. Which way do I pick up? With an inexperienced boat crew, maybe I'd better go to leeward of the folks we're picking out of the water in case someone slips up... don't want to roll them under the boat.* "John, there is a steel boarding ladder hinged at the front of the afterdeck, starboard side. When we get ready to pick up, swing it over – gravity will keep it there. And in the stern locker, starboard side there is an orange horseshoe rescue sling like they use for ice rescue... maybe get it out and ready just in case someone can't do the ladder. I'll come up on them on the down-wind side, starboard so get a rope to them quickly. Are either of your crew good at water rescue so they can go overboard and help?"

"Yeah, me. I'll take off my gun and gear just in case. Andy," he called out, "you're our sharp-shooter. Watch that shoreline closely in case the perps are in there and ready to shoot at us. Ajay and I will try to handle the rescues alone."

The Seaswirl and the chopper were downwind of the island and fairly close to shore, so the waves were more confused but not as rough as they were in open water. Anderson went for the boat first. It was still busy turning itself into a lump of molten plastic, but the two officers were clearly visible in their lifejackets about 150 feet downwind. "Stand by, crew, coming alongside to starboard. Put down the ladder, both men look okay to board."

Well, not quite. One officer had a severely damaged left arm where a bullet had shattered his elbow and would have a problem with the ladder, but with help from his crewmate and the sergeant he was onboard and sitting on the bottom of the well deck in less than a minute, followed by the other officer. Anderson shoved the throttle forward and made for the helicopter.

As Anderson manoeuvred *The Beaver* along the downwind side of the upside-down machine, he fervently hoped there were no stray pieces of rotor blade close to the surface that could get caught up in the boat's propeller. Both men were in lifejackets, but one was unconscious and the other looked exhausted. Sergeant MacLeod went into the water with the horseshoe and with the other officer's help slipped it over the unconscious man's head and under his arms. Anderson left the boat in neutral and ran back to help hand-over-hand the man up the side, across the gunwales and into the boat. By the time they had him settled in "rescue position" on the well deck floor, the other officer had made it up the ladder, followed by the sergeant.

The launch had drifted clear of the chopper so Anderson pulled a little further off the shore of the island and aimed into the wind at dead-slow speed until next steps could be decided. He called to Ajay to grab the blankets and pillows from the forward cabin to make the injured men more comfortable and keep them warm to guard against shock.

The sergeant flipped off the radio speaker and called in to Maple Falls: "Daniels? It's MacLeod here. Good news, all four men rescued, bad news is we do need the medevac – one man is walking but has a smashed elbow, the other is still unconscious and we don't know why yet. No, we're over two hours from any landing so the medevac team will probably have to use the basket to get these guys off. The other two officers are tired but in good shape, so we can keep them onboard for now. Huh? Yes George we have lots of donuts... yeah, I know – it's all about sugar, right? And the medevac is about thirty minutes out? Good, we'll be ready. Do you need our coordinates? Okay, close enough. Tell me, we can see the other EC135 flying around up there – what is he seeing?"

The chopper pilot broke in: "I was staying quiet until you had the rescue and medevac stuff settled. We don't see much at the moment, except two men picking up heavy sacks scattered around the east end of the island and taking them to their boat. From up here it looks like one guy is doing most of the work... the other one is just walking around close to the boat. He's carrying something like an AR15 slung across his back. Not sure if he's even seen us yet. And one more thing – there is a really fast pleasure boat approaching the west end of the island from the north – general direction of Spirit River village. We're keeping an eye on him because he looks pretty determined to get here in a hurry. Most sport boaters wouldn't bang themselves around so much, for so long. We'll let you know what he does and where he goes."

"Thanks officer. Good eye!" The sergeant handed Ajay his headset and told him to keep his ears on it. "I have a sort of uneasy feeling about this, Frank," and he told him about the fast pleasure boat.

"So, the bottom feeders in Juan's operation slither around in a big old hot-rod boat with machine guns picking up sacks full of pills. What kind of boat do you suppose Juan might choose to drive... the local version of a cigarette boat like they use off Florida Keys and the Baja... fast and fancy?"

"Kinda what I was thinking. Crap, I wish we still had a fast boat out here with armed officers." The sergeant walked across the wheelhouse and brought back two cups of hot coffee and half a box of donuts. "Better stock up – we're gonna get busy in ten minutes."

In eleven minutes the medevac chopper came into sight, circled *The Beaver* once and called in: "Hold your position as best you can and we'll send down a paramedic."

"Tell him roger that, Ajay. I'll just hang tight here." The helicopter settled into place right overhead with open doors and lowered a man to the deck, where Andy and the uninjured officer from the Seaswirl steadied him and released the line.

The paramedic took a brief look at the other boat officer's arm, said "we'll bind that tight across your chest and send you up in harness after I see to the other guy. I'm going to give you a shot to ease the pain a little." After administering the pain-killer, he went and kneeled down beside the unconscious officer – the pilot apparently – and examined him quickly. After a minute or so he stood up and spoke into his headset, asking for the basket. "This guy's lost a lot of blood, I expect from a wound in his upper thigh but he's been in the water for over an hour and it's hard to tell. Let's get him onboard." The basket arrived, swirling around over the deck until the sergeant and Andy were able to get it under control and set it down in the well deck. The paramedic unhooked the line and let the chopper crew take it up out of danger while they manoeuvred the injured man into the basket and strapped him in. The paramedic called for the line once again and hooked it to the basket ring and guided the basket off the boat and into the sky, where it seemed to dangle for an agonisingly long time before being safely taken onboard the helicopter. After less than half a minute, the line reappeared with a harness for the other officer, who winced as he was strapped in and was unceremoniously hauled into the sky and fished in through the chopper door.

One last time the line appeared, the paramedic hooked on and gave a thumbs up... and it was over.

"Those pilots are something else," Anderson remarked to no one in particular.

"They are. Didn't hurt that you managed to keep this outfit so steady in place, however. Let's head east toward the mainland and try to learn what's going on at the other side of the island. Ajay, are you getting anything from the cheap seats up there?"

Ajay called the pilot and flipped open the speaker. "That speedboat, the pilot answered, looks like the mother of all wakeboard boats. It's just approaching the other boat along the shore and it looks like he's landing on the beach right beside the other boat. The two gentlemen who were loading sacks seemed to have finished about five minutes ago, because they're both at the beach now, maybe talking to the guys who just arrived. Looks like there are two onboard the wakeboard boat as well, but one is just sitting there. Can't tell from here – small – might be a woman. Incidentally, Command, I will need to re-fuel in about 40 minutes."

"Let's hope they get done what they're gonna do before too long then," said the sergeant. "Where do you fuel up?"

"We're set up at the landing strip at Spirit River – that's about fifteen minutes from here... hold it, this is interesting... Genette – my observer – says they are now transferring all those sacks from the old boat to the new one, and they seem to be in a hurry. The guy from the new boat, I think, keeps looking up. Holy crap, he must have just shot the other two, 'cause now they're down on the ground. He's taken something else from their boat – maybe a gas can. He just threw it in the boat and is getting back into the wakeboard boat in a hurry. He's backing out and... shit, he just lit the old boat and those two guys on fire!"

"This is MacLeod – head out for fuel right away, but on your way maybe swoop down over that wakeboard boat – not too close – just to let him know he has an audience. I'm sure that's the boss and we want to keep him nervous and not thinking clearly."

"Roger that."

Now Anderson could see whisps of black smoke blowing off the far side of the island. *I think this must be what people call surreal,* he thought. In a couple of minutes he saw the wakeboard boat come out from behind the island, headed straight for the east shore of the lake, throwing up huge curtains of spray as it charged the following waves, which had not diminished.

"Frank, follow that boat, with attitude," the sergeant chuckled. "I realize you ain't gonna catch him, but it's the attitude that counts, and we'll get to see just where he goes. Can you stick this outfit on autopilot so we can talk?"

"Not really. In a following sea like this, she just yaws all over the place and the autohelm over-corrects and it ain't pretty. Actually potentially hard on gear and maybe even dangerous."

"Officer McMichael, can you take the wheel from Sergeant Anderson for a little while?"

"Certainly sir. I've gotten over the shakes. This is a great boat, it'll be my pleasure!"

"Thanks," said the sergeant. "Frank, Officer McMichael was skipper on that Seaswirl but has also operated our biggest boats, so he can spell you off. Let's go have a smoke and a chat about the rest of our otherwise perfectly normal day. You might even get a sandwich!"

Anderson relinquished the wheel with pleasure... he was

getting a bit stiff and sore, and a sandwich and a smoke sounded like a perfect solution. He watched for a moment as McMichael settled in, checked out the controls and instruments, and settled back, focused on following the wakeboard boat. "So, sergeant... now what?"

"Couple of things. It's now after 14:00, and now that the Robertson Logistics airplane has been detained and the personnel arrested, the Mounties have a clear role to play. We set it up that they would descend on Robertson Mines about an hour before shift change, block the roads and their main gate, and check over everyone at the facility. Everyone, executives and all. I think the RCMP planned to have ten personnel and five vehicles in place for that, so it should just be starting to happen. If that wakeboard boat over there is headed for the dock inside Robertson's chain link fence, all the better – he's effectively running into a trap."

"Is anyone checking into Robertson's Canadian head office in Toronto?"

"That's another thing, sort of coincidentally. Yes, at 16:00, two hours from now, a team of investigators – mostly forensic accountants – will move into Robertson's Toronto office and shut it down. The RCMP has reason to believe that they are juggling funds – sort of corporate money laundering – between Toronto and a series of offshore accounts. They – the RCMP – were planning this for months – the drug thing is simply an add-on and provided a good opportunity to go even wider. We got lucky with that!"

"Wow. When that hits the news poor Wendy will be pretty shaken. I just hope she and Marjorie are on the highway to Spirit River by now."

"Yes, I sure do hope so, or at least that she didn't go back to her old office and former colleagues this afternoon to ask more questions. I guess you could call Marjorie and put our minds at rest."

"Not from here. That cell booster just doesn't cut it out here. The tower is in Maple Falls and the signal barely makes it to the lake at all. Reminds me, if that wakeboard boat gets back offshore and heads southeast, I need to tell Marion or Willy to radio his FBI crew that is guarding Anita.

"Huh? There's something you're not telling me?"

"Well, yeah. My turn to say "need to know" and I apologize. Willy, and also Marion indirectly, use ham radio to connect, through Willy's old reserve down south. And he has Anita hidden as you know, but she is being guarded by two strapping big men and one tough broad, all of whom are well-armed and they all come from that same reserve. Not even sure if that's something even I wanted to know, except that Anita has been safe."

"Who calls them 'FBI'?"

"Willy."

"Figures," he chuckled. "Well, you're right, and it's likely that Anita is the only person left alive around here who could connect Juan to the local distribution network, so if he has put two and two together and there is any chance he's headed up there, we have to get word to the FBI so they get her well back into the bush."

"Maybe not. Maybe we get them to bring her out in their boat – it's a big fast jetboat – and we could take her to the Marjorie's and Wendy's little island – and the FBI could guard her there until we shut down Juan."

"Worth a try. You need to get to Willy and Marion, ASAP. Say, I expect the second EC135 will be back out here any time now – wanna chopper ride? McMichael can take care of your pet beaver."

"Sure, put in a call. Let's do it. I'll grab my cellphone."

Twenty minutes later, Anderson had been hoisted out of the boat and into the helicopter and was flying back to Spirit River.

***

Once he figured he was in cell range, Anderson called Arnold: "Hey Arnold, need to come to your place and talk with Willy and Marion, ASAP. Nope, I'm actually in a helicopter. I'll be landing in about five minutes at the landing strip. Huh? Yeah it will take many beers to tell you about today, and it ain't over yet. Things are kinda tight. Good, see you soon."

Sure enough, the chopper was landing when Arnold skidded off the road and onto the landing strip. The pilot asked Anderson if he wanted him to wait, but he said no, the Sergeant wanted him right back there between Robertson Mines and the island. He jumped down, scuttled off to the side and waved the pilot off before jogging over to Arnold's truck.

"Man, you look like you've been rode hard and put away wet! You okay?"

"Oh yeah, just lots of stuff going on. Most of the day felt a little like there was a war going on, and there was a pretty good wind and some wave action going on that's always kind of tiring. Gotta get to Willy and Marion though, we'll talk later."

"They're safe at home, so here we go. I can't speed though 'cause I'm surrounded by cop cars all day and night."

"Well, I don't mean to scare the crap outta you, but that chopper pilot there just watched this Juan guy execute two of his slaves and then burn them and their boat. Happened across the island from us... he be one mean son of a bitch! And that was a half hour after those same two slaves shot down a chopper like the one that dropped me here, and burned up a police boat."

Willy and Marion were sitting in her garden, and both stood up when he stepped around the house corner to join them. "Sit down, for heaven's sake. Arnold tells me I look like hell but actually I'm fine."

"You are doing a lot for my granddaughter and for my family. And I know you need to say something urgent, so please, let's talk."

"Yes. This morning we watched two of Juan's workers shoot down a helicopter with AR15s, then shoot up and burn a police launch. Just after noon, Juan – we are almost 100% sure it's Juan, executed and burned those two workers after they loaded his drugs into his new speedboat. As we are talking here, Juan has taken his drugs in toward Robertson Mines, but if he realizes it's a trap (because the RCMP are now all over that place) he will leave in his boat. He knows he can't come this way, and he knows he can outrun anything we have out there. We also know that the one person who could testify against him is Anita, and I expect he now knows where she is. I want to ask you, Willy, to get in touch with your FBI and their fast boat, tuck Anita under the seat, and come down the river into the lake like a bat out of hell and head for the Webster sisters' island, where you, the FBI, two police forces and I can take care of her. And give me a smoke."

Marion flipped him her pack, and just stared at him. Willy looked at the garden for almost a minute, then asked Marion for her cellphone. He dialled a call, and began talking in Ojibwe. There were obvious pauses as messages were relayed back and forth, and after ten minutes he hung up.

"Okay Frank, they'll be headed downriver in twenty

minutes. They know to talk to no one except Willy or Captain Frank on the marine radio, and they have my cell number. I will take my skiff to the island in half an hour and wait."

Anderson fished in his pocket, pulled out the key Marjorie had given him, and handed it to Willy: "I'll see you there." He turned to Marion: "The girls know to come straight here when they get to the village. Please feed them and care for them and by now you can tell them everything you know. Marjorie will be pissed off because when I talked to her yesterday I left out some of the details from the last couple of days."

Arnold grinned at him: "Airport, sir?"

"Yep. Please."

16:15 JULY 26

While Arnold was driving to the landing strip, Anderson called the Maple Falls detachment and asked for Superintendent Daniels. "I'm back at the landing strip in Spirit River and Sergeant John told me to let him know when I've made my contacts and am ready to be picked up and delivered back to the boat. I'm ready, and please relay to John that Plan A will be in motion in about 10 minutes."

"Is there just one of you?"

"Yes."

"I have another chopper on the way with two officers to spell off your crew and to remove the two drowned rats you pulled out of the lake, who must be really feeling their day by now. John, of course, will remain onboard. Okay if I have them stop by the landing strip and pick you up?"

"Works for me."

"They should be there in about fifteen. How are you doing, Frank?"

"When the clock strikes midnight, I have every intention of turning into a pumpkin, but I'll be fine until then."

"I'll make a note of that, just in case," he chuckled. "Thank you, Frank," and he clicked off.

"Chopper coming?" asked Arnold.

"Different one, I guess, but yes. Geez, it's been a day of firsts, one of which was the first time I ever got lifted off a boat by a chopper. This time I get to be lowered down to the boat. That somehow seems slightly more unnerving! Willy's quite a guy, isn't he!"

"He sure is. Hadn't really got to know him until last night and today. Someday I'd like to hear his story... he's so well spoken he puts the rest of us to shame."

"It's a wonderful story of love and respect, and a sad story of loss and disappointment at the same time. Some day I would like to be as wise, but the only thing we have in common is choosing to go our own way... and here comes my taxi."

The helicopter thundered overhead and churned up a small sandstorm as it settled onto the landing strip. Anderson scrambled across to the open door, acknowledged his fellow passengers as he climbed aboard, and strapped in as the very new-looking helicopter rose quickly and swung over the village into the late-afternoon sky over the lake. He watched as they flew at about five hundred feet over Ship Island and swept along Awan Lake's east shore. Soon he could pick out his launch, hove-to about a mile off Robertson Mines with her bow thirty degrees off the wind and stopped. A crewman opened the port door while the pilot brought the chopper overhead of the launch and dropped to about seventy-five off the deck. The two officers slated to be offloaded were already in harness, and the first one soon disappeared out the door while the crewman worked the winch. One-down-one-up three times... Anderson had been strapped into a harness and was the third man down. He waved at the sergeant, stepped into the wheelhouse and took over the wheel from McMichael, who would be the last man up.

The combined noise from the chopper's main engine and rotor had been deafening throughout the transfer process. When the helicopter pulled away into the sky and headed east to the shore, the sense of quiet was almost like a sedative suddenly taking effect. The sergeant introduced himself and Anderson to the newly-arrived officers, showed them where the coffee was, and came over to the wheel to talk with Anderson. "So Plan A is in motion, apparently?" he chuckled.

"Yes, the FBI and Anita should be coming down the river to the lake by now, and Willy will have left the village for the island in his skiff a few minutes ago. The FBI know to make contact with no one but Willy or Captain Frank; they should be coming into radio range shortly but I doubt they will call until they are quite close. What happened to Juan, his boat, and the drugs he had onboard?"

"Well, he actually landed at a little dock just outside the Robertson Mines' chain link fence, just to the north. I called that in, but by then the RCMP were active within the fence checking worker IDs and interviewing management staff. Our guys had pulled back along the main road, so by the time they got to the beach, he had presumably off-loaded the drugs and pulled offshore. As you predicted, he took off south along the shore at speed. Meantime, our guys are assembling for a search... this extra chopper will be useful. I think we should move in closer to discourage anybody leaving by boat – maybe just parade back and forth along the shore keeping our eyes wide open and ready to respond."

Anderson flipped the wheel and gently pushed the throttle forward, heading into shore directly opposite Robertson Mines. The sergeant took over the radio and set the new officers to maintaining a watch on the shore. It was close to 18:00 hours and the wind was dropping noticeably.

321

***

"Motorboat behind us and further offshore coming up fast, maybe over a mile back." They had been running on the first pass north along the shore, and roughly opposite the former provincial park, when the officer at the stern called it out. Anderson took a glance, but couldn't pick it out against the waves. He checked the radar, but nothing was showing so it was low in the water and probably not steel or aluminum. He twisted the squelch control on the marine radio right to the edge and waited.

A couple of minutes later the officer called out, "Motorboat is moving further offshore and will pass us on the left. Boy, is he ever moving!"

Anderson picked his field glasses off their hook beside him and called the sergeant over to the wheel. "Can you take this for a minute? I want to check out that boat myself."

It didn't take long. He steadied his elbows on the open windowsill on the port side of the wheelhouse and took a glance through the glasses. Returning to the wheel, he resumed his seat and said, "Almost positive that's the FBI. It is definitely a jetboat – you can tell from the long plume of water at the stern – and it looks like there are three men onboard."

"Three guys - what about Anita?"

"I told Willy to tell the guys to stuff her under a seat, or the deck, or somewhere. Poor gal, I hope she doesn't get seasick under there. I used to love being under the deck when I was a kid, but it's not everyone's cup of tea!"

He unclipped the microphone from the marine radio, keyed the transmit button and said, "This is Captain Frank calling FBI. I repeat, Captain Frank calling FBI. You are just passing me to your starboard."

There was a short silence, then: "Captain Frank, this is FBI. Where is Crazy Man?"

"Crazy Man Willy should be getting to the island within a few minutes. You have time to stop and greet. I will stop and hold position when you turn. Come alongside starboard to starboard. You need to know I have three OPPs onboard but they are AOK."

"Roger that, Captain Frank. Turning now."

"John, would you please flip three of those docking fenders over the side? No point wrecking their paint job!"

It was a big jetboat, almost three-quarters the length of *The Beaver*. The crew, too, lived up to their acronym: two men who could have played offensive line for the Ottawa Redblacks and a gal who could join them at tailback. Happily, they all had big smiles. There were quick introductions all around, and Anderson said, "I assume your cargo is safe and sound?"

A small hand appeared from an open hatch under the dashboard, and waved. "Safe, not necessarily sound," said the big voice behind the small hand. Anderson laughed: "Hi Anita. We're all awfully glad to have you safe. Can't wait to talk with you – then I'll tell you if you are sound. I suspect you are, very!" He turned to the jetboat's helmsman and pointed out the barely visible outline of Ship Island to the north. "That's where you are headed, and there is a little bay on this side of the island with a shaky old dock. I think you should be okay to dock on the left side of that, but don't go too far in because there is no beach – just rocks. Willy should be there soon and he has a key to the cottage. He may even be there already. We'll stop by when we're done out here, whenever that is."

"Gentlemen, keep your eyes open and be safe!" said the sergeant. The boats parted company and got underway, with the jetboat continuing north to the island and *The Beaver* headed back south along the beach. "Frank, I've been able to talk freely with Super George (as you call him – hate to think what you call me!) at The Falls. The RCMP are done their sweep of the Robertson Mines facility and found a number of illegal workers – it wasn't just Hassam, after all – and they detained for questioning two senior management staff – one American and one Mexican – both of whom had records. They are on their way to Ottawa, where they will have a long night."

"How about the guys who got smoked on the island – are they still out there?"

"Not any longer. The first chopper (the one that took you to the village) went out to the island and landed on the beach after you took off from the village to come back here. The boat was basically just a lump of aluminum and parts, but the two bodies had really only been scorched. Our team took photos and bagged and loaded them – they are now on their way to The Falls for identification and autopsies."

"Anything on the ground over here, outside the Robertson fence?"

"Yes, a couple of arrests. You will be tickled to know we picked up old man Giordano for possession and a number of possible extortion charges. There were three or four other guys and a couple of women in the camps who had outstanding warrants, so they, too, are headed for an overnight stay at The Falls and arraignment tomorrow morning. The drugs from this morning, however, we have not found so far. It is possible that we can squeeze some information out of the folks we picked up, and it is also possible – maybe more than likely – that Juan still has them on his boat. And we have no way of knowing where he has gone to ground. It seems likely he went upriver to Willy's place, but your FBI buddies told me they never passed another boat on their way down to the lake."

"He could have passed Willy's, I suppose, except that you'd think they would have heard that thing go by even if they didn't see it. Or, he could have stopped along the south shore out of sight in a marsh. It's a fast boat, but it doesn't stick up much! So, Sergeant MacLeod, what's next on the agenda?"

"Several things. First, I'm going to release the one remaining OPS car on the shore over here and tell the two officers to go back to the village, have a relaxed supper, and wait on me for further orders. Second, unless you have a better idea I will release the second chopper, which is wondering if he should return from delivering Andy and Ajay and the other two officers he picked up from the boat. Third, we have some officers onboard who need to get to the village to take over the village patrols. We need that to continue until Juan is dead or arrested. I confess I hardly care which, after he murdered those two guys this morning. And fourth, I think you have a lady waiting for you at the village, and there is another one I'd like to see, so if in an hour and a half from now you and I and those ladies were sitting in the Spirit Inn with a steak, that would be a desirable way forward."

Anderson had already begun a leisurely one-eighty. He fed the engine an almost full diet of diesel and headed back to the village while the sergeant informed the command office in Maple Falls and talked to his staff who had been waiting patiently on the well deck.

***

Half an hour later, they were passing north of Ship Island. Anderson sounded a couple of quick blasts on the air horn and dialled Willy's cellphone. "Willy, you're at the island I assume and your gang and Anita are safely with you?"

"Hi Frank, yes, we're all here and all is well, although

someone has broken into the cottage and made a bit of a mess – likely stole some stuff too. I see you are headed to the village?"

"Yes, we are. Our crew here will be on patrol in the village and John and I will go have some supper. Do you folks have food for tonight?"

"Yes we do. I brought some nice steaks with me and a six-pack, which will be enough for now. Go and see your missus – she's at Marion's and she's worried sick."

Anderson chuckled: "You bet, will do. All of you keep your eyes and ears wide open tonight – you've got a good crew there but although his army is probably defeated we haven't found Juan yet. You have my cellphone... we may come out to the island later tonight but I'll let you know. Depends on what we learn in the next couple or three hours. You and Anita and your team there are our priority. Later, my friend!"

The sergeant brought Anderson one of his own beers from the forward cabin. "Here, I'm passing out one of these to each of us, so we are temporarily off-duty and I promise not to arrest you for having open alcohol onboard. If I did that I'd have to pour it over the side and that would be both polluting the environment and a criminal waste. Anyway, I think the government ruled that this tradition is still valid in the navy, Captain Anderson."

"Thank you, Admiral MacLeod. I'll go to any length to win the battle against pollution." They were about twenty minutes out of the village, so he dialled Marjorie: "Hi Marjorie, it's me!

" Oh Frank, I have heard all about you but I have needed to hear your voice. How long is your boat?"

"Thirty seven feet. Why?"

"Then I plan never to be more than thirty-seven feet from

you, ever again."

"Well, the comfortable part is about twenty-five feet. Will that do?"

"Yes."

"Okay, there are two idiots here who want to invite two pretty girls to dinner at the Spirit Inn in about a half-hour. You game?"

"Yes. Wendy has already booked us a room there, and is over there now. I am still at Arnold and Marion's place."

"You don't need a room. I have an empty one. I'll pick you up... we're about twenty minutes off the dock so... like I said, about half an hour?"

"That would be perfect."

"Love you, lady!" Anderson blurted out, and clicked off. He sat for a moment wondering about himself, then called to the sergeant: "The ladies will have dinner with us – I have to pick up Marjorie at Arnolds, but Wendy is already at the Inn." The docks were ahead, and he slacked off the throttle and began to plan his landing. It was an early weekday night before the long weekend, so there was little or no boat traffic and he was able to get in quickly.

The officers and their sergeant pitched in to tie down and lock the boat. Anderson dipped his fuel tanks and was in the process of shutting everything down, the sergeant came to him and said quietly, "Frank, we are all actually on duty one way or another. The officers here will be on patrol in the village, and you and I are still on twenty-four seven. So, please check over your sidearm and holster it on your belt. And of course, the girls can drink over dinner but we can't. Which doesn't bother me much because I plan to eat a whole lot."

"Works for me," and Anderson struggled with his belt, attached the holster and checked the pistol for action and load.

"Not exactly used to this thing," he muttered to the sergeant. "It's embarrassing, sort of."

"Don't worry. It rides well on you!"

***

There was only one police cruiser at the docks – the sergeants – so he directed his officers to take it, drop him off at the Inn, and sort out how to get another car to the village sometime this evening. Anderson had left his truck at the dock, so after checking the boat one last time he climbed into the truck and headed for Arnold's place. They were sitting in the front garden, and Marjorie ran over to greet him. The hug was enthusiastic and the kiss was long.

"Time for a drink?" asked Marion after they had quit being affectionate. "Either that or we've got a room upstairs!"

"Hey," Arnold called, "look at this! Now quiet old Anderson is armed. Holy crap!"

"Oh, that? John made me wear it. Sorry about that!"

Marion rolled her eyes, and Marjorie looked at his waist and shrugged. "Whatever. I just hope he doesn't have to wear it to bed, and can give it back tomorrow."

"Me too. Thanks so much Marion, and Arnold, for everything. Hopefully we'll all get together tomorrow, but right now I have something to show Marjorie."

"I'll bet you do!" Marion called across the lawn. "That pistol's bad enough!"

"Wise-ass broad, not that!" Anderson laughed, and he bundled Marjorie into the truck and drove back down to the dock.

"Where are you going? I thought we were going to the Inn..."

"Hang on a moment. You'll see." He drove onto the dock

and up behind the launch before he stopped. "There."

Marjorie looked, then suddenly saw the name on the transom. She sat dead still for a moment, then her eyes filled with tears and she slid across the front seat and buried her face on his shoulder. "Oh Frank!" was all she said. "Oh, Frank."

He hugged her close for a couple of minutes, then cupped her face gently and said, "Glad you approve. Dinner?"

"Mmm hmm. Let's."

***

The Inn had a section of the lounge that served as a dining room in the evening, and it was empty except for John and Wendy, who were happily chirping at one another at a corner table for four. "Thought you were lost," said Wendy, who stood up and gave Anderson a hug. Marjorie greeted the sergeant warmly and the four sat down.

Georgina was on shift and she almost skipped across to Anderson and said, "Is it true? I've heard from Marion that you may have found Anita. Is that true?"

"Yes it is. If it wasn't for Willy and his people, and John here and his people, we wouldn't have, but yes it's true, and I'll make sure that you and Fred get to see her tomorrow." He glanced across at the sergeant: "That will be possible John, I hope?"

"We'll make sure it happens, Mrs. Antoine. Yes, she is alive, she still has a great sense of humour, and she is safe tonight."

"Oh my God. Thank you God, Thank you friends... here's a menu, I'm gonna call Fred right now. Haven't told him yet. I couldn't see his heart broken again!" And she disappeared into the kitchen.

"I am so happy for her," Wendy said. "The last three or

four weeks must have been terrible!"

"There will, I hope, be another reunion in the next couple of days," said Anderson. "Fred's dad is Willy, and they haven't talked for many years – maybe twenty. Two nice men like that deserve better... let's hope it happens!"

"Twenty years? That's a very long time for a father and son to be silent," said Wendy.

"Well, it happens. Misunderstood blame, I think. And booze just never helps. I just hope they sort it out. Okay gang, what are we gonna eat? This is on the Crown's tab tonight, so enjoy. And you ladies can even have drinks, too, although Sergeant Anderson and I will have to wait until another time. We're still on the job."

"Sergeant Anderson? Is there something I don't know?"

"Don't worry Wendy. It's a condition I'll get over as soon as everyone else is healthy. Hopefully very soon... I kinda liked being a small-time contractor with a boat."

"Well, okay then," Wendy replied. "I mean, I happen to think that police officers are especially sexy, but I just didn't think of you that way. I mean..."

"Thanks a lot, lady! Anyway, that's a good thing 'cause I think your sister might have something to say!"

"Damn right I would!" And the four could feel the day's tension evaporate as they laughed together.

***

It happened so suddenly. Meals had been ordered – rib eyes, rare, for the boys, and crab-stuffed chicken for the girls who were sipping wine while Anderson and the sergeant drank coffee. A tall, good-looking and well-dressed man with jet-black hair walked into the bar, looked around and saw the sergeant in the corner. He pulled a small pistol from the waistband of his slacks, waved it around the room and strode half-way across the bar where he aimed it square at the sergeant: "You! Fuckin' cop! You've been fucking me around for a week and tonight it's over. Where's Anita, that black whore? You have five seconds to tell me…"

He didn't pay any attention to the others at the table, including the man in blue jeans and a dark jacket, so it was too late when he saw that man bring his sidearm out from under his jacket and fire. Juan toppled over backward with a bullet hole in the centre of his forehead.

The shrieking from the other bar patrons stopped immediately and the silence was almost deafening. The sergeant was the first to speak: "I thought you didn't really know how to shoot a sidearm…"

"No, I just said I didn't like shooting guns. Didn't say I didn't know how." He withdrew the clip, emptied the chamber into his hand and handed the whole works to the sergeant. "I expect you'll be wanting to keep this now."

The sergeant stood up and checked his watch before looking around the bar. It was 20:47, and there was only a handful of people there – maybe a half-dozen – sitting in stunned silence at two separate tables. "I am sorry about the interruption, folks. I'm going to have to ask you to stay here until my colleagues arrive and they'll want to ask you some questions. In the meantime, feel free to enjoy the Inn's hospitality."

He sat back down and called Superintendent Daniels. He talked quietly for a few moments then clicked off, and looked around the table. "I think Spirit River, and indeed all of Ontario, is suddenly a lot safer. However, this will be a long night, I'm afraid. Certainly for me, and Frank – you may have a long night too."

331

The sergeant had asked Flo for a blanket, and when she brought it he respectfully covered Juan's corpse, touching nothing and leaving the gun still clenched in his right hand. He straightened up and suggested they move to a different table on the other side of the bar, close to the door and as far from the blanket as they could get. Even so, there was not much chatter between them, and after a few minutes Anderson turned to the sergeant: "John, that's Willy's stepson – and Anita's step-brother – that I just shot. As soon as your gang is done with me, I need to get out of here and go and talk to them. Okay?"

"Of course Frank. I'll make sure it gets sorted out quickly. Someone will need to take a statement from each of us, so I'll get them to start with you and Marjorie. If it's okay with you Wendy, we may have to hang around a little longer."

The first police officer to show up, only minutes later, was the one they had dropped off at the sergeant's car. He was, after all, now on duty patrolling the village and he had, about forty-five minutes earlier, seen a person who fitted Juan's description arriving at the marina with a big wakeboard boat. He had also witnessed the man getting into his Mercedes AMG Coupe, not a totally unfamiliar vehicle in cottage country, but noticeable anyway. It was now sitting in the Inn parking lot and the keys and key fob were in Juan's pocket.

Three more officers, including the Superintendent, arrived in two unmarked cars in about twenty minutes. There were photographs. Anderson had his hands swabbed for gunshot residue and he answered questions and wrote out and signed a statement. Marjorie was also questioned, more briefly, and signed her statement, then they were released to go home with an admonition not to leave the province without informing the police. An officer was to follow them back to Anderson's home and collect the clothes he was wearing.

When they were leaving the Inn, the Superintendent followed them outside, where Anderson introduced him to Marjorie. "Frank, I want to apologize for two things: one, putting you in a situation where you had to use a sidearm to protect the public and your fellow officer, and two, having to go through all the bureaucratic, but necessary, follow up. That part will continue off and on for a few weeks, I expect, and you should not respond to the media other than by directing them to the detachment communications officer or commanding officer. And, I want to thank you for the outstanding work you and your vessel accomplished today. That, too, will continue, although you will be better paid: I understand we have two burned boats and a helicopter to find and retrieve. That will start tomorrow, I'm afraid, so get a good night's sleep."

"Maybe no earlier than 10:00, because I need to refuel and check fluids and stuff. And you're welcome, George... apart from the last hour, it has been a pleasure, and your folks are great women and men to work with!" They shook hands, and Super George went back into the Inn while the constable followed Anderson and Marjorie home.

***

The only light in the sky left over from today was a faint sliver of red in the northwestern sky. *The Beaver* was making about eight knots in a north-easterly direction toward Ship Island, and Marjorie had pulled up the navigation table stool to sit close to Anderson.

Anderson had changed clothes and bagged what he had been wearing for the officer and bid him goodnight, before he and Marjorie had driven to the dock, checked the tanks for fuel and the engines for fluids, started everything up and turned on the navigation lamps, and now were over half way to Marjorie's and Wendy's cottage. Anderson had phoned ahead to Willy to say he was coming, and asked him to meet them at the dock so they could talk in private for a while.

As they neared the island, they could see a faint light from a window, perhaps from a camping lantern. "Geez," said Marjorie, "didn't you tell them how to start the generator?"

"Nope, I didn't tell them anything, and I also haven't had a chance yet to tell you that your cottage may have been broken into. We saw that boat that burned up this morning pulled in at your dock yesterday afternoon, and for obvious reasons did not follow up because we were basically unarmed at the time. I am pretty sure it was those idiots moonlighting – perhaps Juan didn't pay them enough – but I expect the recent rash of break-ins at the cottages may be over."

She squeezed his hand gently. "You've had quite the week, haven't you! But we're almost at the island, and Willy, and Anita, and I'll bet this is the toughest part."

"Yeah, not looking forward to it. I just wish I could be there when Anita gets back together with her folks."

He gave two quick blasts on the horn and went around the island to the little bay, where he turned on the spreader lights on the navigation mast and one searchlight forward. The wind had completely died down from the day and the lake was calm except for a very gentle seiche effect. He nosed the boat along the dock and reversed to a stop. Willy was there to take the bow line and Marjorie took a short line to the dock from the centre port-side bollard, and they were made fast. The big jet boat was on the other side of the dock and Willy had taken his skiff to the opposite side of that so the dock would be free for *The Beaver*.

"Hi Willy, please meet Marjorie Webster."

"Ah, Marjorie... so you are this very special person I have heard so much about, especially – but not only – from Frank!"

"Marjorie!" Anderson laughed: "You're blushing... or is that a reflection from the port navigation light! Willy, let's go into the wheelhouse and talk for a short while. I have things to tell you."

"Hang on a minute." Willy walked partway down the dock and bellowed, "Hey Monika, you can go back to the house now and tell the guys to turn the light back on. I'll be up soon." He came back up the dock and stepped onto the boat, laughing: "Monika was sitting in the bushes up there with an AR15 aimed down the dock, and Lucas and Little Joe are up at the house with rifles stuck out the windows. They can go to bed now, and Anita is already asleep."

They wedged around the navigation table, lit up smokes and Anderson opened the last three beers. "Willy, I have good news and bad news. First, it's over. All Juan's network has been scooped up today by the two police forces, the provincial folks and the RCMP. The network extended from here to Ottawa, Toronto, and as you suspected, California and likely Mexico."

"That is good news. What about Juan, and Anita's safety?"

"Well, that's where it gets tougher. Your stepson Juan is dead, which is sad. From my perspective, it's even worse than that: I killed him, about two hours ago, with a single gunshot to the head as he tried to force Anita's location from Sergeant John. We were sitting waiting to have dinner at the Inn when he walked into the lounge waving a gun. I'm sorry, my friend. It is not the outcome I wished for."

Willy gazed quietly out the wheelhouse door onto the

silent lake. After a moment, he turned back and smiled, first as Marjorie then at Anderson. "Some days I cannot get over missing my beloved Juanita but today, I am happy she is not here. Frank, I think you know that you saved me the trouble of bringing this to an end myself. I only hope that you are not in trouble because of it. So..." he reached across and covered Anderson's hand with his... "thank-you my good friend. And I will make sure that Anita understands that you are a fine friend and neighbour. I will bring her to her father and mother in the morning, but now, I think I will go up to the Webster sofa and sleep soundly, hoping for happier dreams."

"Good night, dear people," he said as he stepped onto the dock. "I will slip your forward mooring line." And he was gone.

***

"The world is not a tidy place," said Anderson, "but I guess we'll keep on trying to tidy it up piece by piece. But that's for tomorrow: I told Super George earlier today that I had every intention of turning into a pumpkin by midnight tonight, and I think we'll make it home just in time."

"It is a beautiful night," Marjorie said softly as *The Beaver* slithered through the black-calm water on the way back to the village. "And I will happily roll you along the floor and into bed, where I will hold you close and keep you warm."

"Someday, Ms. Webster – perhaps someday soon – we'll relax all day and then keep each other awake all night."

"Soon. Yes Mr. Anderson. Soon."

THE END

ABOUT THE AUTHOR

Peter Kingsmill was born and raised near Montreal but soon after high school chose to move west, first to British Columbia then eventually settling in Saskatchewan. He has worked at an eclectic mix of tasks - reporter and editor, logger, trucker, cattle farmer, and riverboat captain.

Peter and his wife Valerie* live at Hafford, Saskatchewan, near Redberry Lake where his work resulted in his being presented with the Governor General of Canada's Conservation Award in 1991. Peter is past-chair and founding director of the Redberry Lake (UNESCO) Biosphere Reserve. He currently serves as publications editor with the Alberta Society of Professional Biologists and works as a consultant on regional development projects when he is not writing a novel or sailing on his beloved Redberry Lake. He joined Crime Writers of Canada as a Professional Author Member in 2018.

*Valerie Kingsmill is an artist and the author/illustrator of the **Redberry Tales** series of gentle children's books, in the Wind in the Willows genre (but set on the Canadian prairies instead of the United Kingdom).*

peterkingsmill.ca

Made in the USA
Middletown, DE
24 April 2023

29011729R00205